THE EDEN PACKAGE

KINCAIDE'S WAR
BOOK 1

BLAZE WARD

KNOTTED ROAD PRESS

The Eden Package
Kincaide's War Book 1
Blaze Ward
Copyright © 2022 Blaze Ward
All rights reserved
Published by Knotted Road Press
www.KnottedRoadPress.com

ISBN: 978-1-64470-509-4

Cover art:
Illustration 145890990 / Alien © 3000ad | Dreamstime.com

Cover and interior design copyright © 2022 Knotted Road Press

Reviews
It's true. Reviews help. Even a short one, such as, "Loved it!" So please consider
reviewing this book (and all of the ones you've read) on your favorite retailer site.

Never miss a release!
If you'd like to be notified of new releases, sign up for my newsletter.

http://www.blazeward.com/newsletter/

Buy More!
Did you know that you can buy directly from the Knotted Road Press website?

https://www.knottedroadpress.com/shop/

ALSO BY BLAZE WARD

The Science Officer Series

Start with: The Science Officer

The Jessica Keller Chronicles

Start with: Auberon

CS-405 (Command Centurion Kosnett, part of Jessica)

Start with: Queen Anne's Revenge

First Centurion Kosnett (sequel to Jessica)

Start with: Encounter at Vilahana

Additional Alexandria Station Stories

Alexandria Station Collection

Handsome Rob (Alexandria Station Universe)

Start with: Can't Shoot Straight Gang

====================

Corsac Fox

Start with: Flight of the Corsac Fox

Operation Marrakesh

Start with: Trial by Leviathan

Captain Daring

Start with: Revoked

The Hunter Bureau

Start with: *Mirrors*

Fairchild
Start with: *Fairchild*

Last Stand
Start with: *Lost Dreams*

The Lazarus Alliance
Start with: *Escape*

Shadow of the Dominion
Start with: *Longshot Hypothesis*

Star Dragon
Start with: *Birth of the Star Dragon*

Kincaide's War
Start with: *The Eden Package*

Star Tribes
Start with: *Winterstar*

ACTION-ADVENTURE
Pacific Force
Start with: *Pacific Force*

The Red Branch
Start with: *Night Strike*

Swordmistress Zhen
Start with: *Traveler From The West*

FANTASTICAL
The Gunderson Case Files, Volume 1

Augustus Derlyth, Occult Detective
Start with: *Ill Tidings*

CONTENTS

DREAMERS

CHAPTER 1

Kincaide studied the walls around him again, trying to figure out at what point he'd finally assented to the massive stupidity of actually attempting to escape The Gage Empire and flee forever into deep space.

The ship was named *Dashavatara*, after the Tenth Avatar of Vishnu. Supposedly the being that came down to set things right when demons—or aliens in this case—had come close to destroying the world. Hadn't saved Earth from the Gage invasion that had conquered humanity however many centuries ago.

Kincaide just hoped that maybe he'd be able to pull off something better next time.

He was alone tonight, as always. As it should be. Steel walls in his cabin painted with a greenish sealant, but no decorations on them other than that. Kincaide Kataragama didn't need art to soothe his soul. Two chairs facing each other in the middle, in case he chose to have a guest here instead of in the common salon outside his suite. A desk with a research screen and keyboard connected to the ship's Encyclopedia Core, if he found that he needed to look something up.

Off to one side, a small sleeping chamber not much bigger than a large coffin, next to a fresher unit where he could shower in water rather than sonics: one of the perks of being important around here, such as it was.

Not much else. He didn't need much, and chose not to live in some faint echo of The Gage, with all their gothic decorations and expansive, baroque detailing on things.

This was, for all the expenses, a shoe-string budget sort of rebellion. One ship. One crew. One Eden Package of colonists to decant at some future date when they escaped and found a future colony world where Humans might live free from the rules of The Gage, the Alvar.

Tonight, Kincaide wondered why he had ever bothered.

What chance did mere Humans have against a star empire that controlled so many thousands of systems and so many other species? Hell, the ruling family of Alvar, the species that controlled The Gage Empire itself, had been in power since before Humans had emerged as a separate species, back on the world they had originally come from, according to legends and oral stories handed down since the Conquest.

But that world had been lost, along with so much. Deliberately erased from the records by the Alvar and their servants.

It didn't help that the average Alvar lived five to eight thousand Human years. Many of them alive today might even remember First Contact with the Humans, followed by the Conquest and then Exodus.

We are but fruit flies to such as them.

And yet, Kincaide Kataragama was going to challenge them. All of them. Not that anyone should be surprised. At fifty-eight years Standard, he had spent more than a generation in quiet rebellion against the overlords and their pets. Against the domes where the Alvar kept their various conquered species, trapped on an airless moon where they couldn't even walk on the surface without Gage technology.

Because what did a man like Kincaide have to lose? They'd killed his wife Nayani twenty-two years ago. He'd never had a chance to have children with her. Grow old with her. Never would, either, because neither of them had ever been taken into one of the Analogue machines, where the Alvar could make a copy of you that they could decant again and again for as long as they wished. For whatever bizarre experiments they might desire.

Kincaide was one of the few Humans he knew who had never been Indexed—copied—by Gage technology. He sometimes called himself the Last Human because of that. He would live, age, and die. There would be nothing left of him afterwards except records and fading memories, because he would not let the Alvar, those semi-immortal marauders, return him to life.

4

Tonight, however, he could not sleep, for reasons that weren't clear. The ship was not yet ready to fly, but it was getting close. The crew had secretly been recruited from known rebels like him, trained down as much as they could without the Alvar or their pets discovering anything useful. The technology was new and untested, but how do you test an experimental Human engine except to put her in the gestalt generator and see if it destroys her mind?

That was coming soon.

Kincaide was restless. Not fretful. Too wound up tonight with emotional energy to sleep.

Someone knocked.

The suite assigned to him was an entire sixth of the forward hexagon at the end of the long gooseneck of the ship that held the bridge in the middle and this hexagon forward. Not a large space, but his. The entire hexagon only housed three people, each with a sixth of a slice for themselves, with the other half dedicated to a lounge and a kitchen for them, plus the airlock system that connected this forward Engine Section to the neck where the bridge was and, farther aft, the much-larger Crew Section.

Kincaide did not need to live outside the warp-spawn shields. Only the Engine herself needed to do that. He chose to, because no warp-spawn demon was going to frighten him. He was the Foreman of this ship. The Chairman was the same way, in the third chamber and unwilling to live in fear. The three of them would face any warp-spawn themselves.

Kincaide would defeat such monsters, or die trying.

He rose as the knocking continued. One of the crew would have called him on a dedicated line if they needed something. None of them would invite themselves to his quarters, doubly so this late in the evening, when he might have already been asleep. Or at least resting and meditating on his sins.

That list was monumental, but the Alvar had never attached his name to those crimes, or they would have already ended him.

That left two people as he moved to the door and opened it. Chairman Zhubin Prakash, and...

Odtsetseg. The Star Flower. The Engine.

She stood perfectly still, watching him from the larger space across the threshold.

Kincaide wondered what she saw, but the young woman had never been able to articulate her visions, to explain Humans all that well. And she was only mostly Human.

Like him, she wore the crew uniform of this new venture. The ship might run on a shoe-string, but the fashion budget was at least adequate. As Foreman, Kincaide wore a red body suit with a black stocking underneath, a yellow belt and trim, and white boots of a style he'd once heard called Pirate, thigh high but folded over to mid-calf.

The woman before him was dressed as an Engine. Her uniform was a gray tunic to the top of her thighs with matching pants, as tight as his bodysuit. Her belt and trim was the same yellow as his. On her feet she wore simple ballet slippers.

Absolutely white hair, cut short and brushed back, and he had no idea why it would be that color, rather than the dark brown her original genes might have suggested.

Tall. Kincaide was about average for a Human male at one hundred and seventy-eight centimeters tall. She had at least five centimeters on him, making her tall for any woman. Built rail thin, like a skeleton with flesh and little else. Her skin was much lighter in tone, and tended over towards East Asian, with a golden-bronze sheen missing from his browner hues.

Odtsetseg presented physically as nineteen years old. No hips to speak of. No shoulders. Chest like a twelve-year-old boy.

Mostly Human, depending on how you measured such things. At least the DNA from which she had been built had started with Human. At some point, one of the Gods, a Human Scientist named Hasan Ildar, had added in octopus genes. And then *other things*.

Her face had an eight-ray design on it, four red tentacles in her skin like tattoos on each side of her nose: forehead, cheekbone, chin, jaw. Except it wasn't a tattoo. That was the alien DNA in her soul.

The eyes also marked her. Transparent eyeballs that glowed in dim light. Kincaide had heard her compared to an Anglerfish at one point, but had never bothered looking up the comparison.

This wasn't the first version of her that he had known. Ildar had made dozens over the last several years, constantly tweaking the template and decanting new versions after he destroyed the old experiments.

Seeking power.

The face tattoo marked her as a telepath. All the early experiments using aquatic creatures had that outcome, so it had become something eventually to standardize on. And it warned the Humans what she was.

Kincaide didn't really care if she could read his mind or not.

He stared at her, daring the young woman to speak first. He was the Foreman of this ship, after all, just as she was the Engine.

Singular, bizarre as that might seem.

The Gage had used a gestalt design that included a dozen or more of their kind to warp space so they could conquer the galaxy, maybe a million years ago. When they discovered other species, those got plugged in as Engines, saving the Alvar from menial labor.

And the risk of meeting the warp-spawn. Dying at their hands.

Until the day an Alvar ship discovered Humans. Unlike all the other known species, Humans had a functional insanity that could power a ship far more easily than the Mog or the Warednja. Six Humans could replace forty Mori, or twenty Mog, and power a ship.

If Hasan Ildar was correct in his calculations, Odtsetseg would be able to lift this ship through warp-space all by herself.

Kincaide studied the young woman. She felt weak, rather than the normal defiance she exuded. Nineteen years old, virginal, telepath. They had each shared enough about themselves that he knew she saw Humans as emotional signatures in space rather than physical surfaces. She painted in oils and other media trying to show everyone else what she saw.

The images were haunting in their beauty. And frightening to others.

"What?" he finally broke down, when it became clear she would not, could not speak.

He wondered from the way she stood, hunched slightly and arms wrapped around flat breasts, if just knocking had taken all her energy.

Odtsetseg would have felt him, felt his mind and his emotions even through the doorway, as she approached.

It could not have been a pleasant experience. Kincaide was not feeling benevolent to the universe tonight.

"I'm cold," she murmured, barely above a whisper, her eyes averted down and to her right, as if even looking at him might hurt her.

Who knew?

Kincaide studied the young woman. Twelve months old, or nineteen years, depending. So telepathic that she had a hard time telling where her mind ended and all the others around her began.

He started to say something with terrible heat, but saw the fear on her face.

She wasn't cold. She was alone.

He stepped back and to one side, gesturing for her to enter his private suite.

"Come," he said.

The way her face lit up when he moved spoke volumes about the side of her that was a person, rather than a scientific experiment. Or a weapon.

Odtsetseg was lonely.

CHAPTER 2

Kincaide put Odtsetseg in the second chair and closed the hatch. Zhubin hadn't opened his own door at the noise, but might not have heard her knocking on Kincaide's hatch.

And pigs might fly.

The Chairman, Zhubin Prakash, obviously didn't want to be involved. He could be like that. What did that say about Odtsetseg? Or either of the men? Zhubin was hardly younger than Kincaide, but he was a copy of another man. An Analogue aged fifty-one Standard Personal, who had been scanned and Decanted at twenty-four Standard Personal.

Another rebel like Kincaide, but one with his own philosophical problems. Zhubin happily admitted that he had killed at least four copies of himself over the decades. The Alvar thought that they had the perfect assassin to send after the man.

Himself.

Arrogant gits had never learned the Human adage about old age and treachery overcoming youth and skill.

So Zhubin was leaving it to Kincaide to handle tonight. Leaving him to handle her.

Kincaide walked across the room to his chair and sat. They were two meters apart, facing each other, in a bare space painted an industrial green that had been the cheapest hue Ildar could apparently find when he began building his own rebellion in steel.

Not that Kincaide cared all that much.

He had been contemplating tea before she knocked, but going out into the shared space and leaving her here in order to make it seemed like a bad idea, although what strength she might draw from his underlying anger wasn't something that made any sense.

"Because you don't care," she said, as though reading his mind.

She was a telepath. She could probably do that.

"Sometimes," Odtsetseg replied to the unspoken comment. "When it's just two of us, sitting in a quiet place. Usually I have a hard time actually speaking, rather than listening and inserting comments directly into someone's mind."

"So what can I do for you?" Kincaide asked now, using a conversational voice while understanding that they would be dancing on many different levels tonight.

However, only he and Zhubin could handle something like that with her, of all the people who Kincaide had met on this project, or associated with it.

"You have been alone..." Odtsetseg began before breaking off her thought. "I would say since before I was born, but that's not all that long, is it? At least not this flesh. Nor this mind. If I were born of woman, you've still been alone longer."

"Twenty-two years," Kincaide acknowledged.

"You never took another?"

"When I was your age, we took a vow," he said grimly. "A promise until death."

"But Nayani is gone," she said, almost pleading with him to explain.

Nineteen years old. Virgin. Alien. They barely shared enough DNA to even comprehend, but she needed him to try. Perhaps to help her find something Human in herself that she didn't understand.

"Nayani is dead," he said. "Soon enough, I'll join her and we'll be together. Whether that's heaven or hell depends on who you ask."

"Aren't you ever lonely?" she asked, getting to the heart of what had driven this person, this creature, to his door tonight.

Human touch, when she wasn't even Human.

"Human enough," she snapped angrily. "He started with a Human. A woman Indexed and Analogued long before any of you were ever conceived, even Zhubin Prakash. I'm still enough her to want Human touch. To crave it sometimes."

Kincaide nodded, remembering what it had been like at that age.

Young, dumb, and filled with dreams of changing the universe. In love.

"What do you want from me, Odtsetseg?" he asked simply.

"Someone to hold me tonight." She retreated from her anger now, almost whimpering in pain. "Someone to put their arms around me and keep me warm when the nightmares start."

"Nightmares?" he asked, surprised.

At the same time, he'd never spent that much time around the various Analogues of Odtsetseg over the last three years to really know their minds. Their souls.

"I sleep, but the power doesn't," she said grimly, sounding older than him now in her tones. "So I have flashbacks of things as I read the unconscious minds around me. Or alien memories of people I've never met, because somehow they got inserted into my Icon by God when he was refashioning me, layer after layer, seeking perfection."

God. Yes, Kincaide supposed that she might see Hasan Ildar as God. Certainly, the man saw himself that way and told everyone else. Benevolent or Malevolent was an entirely different conversation.

There was a whole pantheon of *Early Human Servants* who had slavishly devoted themselves to The Gage when the Empire had first conquered Earth. Each of the Domes were generally self-sufficient, with all the equipment printers linked to and controlled by *The Catalogue*, that near-infinite Gage database of designs that could be actualized.

Weapons were strictly controlled, but biological research was much less restricted. Ildar's funding had come from an Alvar think tank that was researching a way to make higher quality servants, and in the process, create more efficient Engines, as they had never found another species like Humans to better power their warp-drives.

None of the Alvar had considered that a megalomaniac like Ildar might be a rebel under it all, intent on escaping and taking all that technology and possibility with him, until he could return and destroy the masters.

In that, Kincaide agreed. He just wasn't nearly as much a racist or specist as *God* might be.

"True," Odtsetseg agreed. "You hate everyone equally, regardless of shape."

"Then why come to me?" he asked.

"Because your hatred is honest," she said, finding some strength in her voice. In her eyes. "There are many on this vessel I might seek out for comfort."

Kincaide waited for her to speak. It was her demand that brought her here, not his.

"All of them respect me, Kincaide," she continued, growing more emotional with each word. "Many worship me as a new type of goddess. Most pity me for what God did to me, even as they understand that it might mean their freedom."

"So?"

"So every single one of them fears me," she pronounced her own sort of doom. "They fear what I might do to them if we touched. What I might learn about them. What they might learn about themselves. Do you have any idea what that's like, to touch someone deathly afraid of you at the moment you're seeking comfort?"

"No," Kincaide replied. At least he could be honest with her.

"Might as well draw a knife and start carving on my flesh with it," she said. "That would actually hurt less."

"And me?" he asked the obvious question, but Kincaide Kataragama was fifty-eight years old and had seen more of this stupid universe than he wanted since he'd lost Nayani. Only his promise to her to destroy those rat turds had kept him alive this long.

"You are not afraid of me," she said. "Your hatred I can deal with, because it's superficial. Your hatred isn't personal. I'm nothing special to you. That makes you special to me."

"You're insane, girl," he snapped.

"You think I don't know that?" she yelled at him, almost rising out of her chair with a surge of emotions that rolled over him like the wind from a breach sucking the air out of a chamber. "I'm not Human, Kataragama. Not alien. Not anything, because God needed power, and didn't care where he got it from, as long as all the parts could be assembled into an organic whole that was stable enough to power a starship through warp-space. How many of me have there been, as he tinkered?"

"Dozens," Kincaide replied quietly in the face of her sudden fury.

"Each spit out and tested," she snarled. "Then destroyed while he went back to the Icon and made adjustments to the design, hoping for something better. I'm twelve months old. Or nineteen years. Or I was born nearly one thousand years ago, depending on which Standard Personal timeline you wanted to use. I seem to be the last, but what do

I tell all the earlier copies of me when I get to hell and find them waiting?"

"They won't be in hell, Odtsetseg," Kincaide said. "The True God of Humans claims all the innocents for himself and takes them up to heaven, so they don't have to hurt anymore. I'll miss you when we're both dead and I'm in hell."

She blinked and fell back into the chair so heavily, so bonelessly, that he wondered if she'd just fainted.

Finally, she stirred. Held out a shaking hand to him across the near-infinite gap between them.

Two meters. Thirty years. Different species.

"Please?" she whispered in pain so exquisite that Kincaide thought he could taste it.

He studied her, perhaps finally understanding the various women named Odtsetseg that he had known over the last several years as the project took shape. What drove them. All of them.

There was a fire that the original woman had contained, along with a high degree of native telepathic power.

But she was nineteen years old. And alone.

He held out his own hand and she took it.

"Okay," he said simply. "You'll probably regret it, but okay."

"I'm stronger than that," she said, rising and pulling him to his feet.

"Tell me that again in the morning," Kincaide smiled grimly at her.

CHAPTER 3

Odtsetseg slept.

At least she thought so. With the Power, it was never easy to tell when wakefulness ended, except that her ongoing visions got weirder. Less well defined.

Blurrier.

It was all still a trap. A well she had fallen into even before she was born and could not escape. Even her telekinetic abilities could not lift her enough to fly away from this place.

Odtsetseg was cornered in a dream and could do nothing except accept it.

She *remembered*.

Except it wasn't her remembering. It wasn't her living. These were someone else's dreams.

She was down in Boston Dome on the moon below, rather than aboard the strange, experimental starship known as *Dashavatara*. It was the past.

Strange faces surrounded her, all of them Human. All of them of a particular ethnic genotype that had originally arisen in a place called India. Or Celyon. Possibly Sri Lanka. The dream refused to explain itself to her, but the Humans were all of a particular skin tone and a narrow ethnic range.

Brownish. Not the African genotype that verged on walnut or onyx. Not the Eastern ethnotype that was the yellow of cow's butter mixed with gold. Not the paleness of the northwest.

But this was Boston Dome. Of all the seventeen Human Domes, it had the widest variety of peoples, all calling themselves Human. Even Angeles Dome was not as broad, but it was dominated by a different ethnotype. Brown, but more reddish in some strange way she could not explain.

All the faces around her were South Asian.

The words were blurry. More emotional signatures than discrete communications. It felt like she was listening to music rather than speaking.

Odtsetseg fought the dream and looked around the room.

Small. Cramped. Poor. Identical to any of millions of tiny apartments where the Alvar had left their servant races on the surface of an airless moon, circling the Alvar home world.

Breeding farm. The Alvar needed Humans to power their warp-ships, so they kept a collection handy. It would still be the future when God proposed to a true deity that he could build even better Humans for the Gage to use.

Odtsetseg tasted nine faces around her in this dream. Seated in a living room by filling a wide couch and crammed in mismatched chairs from the kitchen.

She recognized the face to her right and the shock was almost enough for Odtsetseg to awaken, but the dream grabbed her by the throat and held her under water when she thought to flee.

Kincaide Kataragama. Young. Much younger than the man she knew. Her age, perhaps.

She was trapped in his dream. His nightmare.

A distant, obscure part of Odtsetseg wondered if she had triggered it, or whether it was always there and he had just never had a victim to share it with before tonight.

Kincaide smiled at her with a love so warm that she wasn't cold anymore. Except she wasn't Odtsetseg.

She was Nayani.

Voices bickered. Angry music clashing like stormy seas, a thing none of them had ever heard or seen, but something that echoed back to the dawn of Humans, on their own world with open skies and solitude.

Before the Gage. Before the Alvar had arrived and conquered.

She was surrounded by rebels. Human rebels, born of a slice of

Humanity from a neighborhood in Boston Earth that had been loaded aboard a Gage ship under Alvar eyes and carried to Boston Dome.

Kincaide resisted some group action, aggressively negative to the suggestions from a male across the way. Arms crossed and face cross, he exuded disdain for a plan.

Seven others outvoted him, so the motion to commit carried.

Commit what?

Mischief? That was Kincaide's expectation. All risk for little reward.

As Nayani, she was unsure, but not as resolutely opposed as her husband. She loved him, but hers had been the only other vote opposed, and even that halfhearted, as she could not see the thing that drove him to resist.

Time blinked in the dream and she was elsewhere. Home, in bed with her husband. He was on top of her, inside her, carrying her to heights of ecstasy no other man had ever managed with Nayani.

Odtsetseg grasped clutching claws at the image, but it faded before she could truly understand what it meant to no longer be a virgin. Nayani had known, but she was dead and could not share.

Odtsetseg had only other women's memories of such things. All of the Odtsetsegs, across all of time. None of them had been touched by a man. Penetrated. Initiated into a new world of wonders. Made sexual.

And then it was gone in a blink, leaving the two of them lying side by side, just holding hands because even the darkness was too bright right now.

"Stupid plan," Kincaide muttered as she blinked and they were in a living room, just the two of them. "It won't work."

"Nelson has never been wrong before," she/Nayani replied soothingly.

She loved Kincaide for his strength, his courage. That unshakable power at his core that could not be overcome by anything. But he was wrong here.

Still, she loved him.

"Too much risk," Kincaide pronounced. "Not sufficient reward. We do better in the walls like a burrowing rodent. Emerging into sunlight is an invitation to be stomped by the Alvar and their pets."

"The movement needs public symbols," she/Nayani reminded him. "Without that, they might decide to simply accept the Gage as the natural order of things. Accept the Alvar as our lords and masters forever. Forget what it means to be Human."

"They have already forgotten," Kincaide groused. "How many of those rebels are Analogues, love? They have all been Indexed by the Gage. Stored in The Catalogue and decanted time and again as population falls necessitated more bodies. How many Humans in this Dome were born of woman, and not machine?"

"More than half still," she agreed. "As you said when I first met you. We have never been Indexed. Never will be. Will not live forever because we choose to be Human. We will live and die and be forgotten, save for deeds like this that will live forever in Human memory."

He grunted, unconvinced, but he loved her and would do this thing merely because she asked.

Odtsetseg reached out to hold that love. To taste it before it evaporated, but it blinked.

Gone.

Empty.

Bereft.

She stood on a street. Daytime now as the moon was tidally locked with the planet below, where sunlight and darkness each lasted three weeks here.

She held a weapon, but not one she understood. The Gage controlled The Catalogue. Controlled the printers that would allow you to output whatever device you needed. Beam weapons were forbidden, but physics was physics and chemistry unchanged. Simple machine parts could be printed or adapted easily enough.

She held a slugthrower rifle. Brass containers with steel-tipped projectiles. Powered by chemical combustion to hurl death at high speeds and using simple springs to recharge for continuous fire as long as you held a trigger back.

Kincaide was next to her, holding nothing but a bag of explosives, again simple chemistry rather than something truly powerful.

They didn't want to destroy the Dome. Just make a political statement of resistance to the Gage followers around them.

It was night, according to the clock. The streets were mostly empty as Humans and other species slept. Nelson led them along a side alley to a door. Like all doors, it was controlled by biometrics with the addition of a passcode.

If you could decant a dozen such versions of a person, a simple iris print was no longer sufficient. Bank accounts were the same way, and many people set up eternal accounts for themselves at banks against being decanted on some unknown date.

The personal rule was that you should keep half of the funds and then open a second account for future you after changing the passcode to this one.

Nayani wondered how it might have been in the distant past, when there might only be one of you in all of history. When the heirs you left money for were children, rather than future you, decanted by some God or Alvar for whatever project or need that came up before being discarded into the streets.

Nelson set the team up watching both ends of the alley and gestured Kincaide to blow the door. Nayani took up a watchful spot nearby, ducked behind a recycling dumpster designed for metal waste rather than organic effluvia. Others watched from similar cover.

Kincaide moved with calm deliberation as he attached bits of clay to the door in various places.

Something warned her.

Nayani turned to the mouth of the alley and saw the first titan appear.

Alvar.

Two and a half to three meters tall. One hundred eighty to two hundred seventy-five kilograms. Blue skin. Pale hair. Long face. Pointed ears. Heavy bones.

This one was male, at the top of the physical end. He wore armor made of steel with a bronze facing and ornate scrollwork to stop clubs and swords, over the usual insulating suit that would protect him against beam weapons.

In one hand he carried a painstik, scaled up to his tremendous size and crackling with power.

Cries of anguish and fear erupted around her as others appeared behind the first, but Odtsetseg/Nayani focused herself on the first one. She must protect Kincaide.

Nayani/Odtsetseg rose from her crouch and pulled the trigger of the weapon. They had warned her that recoil would drive the end of the barrel into the air, so she aimed low and leaned herself into it like the stiff wind of a shell breach she had to escape before the corridor locks sealed.

The weapon chunked with a sound so immense that she was

instantly deafened. A runner's heartbeat pounded in her ears from the gun, even as her own heart began to race.

The Alvar was caught off-guard. Previously, he had been immune to the puny, tiny mortals that surrounded him. Swords bounced off his steel. Beams grounded.

In his immense, undying lifetime, he had never been hurt.

Alvar blood was green as it spilled. Spurted.

The titan collapsed like a broken tower.

Her rifle clicked empty.

Another titan appeared behind the first one.

Nayani/Odtsetseg turned to a calmly-angry Kincaide and suffered as much as he would ever say to anyone, just looking at her.

He had been right. Somehow, this had been a trap.

Nayani/Odtsetseg loaded another stick of ammunition into the weapon as the second titan pulled a hotblaster and opened fire.

Nelson died first. Fitting, as it had been his idea.

"Run," she yelled at Kincaide as she opened fire again. She wasn't sure he could hear her over the immense noise of so many rifles chattering.

But he nodded at her. She watched him pull a lump of clay from the door, insert a detonator into the wad, and throw it at the mouth of the alley.

It exploded with a flash of light, sound, and wind so intense it nearly knocked her over, but Nayani/Odtsetseg held the line, continuing to fire as Kincaide ran.

She never saw the beam that struck her from behind as she moved from cover to join her lover in flight.

Only pain as it kissed her back.

Only death as it ended her.

Only darkness.

CHAPTER 4

Odtsetseg woke in darkness and confusion.

Warmth engulfed her, and she realized that as both she and Kincaide had fallen asleep, the older Human had wrapped himself around her like a cloak.

Both slept dressed save for her shoes and his boots. She had other memories of sleeping with him, but were those her memories? She had been Nayani, not Kincaide in the dream.

Had felt him make love to her. To his wife.

Where did the dreams end and the waking begin?

He snored quietly in her ear, one hand under her head and the other across her stomach, softly palming the belly button that was the leftover from someone else's birth.

Someone else's life.

She listened with her mind, but he had fallen into a dreamless darkness now.

Odtsetseg considered laying here all night, enjoying the warm comfort of real arms around her, rather than memories implanted or stolen somewhere along the way, but fear drove her now. Moving slowly, she pulled the hand from her stomach and rested it back on his hip. Slid away from the man as carefully as she could, wondering if she could somehow push him back down into sleep were he to start waking now.

Odtsetseg had never tried something like that, but she had precious few memories of previous incarnations of herself. From what she'd seen in Kincaide's mind, God would push and test, then go back and tweak the Icon and decant a new copy of her. Only a few times had he been satisfied at some plateau to make a new copy of her with enhanced abilities as a new starting point. Those were the only memories she had retained.

He was God, so she could find no anger in what he did to her. Only a father's love that he could make his daughter better, in a quest for the perfect Human. A shadow crossed her mind fleetingly, but it fled before she could grasp it.

Odtsetseg made it to the edge of the bed and rose carefully, still listening as Kincaide rolled over on his other side now, never stirring in his dreams.

She wanted to kiss him. To thank him, but her stolen memories suggested that it would wake him. So many years of paranoia that the Alvar had finally identified him. Found him. Were coming for him.

He would rouse with violence in his hands and rage in his heart on that day.

Odtsetseg planted a mental kiss in his dreams, where he might never find it on waking.

Her heart was warm now, but her soul had gotten even colder. She pulled on her slippers and moved out of the sleeping chamber, into the larger space where Kincaide Kataragama lived.

Sparse. Almost empty and utilitarian.

Her cabin had an easel and oils she could mix. Drying portraits that never once suggested a realism school of painting, because she painted Humans as the emotional matrices she saw. Odtsetseg wasn't sure she had ever actually seen a Human face, so intensely did her Power bleed over all her other senses.

She made it to the door and listened, but Kincaide remained asleep, so she took a deep breath and opened it, emerging like a butterfly into the antechamber. Her door immediately to the left, with Zhubin's beyond that. The kitchen door on her right and the lounge directly across. The hallway that was an airlock, beyond which the ship's neck stretched gracefully and connected with the Crew Section like a goose she had never seen except in memories of other people.

Everything aft was protected by warp-shields. Crew, weapons, sensors, environmental systems, generators, even the decant machines that God would use when he found his Eden and could repopulate the world with only perfect beings.

When she wouldn't be alone anymore.

She strode purposefully to the other door, knocking quietly. A mind approached, felt her, opened the hatch.

Zhubin Prakash. *Spear*, in the ancient language known as Sanskrit, at least as it had been handed down to modern descendants who had no memory of such a place.

Tall and mighty, compared to most of the rest of the crew. One hundred and ninety-three centimeters. One hundred and two kilograms. Lighter skinned than most of the Humans, from a section of home once called Gujarat in the far northwest. Back when those sorts of directions had meaning. Dark eyes. Lean muscles.

Like Kincaide, old enough to be her father, had she any besides God. But it was different in Zhubin's case. He was an Analogue, like her. Indexed at twenty-four years Standard Personal, and decanted several times, because the Gage had considered him the perfect warrior. Before he had become The Chairman, she knew his title had once been The Assassin. This copy had been living until he was fifty-one years old, twenty-seven years as a killer and a fugitive.

He studied her like one might a valuable painting. Her own had no value, save whatever her notoriety might instill, but she understood the concept.

"Come," he said, withdrawing into the chamber finally.

Inside, it was somehow a middle ground between the busyness of her suite and the starkness of Kincaide's. Several comfortable chairs and a couch that brought a harsh flashback to Nelson arguing wrongly with Kincaide that the Alvar would never expect such an attack.

Kincaide had never been able to prove that they had been betrayed by an insider or close contact of the group, but he'd been the only survivor, so he hadn't spent time hunting traitors.

Just mourning Nayani quietly.

Zhubin displayed several weapons on the walls decoratively, or rested them in corners and out of the way, but still where he might reach them instantly at need. Most were for melee, from knives to staves, but she saw an unstrung bow, a rifle remarkably similar to the one she had carried as Nayani, and two hotblasters: a pistol and a short rifle, scaled down to Human hands.

This was a man prepared to kill again at a moment's notice.

Art on the walls suggested landscapes by someone standing on the surface of a habitable planet, watching suns rise or set. None of her own memories had ever walked on the surface of any place but the moon below them. Never felt wind that wasn't a breach. Never felt the sun warm her skin.

Zhubin sat her on the couch and took a chair. Like Kincaide, he wore the standard bodysuit of the crew, with his being blue as Chairman of the corporation. It reminded her of Alvar skin. God had just provided the funding, the legal framework, and the Engine for the project. Zhubin had been responsible for the rest, although God would bring the Eden Package with him at the very end, just before they attempted to flee the Gage Empire.

The crew in green all answered to this man. Including Kincaide. Odtsetseg supposed she did as well, although with Kincaide the three of them formed a Triumvir at the peak of the ship. Zhubin's connections. Kincaide's experience in space, after his time as a rebel.

Her Power.

She wasn't sure how God would fit into the matrix they were making, but she was sure the three men had it handled.

"What went wrong?" Zhubin asked her as Odtsetseg found herself thinking.

"Wrong?" she asked, confused.

Zhubin Prakash was a hard man to read. Intentionally so at a mental level, she gathered. His training had included techniques intended to protect him from telepaths like her. She could focus on him and read the man, if she chose, but otherwise her probes tended to slide off the surface of his mind.

"You woke Kincaide and then retired with him," Zhubin replied. "It was long enough that you went to sleep with the man, but did not engage in anything physical, as it is now the middle of the night and you are on my doorstep. Something was bad enough that you came to me for help. I cannot imagine Kincaide Kataragama has forgotten how to fornicate. *What. Went. Wrong?*"

She took a breath to ground herself from the intense emotionality coming off the man like waves of radiation. Odtsetseg wondered if his words might blow her hair back, but he was right. She had come here.

Something was indeed wrong. She lacked the subtlety or guile to dance elegantly around the words. It was too important.

"Kincaide is dying," she replied simply.

CHAPTER 5

Zhubin thought he had steeled himself for anything this woman might tell him. Thought that a lifetime of war and death and deceit had prepared him for all eventualities.

He had been wrong.

"Dying?" he gasped.

Immediately, his mind went to all manner of medical emergencies and he fought to not spring from his chair to summon a doctor. But the Engine knew all of this. She had been programmed with the correct procedures, since retraining each of them would take too much time.

She would have sounded the alarm already, so it was something else.

Zhubin watched the muscles around her glowing eyes and her jaw as they worked, seeking to shape words that a mere Human might understand. That much he knew about her, but he'd also spent much time listening to Hasan Ildar explain the thing he was building.

Human, but both more so and less at the same time.

The Engine. He had to stop and remember that she had a name. Odtsetseg. No family name. Just *Star Flower* in ancient Mongolian. Zhubin assumed that it drew from the design that advanced genetics had added to her face when it gave her the power to alter space.

"Dying," she finally repeated. "Slowly, but surely."

"How do you know this?" he demanded quietly.

"We slept together," she admonished him like she was the elder and he but a mere stripling.

He let the smile appear on his face.

"There was no intercourse," she continued sharply. "Sleep. His arms around me to keep me warm."

She paused and something about the light in her eyes changed.

"He protected me," she said in a quieter voice before it gained power again. "Or meant to. I fell into his dreams."

"Tell me everything," Zhubin ordered her.

So she did.

Most of it he had already known before this. And he had never encountered a telepath powerful enough to become a character in someone else's dreamstate, but he had no doubts. Odtsetseg was too flat of a personality to have developed deviousness yet.

Ildar intentionally kept her design that way, although Zhubin supposed that she might finally reach end-state if this version was intended to live for several years.

"Why do you think he is dying?" Zhubin finally asked when she was done.

"All of you are driven by desire," this painfully-young, innocent waif of a telepath announced in a voice like a goddess brought to space with them. "You. God. Any of the crew I interact with. Forceful, powerful emotions. Fear. Anger. Something."

"And Kincaide?" Zhubin asked, wondering what this woman had seen or discovered that all the psychological tests and notes had missed.

Zhubin had looked long and hard to find a Foreman to build what the Alvar believed was simply a new colony ship. *Dashavatara* on paper had been designed to establish a new arms storage depot colony somewhere on the fringes of Gage Space. Engines were routinely used up and burned out by exposure to the warp. And the things that lived inside it, outside the known universe.

Most Humans were kept nearby on Al-Winoq's lone moon, itself apparently similar to the homeworld of the conquered Humans. Large and gray and uninhabited save for the Domes. Having a new supply closer to the edge of the Empire would allow the Gage Fleet to more rapidly conquer new worlds and new species. The Alvar must always be kept in luxury.

The Engine studied him, like she shared his thoughts. She might. He was not trying to keep her at bay right now.

"The opposite of love is not hate, Chairman," she said in a grown-up voice he'd never heard from the woman. "It is apathy. The opposite of all strong emotions is the lack of any. Kincaide Kataragama has given up even hope."

"How soon?" he demanded. "How much time do we have before he surrenders?"

"I am not Human, Chairman Prakash." She almost snarled the words at him. "Not male. Not old. Not original. I am a young, female, Analogue who has never even been kissed, let alone seen the world in such terms."

Zhubin controlled his anger at the woman's response. She was right. Ildar had not equipped her with the psychological tools necessary to process such things, preferring her in a simpler state.

Innocent, if you will.

Hasan Ildar needed Zhubin Prakash for deviousness.

"Can you show me?" he asked her. "What it was you saw in Kincaide? Can you implant it in my mind so that I can understand and perhaps find the fire that has ebbed?"

"Fire?" she asked, wholly lost now.

"As you said, Odtsetseg," Zhubin explained. "You have youth and femininity on your side, so you cannot truly begin to understand a man like Kincaide. I am old and male and mean."

"Oh," she said simply, eyes opening about as far as her sockets would allow. They lit up when she did that.

Odtsetseg reached out a hand and he took it.

Zhubin tried to express everything he felt in physical terms, lacking the vocabularies that proper telepaths had developed to explain themselves. The Engine had never met any others of her kind to learn.

Or rather, she had, but Ildar had erased those memories and implanted other ones in their place.

Zhubin steeled his mind against her rifling his memories, but she just nodded at him, perhaps still too unsettled by Kincaide to want to experience another Human right now.

He felt hands reach out and take hold of his mind, even as they sat perfectly still, holding hands across a small space and staring at each other. The Engine opened up a portion of his mental shields and put it carefully to one side, as a mechanic about to repair a system would unbolt a panel first.

Something heavy pushed down on his mind, almost driving him

into the chair, but again, it was all mental. He felt her hands take hold of his and lift them up, wrapping them around—...*something*.

"A memory," she explained. "With all the necessary symbolism and emotional loading cataloged for you to understand."

Zhubin felt her hands withdrawing now. Closing up his mind and watching from a safe distance.

He studied this thing cerebrally, rather than falling into it. The woman had added a second memory alongside, almost invisible because the emotional signature was so slight compared to the first.

But then, the first had been the mission that had gotten Kataragama's wife killed and turned a young man into a fugitive who eventually came to be known as Kincaide Kataragama, regardless of who he had been born as. Of course, such a memory would be heavy in the mind.

He turned to the other. It was a vision of this same woman, taken from Kincaide's mind as they lay down and she slid carefully back against him so he could pull up a blanket, in spite of them both being fully dressed, and then cuddle.

If such a term could be used here. There was no romance. No love. No hate, beyond that background radiation that marked Kataragama's entire existence of hating everyone. Kincaide had no aspirations to strip this young woman naked and experience her physically, even if she might not have resisted such an action.

She just didn't know what she was doing. Zhubin wondered if he should task a crew member with initiating her into the adult glories, but then he saw her explanation of the rest of the crew. The adoration. The worship.

The Fear. Of her.

Only Kincaide was not afraid of this being.

Zhubin leaned back in his mind. Was he afraid of her?

He supposed so, at some non-intellectual level. Fear of her power, as all Humans had.

No. Most Humans. Kincaide Kataragama had no fear of her at all. She could not hurt him, after all, any greater than Nayani's death had. She could only kill him, if she dove deep enough into his mind, which was why Zhubin found he did have a fear of her.

Nothing could stop an angry telepath from doing such things, save another one.

But the Star Flower had no rage in her soul. Only love and inquisitiveness.

As designed.

Odtsetseg saw Kincaide grown old and tired. A generation removed from the loss that defined him and approaching an age when death might be coming for him.

After all, the man had undergone no treatments that might extend his life. Had never been Indexed and corrected before a new copy was decanted.

He was Human, with all that such a silly thing implied.

Zhubin had no idea how long he himself would live. Or even how many copies of himself the Alvar and their servants in the Gage Empire had decanted over the years. Centuries? Time was an odd beast when you might awaken tomorrow and step out of a small coffin.

To you, it would be as though no time at all had passed, but the world outside would have aged and moved on. At least as far as the Gage would allow their Humans to advance, which was not much.

But she was right, this Star Flower.

Kincaide was preparing himself for death.

Whether he expected this mission to fail, or succeed, Kincaide had largely given up hope of anything and begun to withdraw. Odtsetseg would not understand, because she was young and female. Beautiful, in her own way, although Zhubin preferred a woman or man with far more meat and muscle.

Kincaide's fire was guttering. Odtsetseg was not the woman to revive it, because she lacked the tools to understand what a man like that would need.

Kincaide had duty driving him now, and not much more. Odtsetseg had misunderstood that power, because for her it was genetic, rather than volitional.

Zhubin leaned back physically now, breaking contact with the woman, but only after she had been given the opportunity to see his own thought processes in motion. Ildar had designed, programmed, and built this woman, and she was a clean, steel blade, lacking nicks and mars.

Zhubin Prakash had perhaps been damascened as a weapon over his lifetimes. Folded and welded and layered as the ancient bladesmiths might have built something. Ugly to look at, but beautiful once you understood the purpose.

"He is not dying?" she asked quietly. Confused but not desperate.

"He is," Zhubin corrected her. "But not immediately. You are seeing the end result of decades of grief coming to something of a focus. Partly, that is you, because you remind him of what it meant to be young and innocent, Odtsetseg. He looks back forty years and wonders what he has accomplished with his time. Precious little, because he does not count staying alive that highly. This mission will probably define his mark in the history books, and so he looks beyond it and sees only darkness."

"But he will carry us there?" she asked tentatively.

"You will carry us, Engine," he replied forcefully.

"No," the young woman countered, just as sharp. "I will carry this ship on my shoulders. Kincaide will carry the mission on his."

Zhubin lapsed into silence in surprise. He didn't think the Analogue had developed the touch to understand such a fine distinction.

But she was not wrong.

Now, he needed to find a way to relight the fire in that man's soul.

FLYER

CHAPTER 6

Kincaide was still forward today from the rest of the ship, but not all the way out on the tip. Warp-shielding required a strange architecture to a starship, at least as Ildar had designed and built it.

The hexagon bow of the ship that Kincaide shared with Odtsetseg and Zhubin. Then the airlock sealing the forward quarters off from the rest of the ship. A long gooseneck connected aft to the much-larger Crew Section, where Ildar's design had put himself and most of the crew safely inside the warp-shields.

But the bridge was midway, atop the center of the gooseneck. Outside the warp-shields, because the Engine had to be there in order to twist space with her mind.

The space was unlike any ship he had served on in the last twenty years. Most were crowded and grubby, only fit for any of the small species, since most were tiny compared to the Alvar. Only the ships of the masters had space and beauty inside and out.

Ildar, however, had designed something more like a cathedral than a bridge. Rather than individual stations with seats, there was a single hollow square counter filling the center of the room, broken up every meter into stations and with a variable incline almost like a drafting table. Crew members stood at a station and talked to each other sideways and across, with two of the corners open for access. Each station had personal holograms available, as well as the large projector at the center of the square.

Kincaide had a small office at the rear of the space, up a shallow half-flight of stairs with a wall that could be open or closed as he needed for meetings and privacy. He had a standing desk that mirrored the work stations outside. Odtsetseg would sit in the only chair in the space, at the front of the bridge and up an entire flight of stairs onto what a building might call a mezzanine.

The walls and ceiling were a clear dome, just like Boston on the moon below them, with invisible wires, equipment, and cabling built in to provide lighting and handle both information technology and environmental systems.

Flying through space today was like walking on the surface level of Boston, rather than down in the warrens or up on a tower where the poor lived.

A head appeared from the stairwell to the main deck hallway and Kincaide recognized Chairman Prakash joining them. He checked a readout and decided that three minutes early was close enough for this test flight. Odtsetseg would not be needed, so she was forward in her quarters right now.

Except that she was not. As Kincaide emerged from his office, he noted the young woman following in Zhubin's wake. Odtsetseg did not ascend to her throne. Instead, she simply moved out of the way into as much of a corner as a hemisphere could invoke, ninety degrees away from her station forward, and across from his office on the port side.

Out of the way, but he noted the way the bridge crew seemed to track her unconsciously in how they stood and where they glanced.

"Bring Information Systems live," Kincaide ordered as he descended his own steps to the main deck.

A face appeared in the big projector. Human, but ethnically vague in construction. Caucasian, only in that it wasn't African or East Asian in the bones. Male, although the system randomly selected personalities every day.

"Good afternoon, I am Hubert, our Computer Personality of the Day," it said in a warm, masculine voice best suited to reading books on the comm for those folks who consumed things via audio.

"All sectors check in prior to free flight," Kincaide called to the oldest man on the bridge right now.

Reyhan Herath had served with Kincaide on other vessels in the past, one of the best Information Systems technicians around. He still maintained those strange sideburns that were trimmed high and forward, almost like horns across his cheeks, even as the top of his head had precious few hairs left, all those combed back. The ring around his skull had stopped being gray finally and things were fading to white now. The rest of him was still thin and fit, even as they both were getting old.

The man nodded a smile Kincaide's direction and pressed buttons.

"Life Systems are green," Dr. Dissanayake replied, the man speaking for the terraforming section, decanting systems, and the huge botanical forest that took up most of the top deck of the Crew Section aft.

"Behavioral Medicine as normal," Dr. Perera replied a moment later, her voice pert and sharp. Professional and expert. All you ever wanted in the person responsible for the physical, psychological, and emotional quality of the crew.

Around the square now as Reyhan nodded to his underlings.

"Helm answering all commands," Dinushan looked up and smiled, his face cheerful since today was finally his chance to fly something other than a simulator.

"Weapon Systems pass all checks, but remain locked down," Hanishka spoke. She wouldn't get to play today, but took it all in stride.

Dashavatara was heavily armed for a vessel of its size, but it was still an explorer, not a Gage warship in combat service. Hopefully Hanishka was nothing but an insurance policy he would never need to cash.

"My systems are within acceptable tolerances," the Power Systems tech spoke now.

Tharushi Sampath was young, but Kincaide had specifically picked her over some of the more experienced candidates for the job. Everything here was experimental. Pushing the limits of what Humans had been able to learn, research, or steal.

At twenty-three, a woman like Tharushi didn't have any bad habits to unlearn, as *Dashavatara* pretty much represented the entirety of her advanced educational outcomes.

"The Encyclopedia Core is fully operational with stable backups," Hubert announced professionally.

Reyhan looked up then nodded to Kincaide. The man always kept his sideburns shaved to look like a bull about to charge. Otherwise, he had just a few wisps of gray hair on top.

Reyhan scowled today at the seriousness of things. Kincaide

grinned in spite of himself, since the man was mostly bluster and brains, rather than deviousness and violence.

That was Kincaide's department.

"All sectors ready, Kincaide," Reyhan announced anti-climatically.

Kincaide turned to Zhubin, but the man had taken a spot along the wall close to Odtsetseg. Out of the way on one side where he could just watch, rather than being involved.

Prakash was the Chairman of the Board of Directors. *Dashavatara* was an experimental colony ship designed and built by Humans for a Human crew to transport a Catalogue package, once other Gage vessels dropped enough prefab housing and industrial systems onto the surface of some world to create a forward arms depot.

Said so right there in the paperwork that some Alvar senior bureaucrat had signed off on. The Alvar controlled the Gage Empire. Even something as innocent and innocuous a project as *Dashavatara* would not be entrusted to the servants. Especially not if success here opened up whole new vistas of the galaxy to easy conquest, with a stockpile of Engines staged safely at a forward base.

Kincaide wondered how long it would take the Alvar or the rest of the Gage to discover they'd been hoodwinked.

"Helm, detach from the dock and prepare to exit Al-Winoq Glide for open space," Kincaide said in a louder than normal voice.

Perhaps the emotion of the day would allow it, as the ship had never been ready for free flight until now. But they had arrived.

Once this flight was successful, and any last little surprises corrected, Hasan Ildar would arrive with his Eden Package and *Dashavatara* would set out on a mission it would never complete. At least as far as the Alvar were able to determine.

Assuming they didn't arrive with Gage Killships or Warp Voyagers while *Dashavatara* was still transiting the system on that fateful day, making the run to the edge of the solar reach so they could jump into warp and flee.

Dashavatara had only been held in place by a handful of struts today. The gooseneck began to turn, stars moving against the night sky. Aft, the larger Crew Section would drift some as the four engines, arranged on the cardinal points, would begin to slowly push the mass of the mighty vessel forward.

Out of the dock. Out of the planetary Glide. Into the darkness between worlds.

Eventually, the darkness between stars and then the cold of warp-space. Tomorrow.

Kincaide wondered if a powerful Engine like Odtsetseg would draw in warp-spawn or repel them. Nobody knew what would happen, because there had never been a thing in creation like her.

Most ships this size had six Humans to power the matrix. It generally only required five, with a spare, and smart ships kept a small crew of extra Humans around against emergencies in the same way that *Dashavatara* had a few cats. Protection against surprises.

Nobody knew what actually happened, other than warp-spawn would sometimes possess an open mind and destroy it as you transited their realm.

"Kincaide, we're clear of the dock," Dinushan said as he looked up from his console.

"Ahead three points until we clear the Glide," Kincaide said. "Then bring it slowly up to ten points to test Tharushi's systems. Stay clear of all nav corridors and let me know when we can push things a little with maneuvering."

Dinushan smiled like an eight-year-old in a candy story with credits in hand and walls of sweets galore.

Kincaide looked over at Odtsetseg, but she was lost in the view of the stars overhead and the other stations in Glide orbit, slowly falling behind until they were hidden behind the larger bulk of the Crew Section and engines.

warp-spawn. A religious man might call them demons. To Kincaide, they were just a fact of life. Supposedly, early Alvar designs, epochs ago, had used one crewman, just the Engine, until they discovered that they could shield a section of the ship in warp-space and protect anyone else inside it. But the Engines still had to be outside the warp-shields.

Even *Dashavatara* followed that design, with the gooseneck and forward section small and thinly populated, compared to the mass aft. In space, the crew around him would fly the ship from here, but once they prepared to jump, most of these men and women would retire and hide behind shielding.

But only most.

Kincaide had modified the original design to include a cabin for him, up next to Odtsetseg's. Zhubin had insisted on joining them in living dangerously, so the bow had been rebuilt from a point into a small, bulbous Hexagon where the three of them could remain physically isolated from the rest of the ship while in warp-space.

Not today, but soon he would confront those demons. Today, he just had to run down a punchlist to prove to everyone that *Dashavatara* was ready for the last and greatest step.

And the biggest adventure in the history of Humanity.

CHAPTER 7

Hasan Ildar studied the Alvar bureaucrat who was his nemesis today. The one who had been an issue for the decade and a half it had taken to get this far.

Dark blue skin, like all of his kind. Fine hair on his head so pale as to be almost white. Enormous compared to a Human, but only average among the giants.

Songkram Sangsuriya. Colonial Dispatch Administrator of the First Rank. A being at the top of the civil service, as such things went, where those above this person were generally scions of the Great Families appointed to manage the Gage.

Sangsuriya was young, as Alvar went, being roughly only forty-five hundred Human years old. In another five or seven hundred years, he would probably be promoted into the ranks of management, but for today, he was a thorn that Hasan could not pluck.

That day was coming. Sooner than the Alvar believed possible, but they measured military campaigns in centuries. The fruit flies beneath their notice had to move with far greater alacrity to get things done.

"The project is close to culmination?" Sangsuriya inquired in a lazy voice that gave lie to the attention the creature had centered on it.

A Colonial Dispatch Administrator of the First Rank did not bother himself with such petty details as this project without good reason. He had layers of underlings to sign documents and file reports. *Dashavatara* only rose to the man's attention because Hasan Ildar was close to proving Songkram Sangsuriya wrong. Proving that Humans were good enough servants to rise in the Gage, relative to many of the other subject species.

Heaven's Anointed were never wrong. That was the whole point of the Creator showering them with *Her* love. The Alvar were the physically largest sentient species in known space. Simply the most powerful. Intellectually at least the equal of all others. Politically, they were in control of the strongest and most extensive empire in the history of sentience in the form of The Gage.

But they could not power starships.

Oh, they could. Doing so had once allowed them to be first into space nearly a million Human years ago, when they chose to risk themselves as Engines and travel across warp-space, however slowly and dangerously it had been then. There had been fewer warp-spawn incidents in those days. Or perhaps the outsiders hadn't noticed the Alvar until later.

One Engine to a ship turned into two. Three. Six. Twelve. Etc. Larger and more powerful vessels plying the space lanes, until they found the Mori. The largest of the Mori in those days had still been smaller than the average Alvar, and starkly primitive in comparison.

They got added to The Gage. And began powering starships to protect the more important species. The Gage Empire became expansive at that point, locating and assimilating the Lop, the Ayotochtli, the Mog, the Cassoway, the Warednja, and even the silly kangaroo-like creatures everyone simply called Boomers.

Twenty-four individuals of such lesser species drove the war vessels of The Gage in those days, the Warp Voyagers. Ninety-six engines were necessary to transport the gargantuan landers that brought combat legions to the ground: the mighty **Starfall** vessels.

And then The Gage discovered Humans. A species so radically insane that half as many or even fewer could power a ship through warp-space. Of course, the Gage conquered the Humans. Carried off as many as they could locate and brought them to Al-Winoq where they could be bred like rabbits to provide as many Engines as possible.

The Gage even looked with favor on those Humans willing to experiment on their own kind to make better Engines. Men like Hasan Ildar, who threatened a technological breakthrough so stunning that it would forever alter the shape of The Gage.

If it worked.

Hasan studied the man across the desk. Alvar tended to dress in an outfit similar to the primitives of Earth, in the late Bronze age. A long bolt of fine, white cloth with a hole for the head, passed over and draped to knees front and back. Belted at the waist with heavy brown leather and an ornate buckle.

Bureaucrats such as this man covered both shoulders, while politicians and the upper classes normally only covered one shoulder, showing off the muscles and definition of being an Alvar, where the males were stocky and ripped for all their immense size, and females tended to be leaner, but just as muscled.

In spite of their other differences, Humans and Alvar looked the most alike of all species in space, not counting differences in scale. All the same parts in roughly the same locations and serving similar purposes. No fur, unlike Mog or Mori. No feathers like the Cassoway. No scales like the Ayotochtli.

Humans were thus the favored pet species of the Alvar within The Gage.

Hasan considered his response to the simple question posed. Alvar lived for eight thousand years, so they were never in a hurry in conversation.

"*The project is close to culmination?*" the creature had asked.

"We are indeed close to success," Hasan replied evasively, letting his face even relax into a disarming smile. "The vessel I designed has completed a test run around the solar system and docked with a short list of repairs and adjustments to make. It is actually a shorter list than I had anticipated. When that is done, we will be ready to test the warp-capabilities of the new Engine I have designed."

"One Human, to power a vessel that large?" Sangsuriya probed, tasting the words it seemed.

"This model is no longer entirely Human, Administrator," Hasan countered. "I have modified the base form extensively, adjusting the Icon nearly a thousand times to bring out the power needed."

"And when you are satisfied?" the political monster in blue before him asked.

"I will upload her to the Catalogue and all vessels might be capable of flying with only one Engine, as in the ancient era," Hasan smiled.

"Your kind will become less valuable as servants," Sangsuriya noted.

Hasan laughed out loud. It was a biting, penetrating harshness that caused the slightest flinch to emerge from that massive creature.

"She cannot breed even remotely true, Administrator Sangsuriya," Hasan smiled. "That was one of many things I had to adjust in this model. However, with another few centuries of research, I should be able to produce even better models. Advanced Humans, perhaps, who will serve the needs of The Gage nicely."

He didn't say Alvar. The Gage Empire was more than just the blue giants in control of it right now. Give him another thousand years of tinkering, and Hasan and his descendants would be able to subjugate the Alvar and swap places with them.

Assuming he didn't just wipe them out everywhere.

Hasan Ildar did not remember Earth. None of the generation that had been originally Indexed into the great Catalogue from the surface of the conquered world were decanted these days. The Alvar had carried off copies of nearly one billion Humans who had survived.

That a person did not emerge alive from the scanner was not a problem. To the person scanned, they stepped into the box and felt a brief pain. Then they could be decanted later, never knowing that they had been ripped apart at the molecular level and transformed into information to be stored in the Catalogue of the Alvar and The Gage.

The Alvar had decanted Humans into the Domes at Al-Winoq's moon and left them for several hundred years, not Indexing new ones until the first generation was all dead and gone. And claiming new Engines as they needed them.

The only memories left of Earth were oral and cultural.

So the Alvar also didn't care if Humans experimented on each other, as long as the results would enhance the power of The Gage. Hasan Ildar was himself twelve hundred years old, and well on his way to immortality.

He had been his own first significant experiment, striving to understand the technology at hand by getting the Alvar to let him keep tweaking and decanting copies of himself, until he knew that age would not ever bother him again.

He would be forty years old forever. Mature enough to be taken seriously by other Humans. Fixed of all injuries and age-related ailments, and then decanted in a perfect form.

A god, if you will.

"Why will it take a few centuries to produce a better model?" the Administrator asked, voice heavy with something approaching malice, however faintly.

"The Gage will need to test this one exhaustively," Hasan smiled. "I have not put her out against warp-spawn to see what they will do. Nor pushed her design to carry something as heavy as a Starfall."

"The demons might take her?" Sangsuriya asked, apprehension now evident.

"Which is why this first mission will include only Humans, Elder," Hasan replied. "None of the Alvar will be at risk if something goes wrong, and I will have her Icon at hand if this model is killed and I need to decant a backup in the field."

The man nodded, as though hearing sage advice.

Hasan clenched hard not to laugh triumphantly in the monster's face.

There would be no Alvar because Hasan Ildar was going to create a perfect future where there were no aliens. Only Humans. And only Humans like him, genetically drawn from a particular slice of the species marked by having originated in an area of Earth known as Caucasus.

Hasan was Tartar, according to his original genetic results. Most of his crew were from the south east, the area known as India on an ancient map. And those had been selected only after seeing their genes.

No Arabs, polluted by exposure to the Africans. No Americans, who were mongrels of all kinds, depending on which wave of settlers you wished to mark. No Chinese or any of those barbarians from the East. Not even Siberians.

Only the purest blood he had been able to locate, working within the Dome known as Boston and occasionally locating a few recruits from Chennai Dome or Tashkent Dome, but both of those had been horribly corrupted early on, because the Alvar had just loaded everyone into landing ships and carried them to camps near the only cities to survive the bombardment that had preceded conquest.

Hasan Ildar would live to see the galaxy conquered by purebreed Humans, with monsters such as Odtsetseg as just another tool at his command. The Alvar would join the Mori and the Warednja as servants of a **Human** order.

Or he would just kill them all. Alvar did not understand disease as a vector. Not like Hasan did.

Not like the Gods of Humanity might.

Hasan smiled at the Alvar bureaucrat and hoped that the creature lived a long and healthy life. Enough so that he was still around when

Hasan's Human armies swarmed out of the darkness and destroyed the Gage.

"So there is one mission remaining?" Sangsuriya asked.

"One," Hasan agreed benevolently. "And then we can begin to conquer the entire universe."

CHAPTER 8

Zhubin considered those that he might contact in his quest to save Kincaide from succumbing to *ennui* and entropy. Professionals would not succeed, because it was not a physical problem that beset the man. Nor even psychological.

The solution needed to be emotional.

Dashavatara had returned to the Glide and docked again into the cradle from which it had been born. Workers were making adjustments and repairs, but they were small and non-critical. The ship could have launched immediately, according to Kincaide's professional assessment, behind closed doors at the far end of their quick cruise.

Zhubin was descending to the Boston Dome in a shuttle, crammed into the poor, third-class seating that was good enough for the bipeds with forward hinged hips. Cassoway had their own shuttles for the few times they left the surface.

Alvar rode forward in luxury, as was their right by conquest.

Zhubin kept his murderous intent to himself, lest some semi-telepath nearby accidentally pick up emotional leakage.

Zhubin Prakash, like Kincaide Kataragama, was a facade cloaking another name. Another face in his case, as doctors had made adjustments to his over the years.

The Alvar had not managed to send a single copy of himself as an assassin in over a decade, but that was because Zhubin hid, not because they had forgiven. Or forgotten.

Third-class had no windows. No entertainment. You brought your own or suffered in silence. At least the shuttle and the Domes had gravity generators sufficient for comfort.

He could only imagine what it would have been like to try to live in one quarter gravity on a natural satellite.

Zhubin let his senses track the compartment. A Mori woman rode immediately next to him, her fur at times auburn or russet, depending on the lighting. Humans had once known horses on their homeworld, and the design implied a universality of physics, that had raised something similar to intelligence and tool use. Hooves had evolved into pads on the upper palms with four fingers and a thumb. Tall and heavy, but still lesser compared to the Alvar.

Fur covered her over, including the long, square skull that ended in a snout with a wide mouth and enormous nostrils. Delicate lashes protected eyes set just behind the front ridge, giving her exceptional vision rearwards, at the cost of the binocular vision of a hunter.

She had dyed her mane Alvar blue, for reasons he didn't care to even consider. But he was a rebel in a sea of conforming worshipers of the elder race. And even his uniform was the same shade of blue as Chairman of the vessel.

On him, it was all protective coloration. All a ruse.

As they descended from the heavens of Glide, his handheld began to pick up signals from Boston Dome as they approached this first stop. He would disembark the shuttle and then it would fly on to Cairo Dome, and finally Montevideo, before returning to the Glide and the orbital factories.

Kincaide needed help. Zhubin ignored the sly smile and batted eyelashes of the Mori woman next to him, pausing only to wonder at those creatures for whom species was not a boundary to...physical encounters. There was probably even a verb to describe the act, but Zhubin Prakash considered himself lucky enough that he had never had to know such a word.

And Kincaide didn't need an alien to tumble with. Rut with. However you wanted to classify such a debased activity. Zhubin closed his eyes and considered those memories that the Engine had stolen from the Foreman.

Kincaide had been driven into rebellion by anger at the Alvar. But not just the blues. At all their willing servants that made up The Gage. The mission had been to blow up a bank, but one that catered to the common folk, and not the masters in their elite towers.

Such as those didn't have banks they visited. They had bankers who called upon them, but even Nelson and his contacts had been able to find a chink in the armor they could exploit.

Zhubin wondered if someone had set Nelson up without the fool knowing it, but that was water twenty-two years under a bridge, and Kincaide Kataragama was the only survivor on this side of the equation.

Still, Zhubin made a note to inquire. It might be worth killing someone who had grown complacent because so much time had passed without retribution. Not that he would tell Kincaide. The man would not care. Would not find solace.

Zhubin meditated as they descended, hoping that he had found a match that he could use to set fire to Kataragama's soul once again.

CHAPTER 9

Zhubin emerged from the flight terminal and took in the surface crowd of Boston Dome as he began to walk. The skies were dark with the long night of orbital physics, but the clock still said day, however barely. Night as the locals measured it would fall shortly.

The streets seemed abandoned as he went. The city was massively overbuilt for the current population, but most of the empty housing was below ground. The poor could still be forced to live in sub-standard barracks, while the small cast of elites did quite well for themselves by knocking out walls and expanding their flats and mansions.

The middle had been what was hollowed out. Shopkeepers and Services. Small entrepreneurs who might keep an economy humming along. The rich had their own exploited servants, with most gladly aware that they aped the Alvar in how they treated those below them on the social scale. The poor who they felt existed to be exploited.

To serve.

Zhubin Prakash disliked even the word *aristocrat*, but that was what the Domes had evolved into over the centuries. Worse, lacking hope, the poor had largely ceased to breed, necessitating that the Alvar and their trusted servants decant copies of Humans from the Catalogue on a regular basis, just to keep the population up.

Humanity was failing. But all systems did when they had no way to grow, and the Domes were a hard, cold, psychological limit on Human potential. And the aristos did not help, trading slavish worship of the Alvar for the ability to sometimes hold the leash themselves.

Zhubin in his current Analogue had been an early, willing member of the resistance that would overthrow such a civilization and replace it with something better.

Nobody made eye contact with him as he walked, save for a woman seated in a second-story window and watching the street. From the way she was dressed, she would take suitors by the hour for some entertainment, with money changing hands, whether furtively or openly depending on the man or woman with a desperate need.

He found professionals to service those needs, and not in a tower overlooking a street where the poorest resided.

Boston Dome had not changed much since he had been first Indexed centuries ago. But it was emptier now than it had been, and he agreed with his earlier self that this was no place to bring a child up. Or even to decant the unwilling, most of whom had to take up living in the towers and serving Alvar who happened to have a skin tone other than blue.

Dashavatara would take them all someplace else. Zhubin Prakash did not expect to enjoy it there, but he had a dream. Aboard the ship, hidden in his personal quarters, he had an Icon of himself. A copy of the original Index. Aged twenty-four. A young man like himself, but one two years from meeting his future wife, another woman like Nayani who had been killed by the Alvar.

At the same time, Zhubin had managed to steal an Icon of Aysha, captured when she was twenty-eight Standard Personal and already secretly married to him for a year in her timeline.

He didn't have it in him to decant her now to deal with him as a fifty-one-year-old copy, when she would be so young and vibrant, but he hoped that when they got to Eden, he could introduce the younger version of himself to the woman he had considered perfect when he met her two years of personal time later.

Those two could find love and happiness, without a jaded, aged assassin intruding as anything more than a favored uncle.

How do you explain personal timelines to people when they are no longer anchored down by time itself?

At Eden, he would try.

Kincaide did not have such a thing. Nayani, like her husband, had never been Indexed. She had lived and died and been lost forever, except in the memories of three people now. She could not be brought back later to give him hope now.

Zhubin walked past another empty storefront, closed and abandoned unless and until the Humans of Boston Dome found purpose again, or the Alvar decided to refill the place and generate new hosts of Engines for conquest of the universe. As he walked, he continued to consider the many contacts that he had accumulated over two and a half decades in the shadows.

Finally, a name popped out of the murky darkness. There was one who might work.

CHAPTER 10

She had finally seen the stars with her own eyes. Odtsetseg didn't count sitting in dock in Al-Winoq Glide orbit, because she was still surrounded by Alvar technology. Or the memories of standing on the surface of Boston Dome, when those had been other people. But the ship had slipped the surly bonds and soared outward from the planet. Left the Boston Dome that another woman had been born under.

Flown.

She had spent the entire trip on the side of the bridge, staying out of everybody's way by not moving, trying not to press her nose against the glass. At the same time, the crew had—every single one of them, consciously or unconsciously—walked the other way around the square to get places, not drawing any closer to her than they needed.

Only Chairman Prakash had spent any time close to her. Kincaide had been neither warm nor cold to her, but she had watched his mind shift into a new focus Odtsetseg had never seen before as the vessel moved.

Harder. Tighter. She might have said happier, if she hadn't known better, but Odtsetseg supposed that would be a low bar to clear in any instance with that man.

Kincaide was who he was. A man not given to great troughs and crests of emotion, running on an impossibly long wavelength that carried him forward.

She did not understand a Human like that, but none of the women she could remember had ever met a man like Kincaide Kataragama. Even Chairman Prakash fell short in the comparison, for all his lethal skill and long experience, but she supposed that was exactly why he had chosen Kincaide as a Foreman for this ship and crew.

Competence.

It tugged at her, but Odtsetseg did not understand the emotions roiling beneath her surface.

At least she was away from the crew tonight. Proximity brought noise on the mental planes where she lived. The only time she had found peace was when they had tested the warp-shields in station dock, and everything went silent around her.

Blessed silence.

At the bow of *Dashavatara*, stuck out like a middle finger from a fist, the noise was much abated. Prakash had gone down to the Domes on some mission she hoped might help Kincaide. Only the Foreman remained close enough that she could hear him.

Aft, the repair teams working with the ship's crew amounted to a dull hum as she listened.

Something approached her door, but it was not Kincaide.

The hatch beeped twice, indicating that one of the ship's improved cats had arrived and was waiting. Each had a collar which the ship could read. It allowed them to open hatchways that were not locked, but personal quarters required the assent of the inhabitant before they would open.

The cats had been tweaked enough to understand that.

Ship's night hung high in the sky. Odtsetseg supposed that she should be asleep, but she was restless, seated in a little bubble at the very bow of the ship, an enclosed balcony just for her.

"Enter," she called and turned back to see who had decided to cross all the way forward out of the Crew Section, along the gooseneck, and into the forward dome.

She had been expecting Snuggle, the black male with three white socks who was the biggest love bug of the three. Lap kitty, content to climb up as soon as you sat to then flop over on his side, happily purring as long as you had a warm hand on his butt.

Or perhaps Shadow, Snuggle's sister that was the all-black hunter of the crew, stalking any little creature that might have slipped aboard in a cargo shipment.

But no, Blur bounded right up to her and meowed happily with a smile on his face. He was the goofball of the crew, a gray tabby with a stubby tail and big haunches. Performance Artist was how Prakash had described him, forever racing madly about as though on stage, or late for some rehearsal.

Odtsetseg was in her chair, surrounded by night sky and repair dock. She studied the little goof and patted her lap.

Blur surprised her by immediately leaping into her lap with a fierce chirp of concentration to let her know he was coming. She remembered from somewhere that cats did not vocalize to each other. That was for communicating with the furless weirdos who provided food.

Or, in this case, scritches, as he butted his head against her hand, as if to remind her why he was here.

Odtsetseg turned her chair back to the darkness and let her mind run free, listening to the purrs of bliss in her lap and wondering what it would be like out there.

Warp-spawn. Nobody knew who or what they were, save that a certain percentage of all Engines passing through warp-space went insane and destroyed themselves every year.

It was not cumulative. God had shown her statistics where some died on their first mission, while others retired ancient and decrepit after a lifetime in service.

All that anyone had been able to determine, across a timeline so long as to be mind-boggling, was that the attacks were growing more frequent with every century. Whether that represented more Gage ships crossing warp-space or the growing awareness of the Gage by the demons of netherspace, nobody knew.

Those who met the warp-spawn died. No one else could predict or explain.

Odtsetseg would be Indexed only to *Dashavatara* before the final flight, once God was certain that she was ready. Not for any other reason than to have another Engine available if something came for her in the night.

Blur yarped harshly in her lap, suddenly reared up and hissing at something in the invisible distance.

Or in his mind.

She sent a soothing pulse and he settled.

"You'll protect me?" she asked.

His purring became loud enough to hear back in the main chamber. She scratched that spot between his shoulders.

Blur was the explorer of the three. He reminded her of Kincaide that way. Did that make her Snuggle, or Shadow?

Only time would tell.

CHAPTER 11

Zhubin entered the building with a moment of trepidation at what he intended. The foolish risk.

The ancient who had trained him so many decades ago had always held that there were only two kinds of action in the universe. Necessary ones, and mistakes.

Zhubin had convinced himself that this fell into necessary, but it was a thin soup as he crossed the threshold into an old, abandoned church cathedral that had been reclaimed a millennium after the Gage had constructed this place for their new toys.

Italian Universal, he thought, finding the faintest hint of a smile as he considered the implications. True believers were few and far between these days, and the kirks assembled in the early centuries had faded as the various gods of the old world had been proven to be liars and frauds.

It was not possible to reconcile a deity who loved you with one who let you be enslaved by blue, alien giants. Or perhaps everyone had misunderstood Epicurus in the first place.

The interior of the building he entered was lit by two rows of powerful lights, pointed up at the massively vaulted ceiling to reflect back down like sunlight instead of rain. When the sun was above the horizon, there would be three weeks of day, but it was night now, and Zhubin found it most appropriate to sneak in here thus.

A few worshipers knelt in various pews facing the front of the building where the ancient icons had been long-since removed. None was any closer to anyone else than they could manage, according to some specialized geometry that Zhubin didn't understand, but was truly impressed by.

He moved to his right and walked across the rear of the enormous, gray space. It had been painted once. Decorated with gold and silver and bronze. Rich carpets. Wall hangings.

Hope.

All of that was gone today. Even the air filled his nose with futility and age. Raw stone floors. Polished walls bare. Fools and believers.

Zhubin wasn't sure which category was a better fit for him as he reached the corner and slowly moved forward.

There was a small booth here. Empty, he slipped in and knelt as though in prayer. The door folded shut and he was alone.

He waited, certain that his entrance had been noted, even if it had not been understood by those watching from the floor. They did not have to. Merely to pass the word up the chain of command that a stranger had come to confession.

Zhubin had no doubt that invisible scanners in here were measuring his blood sugar and gastro-intestinal health. As they should.

He waited.

Several minutes passed while he studied the interior of the booth. Wood, but no tree had ever died to make this place, as Alvar printers had enough Earth records in the Catalogue to mimic things.

Padded floor for the penitent to kneel, facing a small window covered over with a fine mesh that would allow words and air to cross, but not sight nor hands. One could stand, if you were shorter than average for a Human, so Zhubin didn't even bother trying.

He would have to withdraw on his knees into the open air in order to rise. Zhubin smiled to himself at the image.

There was a new symbol, added to this confessional long after it had fallen into disuse, matching the one on the front wall for the worshipers to bow to. A circle, with eight rays coming off of it, four on each side.

Zhubin found it interesting how much the image reminded him of the Engine, but as far as he knew, the similarity was random. That combination of genes that gave her Power presented with the same design on her face, from the tentacles of the octopus that had been merged into her being.

Nature repeating herself time and again.

The portal between the confessional and another world opened with a slide. Zhubin could hear someone breathing on the other side of the wall, but nothing more. Darkness over there allowed no image, not even a shadow.

A moment passed.

"What sin brings you here?" a woman's voice asked slowly. Carefully.

She had a lovely speaking voice. Zhubin suspected that she might be one of the great singers in this Dome, or perhaps even the galaxy if she cared, but as far as he knew, nothing would draw Euryale out of the shadows.

"Arrogance," Zhubin answered. It was as honest a response as any other, and he had given it much thought. Euryale would appreciate that.

"Which is almost as common as breathing for you," she replied coldly.

He would not dispute that. She was not wrong.

"I have a problem, a request, and possibly a boon to offer," Zhubin said instead of fencing with Euryale all day.

Her mind had been designed by another one of the Human gods to be right at that upper end of intelligence before it crossed over into a place called madness. But a man like Brakiee Goaulda had already been mad, so he had kept all his wives a little dumber than him.

Just smarter than ninety-nine percent of the sane beings in the universe. Probably including Zhubin Prakash.

"What could Zhubin Prakash offer me that I would find even remotely interesting?" she asked after a pause to digest his words.

"Not just you," he countered. "All of you. All of the wives."

"Then you have grown into an even greater fool, Prakash," Euryale snapped. "Is senility programmed into your Icon?"

"Programmed?" he asked. "No. I'm sure I've stumbled into it myself without the help of the Alvar or their other pet gods."

He listened to her breathe for several seconds.

"All of the wives?" she finally demanded in a hard, quiet voice, dripping with metaphorical acid, rather than the literal her name would suggest.

"I wish to speak with Lilith, Euryale," he said. "Megaera. Kali. Niki. Koralia. All of them. I do not know if they will find my proposal interesting enough to consider. Nor if the deal I would offer would tempt them. But I am the Chairman, and my word will pledge the others to a deal I make with you now."

"It is your death, Prakash," she finally said, about the time he expected her to close the window and cast him out. Instead, the entire inner wall opened away from him on a hinge, revealing a wide, dark hallway that was not obvious from the outside and not part of the cathedral on any map ever published. "Welcome to hell."

He rose, stepping forward to stand.

Euryale slithered backwards slowly, giving him a moment to appreciate the new symbolism.

Take a Human woman. Slice her off at the top of the hip bone and attach six meters of snake body covered over with green and black scales and a white belly.

Cover most of her nudity with those scales like a tunic, leaving her full breasts, neck, and face uncovered to remind you of her lost Humanity. Exchange her hair for tentacles, except that as a god, you have engineered those tentacles to end in snake heads, sniffing and tasting and biting with poisonous glee if she grows angry.

A circle with eight rays coming out, four on each side.

It was still a beautiful face, if you could get past the fact that Brakiee Goaulda had turned her into a Gorgon from ancient legend. A Medusa.

Perfect breasts that would never age. Never sag.

A body that was as immortal as her maker, because that vulture had intended that his entire harem would live forever with him, servicing his needs with their variety.

At least he was dead now and truly roasting in hell.

"Come," Euryale said as she turned and went deeper into the complex.

Zhubin followed, wondering what the Monster Wives would say when he spoke with them.

CHAPTER 12

Lilith had followed the conversation in the confessional. Zhubin Prakash was a rare and exceptional visitor to the cathedral. Dangerous, both in himself and in those people and ideas he might represent.

And still possessed of that enormous ego that she had first encountered a decade ago, on some other scam the man had intended to perpetrate on the Alvar.

Rebel.

Underground warrior.

Analogue like herself, but unlike her in any of the ways that mattered.

Except for the shared hatred of the Alvar. That much he could probably expect. Would be what he was counting on to have walked in here openly.

The man wanted to speak with all of the wives, but that would not happen today. Perhaps ever. Unless the con game he was peddling today was interesting enough.

She led the Wives. It would be her decision, regardless of the other names Prakash spoke out loud.

Euryale had a radio in her ear, covered over by the questing snakes that were her birthright.

"Bring him to me," Lilith spoke into her own microphone, leaning back now and watching the scene unfold on two screens, one a simple camera and the other a scanner.

Prakash had no weapons on him, but the man himself was a

weapon. Even Human aging would not rob him of that. At least, not yet.

Time would erase the man soon enough. Only a precious few might envision living longer than even one of the Alvar. Goaulda had intended to be one of them himself, once upon a time, before his own impossible arrogance undid him.

Lilith was free now. All of the Monster Wives lived without a master. A fruit fly like Zhubin Prakash would have to dangle something enticing indeed to rouse them from the shadows where they lived.

She was Human. Every bit of her DNA had started out of woman, however much Goaulda had twisted it along the way. No matter what *things* he had done to her or any of the other Wives.

But you could not convince the mundanity of Humans of such a thing.

They would see her as a monster. Perhaps the worst of the monsters, because Goaulda had finally gone well beyond the realm where mere Human females might interest him.

No, that fool had decided he was a god. Every century or so one rose from the depths of Humanity to lay claim to such a title, usually by exploiting the Alvar's desire for better servants.

No other species so willingly modified themselves, twisted one another into monstrous caricatures of Humans.

Lilith rose from her nest and stretched, eight legs flexed and carried her thorax two meters into the air before lowering again.

Like so many of Goaulda's pets, she fit the upper/lower design he had perfected early on. Euryale had a snake for her lower. Lilith had the abdomen and eight great legs of a spider, down to the red infinity symbol on her lower back.

Centaur, but not horse. Human/Spider hybrid, down to even spinnerets and a web gland, because Goaulda's perversions elevated his sex drive beyond even the impossible.

Right up until it had killed him.

Euryale led Prakash through the complex, down a flight of stairs into the true church of the Monster Wives. A rap on the door and she opened it, gesturing the Human Analogue into Lilith's office and then closing the door behind him when she did.

They were alone.

Always, that faint twitch when a Human first encountered her.

Black hairs on those legs like spikes. Raven-black hair on a Human head, natural curls that still tumbled past her shoulder blades.

She had dressed today for business, although she supposed she could have met the man nude, if she really wanted to get under his skin. Humans all had some fear of spiders, and few of them could control it.

But she wore a simple half-kimono today. Golden fabric soft against her skin and belted with a long sash she had knotted on one side. An All-seeing Eye on a gold necklace hung from her neck, not quite between her breasts, where it would draw the eye and induce another shudder.

Lust meets fear. Goaulda had considered her his ultimate design piece, but he would never have shared them with others.

Not until he had created Enkya, the so-called elf maiden that he had been looking to mass-produce for any man who wanted a long, slender blond with perfect breasts and a sex-drive that could not be turned off, only sated for a time.

Lilith gestured for Prakash to sit. There was a chair designed for bipeds. About half of the wives were, after all, and might need to come into her office with some need or complaint. Or just to gossip.

"Lilith," Prakash began with a bow of his head. "Thank you for seeing me."

"To what do I owe the honor, Prakash?" she asked.

It could be anything, but it would not be a small thing. Prakash didn't do *petite*.

"I have been working on a new project for the last several years," he replied.

"*Dashavatara*," she interrupted before he got too far. "I'm familiar with the public bits. And Hasan Ildar."

She didn't spit on the floor at the name of one of Goaulda's disciples. Or intellectual descendants, depending on how you wished to parse such a thing.

"Just so," the man nodded again, apparently willing to be derailed for now.

She knew about the colony ship. The plan to haul more Humans to a new world, far out on the Gage frontier, in hopes that they would breed better if they didn't live in Domes. Might choose to survive as a species, even.

The Gage needed to keep conquering new worlds. New species. To ambitiously rape and pillage where no sentient being has ever gone before.

"Then let me begin with my problem," Prakash pivoted smoothly. "I have an issue with my Foreman, Kincaide Kataragama."

It wasn't a name she knew, but Boston Dome had a million beings. The others were similarly half-full.

"So kill him and eat him," she suggested, playing on the night terrors she could see in the back of his eyes.

Even a killer like Zhubin Prakash.

"That's not the problem, actually," the killer Human smiled now after his skin stopped puckering. "He's depressed."

Lilith blinked. Utterly shocked as the word derailed her train of thought entirely.

Then the rage took hold of her being.

"And you think he needs a sex object?" she snarled quietly, unwilling to control the heat. "Have Ildar build you one. The Wives will never fuck again. You, of all people, should know that, Prakash."

"I am aware," he said in a smaller voice than before, this one lacking the arrogance that might have flavored his words as he realized that even his skills and lethality might not protect him from her.

Lilith couldn't lay eggs in his corpse, but that was about the only limit, as he was already trapped in her web by locked doors and many violent women behind him.

All of the Monster Wives.

"Then what exactly do you think we can do to help a depressed Human, Zhubin Prakash?"

Her voice was Death itself now, a rage she had not felt in centuries.

"Give him hope," the man replied.

CHAPTER 13

Odtsetseg watched the two men from a spot on the couch, out of the way of the emotional holocaust raging about her. It was all she could do to hold her mental defenses in place, like warp-shields keeping the night creatures at bay.

This room took up more than a sixth of the forward dome, with her and the two men taking half between them. A single corridor airlocked down the middle on the other side, with the kitchen on one side and this salon on the other.

It was big enough to hold small receptions in here, if you wanted an event with twenty close friends.

Odtsetseg wasn't sure it was big enough to hold the two men standing at opposite ends of the room screaming at each other. None of the cats were here, but maybe they'd smelled it coming and gone to hide or hunt in the arboretum.

She held a travel mug filled with richly spiced tea, keeping the lid mostly closed so she didn't spill any on herself when her hands shivered.

"I don't care!" Kincaide snarled across the room.

The whole space separated them, as if the two men understood that getting any closer would result in punches being thrown.

Odtsetseg could smell the suppressed violence in the anger surrounding her.

"It's necessary," Zhubin countered, just as loud but perhaps not as angry.

He sounded angry. Just as filled with wrath as Kincaide.

The smell was wrong.

Odtsetseg took a sip and turned her head to study the two men directly, instead of ducking the tides of madness around her.

She understood that she needed to be here. Witness? Referee? Mother of rambunctious children?

She didn't know. But something was off. Zhubin was only sounding angry with his voice, not his mind.

What was going on?

Both men took notice of her movement. It was like they had forgotten that she was even here, except that the tone changed, like dropping red hot steel into a bucket of water to quench it.

"Why the fuck are you changing the parameters of the entire mission this late, Prakash?" Kincaide growled now, his voice dropping several dozen decibels to a hard curse that didn't hurt her ears nearly as much. "And don't tell me that it was always the plan, because I helped design the damned ship. Oversaw construction. What you're proposing to do now requires almost ripping out an entire deck and redoing it. What has gotten into you, damn it?"

"We're taking on last minute guests," Prakash replied, his voice also coming down to something only marginally painful for her to be so close to.

"Those modifications are not Human, Prakash," Kincaide said in an ugly, deadly tone. "Either we're about to haul off a new alien species nobody has ever heard of, or we're going to be hauling a group of blues with us."

"Human," Prakash countered. "Completely Human."

But Odtsetseg could tell he was lying. Something. Shading the truth in ways that might be legally acceptable in an Alvar court, but threatened to shatter the cohesiveness of the crew.

She had watched things come together slowly, like an oyster making a pearl, until the crew of *Dashavatara* was a gem she would hold in her hands as they leapt across warp-space.

"Humans do not need six-meter corridors or four meter ceilings, *Mr. Chairman*," Kincaide spit the words out coated with sarcastic bile as she watched and took another sip of her tea.

"If you would sit down and shut up long enough, Kincaide, I might have been trying to explain all this when you went apeshit on me," Prakash said in a quiet, almost professional voice.

Utterly at odds with the last ten minutes she'd had to live through.

At least her presence had kept things merely emotional. She didn't need one of them trying to kill the other. How would she explain something like that to God, when she might have had the power to stop it?

Did she?

Nobody else knew what her limits were and she'd never pushed herself.

How much psychic power did she really have? What were the limits to her telekinesis?

The most powerful telepaths could generally blink an orange across a room. But they didn't lift starships. The terrible, powerful generators aft did that, though they needed an organic focus to harness all that raw energy.

She had moved things similar to an orange, but had gone beyond and actually teleported herself a little under thirty meters the most recent time she had tried.

She hadn't told God about that. Or anyone else.

Odtsetseg had been in the kitchen, preparing a meal for herself alone. She had slipped and was about to drop a small pitcher of milk into a pan of hot grease for gravy, knowing instantly that it would flip backwards and spray her so badly that God would probably decide to decant a new copy and start over, not having lost much in the way of recent testing.

In that eyeblink, she had recognized her semi-death and stepped sideways to avoid it, landing in her cabin.

Farther than any creature had ever stepped without an entire starship pushing.

How much power did she have?

Odtsetseg studied the two Humans, now moving to chairs that would face each other, with her on the midfield line watching. She reached out and tried to calm both men.

They were headstrong, compelling figures.

Stubborn.

She moved like a spider web descending.

Something stuck to her web and the room turned quieter in her mind.

Maybe it was her. Perhaps both men had looked at her shaking and realized how much it hurt a telepath to listen to such raw, emotional fury.

They grew calm.

"Talk." Kincaide blew out a heavy breath and even leaned back into the chair.

Prakash remained poised, but he had never been as close to violence as the Foreman.

"It is an old debt," Prakash said. "I will honor it by transporting an additional nineteen Humans with us as part of the crew."

"That is a load of horse shit," Kincaide replied deliberately, adding a wry smile now as he slowly spoke the words.

"What is the purpose of this mission, Kincaide?" the Chairman asked deliberately. "The actual one, and not the pile of manure that Ildar is selling the Alvar."

"To escape Gage control for all time, Zhubin," the man replied. "Fly this ship into the darkness and never ever return, regardless of what Ildar thinks about coming back after he's built himself an army. Either way, long after I'm dead and you've either joined him as a god or joined me in hell."

"And do you think Ildar would countenance hauling aliens on his triumphant operation?" Prakash pressed. "Have their very presence soil his perfection?"

"Impossible," Kincaide agreed. "He's not just a specist like the rest of us, but an honest to God racist on top of it, Zhubin. Personally, I'm surprised that he started with an Indian crew, when he considers himself Tartar, and above all the rest of us."

"You cannot make bricks without hay, to quote the old adage." The Chairman relaxed and leaned back in his chair.

To Odtsetseg, it was almost like being in a regular meeting with the two men, but the undercurrents had gotten louder as she listened, not quieter. Fencing, perhaps, rather than wailing away at each other with greatswords.

"Is that what we are?" Kincaide asked. "Bricks?"

"If you listen to the man mutter, the Tartars are God's Chosen People, Kincaide," Prakash noted. "The Russians he would claim were all apparently tainted by Mongol invasions, either early, during the Golden Horde, or later, when Russia was a fading superpower, towards the end before the Alvar appeared overhead. All of them remind him too much of the Chinese, and you know how he feels about those people."

Kincaide laughed harshly. Braying, almost, to Odtsetseg's ears.

"Close enough to white, are we?" Kincaide asked after he took a bracing breath.

"Boston and Chennai Domes had the best mix of what he thought of as pure-blood Humans," Prakash agreed. "Those were just some of the requirements he placed upon me when it came time to recruit a construction crew for this vessel."

"And you are about to fuck it all up by bringing someone aboard at damned near close to the last minute," Kincaide circled back suddenly. "Who?"

Odtsetseg had been listening. Zhubin Prakash could keep her probes at bay, if she didn't push really hard. Nothing could stop her if she chose, save another telepath, and maybe not even then, if she was that powerful, but she could not sneak into his mind.

He seemed to be aware of that, because he turned to face her now and smiled.

Odtsetseg had an image of a monster of Human mythology, but she was not a legend. She saw the woman alive, down in Boston Dome. Picked out a memory that Prakash was letting her see right now, of a conversation with a creature that had the torso of a woman and the lower body of a...giant spider?

And that was Human?

"She is," Prakash said unequivocally.

Odtsetseg felt the blood drain out of her face. Maybe out of her soul. She felt a sudden chill and took a drink of her nearly-forgotten tea to try to warm herself.

"What did you see?" Kincaide asked, scared now, but scared for her, not himself.

Kincaide was never worried about himself. All anyone could do to the man was kill him, and he saw that as an admission of failure, that they could not change his mind.

Nothing could change the mind of Kincaide Kataragama if he didn't want to.

He was *The Foreman*.

Prakash turned back to Kincaide now as she fell into herself and watched.

"There was a man," he began slowly. Carefully. "Much like Hasan

Ildar, and rumor suggests that he might have even helped a young Ildar, centuries ago when that one was just deciding to become a god."

"He got a name?" Kincaide growled.

"Brakiee Goaulda," Prakash replied evenly.

The obscenity Kincaide muttered was too quiet to hear, but he yelled it with his mind, then glanced over at her sharply when she winced. "Sorry."

She nodded and went back to hiding behind her barriers now, instead of trying to listen to the men. The emotions were about to come back. It would be like drowning again.

"Are you serious?" Kincaide turned to the Chairman. "They're not Human, Prakash."

"Actually, they are," the Chairman said with a wry smile. "In those days, the Alvar hadn't realized that Humans could be merged with other creatures to create new things, so everything Goaulda did had to be contained within Human DNA."

Odtsetseg shivered uncontrollably, nearly spilling her tea all over herself but she managed to teleport it to a table nearby.

Both men flinched as they realized what she'd just done. She was already flinching.

Kincaide rose from his chair and moved to sit next to her on the couch.

"Are you okay?" he asked, not touching. Carefully not touching her.

She leaned into him anyway, trying to steal his warmth again, like she had done that one night.

Kincaide wrapped an arm around her back and pulled her onto his lap.

"Get me a blanket," he ordered Prakash.

Wonder of wonders, the Chairman rose immediately and located one in a trunk, returning and draping it over both of them.

Odtsetseg could not get warm, even with both his hands on her back and his chest pressed against her side. She felt him mutter nothings into her ear and that seemed to settle her.

It was like being in a nightmare from which you could not wake, but she did not sleep.

Eventually, she regained control of herself. Somehow. Warmth from the man filled a hollow spot in her soul.

"Better?" Kincaide whispered in her ear.

Odtsetseg nodded and he picked her bodily up and set her down next to him on the couch, still keeping one arm around her and the blanket across her body.

He spoke with calm deliberation.

"The Monster Wives?" he asked the Chairman.

Prakash nodded.

"How are you going to convince Ildar?" Kincaide continued.

Odtsetseg knew. She'd seen it in Zhubin's mind as she saw the creature who called herself an Araneae.

It was wrong, because it violated everything God had told her was right in the universe. But it was right, because they were Humans, as far as Prakash was concerned.

She did not know what to think anymore.

"Personally, I wasn't planning on telling the fucker," Chairman Prakash said with an ugly smile.

CHAPTER 14

Kincaide bloody hated going back to the surface of the moon. Didn't really matter which Dome, although Boston had been his home for the first half of his life, until he got a new name and identity then started flying in spaceships hauling cargo to the orbital Glide and back.

Anyplace to hide from the seekers, blue or otherwise.

The shuttle had landed and forced him out. It had only felt like gunpoint, but that was in his head.

The frantic lizard at the back of his mind didn't like walking on the streets of a Dome, where it kept expecting a big, blue freak to step around a corner with a painstik in one hand and a cruel smile on his face. But looking panicked right now was a sure way to get the authorities interested in him.

The ID in his pocket was good enough, as long as nobody dug really hard and discovered a record of the same man dying fifty years ago when he was just a child. It was an old scam, at least according to Humans. The Alvar didn't really understand underhanded.

Too busy being Alvar, or something.

Boston Dome was mostly Human. Some of the others didn't have that insular quality and welcomed aliens, but not Boston. New England Freeze as a social thing.

He kept his head down and walked like a normal person with someplace to go.

Kincaide considered stopping at a bar for a drink and maybe some food, but he had an appointment and they would be expecting him. Whatever they were.

Nobody knew. The Alvar were aware of them, but didn't bother, as long as they kept a low profile and didn't bother anyone else.

That sort of attitude was the same reason a guy now known as Kincaide Kataragama could walk around free. Nothing to connect him to a small rebel cell that had been crushed so long ago that hopefully everyone had forgotten.

Grumble.

The city hadn't changed from when he was a kid. Maybe more grungy. Fewer people, but it was late afternoon local clock, so maybe people were at work or in one of those bars drowning their sorrows and watching a match of sport.

He kept walking.

Zhubin Prakash would let him decide, which Kincaide found even more frightening than the man pulling rank and ordering it. He could do that. That's what *Chairman* meant around here. Everyone else was just an employee, including a Foreman.

Only that asshole Ildar didn't have to listen.

But he was going to get what he had coming. Kincaide didn't really care. Ildar's racism was just louder than most of the crew. Not more strident. And they were all specists.

That had been the first cut-off for recruiting. You had to hate the Alvar enough to want to see them destroyed, along with all the rest of their pets. Kincaide had apparently been the third choice for Foreman, but the first two had friends who were other species.

He hadn't cared enough to have friends.

Just another reason to look in Boston or maybe Chennai for people.

Kincaide turned a corner and saw his destination.

Some enterprising soul had rolled a hot dog cart near the front of the place and was hitting up pedestrians and believers with equal fervor. They made eye contact as Kincaide got close and the man nodded at him.

It wasn't a carnival barker kind of nod, so much as a recognition of who he was. Or maybe what.

Kincaide wondered if the spy out front worked for the wives, or the Alvar. He'd spent thirty years having to judge strangers for loyalties and deceit by the way they combed their hair or held their hands when they talked.

This man was a spy.

Kincaide considered just walking past the door and turning a corner, but he'd been made. They knew he was here. Running would just make them chase him, since he was unarmed.

Honest citizens didn't need guns. He would appear to be an honest citizen.

Right up until it became necessary to execute him for treason.

Kincaide climbed the nine steps, each stretched back nearly a meter, to reach the five sets of double doors that covered the front. Only one of them was open right now, but he didn't suppose they had the sorts of church services that packed the place standing room only.

Or a lot had changed in the last twenty years that he'd been gone.

He'd never walked inside, but had taken a quick architectural tour from the Encyclopedia Core to familiarize himself with the basics. Rows of pews. The place where the old altar had been removed.

He felt eyes on him, but Kincaide just assumed that it was his paranoia speaking. None of the old people kneeling or the mendicant seemed to give a shit that he was here.

He approached the little box where a penitent man was supposed to offer truths to a conman of a priest, who would offer absolution and peace of mind for a good rattle of coin in a box or jar.

No, he didn't have any purpose in a church. At least this place was a former church repurposed to more interesting things.

The old churches, still filled with believers, had all come to see the Alvar as their saviors.

He'd never been able to convince Nelson to let him blow up one of those places, back in the old days. Shame, really.

He closed the door and knelt, wondering who was the greater fool here.

A window slid open almost immediately.

"I'm here to apparently contemplate sin and redemption," Kincaide told whoever in a dark voice. "What have you got for me?"

"Would you prefer sin or redemption?" a woman's voice countered neatly.

"I continue to sin by merely breathing, lady," he said. "Pretty sure God won't be redeeming me without a lot of time in hell first."

"Then why bother, Kataragama?" she asked.

"Dying would be too easy," he snarled quietly at her. "Then they'd get to win. I won't allow it."

He left the *they* part vague. Most people really were not equipped to grasp the scope of his anger at God and all the rest of Creation.

Or what he'd do if he had the power. Probably safer that Odtsetseg was such a fragile flower at times. If she had something like his rage inside her, she might scour the surface of the moon bare.

Then turn her attention to Al-Winoq below and treat them to an afternoon of fireworks.

"You won't allow it?" the woman pressed, a bit wonderstruck from her tone.

"That's right."

He wondered if he'd be stuck all afternoon fencing linguistic fineries with the woman, but the wall in front of him suddenly gave way and pivoted into the hallway that Prakash had warned him about.

He stiffened for a moment, recognizing an Alvar woman standing there, but then he looked closer.

Her skin was green, rather than blue. She had the muscles of an Alvar male, but they were leaner, without the bulk that always looked like a layer of fat over them. Wore an outfit emphasizing her breasts, muscles, and tattoos covering lots of skin. Two big canines emerged from her mouth, pointed up to either side of her pretty nose but not that long. Not even that bad of an underbite, but then, she'd been designed to be perfect, just like all the others.

Gorgeous, if you liked them two and a half meters tall, broad, powerful, green, and close enough to Human.

Kincaide didn't give a shit. Wasn't like he'd ever want to see her naked.

"You got a name, princess?" he asked in a grumpy voice as he rose and stepped into the open space and looked up at the giantess.

She scowled down at him, but he already knew she could fold him into a pretzel if she felt the need.

Kincaide just really didn't fucking care.

"Staci," she replied, turning away after closing the door. "Follow me."

CHAPTER 15

Staci took her usual job as a bodyguard seriously around here. She'd been designed and built to be the physical equal to the average Alvar male, which meant better, tougher, stronger, and meaner than any other species in the galaxy.

She didn't weigh as much as the blues, but she had hips and curves. Alvar females tended to be straight-sided and a little skinny compared to Humans. Males tended to be blocky, but they came with shoulders wider than hers. The only advantage they would get would be mass from denser bones.

And that sort of thing just slowed them down. She could still dance with Human professionals. While lifting any of them up over her head one-handed.

This Human didn't seem impressed, which impressed Staci. Fascinated her, even.

Staci was used to the hard flinch every Human gave off when they realized how big she was. Then that second flinch when they realized she had green skin and black hair, utterly at odds with the Alvar that their unconscious mind expected.

Supposedly, her design had originally been considered for a sex object for Alvar males who liked it rough. Or one of the smaller species that wanted a similar experience. Green like an ork from ancient mythology meant that she wasn't seen as an infiltrator, although she'd often wondered if Goaulda had originally had plans that

74

would have involved tweaking her design for blue skin and white hair later.

Or just using paint and dye.

In the dark, she could pass for a muscular Alvar woman right now.

This Human looked her up one side and down the other, but that was it. About as much emotion as a man rating a cat for adoption at a pound. She wondered if Zhubin Prakash had warned him, or just the legends that had accumulated over the last half millennium told Kataragama what he needed.

He made no comment as he followed, just moved so quietly that she had to glance back to make sure he hadn't slipped off.

The second time she looked, he grinned up at her.

Staci managed to keep her snarl to herself and took him down the stairs into the catacombs. This wasn't Prakash, needing a private meeting with Lilith.

Instead, they entered an underground vault. The sides were stepped down like an auditorium, but each level was flat for people stand, sit, rest, or coil. Plus Niki and Serena in their private swimming tanks.

She let Kataragama walk beside her now so she could gauge his reactions. She was, at the end of the day, really just an extremely large Human, after all. The others ranged deep into the realm of Human nightmare.

Even Lilith wasn't that bad, comparatively.

Theodosia and Koralia guarded the bottom of the steps as she approached. Both were designs like hers, but smaller. Just big Human women rather than Alvar-scaled. Muscular babes covered over with fur.

In Theodosia's case, fine black fur reminiscent of a Mog, and apparently based loosely on a Human Puma, from the memories of the home world.

Koralia's was brown and heavier, named after the tatanka legends. *The Bison*. Thick fur covered her back and rounded her shoulders, engulfing neck and head, with finer, straighter hairs than the heavy curls. Inward curved horns on her forehead completed the look.

Any of them would be a match for even a well-trained Human like Zhubin Prakash. Kincaide Kataragama was a spacer, not a warrior.

Lilith was making a statement, having all three of them down here, as if protecting him from the others up on the levels above.

Kincaide came to rest and turned slowly, counting Wives to make sure all were present, if she had to assign meaning to his behavior.

"Good," he said abruptly, staring up at her. Or rather, her breasts.

But she had been designed as a sex object, once upon a time, as well as a killer. Or maybe both tasks at once.

She would never mate with another being, even if she lived forever.

Because then someone might discover the secret all the Wives held dear. Goaulda had programmed them to be instantly willing for sex with him whenever the mood struck the man. In whichever perversion he delighted in today. All of them would lose their minds and be drowned in unquenchable desire, unable to stop the act of fornication until they had achieved orgasm. Or however many occurred.

At least Enkya had killed him, however accidentally. Fucked him literally to death, her legs holding him in place as he had a heart attack and was unable to call for medical assistance over her screams of passion. His notes had detailed all the drugs he had taken beforehand to extend his performance, in order to test the new design.

He had missed a bad combination somewhere.

Staci didn't really miss Enkya, but she'd never known the woman that well. Just a little elf designed to be sold to rich Humans and kinky Alvar.

After Enkya had self-terminated, Lilith had decided never to decant a new copy. Had, in fact, destroyed all of Goaulda's design Icons, so that the nineteen of them were all that would ever exist.

"Good?" she asked, looking down at Kataragama.

"Prakash seems intent," he growled up at her like a small dog barking at a mastiff. At least he met her eyes now. "I have my doubts, but unless I want to commit suicide elsewhere, I'm stuck with you people."

"You could not just quit?" she asked, wondering why she was the one speaking for the Wives now.

Except that she'd been the one to try to intimidate him. Had he seen that as a challenge? Or a threat? Or an arousal?

Humans.

"I know far too much to be allowed out now," he smiled, turning to look both ways at Theodosia and Koralia. "Prakash or someone else would just kill me and be done with it."

"Does that fill you with dread, little Human?" Staci asked now, leaning forward just a little to make him stare that much more up at her.

"Not particularly," he shrugged. "Hell will be along soon enough to claim me. If it takes a few thousand years for the rest of you to catch up, that'll be your problem, not mine."

Staci blinked in surprise.

Humans were programmed by their very DNA with a strong will to live. The modified versions like her and the other women had had that heavily reinforced, because Goaulda didn't want them listening to the whispers and deciding that they really were monsters.

Or, at least, that they should self-terminate over such a thing. Enkya had only been overcome by the grief of committing a *deicide*.

They were all of them monsters. Goaulda had designed them that way. Normal Humans had no longer aroused him sufficient for completion by that point. He needed to fuck his nightmares, to dominate them.

Staci's own studies had suggested that in an alternate universe the man might have turned into a serial killer, but he had instead been able to play at being a god, and give his bizarre fantasies breath like a modern-age Pygmalion.

"We are here, Kincaide Kataragama," Kali announced from where she sat on a level just above his eyes.

Unlike all the other Wives, her skin was blue, but that was a vision dating back long before the Alvar. Four-armed goddess of destruction from the Hindi region of the world. Front-back shoulders with the front pair of arms shorter than the outer pair, so that she could hang all flat to her side when she stood.

Like the rest, designed and built for immortal perfection, however many tweaks and indices it had taken Goaulda to get his kinks just right. And immoral perfection, too.

"Prakash tells me that you are exercising a marker on him," Kincaide called bluntly, still scanning the room, even as he stood at the bottom of a small bowl, with her, Koralia, and Theodosia around him on the points of a triangle. "That you're to be transported with us aboard *Dashavatara* when the mission departs."

"And?" Kali asked.

Apparently Lilith had chosen her to speak. Staci wondered if it had anything to do with his cultural matrix having originated geographically close.

Except that this was Boston Dome. One of the supposedly most socially advanced, at least compared to the others. Stolen from the Golden Land of Opportunity by invaders who saw all Humans as tools and insects.

Staci fell to rest and watched, confident that she could move faster than an unarmed Human male past middle age. That she was five hundred years older meant nothing. She was still physically twenty-four years Standard Personal, locked that way forever.

"And the ship was never designed for it," Kataragama snapped at the woman. "It's a Human vessel."

Kali started to speak and Kataragama just waved her off angrily.

"I know," he said angrily. "All of you are supposedly Human to the nth degree, unlike many of the more modern models."

Staci watched him glare angrily at all of them, one at a time, beginning and ending with her, interestingly.

"I. Don't. Care." His bile was pungent, but harmless.

His turned to her and stepped close enough now that they might dance, but his hands were crossed behind his back.

Just his jaw jutted in her direction.

"The ceilings everywhere are set at two point three meters tall," he challenged her now, aware that she was two point four five. "Because we didn't need anything high enough for an Alvar to walk our decks."

He spun now and lined up an accusing finger on Lilith, but hadn't moved out of a range where Staci could bite him, let alone grapple.

"The hatchways in all places are the standard one hundred and ten centimeters wide that Humans always use," he growled at the woman.

Lilith's abdomen was wider than that, even before you added the eight legs emerging from the sides.

Kataragama turned again and noted Niki and Serena in their tanks. Each was a standard top half/bottom half design, with a beautiful Human woman chopped in the middle. Serena had a flat, flared tail with a vertical motion to her swimming, taken from a porpoise or killer whale.

Niki had the tentacles from a red octopus, or perhaps a vampire squid, depending. Eight flexible limbs that could wrap around Goaulda's entire body as he stood in chest-deep water, or perhaps wore an underwater breathing apparatus.

Both women could breathe air into lungs, as well as use their gills, but neither had legs upon which to walk.

"*Dashavatara* is not rated to transport amphibious crew," Kataragama said simply.

At least there was no bile in his voice there. Just a harsh statement of fact.

"What is your point, Kataragama?" Kali asked in a bored, disdainful voice.

The man smiled at Kali as Staci watched. It seemed to be a genuine thing, utterly at odds with all the emotions he'd portrayed up until now.

"My point is that at no point was the ship designed to handle you," he gestured wide with both palms now, encompassing all of the Wives into one. "You didn't tell him that you were coming along until extremely recently, because there are things we could have done had we known."

"Oh?"

"I have a cargo deck that we could functionally rip out and transform into some sort of living quarters for most of you, but in doing so I lose more than a month of sailing capacity in consumables. And we won't be able to just sail up to an Alvar system and ask for them to top everything off, once we go rogue, ladies."

"A deal is a deal, Kataragama," Kali pressed hard.

Staci wondered if the truth of the situation would ever come out. Or if Kataragama would even care.

If the Monster Wives hadn't gotten a rise out of the man, what would?

The Human moved.

Staci nearly tackled him, until she realized that his hands were still behind his back. He reached the edge of the platform and pivoted.

Pacing.

Koralia was closest now.

There was a twinkle in the man's eyes that hadn't been there before.

She locked eyes with him across the distance and she saw the smile emerge from the sorts of black depths that a shark might patrol.

Staci discovered that she could indeed feel the beginnings of fear. That sudden catch of breath. The pulse racing to catch up with a heart already banging away in her chest. Hairs on her arms standing up as her flesh prickled.

He spoke to her directly, in a voice loud enough for the rest to hear cleanly.

"Hasan Ildar will hate all of you," he announced proudly. "The product of some other megalomaniac god. Outwardly inHuman. Monsters, for all your DNA. Not the sorts of medium-brown, black-haired folk from which he wants to extract his future master race."

"You think we care about all that, Kataragama?" Kali yelled.

"No," he smiled serenely. "But you've complicated the hell out of my life right now, lady."

Staci heard growls of discontent, but the man waved them away like a conductor leading an orchestra.

How could a mere Human have such charisma? Because he did. And was aware of it.

Using it.

"What I would like to propose to you is a delay to the mission." He turned to Kali now on his heels, falling sharply into some sort of military stance. "I want you to blow up *Dashavatara*."

Staci's voice joined the chorus of howls and indignation.

Again, one hand waved them to silence like a magician.

"Only a little," he reassured them. "Nothing critical or big."

"To what purpose, Kataragama," Kali snapped.

"Then I have an excuse to rebuild a whole section aft," he snapped back at her. "You think the Alvar wouldn't notice if the timelines suddenly imploded with unforeseen modifications to the ship? But a terrorist attack? That's an entirely different matter. They might even decide to let me up-gun the ship beyond the pitiful weapons I have, if resistance crazies are threatening to destroy us. I mean, *What do they know???*"

She watched him turn that serene smile on each of them like a lighthouse, and Staci finally understood why Prakash had chosen this man as his Foreman.

Kincaide Kataragama's brains and charisma made him *dangerous*. Alvar or Monster Wives, this was not a man to be underestimated, regardless of what she'd thought all of ten minutes ago.

CHAPTER 16

Kincaide paused just inside the door to the great converted cathedral before he emerged and drew a breath of harsh Dome air into his lungs. Ships always kept the atmosphere cleaner. Smaller volume. Less margin for error. The risk that an unhappy crew quits and signs on with some other ship to haul cargo around.

Outside, it would be chewier. Smellier. He hadn't walked on the surface of a Dome more than one day a month in years. Building *Dashavatara* had required the last six months be spent in blessed space.

And he loathed Boston Dome above all others, for all that he had been born here.

Nayani always appeared at the edge of a crowd, out of the corner of his eye, until he turned to look and she turned into some other young woman. Or was just the way a shadow of light fell onto a storefront.

Something.

She was gone. Only she still had hold of his heart and soul.

Kincaide squared his shoulders and emerged.

That idiot spy with the hotdog cart was still hard at work, busking for customers.

Kincaide thought of a vid he had seen once, supposedly set on the surface of old Earth using the sorts of cultural memories written down or passed forward orally.

Weather. In an era of primitive industrialism. A kid selling newspapers, when the term meant a large piece of wood paper stock printed with ink, folded, and disposed of in a day because the news was an ever-changing beast even then.

The boy had worn a heavy jacket. A scarf designed for cold had been tied around his neck. A strange hat pulled down over his head and fingerless gloves.

They had even gone so far as to simulate wind with giant fans, suggesting the real Boston.

The fool selling brats from his cart was trying to convince people he was that kid with disposable newspapers for sale. None of the passersby had taken their chances before with his food. There was an older woman there now. Kincaide might have recognized her from inside the cathedral, but he wasn't close enough to be sure.

He began to walk.

Fool with cart marked him as Kincaide exited the shadows of the building.

Eyes locked.

Kincaide kept the curse and the grimace inside, letting his face fade to blandness, even as he calculated all the possible routes he could run to escape.

Someone wanted to talk to him.

Twenty-two years and either someone had recognized him, or they were marking strangers visiting the Monster Wives.

Any minute now, a car was going to appear. Land somewhere close. Men or women with navy blue uniforms and guns would get out and ask for his papers.

He could survive that scan. Kincaide had paid good money for the identity. And if pressed, he could honestly say that he'd been meeting with a group of potential investors to let them know that the ship was not currently taking on any additional passengers.

Currently.

Things might change.

However, if they arrested him right now, he had a feeling that these papers wouldn't be enough. Someone would take a hit of his blood and put it through the impossible records of the Catalogue.

Kincaide Kataragama was a mask he wore. The Alvar or their pigs would rip it from his face. The best he could hope for was that they rated Zhubin an utter fool, to have fallen for it.

Otherwise, they might start investigating *Dashavatara* and her crew a little more closely.

Then everyone would be dead.

The busker was busy with the old lady, so Kincaide turned right, even before he got to the bottom of the wide staircase. He'd come from the left originally, so hopefully whoever it was had been expecting him to return that way.

He'd burn that bridge when he got there.

The surface of the Domes was set close to Human normal gravity. Some ships were higher, others lower. Kincaide always liked keeping it just a shade hot, to keep his muscles in shape.

He started moving faster. Not a run. Not even a jog. But no longer an angry saunter, like maybe he'd been guilty of before.

A man with a purpose, possibly late to his next meeting, but not that late. He could still make it if he didn't stop for coffee or to deal with that one hooker watching the street below.

Kincaide wondered if the man was really a spotter for the authorities. Or the underground.

Hell of a cover. Maybe he'd need to make some inquiries when he got out of this mess, just to be sure.

Always positive. He would escape. Just a matter of time.

He'd never been wrong before. That attitude had kept him alive for two decades of stupid shenanigans.

Faster.

Somewhere behind, he felt the presence of the busker finally reaching for a radio and calling down doom on Kincaide's head. The air changed, picked up a charge like a battery wall about to overload and violently ground. Assuming it didn't just explode and take out a section of your ship, venting people and atmosphere to deep space.

Move.

That particular low-pitched hum of engines above and behind him. Short-range repulsorcraft. Dome-capable only, where they didn't have to climb to orbit so they could be light.

Kincaide risked a quick glance back to confirm that it was a police cruiser. They'd been hiding somewhere. Lying in wait.

Which organization had a leak? This had been a set-up, but if the Wives were trying to kill him, they'd picked an amateur hour, clown-shoes way to do it. And if *Dashavatara* had a traitor inside, why hadn't they already arrested everyone?

Or had Prakash thrown a banana peel into the works by visiting the

Wives the first time? And now Kincaide was there. *What they hell were those dangerous rebels up to, anyway?*

He smiled grimly, wondering if there was any chance in hell he could get away.

They were airborne. He made his way towards the tube station. It wasn't far, and would at least get him away from them. They'd still have to dismount, or call for backup if he did.

He'd be trapped in a hole in the ground with only a limited, predictable number of escape routes, but out of sight.

How bad did they want him?

"You there, stop moving," an angry voice came over the public address system.

At least they were still flying. Hadn't set down yet to chase him.

He had thirty meters to make.

Kincaide started running. Screw the soft jog. He put his head down and took off like a rabbit, whatever those were.

"Halt!" came the angry order.

He nodded at the stupidity of it and pushed.

Movement out of the corner of his eye as they came even. Probably shoot him on general principle right now and sort out victims and perpetrators later, like the cops normally did.

A strange sound cut through the scene. Kincaide couldn't identify it, against the normal background noise of the Dome. A dull thump. A hiss. A crack.

An explosion engulfed the flying police car and knocked Kincaide on his ass. At least his red bodysuit was fireproof and did a pretty good job against roadrash. He ducked his head and raised his arms to keep any flash of incendiaries out of his hair.

The sound finally arrived, like it had been traveling in slow motion to cross the twenty meters between him and the boom.

The burning wreckage of the police car fell the last few meters to the street with a clang. Somewhere, every AI system in the Dome would be waking up and screaming right about now. Fire was the one thing that threatened everyone. Stone buildings wouldn't burn, but if something caught, oxygen was being depleted faster than the systems could generate it.

Extinguisher drones would be lifting off from their light poles, sniffing the air and racing to smoother the flames with neutral foam.

Manned rescue vehicles would be sounding alarms and springing into action to protect and serve.

Kincaide rose shakily and staggered away from the scene.

His comm chirped with a message. He pulled it out and tried to make sense of the words.

Maybe he had the slightest concussion.

Take the tube south one station. Will meet there. Prakash

Kincaide shook his head and nodded to the gods. He put his feet into motion and went down the well into the tube station. Hopefully, nobody had gotten a good description.

Red was only a uniform color on *Dashavatara*, and only then because he'd needed something to stand out against the green of everyone else. Or Prakash's blue.

Pedestrians were emerging from underground in shock and wonder as he wove his way into the depths of the moon, hoping he wasn't being followed.

At least not by any bad guys.

Zhubin had obviously been expecting this.

CHAPTER 17

Zhubin folded up the tripod holding the launcher and tossed it into a corner. Rough piece of mechanical work done in a backyard shop. It would be untraceable when the authorities finally backtracked the shot to this abandoned apartment. However long *that* would take.

There were so many empty ones around here to choose from. One of the reasons the Wives had been able to buy the church so cheaply.

That and nobody really gave much of a damn anymore. If rooms were going for the wanting, he could pick.

Knowing Kincaide, Zhubin had expected the man to move this way. That had caused the police to spend an extra five seconds getting caught up, because they had expected an amateur.

Zhubin snorted under his breath as he abandoned the empty box that had originally held a seeker missile. The kind designed for indoor work. Small charge to launch the main warhead and give it spin. Rockets ignite a moment later, so you don't need to worry about back blast. Motor that burns out in less than three seconds, because the Domes are never that far across.

Seeker head had locked onto the flying police car and happily annihilated it. Zhubin wondered if there would be enough rubble left over to figure out what had happened. Simple electronics like the ones the Alvar allowed Humans could be programmed to do much of anything, if you had time and patience.

And a killing desire.

He exited the room and hit the stairs going down at a dead run, almost free-falling from level to level as distant alarms began to sound.

Out the back door, he hopped into a little six wheeled flatbed cart for hauling supplies around. Car theft was almost unknown, with nowhere to take them, but they still went missing from time to time. Generally juveniles out for a joyride. Zhubin wore meaningless grays and pulled a scarf around his face just before he entered the alley and climbed in.

They would investigate soon enough, but not yet. There was still a terrible accident back there. Nothing more. Only when eye witness reports began to be collated would someone understand that this had been an assassination.

Done by one of the best assassins ever decanted.

The tunnels ran diagonal to the street grid to make it easy to get around. Zhubin navigated the little truck like a salmon swimming upstream to spawn, as emergency vehicles and journalists both raced to get to the story first.

Zhubin abandoned the sled near the next station and pushed a button on his sleeve as he started down the stairs. The process took nearly fifteen seconds to complete, so you'd have to have been paying attention the whole time to watch his bodysuit change from gray to the bright Alvar blue that he wore in space.

Eyes averted nervously from him as he walked. His height would not fool anyone, but anyone wearing that color either was looking for trouble, or had the backing of the giants behind him.

Nobody wanted to be collateral damage.

A train car pulled into the station and stopped. Zhubin spotted Kincaide and nodded for the man to remain while Zhubin joined him in the car. A moment later, the doors closed and the lifters engaged again.

Zhubin moved close, noting that this car was only mildly crowded but not packed cheek by jowl. He slid close to the Foreman and smiled.

"Three stops," he murmured at the man.

Kincaide nodded like a shadow and grabbed onto an overhead rail again, looking for all the world like just another office drone sneaking out of work a little early. Like so many others in the car.

Three stops later, they emerged, crossed the platform, and climbed the stairs out onto the street.

This was about as far as one could get in Boston Dome from the space port, which was the point. If they had spotted Kincaide and identified him they would expect the man to try to fly away.

Zhubin had other options available, if push came to shove. He just hoped that it wasn't time to start using up odd plans he had made against crazy circumstances.

Crazier circumstances.

This was an industrial area. Warehouses rather than mixed use flats and business. Factories that made widgets for people and occasionally parts for space, if the Alvar had any particular need that Humans could solve cheaper than anyone else.

They turned and moved down a side street not much larger than an alley. Just wide enough for a pedestrian and that truck he had stolen earlier to not touch while passing.

"Prakash," a low voice called out.

Zhubin spun with a hotblaster in one hand and a knife in the other.

The alley was empty.

Kincaide slipped back and sideways to watch their backs. Zhubin checked overhead, but they were still alone.

"Here," the voice said, and something appeared on the ground.

A hand, covered over with fresh dust since the area hadn't been cleaned recently.

The hand floated in the air, then gestured behind them.

"You're safe," it said.

She said. It was a woman's voice.

Enlightenment arrived.

"Ghost," he said simply.

"Correct," she replied. "I wanted to get your attention before you arrived wherever you were going, in case you had sensors that might detect me and cause concern."

"Noted," Zhubin said. "You follow and I'll hold the door for you."

"Following," she said.

The hand did something that took him a moment to understand as brushing the dust off and then she was gone.

He studied the area closely, and could just make out her faint outlines, almost like a true ghost, rather than a modified chameleon form that Goaulda had created at one point.

Invisible in the normal, Human vision range. You needed high UV or a good IR scanner to detect her.

If there was a way to turn it off, he might have considered such a treatment, just for the advantage it would give someone like him.

He led Kincaide to a door and unlocked it with a mechanical key that had a chip embedded in it. Sufficient to keep out almost anyone, and his name didn't appear on any record of ownership of the property until you got seven layers into holding companies.

Still, he opened the door with the hotblaster in hand.

Inside, the space was broken by crates and racks of equipment, most of which had been here when he acquired the warehouse. Some weapons and other things were carefully hidden, but nothing of immense value.

"In," Ghost murmured as she slipped past, the breeze of her passage caressing his skin and leaving an afterimage on his retinas, which was about all you ever saw with the woman.

He knew from his studies that she would appear Human. A little above average for height. Muscular and athletic because that had been Goaulda's signature with his sex objects. No waifs for that man.

Zhubin closed the door and set both the lock and a secondary section of pipe across it to hold against anything short of explosives or a cutting torch.

Kincaide had found a spot to sit and was breathing a little heavy, but that was excitement and old age. Nothing more. Zhubin was just in better shape.

"Which way should I face so you can hear me?" he asked the air.

A moment later, a half-cloak he'd worn from time to time lifted off a chair and swept around her shoulders, coming to rest and framing Ghost's shoulders, neck, and jutting breasts in black silk.

"Thank you," he said with a nod.

"What happened?" Kincaide asked. "I appreciate that you were there, but why was it necessary? What haven't I been told?"

"The Wives are always under observation," Ghost's voice came now. She had a pleasant, throaty alto.

Goaulda would have been able to enjoy her in the darkness like any other man. Perhaps that anonymity had been the point.

"So neither organization is penetrated?" Kincaide pressed.

"As near as we can tell, no," she said.

"I was there because I'm more paranoid than the rest of you," Zhubin said simply. "I know you don't like coming to the surface, Kincaide, so I was your guardian angel today."

"Will they make us?" the Foreman asked.

"The second shot took out the flyer," he smiled.

"And the first?"

"The hotdog vendor," Zhubin said. "Can't have him around making suggestions to a sketch artist or AI program that might come up with a reasonable approximation of your face, can we?"

He turned to the naked woman now. It was strange, being able to just make out her outline when she stood perfectly still, like smoke drifting. Something about the surface of her skin made the eyes slide off her when she moved.

Zhubin wondered what color eyes her original Icon had contained.

"Why did Lilith send you?" he asked the woman.

"Similar logic," Ghost said, "But it was Kali and Staci making the suggestion, rather than Lilith. She's an administrator, not a warrior."

"Agreed," Zhubin said. "What did I miss inside the cathedral?"

"Kincaide made a suggestion that we wish to investigate," Ghost replied with almost a laughing lilt to her voice.

Zhubin turned to the man that both he and Odtsetseg agreed hated everyone equally, wondering what deviltry the man was up to now.

Kincaide's smile promised something grand.

"So had you folk given me more time, I could have done some things without making it obvious," Kincaide said.

"Understood, but it was rather last minute," Zhubin said.

The Wives understood that Zhubin Prakash had asked them a favor, not the other way around. Just seeing the excitement in Kincaide's eyes now told Zhubin that he had made a good call.

The man was alive in ways he hadn't been since early in the construction, nearly two years ago. He needed purpose, and the psychological profiles had been correct in suggesting princesses to rescue, however bizarrely alien they might appear.

Not that anyone would ever tell Kataragama.

"So what I needed was a reason to delay the flight until we could do some radical engineering aft," Kincaide continued. "The arboretum has the necessary overhead volume, but it also defines the top deck, because of the way we needed lighting and plumbing run for everything."

"Go on," Zhubin prompted the man.

"There is a way," Kincaide said. "I can stretch the top deck aftwards with a couple of flanges sideways from the engines, which will also reinforce them a little, while supposedly extending the arboretum another forty meters or so. And if we do it right, Ildar won't suspect what we're up to. What story were you going to feed him, anyway? The man's not *that* stupid."

Zhubin had wondered when Kincaide would put all the pieces together. The man was smart, even with the holes Zhubin had left in the original tale of things.

Rather than answer, he pulled a small device from a pouch on his belt and held it in the air. A button press served to turn it on, and it hovered a few meters overhead, turning in place as it scanned everything, warbling quietly to itself while the others remained perfectly silent, just in case someone had left a voice-activated listening device.

It chirped happily to itself a few moments later and dropped down in front of him. Zhubin grabbed it and returned it to the pouch.

"This is a secret known only to you two, as of now," he said, watching Ghost's body language for the nod, in the way her shoulders and breasts moved down and then back up.

Weird, but not even all that weird, considering some of the things he'd seen and done in his life.

"At the last moment, *Dashavatara* is going to back out of the repair dock," he said. "Instead of shifting over to the platform where Ildar is waiting, we're going to turn and run like hell out of the Glide for deep space."

"You're leaving him here?" Ghost asked, shocked.

"If he were aboard, I'm certain that the Wives would cause no end of trouble with the man, regardless of your DNA," Zhubin said. "He will see you as monsters, and you both know what a racist, specist shit he is. Our future is better without him in it."

"What about the Eden Package?" Kincaide said. "All those lives to decant on some new world. Who will be able to run the equipment?"

Ghost laughed now, a mirthful, warm sound that reminded him almost of a mother that had been dead for centuries now.

"You are a delightfully wicked man, Zhubin Prakash," she said.

"What am I missing?" Kincaide asked, bewilderment giving way to anger that he was on the outside of some joke.

"The Monster Wives," Ghost said. "We are all experts on those machines. Goaulda needed us to be able to run everything to help him in his experiments."

"So we're swapping an asshole for a troupe of monsters?" Kincaide asked.

"So to speak," Ghost replied.

Zhubin watched him smile broadly.

"I like it," Kincaide said.

CHAPTER 18

Hasan had awakened today with a spring in his step. He lingered over breakfast this morning, enjoying the view of his most recent cast of servants as they cleaned and worked around him.

All of them presented as young Chinese women, ripe for the taking and even genetically aroused by the prospect. They were not pure sex objects, because keeping such creatures around for only that was a waste of time and resources. Instead, he had acquired a set of four who were all primarily trained as domestics. Or rather, numbered copies of an original Chinese maid, with the woman's mind adjusted by Hasan to be happy with her lot in life and excited to serve.

And Chinese, because it allowed him to enjoy himself debasing such a lesser race personally.

The original had been an exceptional cook. The copies retained those abilities, and he had provided them with the recipe book that covered his preferences. The four of them could feed themselves as they desired, with the market delivering everything.

Life was good.

This morning, Hasan sat in his breakfast nook with the wide, transparent window, staring out at the stars and watching the sunlight glint off of the three stations that he could see in the distance from this one. The platform containing *Dashavatara* was not close enough for him to see from here, even if he faced the correct direction, but the ship was high in his mind this morning as he sipped his coffee and scrolled through the reader board for the latest news and scientific research.

Chun 11 was cooking this morning. Or rather cleaning up after cooking, wearing nothing but an apron to protect herself against the grease from his bacon.

He preferred the Chun model to the Arabic *Hadiyas* that he had dabbled with last year. They looked too close to real Humans for him to enjoy, so he had reverted to Chinese maids for a while. Perhaps next year he would decant some African servants, or perhaps reach a deal with a cohort who had connections to the Montevideo Dome for some South Americans to try.

It was awesome, being a god.

He paused, the mug of fresh coffee halfway to his mouth as his handheld beeped with an important message. Hasan drew it from the pouch on his thigh, flipping his half-cape back out of his way as he sat up straighter.

The message from Prakash caused his stomach to turn to lead.

Terrorist attack on Dashavatara. Damage extensive but controlled. Ship safe. Crew safe. Engine safe. Security quarantine in effect.

He rose with an inarticulate screech of psychological pain.

"Damn them!" he snarled at the heavens.

At least the ship was safe. He could always recruit a new crew. Decant a new Engine, although the current design was nearly a year old at this point, so maybe he should consider snapping a fresh backup now, instead of just before departure.

Except that the ship was quarantined. The Alvar would demand an investigation.

Would Administrator Sangsuriya tour the wreckage himself, or send a flunky? Which flunky? Not all of them were as corrupt as their master. Nor as addled by the vision of Alvar species perfection.

Chun 11 had stopped cleaning and stared at him with wild, almond eyes and a quivering lip.

"Out!" he screamed. "All of you."

Another of the Chuns had appeared at a doorway. Both fled.

Hasan stomped to the center of the bubble, surrounded now by raw space on all sides except backwards. He howled a curse at whatever gods had allowed this, because someone had tried to thwart him.

He would see whoever it was dismantled slowly in an Index. You could lower the sensitivity settings on the scanner such that it might take someone fifteen minutes to die as they were peeled like an onion. Painfully.

Someone.

His handheld warbled with an incoming call. He checked the identity of the caller.

Colonial Dispatch Administrator Sangsuriya himself. Or perhaps his office.

Of course.

"Ildar here," he answered, forcing his voice to sound normal.

"Have you heard the news?" Sangsuriya asked in a quiet voice.

"Only the barest details, provided just now by one of my crew," Hasan replied, drawing the venom back into his throat before speaking the words. "What has happened?"

"It is unclear, Ildar," the Administrator said. "Our scanners note an explosion of some sort in an aft storage area that had been loading supplies. No crew were nearby and the explosion did not penetrate the outer hull or any of the frames forward, but the ship will need to be repaired."

"One of my enemies, or yours?" Ildar asked, just to get it out on the table.

"They differ?" Sangsuriya asked in a sarcastic tone.

"In scale, if nothing else," Hasan replied tartly. "Many Humans loathe the Alvar and The Gage, but lack the ability to do anything about it. I am seen as something of a traitor in certain circles for not just working with you, but improving your power, presumably at the equivalent loss of power and prestige among Humans, if their value to the Gage is reduced to that of any of the other species."

"You suggest a war within your kind?" the creature asked, apparently surprised.

But then, the Alvar considered all others in The Gage beneath them, regardless. They were not the Anointed.

"Each of the Domes represent a difference facet of Human culture," Hasan reminded the Administrator. "There are at least four major ethnic varieties of Human present. The Chinese hate everyone, so perhaps they seek to throw down all other Domes that they might rise preeminent."

"Interesting," the Alvar noted. "So if we investigate your crew for disloyalties?"

"My officers will handle that investigation," Ildar put his foot down. "I hand-picked those men and women. They will find any flaws in their crew. You should find out who shipped us a bomb and shatter their lives."

"There was an incident in Boston Dome, perhaps a month ago," Sangsuriya said.

Hasan remembered seeing something about that, but the details were fuzzy.

"Ideologues attacking a police station or something?" he asked hesitantly, still staring at the stars that would provide his refuge, once this setback was overcome.

"A police vehicle was destroyed by a missile," the Administrator said. "As you noted, perhaps ideologues. Much of your crew was recruited from Boston Dome. That was why I had an interest."

"I recruited there because the Chinese, African, and South American Domes are filled with untrustworthy scum," Hasan snarled. "Of course, one of them probably took offense. When this project works, you might not need as many Domes to worry about, and can just shut several of them down or something."

"You do not seem to care for your fellow Humans, Ildar," the Administrator said.

"They are not my fellows," Hasan snapped. "I am working on creating an advanced being. A perfect one. A Truebreed that will serve The Gage far greater than any of the other species might. I plan to live almost as long as an Alvar, in order to see such perfection achieved."

He didn't bother noting that if his most recent gene mapping had been correct, he would live for at least another ten thousand years. The blue ignoramuses didn't need to start fearing him yet.

Yet.

Their time would come.

"Interesting," Sangsuriya said simply. "I will make sure you hear anything that comes up from my investigation. I will expect the same from you."

"We will bring the scum down, Sangsuriya," Hasan replied. "None may jeopardize my plan."

CHAPTER 19

Kincaide tapped his faceplate once, just to confirm that it was in place and sealed. It was a nervous habit he had picked up twenty years ago, but it had saved his life more than once. Beside him, Zhubin was doing the same, whether a similar tic or just mimicking him was uncertain.

"Shall we?" the man asked.

Kincaide looked back and confirmed that the hatch behind them was also sealed. The air systems had locked down tight on the other side of this wall, rather than allow fire or smoke to spread, so he knew there wasn't much oxygen over there. Pressure, but all poisonous for now.

He needed to see it with his own eyes before he would send crews in to repair everything.

Captains going down with their ship, and all that. Older than the Alvar. Older than space.

He keyed the hatch and watched a puff of haze enter this room. Which was why they'd sealed it off as a pseudo-airlock.

Beyond, the hallway looked normal. He hadn't been able to do anything aft to prepare, except to make sure a week ago that new door-seal procedures were in place and followed religiously, with the penalty being points accrued against your record. Without those points, you couldn't buy certain luxuries from the commissary, so it kept people sharp.

All the frames had held, but that wasn't a surprise. The bomb that had been smuggled aboard had been intended as an incendiary, not a shaped-charge to vent the section to space.

That would have spoiled all the fun.

He heard Zhubin close the hatch behind him. Engineers would be monitoring the room and probably turning the fans to overdrive back there.

Forward. The next hatch had also held, which was good. It would remain in place when he redid this section for the ladies.

Not even Kincaide wanted to think of them as Wives. That suggested husbands. Even dead ones.

Widows, perhaps, but didn't those silly Christians once demand that a brother marry his widowed sister-in-law or something?

He let the shiver pass through his whole body at the thought of dealing with one of *those* women *that* way.

"All good?" Zhubin asked.

"Someone just walked across my grave," Kincaide joked loosely.

"We're not there yet," Zhubin joked back.

Kincaide opened this hatch and could see the dark stains on the walls now. Fire had flashed and erupted like dragon's breath from some bad fantasy vid, scorching. Eight-meter ceilings showed a variety of black stains from smoke and detonation.

This first space was the staging hold, surrounded on three sides by the five larger cargo areas with temperature controls, so you could set them as needed and keep enormous amounts of cargo against future demand, pulling it out of the five as you started to access it, such as cracking open a six-ton container and pulling two or three boxes for use.

Hold One on his left had ruptured, just as Kincaide had expected. The wall itself separating the two spaces had been breached by fire and pressure. It would require time to pull everything out and repair it before he could certify that the ship was ready to sail again.

Zhubin could figure out how to smuggle Lilith and the others aboard, once he had built them personal quarters here. At least he still had an identical set of holds on the starboard side, beyond the bottom engine pylon.

Kincaide stepped around a pile of something that had been burning pretty good when the oxygen ran out and smothered it. It was crunchy to the touch when he reached out with a foot. Probably everything in both holds would just need to be boxed up and sent to recycling.

"I've seen enough here," he announced. "Let's check the rear."

"Following you."

Kincaide slipped around a box that had melted like a dead frog and headed to the freezer compartments at the rear. Both looked intact. Sensors had registered the same lack of oxygen, but more of the contents here were sealed in plastic, so they could probably be wiped off, if you didn't mind the faint smell of smoke.

"Pressure still good," Kincaide said on the radio, speaking to Reyhan and Tharushi up on the bridge. They were half-blind from sensors that had cooked. "Temperature reads acceptable as well. Opening Hold Four."

Inside, stacks of boxes eight meters tall showed no obvious damage. They would require personal inspection later, but had held. Checking the nearest one, he had enough ghee to keep the crew happy for six months, even after they had gotten addicted to English-style muffins.

"Switching to channel seven now," Kincaide announced with a hand on his left wrist controls, turning to Zhubin and nodding.

The Chairman joined him on the short-range circuit. This one wasn't powerful enough to penetrate the walls in here, so they were functionally private for now.

Kincaide headed back up to the damaged area. Zhubin followed.

"I still think we should move the inner bulkhead between One and Two aftwards about four meters as part of the refit," he told the taller man. "Two decks inside what had been Hold One, both about four meters of clearance with steps for most and a cargo lift for Lilith if she needs and personal space for Niki and Serena down on this level. Only five of them really need something exotic. We can shift spaces around forward and occupy some of the currently-unused cabins with Wives. They'll have workout space, meeting rooms, and a dozen personal quarters here."

"Will the crew handle dealing with Monsters?" Zhubin asked.

"You recruited them, Zhubin," Kincaide reminded him. "I presume you'll have a certain subset that have specist issues, just because of what Humans are like. A number of them are like Ildar that way."

"And you don't care," the Chairman noted.

"They are nothing but statistics," Kincaide replied with an edge to his voice. "Consumables that have to be accounted for, at the same time I'm losing storage space here. That's why putting the bulk of the women forward would be helpful, because I can build out a conference room between now and then and pack it with boxes. Same with some spare quarters. We'll need space when we get wherever, because we'll have to build up an entire civilization on the ground, instead of just taking occupancy of stuff someone else has put in place for us."

He watched the tall man think. Everything had been theoretical up until now, because the amount of damage would have to be reported with visual scans. The repairs just had to meet with the Foreman's approval before the ship was declared safe for another test flight.

"Should we use Odtsetseg?" Zhubin asked. "To verify the crew's true loyalties?"

"You could *ask* her," Kincaide sneered, reminding the man that the woman was a person. "She needs to know the truth at some point."

Like Ildar, Prakash tended to see the Engine in all her various incarnations as nothing more than a cleaning robot at times. But then, how many times had she stepped out of a decanting chamber fresh and ready, unmindful of what the previous woman had known, depending on which Icon was tweaked and used.

Zhubin nodded. Kincaide caught the wry grin on the man's face through his helmet.

"Touché," he replied. "I will inquire."

"Good." Kincaide started forward again. Time to start ripping out plates and throwing away garbage. "We're walking a tightrope here, Prakash. I've got no more margin for error."

CHAPTER 20

Odtsetseg listened to the two men approaching with her mind as much as her ears. Chairman Prakash was still keeping her softer probes mostly at bay, but Kincaide just walked along and sipped tea from a mug, his mind relaxed and open, like he was inviting her to rifle his memory as Prakash spoke.

She stared hard at the Foreman and the man winked at her.

Odtsetseg started and nearly fell off the stool she had seated herself upon when the two men asked her into the lounge for a chat.

"Repeat that?" she asked/demanded in a voice that sounded plaintive even in her ears as she turned back to Zhubin.

The Chairman took a quick breath and focused on her, then glanced over at Kincaide with something like irritation on his mind.

Odtsetseg was familiar with the Good Cop/Bad Cop concept, but this didn't seem to follow that pattern. Prakash was grumpy at having to explain, and Kataragama was laughing at the man.

Not at her though. She could sense only warmth from the man directed at her. It was strange, after he had been so distant and cold to her for so long.

Did Kincaide see her as Human now?

If anyone might, it would be him.

Or did he see her as Nayani, somehow still there in his dreams playing that role?

She didn't believe in reincarnation or a true god who loved people. If there was such a creature, he obviously loved the Alvar more.

But her God was more personal. Hasan Ildar. The father who had taken a broken child and turned her into something great and powerful.

And Prakash proposed doing what again?

She scowled at the man as he turned back to face her, taking another breath.

"The plan calls for us to abandon him here just before we depart Al-Winoq Glide, Odtsetseg," the Chairman did repeat the words, but they made no more sense the second time.

She felt her face fall slack.

"Why?" she finally demanded, emotions rising.

Abandon God himself? He would strike her down. Erase her Icon. Cast her into permanent darkness!

"For the good of all Humanity," Kincaide spoke up now.

"But we're going to rescue Humanity," she cried out quietly. "That's the mission. Go found a new colony of only Humans, so the blues can never find us again."

"Not all Humans, Odtsetseg," Kincaide crooned quietly, breaking through the fragile shell around her emotions right now.

"Not?" she squeaked.

"Ildar is bringing a package with him that only contains those Humans he considers worthy," Kincaide said, rising from his chair with a sigh and setting his mug down. It would be time to pace. He did that. "Only Caucasians with a certain purity of blood and genetics, Odtsetseg. Not all Humans qualify."

"But...?"

A small fraction of her mind noted Chairman Prakash mentally stepping back and sitting, so that he was out of the way. Kincaide would try to explain now.

Odtsetseg wondered if anyone could. Or if she needed to destroy these two men and then tell God. Or go along with their ultimate betrayal until she could triple cross them later.

Betray God?

"No East Asians will be transported in the Encyclopedia when he loads the final package, Odtsetseg," Kincaide continued. "No Chinese, no Japanese, no Indonesians. Nothing. Similarly, no Africans or blacks of any kind, regardless of culture or Dome. No First Nations or South Americans. Not even Russians or Arabs, because he believes they have been irrevocably tainted. Only certain people from South or Central Asia, or Euro-descended whites."

"But, why?" she managed, feeling something tear in her mind. Or maybe the man's words had slammed headlong into a barrier in her mind that she had never encountered before.

Had God put it there? Why would he do that? What was wrong with her?

"If you hate the Alvar or the Mori or the Mog indiscriminately, if you consider them a lesser species by definition, the term I would use to describe you is a specist, Odtsetseg," Kincaide's voice dropped to barely a murmur, like she was a wild animal about to spook.

Was she?

Odtsetseg realized how hard her hands were gripping the sides of the stool and forced them to unclench. At the same time, she lifted her feet from the deck and tried to relax.

To listen.

To not lash out at the man verbally or psychically at his heresies.

"Are you a specist, Kincaide?" she fired a heavy bolt of anger at the man.

Maybe she also hit him with her psychic power, too, because he seemed to slump for a moment before recovering.

"I have been called that," he replied, mind still open for her to see the honesty behind the statement. "But I only hate the Alvar for what they have done to everyone else. If they left us alone, I'd like to think I felt differently."

"Alone?" she asked, confused. "How could they do that?"

"What if they had arrived on Earth and offered mankind the stars?" Prakash spoke up now, drawing her eyes and giving Kincaide a moment to breathe. "What if they said that Engines might die, but you could see the galaxy? Many Humans would have taken that chance."

"They didn't do that," Kincaide said now, and Odtsetseg could see the rage that he kept buried deep most of the time. "They arrived and killed people. Conquered the planet. Took the survivors and turned them into pets. Keep us in the seventeen Domes like animals in a zoo. Decant Humans from the Catalogue as they need more. Allow people like Hasan Ildar to experiment on Humans as they desire, to make them better servants to the Alvar."

"I'm a better servant," Odtsetseg snapped at both men. "Without that, I'd have never existed."

"Wrong," Kincaide fired right back, his voice and face turning so hard it might be steel. "The woman who you were before would have existed. She might have gone on and had several lives, depending on her Icon. We know she was already mildly telepathic so she'd have been valuable. That was why Ildar chose you at the beginning. You'd have made a good Engine or breeder in your base form. What he did to you was not ethical."

"He gave me power." Odtsetseg felt her anger rise.

"And he took you and forced you into someone, *something* you were never meant to be." Prakash remained seated, but leaned forward now. "I've known seventeen different versions of you to date, Odtsetseg. Only four of them were re-Indexed as new baselines. The others were disposed of when you developed some unforeseen problem or limit. Ildar went back to the Icon and adjusted it before decanting a new edition of you that was closer to his vision of perfection."

"So I'm perfect?" she asked, letting her anger channel over into something she might call godhead.

"The perfect tool," Kincaide interrupted before she Ascended.

She felt her anger at the man boil up and threaten to splatter on him.

"Ildar doesn't see you as a person, Odtsetseg," Prakash continued. "You are a model he wants to sell to the Alvar when he gets it finalized. Thousands—millions—of you. That was how he got all the funding for this project. The Alvar provided it, on the promise of a better *Engine*. Nothing more. The project involved putting a spare Human colony at a new forward depot, but that was mostly a bureaucratic cover by his Alvar allies to prove that the *Engine*—you—worked as well as intended. The first betrayal is Ildar double-crossing the Alvar and The Gage so that he can instead go set up a Human colony on a secret world."

"I know that," Odtsetseg snarled at the man. Men. Both of them. They were founders of that conspiracy, more or less. "You know that. You've gone beyond that now."

Both recoiled from the venom she had found in her voice. In her soul.

They were talking about betraying God. He would strike her down.

"Tell me why I should not destroy you right now," she seethed.

Prakash's mental shields faltered finally as her rage bubbled out psychically. Her anger, her emotion, made it hard for her to even see his flesh. Kincaide, alternatively, took it all in stride, with a phlegmatic mental shrug in her direction that almost completely derailed her in a single heartbeat.

How do you threaten a man who doesn't care if he lives or dies?

Odtsetseg blinked. They both knew it, but she didn't think Prakash had recognized the moment, or caught the implications.

"We need to talk about racism now, Odtsetseg," Kincaide said quietly, both hands out at his sides like he was about to step forward and embrace her.

"Racism," she repeated the word, striving in her mind to hold on to the anger and power she'd had a moment ago, but watching it somehow slip through her fingers like sand. Or maybe water.

How could Kincaide do that to her?

Odtsetseg paused for less than the blink of an eye and looked inside herself to see if there was some button, some something he had pushed that could manipulate her like that.

She found nothing of the sort.

What she found were other walls. She recognized none of them.

Had they always been there? What were they?

She listened inside herself with mental ears and felt the hands of God himself in their construction. Hasan Ildar had put them there when he built her.

Why?

Kincaide was speaking now. She leapt up out of herself and focused on the man's words.

Less than a heartbeat had passed, and already she was calming, listening.

How did he do that?

"Racism," he was saying.

He even paused for a moment as she recentered herself, like he'd been following her conversation with herself.

"Ildar is a specist," Kincaide repeated. "Much of the crew is, but that's not unexpected, with what we're doing. The damned blues don't need to know that."

"Okay," she prompted.

"Ildar is also a racist, Odtsetseg," he continued. "The Icons he is planning to transport to his new world is not all of Humanity. Only those sub-sets he personally considers valuable. Nothing more. Not the entire wealth of the Human species. South Asians like me or Zhubin and much of the crew. White Euros. A narrow band of cultural geography running northwest to southeast for a few thousand kilometers, but excluding most Humans."

"Why?" she asked, feeling small and young compared to this man somehow.

"Mindless hatred," Kincaide replied.

"You hate everyone," she poked at him with her mind.

"Perhaps," he agreed. "But I hate everyone equally. It's not personal. I don't look at a Chinese woman and see an animal. Or a black African and see a primitive, unevolved form of Human. Ildar does."

"And you're going to betray him over that," she sneered now.

"Fundamentally, yes," Kincaide nodded.

"Why?" she asked again, tiring of the word and wondering if she should have to kill them both right now.

Could she?

"Because Zhubin Prakash promised me that we would not bring Ildar's package of Icons when we went into deep space, Odtsetseg," he said. "We're going to replace it with a different one, representing a new Eden. Every flavor of Human will be represented, from all ethnic groups. As far as I understand that includes over four hundred different telepaths like you, although none nearly as powerful. And that we'll transport most of the aliens as well."

Her gasp caused her hands to let go from the stool as they flew to her mouth. She started to fall over, but Kincaide was there to steady her with a hand.

"Yes," he nodded to her enormous eyes. "We're taking Mori with us. Mog. Cassoway. Warednja. Ayotochtli. Lop. Even those goofball Boomers. But no Alvar."

"Why?" she whispered, wondering if she was completely broken and she could only say the one word over and over until God created a new version of her that didn't have a shattered mind.

"We are all victims of the Alvar," Kincaide said. "The Gage. Ildar's plan was to spend a few centuries in hiding, designing and building perfect Human warriors who were probably Alvar-sized, so he could come back and conquer The Gage. Take over the entire galaxy and eventually the universe. That would make him, and us, no better than the Alvar, Odtsetseg."

She stared at him, her jaw feeling broken from the way it fell open and just hung there.

She studied him with her mind, and could detect no falsehood in him.

None.

This man who hated everyone had suddenly decided to love everyone instead. Somehow.

She pressed. Caught a fleeting image of a woman's face, framed by black hair in long, luxurious curls.

It wasn't Nayani. Odtsetseg knew what that woman looked like. This stranger had skin Odtsetseg associated with Northwest Euros.

Then Kincaide did something she didn't think he was able to do.

He closed his mind to her. Shut it like a door and set the bolt.

"No," he said.

"No?" she demanded, feeling only a faint echo of the anger that might have destroyed the Chairman just a moment ago.

How did Kincaide do that to her?

"Not yet, perhaps," he corrected himself.

"Why?" she fell back on the question, seemingly the only word left in her spoken vocabulary, but there was so much she didn't understand.

"Someone reminded me that we can be a force for good in the galaxy," Kincaide said quietly. "That we have the chance to save everyone. To protect everyone from people like Hasan Ildar or the Alvar."

"Oh?" she asked, shocked at the change that had come over the man in the last month or three.

This was not the Kincaide she had fallen asleep protected by. And yet it was.

"You're not Human, Odtsetseg," Kincaide crooned in a soft voice. "If we draw the lines the way Ildar wants, should we leave you behind?"

Odtsetseg started to rage again, but his words shattered her mind. But for that hand that was there again, keeping her upright on the stool, she would have fallen off and possibly hurt herself.

Kincaide hated everyone equally. But it was equally. He could love them just as much.

From a safe distance. That was his secret. Her secret now. As long as everyone was far enough away, he didn't register them as a person to hate.

Just a people to be protected from predators like God.

Like God?

She shivered so badly that Kincaide stepped up and wrapped arms around her. Held her against his chest.

Warmed her. Just like that first night, when she finally began to understand the Foreman.

She touched flesh and was inside his mind again, like a waking dream.

Kincaide Kataragama's mind lay spread out before her. She could even see the other man, the one who had come before Kincaide and been deeply in love with Nayani.

Was deeply in love with her, even today.

Never forgotten, only waiting until death brought them together again.

Odtsetseg had never been loved. Tears spilled from her now, soaking his shirt.

God did not love her. Not like Kincaide did Nayani.

God saw her only as a tool. A better Engine that he would use to extract power from the Alvar. To eventually help him conquer them, when he could upgrade her several more times to carry the warships that he would bring like a plague upon them in a thousand years.

She saw God as Kincaide saw him. Saw memories of conversations between the men, talking about her as a tool to be used and discarded. Another alien on his path to ultimate power.

One of the walls in her mind broke. Crumbled.

She had no vocabulary to describe it, except that God had placed a stricture upon her to never question his will, and Kincaide Kataragama had just broken it.

Hasan Ildar was a predator. A would-be conqueror with plans to replace the Alvar, not save the galaxy from them. She remembered seeing such things herself with her power.

Accepting them as correct at the time.

Because he was God.

What else had that rotten son of a bitch done to her?

CHAPTER 21

Hasan sat in his lounge and studied the updated plans that Zhubin Prakash had sent as part of the repair work. It was a place of serenity, when he wanted to relax and contemplate the future.

A comfortable chair designed to his dimensions. End tables and bookshelves intended to sooth his mind. The nearby desk where he could spread out printouts or various computers if he needed to.

Hasan would retire to his office or his lab later, but for now, he needed to take a moment and understand how Prakash and his crew were coming along. It had cost him nearly six months on his schedule timeline, but nothing irreparable.

It wasn't like he ever intended to arrive at that forward arms depot the Alvar had already caused to be built.

Dashavatara was a thing of perfection. A bow section like a Goose flying into the future. Or a middle finger raised to The Gage. The vast, squarish aft section where most of the crew would fly, protected from the warp by powerful shields.

He still did not understand why Prakash and Kataragama had chosen to live at such risk forward, because his own quarters were almost at the center of the vessel, protected on all sides against injury. Hasan Ildar had plans to see the Alvar fall, and that would take centuries to achieve.

Still, the changes were not great. Extending three middle decks aftwards some on either side of the vertical engine pylons would improve stability and add cargo space, giving the ship perhaps an entire additional month at sea before they needed supplies of any kind. And even then, most star systems had the raw materials available to load into Decant machines or industrial printers.

The modifications should improve the four mighty engines that pushed the vessel through space outside the warp, with the larger pair on the same plain as the flat body of the ship, and the other two at the cardinal points top and bottom.

Power.

Sufficient to travel through warp-space. To engage anything smaller than a full Warp Voyager in combat.

But more importantly, enough for his Engine to transport the entire vessel on her shoulders.

And he was just beginning. As he improved his TrueBreed Humans, so would the Engine be improved over time. He could be patient as he made her more and more powerful because she could never herself breed. No risk of those genes ever polluting his other projects.

A sound caused him to look up. Chun 8 delivering coffee. Since she was not cooking, she wore nothing but a collar with her number.

She smiled at him as she held the tray with a mug.

The Chuns were acceptable. More than acceptable, as he smelled her musk, the excitement of being able to serve him. The arousal it caused her to stand here with a mug of coffee and be noticed.

For a long moment, he considered taking a few designs like her with *Dashavatara*. He would have centuries to work. A man should have pleasant diversions.

"Put the coffee down here," he pointed, rising and setting his handheld on the end table.

Chun 8 immediately moved to please him. The mug was placed with a happy smile at bringing her God any amount of joy.

Yes, he approved of the changes he had made to the base design. He would not ever incorporate it into the TrueBreed design, but he would probably take a few pleasure Icons with him.

"Bend over the desk," he commanded the Chun. "I will take you there."

The object squealed with delight and immediately pressed her chest flat on the surface, presenting her bottom with a wiggle as he undid the fly of his pants and moved behind her.

The coffee was in a sealed mug, so it would remain warm. And he wouldn't be long. He had also added modifications to the Chun design to make it quick and pleasurable for him.

Hasan stepped up and entered her with a hard thrust, forcing her muscles to give way, even as the creature was already soaking wet with anticipation. He reached down and grabbed a handful of that shoulder-length black hair, wrenching it back roughly and bending her spine up.

She emitted a sound midway between a scream of pain and a small orgasm as he did, just as he had designed into her, making him wonder if he should pause to retrieve the leather strap that would cause her to collapse into a near-unending string of orgasms. That sounded like too much work, even as much as he might enjoy beating a Chun this afternoon.

A chime interrupted his thrusts, bringing Hasan's mind back to the present.

"Answer," he ordered the home system.

Another sound and the system was on conference mode.

"Hello?" a voice asked. "Ildar, are you okay?"

Colonial Dispatch Administrator of the First Rank Songkram Sangsuriya.

"Just fucking a sex object, Administrator," Hasan replied, slapping the creature on the ass once with an open palm to get that cry of pain he needed from her so he could reach his satisfaction. "How may I serve you today?"

She found the correct rhythm now, pinned to the table, bent back by her hair, and violated in the way he had designed her to enjoy. His orgasm began. Hers followed immediately on, not that he cared, but he supposed the sound would make it even better for him.

"I have been reading the reports from *Dashavatara*, Ildar," Sangsuriya spoke now, raising his voice a little to overcome the cries from the Chun being fucked. "The vessel approached a new completion?"

"So I understand, Administrator," Hasan grunted and finished. "Has the investigation found anything useful? And will the quarantine be lifted? I need to retrieve my Engine and make a final backup copy of her before departure."

Hasan stepped back from the Chun and gestured to the servant.

"Clean me," he ordered.

The creature staggered from the lounge into the salon, returning a moment later with a towel. She knelt and proceeded to use mouth and rag on him. Hasan ignored her to study the far wall, as if he could see *Dashavatara* in the distance.

"There have been some changes decreed, Ildar," Sangsuriya began, almost apologetically.

Hasan felt himself tighten.

They had reached endgame. What surprises would those blue shits spring on him at the last moment? How would he be boxed in, if he allowed it?

"The delay has given the fleet time to reconsider and study some of the feasibility reports they had ignored earlier," the Administrator continued. "They wish to transport an embassy of administrators to the depot, as well as supplementing the package of Icons to include several other species."

Damn them!

Hasan gestured the Chun to depart as she closed his fly. The servant fled.

Hasan kept himself perfectly silent for a long moment lest he rage at the nominal ally he had been planning to betray.

"Ildar?" the creature asked.

"Here," he replied. "Contemplating the logistics, Administrator. It may be impossible."

"Impossible?" Sangsuriya replied with a huff verging on a snarl.

Hasan wondered if the man had been told no by an underling in the last millennium.

"Scale, Administrator Sangsuriya," he offered. "Because the vessel was never intended to risk Alvar lives, we purposefully built it much smaller inside. An adult such as yourself would be thirty centimeters taller than most of the decks, with exception of the cargo storage areas and the arboretum. I would not wish to cause your kind distress, even over such a short voyage."

Hasan said a silent prayer to whatever Human gods might have survived the Conquest and Exodus that The Gage Fleet didn't just order him to rebuild the entire ship. Or build a new one that would be comfortable to them.

When individuals of a species might live eight thousand years, what was a decade to them? They didn't see the need for alacrity that the short-lived species were consumed by.

And the longer this went on, the greater chance that his conspiracy would be discovered.

"That small?" the Administrator asked, amazed.

"We are tiny creatures, compared to the mighty Alvar," Hasan replied, striving not to gag himself with such pretty lies.

We will also see you all cast down like the lowest Boomers, Alvar scum.

But he could not say that. Not until he had escaped. Maybe not even then.

Hopefully, Songkram Sangsuriya, the Alvar who was currently a Colonial Dispatch Administrator of the First Rank, would still be alive when Hasan Ildar's fleets and armies descended on The Gage on some fateful, future date, and Hasan could have the creature dragged before his throne in chains, just so the beast could see what he had wrought before Hasan had his eyes put out.

"How long would it take to rebuild the vessel?" he asked, sending Hasan off on a binge of cursing in his mind.

"I would need to consult with my Chairman and my Foreman to be conclusive, Administrator," Hasan replied, hoping that he would have a chance to prepare the two men for whatever lies they needed to spin.

"I will summon them from *Dashavatara*," Sangsuriya commanded. "And the Engine as well. You will attend me this afternoon at my office."

And he cut the line. Just like that. Not even the politeness of a goodbye-for-now.

Fucker.

And there was nothing Hasan could communicate to Prakash.

Hopefully the man was smart enough to lie to everyone when he arrived.

CHAPTER 22

Kincaide looked up at Zhubin, standing in the doorway to Kincaide's suite. He didn't appreciate that Zhubin had just opened without knocking.

"All of us?" Kincaide asked.

He could see Odtsetseg standing behind the Chairman, so Zhubin had told her first. Or found her in the lounge or the kitchen when he got the news.

"All of us," Zhubin agreed.

"Are we made?" Kincaide asked. "Did those sorry shits finally put two and two together?"

"Maybe," the Chairman replied. "Except that I wouldn't have asked for Odtsetseg to accompany us, if you and I were about to be arrested and executed. Too much risk of damaging her if we went insane or decided to go out with a bang."

"But they want all three of us to fly over to the Administrative Station to meet with the Colonial Dispatch Office now?" Kincaide confirmed.

"Ildar's project was funded by those fine folks," Zhubin grinned grimly.

Both of them had wandered far enough past the hatch now that it closed itself up.

"Why?" Kincaide asked bluntly.

"They instructed me to bring the ship's plans," Zhubin said. "The ones we filed. Not the actual as-built we're flying."

"Someone going to ask us to collapse a few decks to allow a three-meter-tall blue fucker to board and travel with us?" Kincaide wondered aloud.

"Maybe," Zhubin shrugged.

The Chairman turned to Odtsetseg.

"I need to know which way you intend to jump, Star Flower," the man said, invoking the common meaning of her name, translated from the ancient Mongolian. "You'll be with us when you see Ildar again, so you can denounce us to him, but I would do it privately if you intend to."

"Privately?" she asked, stepping around him with a wide berth, as if he might lash out.

Kincaide could have told her that the man could reach her anywhere she was in this entire chamber, probably faster than she would even notice. He himself remained seated in his comfortable chair and watched.

"Neither Kincaide nor I have been Indexed in the current. If they destroy us, we're gone forever and the best the Alvar could do would be to decant another copy of the kid I used to be," Prakash said. "On the other hand, if you just tell Ildar and not The Gage, he might have us quietly killed later, but the *Dashavatara* could still escape."

"You don't want that outcome," she pointed out in a tart voice that sounded like it came from a much older woman.

Weird, when she was nineteen and built with no curves at all. Like there was someone else inhabiting that flesh. But wasn't that as close to a truth as you might get, depending on your epistemological tendencies?

"I still prefer that outcome over The Gage killing all of the conspiracy and keeping you as a new and improved Engine with which they can extend their power over the entire galaxy," the Chairman said. "Second best, but letting The Gage win is third."

"So I should betray God and the Alvar, but not the two of you?" she asked angrily, looking at both of them in turn.

Kincaide made a noise to draw her eye. It was time.

"Odtsetseg, there are others you would be betraying, as well as us," he said. "Those people who are the reason we risked the delay that might cause our deaths today."

"Who?" she demanded.

"The Monster Wives of Brakiee Goaulda," he said simply.

Kincaide relaxed and tried to open his mind to her, knowing that she would immediately rifle his memories to understand what he was saying.

He thought of Lilith first. Staci. Niki. Ghost. Megaera. All of them.

She gasped, hands to her mouth in a nervous tic she probably didn't even know she had.

"What are they?" she asked now in a quieter voice.

"Humans," Kincaide said unequivocally. "Before Hasan Ildar figured out how, people like Goaulda could only work within the confines of Human DNA to make changes."

"Do all men immediately turn to creating sex objects when given that kind of power?" Odtsetseg scowled at him.

Kincaide had wondered much on the topic over the years, more so when Prakash had found him and recruited him to build *Dashavatara*.

"Absolute power corrupts absolutely, Odtsetseg," he replied. "I suspect that the ability to make those changes is the honey that draws in that kind of man in the first place, rather than the other way around."

"I know at least one woman of a similar bent," Prakash spoke up. "For her, she created the perfect domestic servants as she saw them. Happy to serve her, pretty to look at, adequate in bed when she had an occasional itch."

"The evil lies in twisting the minds to enjoy something," Kincaide picked up the thread now. "Ildar routinely decants new domestics and turns them into sex objects, because he doesn't see most people as his equals. They happen to be pretty females because Ildar expresses hetero, but if he liked boys, I'm sure they would all be buff Adonis types, half-clothed as they vacuumed or cooked. Perhaps twelve-year-old boys, depending on his perversions."

"Evil is as evil does?" she sneered.

"You have the power to change us, if you got angry enough," Kincaide pointed out.

"How would you know that?" she rounded on him, hunched forward a little and breathing heavy, like he'd pushed just the right button.

But then, he'd known which one to push.

"Because that night when you fell into my dream, I fell into yours," he smiled grimly at her.

Odtsetseg turned so white he thought she was about to pass out.

"Sit," he ordered her lightly, gesturing to the other chair.

Prakash moved to keep the power triangle of their personalities intact. Kincaide nearly laughed, because all of them seemed to do that unconsciously these days.

"What did you see?" she asked, frightened now.

"You were you," Kincaide nodded. "I was Hasan Ildar, except as you saw him then."

"Then?" both she and Zhubin asked in harmony.

"Taller than Zhubin here, and broader in the shoulders," Kincaide gestured. "Handsome and commanding in ways that confused you, but I suspect that that fucker has done things to your biology to make you more controllable at the same time he made you stronger, or just because."

"Such as?" she demanded, but he let her derail the conversation. They had time.

"A woman your age should have a menstrual cycle roughly every twenty-eight days," Kincaide said. "Have you ever had one?"

"No," she whispered. "He said I could not, because of the octopus genes."

"He might be right there," Prakash interjected. "An octopus female breeds once, lays her eggs, and then starves herself to death protecting them from predators. Dozens or hundreds might hatch, for only a handful at most to survive to mate themselves."

"Oh," she said.

Kincaide watched her eyes grow huge, the epicanthic fold of her Mongolian heritage normally making them wide and slim compared to his. Almond-shaped, to use the traditional insult that history had handed down, but containing a kernel of truth.

"In the dream, I suspect, like you, I fell into a memory, but not one you consciously remember," Kincaide said. "Or one either you suppressed or he did. I couldn't tell and wasn't in it long enough."

"What did I do?" Odtsetseg leaned forward now, her eyes and mind boring in on him, so he let her see it as he spoke.

"Ildar—me, I suppose—had you modify someone's mind," Kincaide said. "Adjust their personality radically with your powers, just before he put them in the machine and Indexed them, so he would have a solid baseline against which to measure changes. If I remember me as him correctly, I could do the same thing with genetics and tweaks to their chromosomes, but he wanted to know if you could do it directly, because I think he wanted to maybe give himself that power at some point."

"He wouldn't be Human?" she whispered.

"Which was why he never did, but you can," Kincaide said.

"Why are you telling me this?" she cried.

"Because we're about to go visit Hasan Ildar and his Alvar masters, Star Flower," Zhubin Prakash said. "You have to decide which side you are on, and there is nothing Kincaide or I could do to stop you. You could alter our minds if you chose."

"That would be evil," she said, almost automatically.

"Yes," Kincaide agreed. "But Hasan Ildar does not agree with you. Nor do the Alvar. That's why we're going to betray him, as soon as we get that chance, because nobody should have that power, Odtsetseg."

"What do you want from me?" she demanded, voice grown tiny and fearful again.

"Your help," Kincaide explained. "Rescuing the Monster Wives, saving Humanity, and maybe someday freeing the galaxy from The Gage."

"Oh," she said, eyes getting big again. "I can do that."

"We're counting on that," he smiled. "Because you are a good person."

CHAPTER 23

Odtsetseg followed Zhubin into the chamber, amazed as always at the size of Alvar architectural design. The largest of the males could reach three and a half meters tall, though they rarely wore footwear with any heel to it. Mostly sandals that were a single flat piece of leather and laces that ran up the ankle and calf.

But they built cathedrals, at least from a Human perspective. The dome in here was four meters high at the edge and more than twelve at the center. More than that, because you entered along a mezzanine-style area around the edge of the dome and then took several Alvar steps down to the pit in the center.

At least they understood all their shorter, servant species, and always added a narrow set of steps to one side fit for Human-sized legs.

God was here already, dressed in the color pattern she had come to associate with godhead in her mind. Brown tunic long over black pants and black leather riding boots. A wide leather belt around his center held a variety of small pouches, most concealed under the brown opera-style half-cape he wore.

The beret he affected for style, this one in black with a red pin on it that always reminded her of a bird. Odtsetseg had a flash of insight that identified the bird as a phoenix, the symbol of death and rebirth.

Indexing and Decanting.

God.

Truly?

The man had shaved his head to a gleaming polish since the last time she had seen him. A short, black goatee and mustache framed a cruel mouth with full lips, although Odtsetseg couldn't remember such details from before.

Had Kincaide and Zhubin broken her? Or merely broken the complete hold God had once had over her mind?

Should she betray these men? Both of them? All of them?

Odtsetseg found the sudden liberty to think for herself almost painful.

Had she always been merely a tool to God? Never a person?

She studied the room as she walked in Zhubin's wake, with Kincaide behind her. Both men emanated protective thoughts that warmed her.

Three Alvar, plus God. They sat on a dais on the far side of the space, staring down at the three intruders.

Odtsetseg noted that the three Alvar included a female, one of the few she could ever remember seeing in the flesh. Humans were the closest to the Alvar, in terms of overall physiology, of all the servant species. This woman was perhaps two hundred and forty-five centimeters tall, so a little below average for their type. Like all Alvar females, she lacked the wasp shape of a female Human torso, where the shoulders slopped in to the waist before flaring out again over hips.

Odtsetseg had no curves, either. She had seen too many minds unconsciously compare her to a pre-pubescent boy, but with a start she realized that she was really built more like an Alvar female, lacking only the enormous breasts of that species and scaled down to a three-quarters model.

All the Alvar wore the white toga-style tunic that marked their kind and station. Pure linen the color of fresh snow, with the biggest male having it on both shoulders, and the other male and the female on the right shoulder only. Both had purple aureole against blue skin.

That style marked them as nobility. The true power of The Gage.

Interestingly, all wore an identical piece of jewelry around their necks, a choker, done in bronze perhaps, with a large, faceted diamond in the center, bigger than her thumbnail.

Each was protected by an invisible force field of some sort that she studied as Zhubin descended into the arena and she followed. There was no other term to describe this. A Star Chamber filled with four aliens.

Four?

Yes. She was no longer Human, even as much as Kincaide would argue with her. The Monster Wives she looked forward to meeting were more Human than she was.

God was a Human, but a bad one. An Inquisitor.

She forced her mind back to the three Alvar. The diamond was the thing that generated the field.

Odtsetseg pushed, noting that it would be sufficient to keep a lesser telepath at bay, a solid shield of energy on several wavelengths that would prevent her from doing anything.

God did not wear such a thing. Did he understand that her design was powerful enough to see and work through it anyway, or did he think he still owned her soul and that would protect him from her type?

Zhubin moved to the left, standing across from the woman. Kincaide ended up facing God. She was in the middle, looking at the Administrator she recognized from before and the stranger who had the look of his well-bred superior. The Administrator was older, but Alvar didn't age like Humans. They got stockier with the centuries, at least the men did. Older Alvar women grew thinner over time, although Odtsetseg didn't know how she knew that. Perhaps some knowledge implanted by God somewhere along the way.

"You are Zhubin Prakash," the Administrator began, looking down at a sheaf of papers on the desk in front of him, invisible from down here.

"That is correct," Zhubin said.

"Your role?"

"Chairman of the construction company founded by Dr. Hasan Ildar to build, test, and operate the experimental warp-ship known as *Dashavatara*, Your Eminence."

"Kincaide Kataragama."

"Here, Lord."

Odtsetseg worked on maintaining a perfectly innocent, emotionless facade as she listened to Kincaide's mind, watching the outward subservience so desperately at odds with the bile and vitriol roiling angrily inside.

Yes. She could see the mistake she had made with the man. Everyone did, so it was an easy trap to fall into.

Kincaide didn't hate all the other species. Or even individuals. He just maintained a mask of disdain around him, and very few people were ever admitted into the ranks of even casual friends.

Reyhan Herath, the Information Systems expert on *Dashavatara* who was also the Assistant Foreman, for example, with most of the rest being merely crew.

"Your role?" the Alvar asked Kincaide next.

But Kincaide's hatred today was a palpable thing in the face of Alvar. Disdain gave way to a rage so intense that she would have burned out minds, even behind those pitiful shields, if she felt that way.

How did she feel?

Odtsetseg found she didn't know. A glance at God did not elicit the pangs of worship that it once had. She did not feel the need to prostrate herself before the man and bask in the sunlight of his approval.

"Foreman of the crew of *Dashavatara*," Kincaide was saying as she stepped back into herself and studied the Administrator speaking.

His mind was hidden, but behind a mere piece of cheesecloth, rather than a steel and stone fortress.

"What does a Foreman do, Human?" the Alvar asked with obvious disdain.

"Ship Systems Manager, sir," Kincaide bit the words off carefully, lest he drip acid on them.

Odtsetseg was amazed at the man's control. But then, he'd been hiding for thirty years now.

"Oh?"

"I am the senior officer in charge of flight operations," Kincaide continued. "Chairman Prakash exercises oversight duties, but lacks the technical knowledge to order my crew effectively. It follows an ancient, Human model, where a noble with no maritime experience would often command a sailing ship that was crewed by experts who could translate vague orders into practical seamanship."

"You also helped design the vessel?" the blue giant asked.

"Redesign, perhaps," Kincaide corrected the man carefully. "Refine Dr. Ildar's original design against the practicalities of space and knowledge won from the construction of the vessel itself."

"It is scaled to Humans," the Administrator stated.

"My instructions from Dr. Ildar were that only Humans would travel on the experimental ship," Zhubin spoke up now. "Not even Lop or Mori, to say nothing of Alvar, so we could construct a much more compact vessel and thus save significant resource expenditures on the project from the initial budget estimates."

"And the recent rebuild necessitated by the terrorist attack?" the man turned to the Chairman now.

"We still retain twenty-four percent cushion," Prakash smiled as she glanced over. "In addition to the standard ten percent allocated to cost overruns from unexpected difficulties."

"Kataragama, have you built larger vessels?" the man asked, ping-ponging back and forth past her as if she wasn't present. Or was invisible.

But didn't they all see her as just a piece of organic hardware? Looking at minds supposedly sacrosanct, she could see that.

Just a tool. A better *Engine*.

"I have worked on crews that have built to Alvar scales, Administrator," Kincaide replied evenly.

"How hard would it be to rebuild the ship to fit my kind?" the man pounced, as if he thought it would be a surprise.

As if Zhubin and Kincaide hadn't spent the flight over discussing that exact outcome. Gaming out the possibilities.

Did the Alvar have such a low opinion of Humans?

But then, they worked with people like God most directly. That might skew their view, all things considered.

Odtsetseg caught herself from blanching. Gasping. Something.

What had been the thing where she finally stopped seeing the man as a God?

Niki.

Not Ghost. Not Lilith. Not even Euryale.

Kincaide's memories of Niki, the Aomi. Half woman and half octopus, like Odtsetseg was, but all Odtsetseg's inHumanity was generally hidden, other than the marks on her face and the way her eyes weren't normal.

But Niki had no legs at all. Just tentacles and that blood-red webbing of her mantle. Designed to serve the kinks of a man pushing the envelope to find stranger and more horrifying ways to degrade a woman while dominating her via fornication.

The others could at least walk on dry land. Niki and Serena would have to crawl with only their arms.

Even Serena would at least remind people of a mermaid.

Niki was trapped as a nightmare.

Kincaide had paused, as if in thought.

"Not sure the ship can be entirely rebuilt, Administrator," he finally said. "Too many places where Human scale sets everything around it, plus we'd have to recalculate everything from scratch, including the thrusters."

Kincaide turned to her now, standing only a meter away, and smiled.

"And nobody knows just how much mass Odtsetseg can transfer to warp-space easily," he continued, turning back to the Alvar. "I'm still looking forward to the first flight, just so we can establish a clean baseline. I'd hate to add a third or more of our mass to the ship and only then discover that we'd passed some critical threshold and have to start over."

Odtsetseg felt six pair of eyes center on her, but Kincaide and Zhubin were friendly. God was august and aloof. The two Alvar nobles appeared bored. The Administrator was suddenly at a loss for words, his mouth falling a little open in an almost Human manner.

She decided to take a small risk, and pushed forward into his mind. The machine generating the field slowed her some, and made her control less than perfect, but she could see his thoughts almost as well as she had with Kincaide, back on *Dashavatara*.

Songkram Sangsuriya, Colonial Dispatch Administrator of the First Rank, was unsure of the best way to sideline God from the project, but betrayal of the Human was high in the Alvar's mind. His opinion of Hasan Ildar was only slightly better than that of Kincaide, to say nothing of Zhubin.

So, at the end, the Alvar intended to cut God out, but wasn't sure how to do it. Worse, she rifled into his memories for a moment, pretending to think about the unvoiced question. If the Alvar had to speak it aloud that would buy her time to study his mind as well, in addition to perhaps making him think her more of a fool than she already might be.

More engines? Better ones? That was the prize God had dangled in front of the Colonial Dispatch Office. Ships that only needed one Engine and the ability to decant new ones in an emergency. Or could use a handful, like most Human-powered vessels, and scale up in size from the already-enormous Starfall landers to things the size of stations?

She watched Sangsuriya weigh immediate value today against whatever he could fund Ildar into producing next.

"Engine," she heard him say before the words even reached his mouth. "How much can you lift?"

Tool. Organic component and not a person. Even less than a man like God considered her, because he at least saw her as *his* creation. Zhubin valued her as a means to a specific ends in a declining logic tree.

Only Kincaide saw her as a person.

Was she?

Odtsetseg found that she didn't know. Knew even less now than she had a month ago. Even a day ago.

Before Niki.

"My design is optimized for *Dashavatara* at heaviest load, Eminence," Odtsetseg fell into a mechanical sort of sing-song tone.

Words, without opinion on their value. Almost the opposite of the two men flanking her, who weighed every syllable with a micrometer and parsed them with a cutting laser.

"Heaviest load?" he asked her, but she shrugged.

Odtsetseg took a risk and pushed the man to turn his eyes on Kincaide. Felt it work as his entire head rotated five degrees.

It was like a spotlight that had been shining in her face suddenly went out.

"Our design, fully loaded and with the hallways packed beyond reasonable safety in an emergency, represents about a ten percent increase over the current dead weight of the ship, Administrator," Kincaide noted. "But that is purely theoretical, as we did not get a chance to take that initial test-flight into warp-space. It was next on the construction schedule when the terrorists planted a bomb and damaged the aft section sufficient that we were under an investigation quarantine until now. Have you located the terrorists?"

Odtsetseg stepped back out of the man's mind now, carefully watching where she put mental pegs, to see what he would do. Or remember, when she was still close enough to perhaps make further adjustments.

God was seated next to the man, and wore no shield protecting himself against his creation. She listened to the vocal conversation while most of her mind went at the man who had made her.

Changed her.

Mated her genes with an octopus, among other things, in his self-given mission to make the perfect Engine. To overthrow the Alvar.

To conquer The Gage.

To give the galaxy to Humans, while mongrels like her remained nothing but servants of the TrueBreed Humans he intended to build.

The name brought an image to the fore as she stepped into his memory.

TrueBreed.

Human. At least in genetics. Redesigned and improved to be the physical equal of an Alvar, so ranging up to three meters tall for the males and weighing around six hundred kilograms.

Females would retain the lesser scale of size and mass when everyone was just Human, because Hasan Ildar could not bring himself to see any woman as his equal.

She refrained from striking the man with her telepathy as she watched his memories of the Chun servants he owned. Chinese women kept as slaves and twisted into sex objects by the man's ingenuity and sadism.

In the outside word, the Administrator was answering Kincaide's inquiry about terrorists finally, but that was a factor of how much faster she was thinking than anyone else could speak.

"Several terrorist cells have been crushed recently," Sangsuriya was saying. "None claim any responsibility for the attack on *Dashavatara*, but none have been subjected to advance interrogations techniques yet."

Odtsetseg shivered in her mind. Torture, where an expert like God could make it so that telling any lie, or even withholding the truth, caused you to burn. Physical pain. No one could resist such elements, which was why Kincaide and Zhubin were prepared to self-terminate rather than be captured.

Every sentient would confess eventually.

She watched God now from the inside of his head. The original double-cross that would see the Alvar pay him to develop the tools that he would use to conquer them in time. The plan to assassinate Zhubin and probably Kincaide when he found the new Eden he wished to build, as the men were too smart, too capable, *too dangerous* to keep around after that.

She stewed in rage. Even Kincaide and Zhubin only intended to leave Ildar behind, when they could have done the same and arranged an accident on *Dashavatara* that would destroy the man.

Odtsetseg finally found the line that separated good from evil, watching how both men, Hasan Ildar and Kincaide Kataragama, approached such things.

God considered all beings as beneath him and would treat them thus.

Kincaide didn't give a shit about other people, unless they were friends to protect, or threats to destroy.

And he considered her a friend.

That made her warm.

CHAPTER 24

Kincaide watched the foursome up on the stage, because that was what all this was. A performance, but he didn't think the three of them down here were important enough to be the target audience.

The two Noble-born hadn't stirred themselves, so they might just be here because one or both of them were major investors in some project that either *Dashavatara* or Odtsetseg represented. The Administrator was a bureaucrat playing long games, but Kincaide already knew that from having to file regular reports and answer detailed and largely irrelevant written questions that seemed to exist just to fill databases with volume.

Data, rather than information, but he wasn't going to correct the man.

Ildar was being his usual sneering punk self today.

Zhubin had fallen silent in that way that Kincaide knew he was supposed to carry most of the conversational load for now. That was fine. Prakash was one of the few people out there that Kincaide considered smart enough and competent enough to actually listen to when Kincaide expressed an opinion.

"How long would it take to make modifications to the ship to carry a few Alvar?" the man in the middle asked him, turning those dark, beady eyes this way.

"You wanna live rough, I can transport you now," Kincaide smiled at the man with just the right degree of insubordination to ignore unless you wanted a bigger performance. "Alvar luxury would require ripping out two full decks somewhere and recalculating everything from balance to generators. But it's your money being spent."

Those eyes narrowed, but the rage Kincaide saw in them wasn't aimed at him. They flashed in the direction of Ildar for just a blink. Nobody on the stage would see it, but Zhubin would catch it.

Triple-cross coming.

"We would like to send along observers for the test flight," the blue punk in the pretty toga said in a slow, meaningful drawl.

Kincaide felt time run out. Hopefully, Zhubin did, too.

Observers would be either Alvar giants down in the arboretum living like hippies, or the most loyal servants they could dig out of the swamp. Mori had been the first species conquered, and tended to be the most trusted today, in spite of others having been around for fifty or one hundred thousand years on some colonies.

Humans were just the most useful, willing to commit all manner of atrocities on one another for a little bit of improvement in their own lives.

A few had even turned into the sorts of boot-lickers that Nelson and Nayani had liked to obliterate, back in another world.

"As soon as you authorize us to put in a full cargo load, we can set the timer running," Kincaide responded, maybe a little more diffident and polite now, but he had the villain aimed in the right direction now.

"Timer?"

"We'll need to get all the cargo properly stowed so we can calculate the balance point on the engines against theoretical design limitations." Kincaide even went so far as to smile. "That's several days to a week. From there, we can fly right over to this station and pick up a short-range personnel pod with you, Ildar, and whoever else you want to bring."

"I will not be accompanying you," the Administrator said, archly "Nor will Dr. Ildar."

Bingo.

Kincaide watched the man turn meaningfully towards the Noble-born now.

Aw, shit.

The female perked up. Small, among her kind. Older, too. Maybe into her sixth millennium now, when the Administrator only had four and a half as far as Kincaide knew.

He took a moment to study the odd man out. The other Noble-born, the male, looked younger. Felt younger, anyway. If he was a Human, he carried himself like a kid just about twenty-five. Past the first edge of stupid and had somehow survived, but not far enough along to have learned any useful wisdom.

Alvar weren't children nearly as long as Humans, relative to their lifespan. Maybe five hundred years, all total, and then that long forever as an adult.

Yeah, he felt like a punk.

Kincaide couldn't see a resemblance to the older woman, but that didn't mean anything. It would be rude to suggest that they all looked alike, but not entirely wrong.

The female was studying him. Specifically Kincaide and not Zhubin. Odtsetseg might as well not even have been in the room, as the woman didn't glance at her once.

"Do you know who I am, Human?" she asked in a slow, sharp voice that seemed to convey great age.

"Alvar," he replied.

"That is a what, Human, not a whom," she observed with a quaint smile cognizant of his verbal games.

"Is that not sufficient, Noble-born?" he volleyed right back at her, not willing to cede a centimeter today.

Kincaide hadn't known many Alvar in his life. They didn't interact with the lesser species unless they had to. Colonial Dispatch Office was one of the few places, but she didn't look like a Paramount to him.

The woman smiled at him. Her face didn't even crack once in the process, so perhaps she had even done so at least one other time in his lifespan. What was six decades to a woman with six or more millennia experience?

"I am Roselani Thammavongsa, Human," she said, introducing herself.

Kincaide supposed that the Thammavongsa name was supposed to mean something to him, but it didn't. He'd have had to care about the species enough to study them in that detail.

"And I am Kincaide Kataragama," he replied with a bow deep enough to not be considered an insult.

He waited, smiling inanely at her as she figured out how to get over herself when someone didn't ask *How high?* on the way up after she yelled *Jump!* at them.

"That name means nothing to you?" she inquired after a frosty moment finally melted.

"It does not, Noble-born lady, but I am a simple spacer hired to perform a task," Kincaide replied, trying to sound helpful. "How may I be of service?"

His mother had always called it her *Dumb Peasant Routine*. You agreed with things innocently, and asked stupid questions that often had the effect of pricking balloons of pomposity.

Mom had been an expert at that sort of thing.

Again, the scowl. Like maybe the Alvar was dealing with someone too stupid to be afraid of her.

As opposed to too stubborn to put up with her tricks and bullshit.

"How far will your so-called test flight go?" she asked in a harder voice. Done with games finally. Maybe.

"Perhaps twenty light-years out and then back," Kincaide replied evenly. "That will give us enough baseline to confirm that everything is working as intended. Not a full shakedown cruise, but if anything breaks while we're out there, we'll have a flight plan filed and the authorities will know where to look for us."

He didn't bother telling anyone that they would never find *Dashavatara* along that vector. Let that be the best surprise yet.

"How long will you be away?" she pressed.

Kincaide wondered if she was going herself. He'd assumed the punk next to her. In his mind, he suddenly wondered if the youngster was an Alvar boy toy or something instead of an investor.

"Departure from Al-Winoq orbit and the Glide to the edge of the solar mass will take a couple of days, since I don't need to push anything at this point," he focused his ire on her. Silently. "Warp-space out there is thin enough that we're a day making that first jump. Again, taking it easy so Odtsetseg is comfortable."

"Odtsetseg?" she asked, confused.

He smiled that particular smile a parent gives a misbehaving child and then turned to the woman standing quietly next to him.

"Odtsetseg," he gestured. "The woman who will be flying the ship through warp-space."

"The Engine," Thammavongsa corrected him disdainfully.

"Your term, Noble-born," Kincaide left a little bit of edge in his tones. "One of my pilots, and the more important one, at that. Not that I have anything against Dinushan Mendis, mind you."

She looked to be grinding her teeth a little right now. Kincaide wondered if the Administrator had some blackmail or something on her, to keep her behaving. He was an important enough piece of the puzzle that just executing him for insubordination right now might put the project back years. Whole budgets would have to be redone if they lost their grip in a fit of pique.

Not that he was pushing. Heaven forbid.

Blue skin flushed more umber, instead of the mauve that Humans got. He didn't know if it was embarrassment or rage.

"All told, I expect to be gone for about nine days, Noble-born," he said as she breathed heavily. "It would be uncomfortable in the current configuration, but I suppose an Alvar could survive such deprivations."

In his mind, he smiled at the thought of an Alvar, standing naked in the arboretum and being hosed off by one of his crew as a way to take a shower in the morning. No hot water down there, unless they brought along a huge watering tub and ran a hose from somewhere.

Might actually be worth it, just to make these turds squirm.

Roselani Thammavongsa's scowl approached epic levels as he watched, wondering when smoke would start pouring out of her ears.

Odtsetseg had fallen so silent he kept expecting her to pass out from lack of breathing, but Zhubin would catch her before she cracked her head on the deck. That was what wingmen were for.

Rather than yammer, the old lady leaned over to the Administrator to whisper in his ears.

Had she been Human, he might have even appreciated the way that one, full breast shifted as she did. The species was exceptionally well-designed, from a physical standpoint, and close enough to Humans externally to make a comparison.

Long faces, rather than the heavier blockiness a Human might have, scaled up to that size. Five fingers and a thumb.

Staring closer at her, he could see the faint patterns to her flesh that all Alvar had, like the geometric decorations you might find on a Shia mosque down in Boston Dome. Normally, you had to be close to see them.

Kincaide wondered if emotion made them flush. Certainly, he'd been pushing her buttons today, carefully as he did. What did that do to a woman like that, to be thwarted by a mere Human?

"This meeting is adjourned," the Administrator announced, catching everyone else off guard.

Ildar flinched like someone had connected his chair to a power socket.

Kincaide just watched, waiting for that other shoe to drop.

"Prakash and the Engine will return to the ship," the bureaucrat continued. "Kataragama will remain behind."

Bitch gave him a smile of superiority, so Kincaide had a pretty good idea what was coming next.

Enjoy it while you can, lady. I'm keeping score.

CHAPTER 25

Odtsetseg stood in a small chamber with Zhubin close by and Kincaide leaned against the far wall, hands crossed behind his back and a smooth mind that she found almost more frightening than the rage she expected.

She crossed to the Foreman and placed a hand on his arm.

"I looked in her mind," she whispered in his ear just loud enough to hear. "All of them wore devices that were supposed to protect them, but not from me."

He nodded. Smooth. Calm.

Not necessarily resigned, but unwilling to fight anyone at this point.

"She's yucky," Odtsetseg continued.

Kincaide actually laughed at that. Broke out of wherever he had gone and turned to her with a grin.

"Ya know, that might be the best term I've ever heard to describe them," he laughed.

"You already know what she's planning?" Odtsetseg asked.

"I can guess," he shrugged.

Zhubin watched the door but didn't intrude. They had asked for a few minutes so that the Chairman could be briefed about anything that the Foreman would have needed to order, but she had spent much time close to Reyhan Herath, Kincaide's Assistant Foreman. That man was almost an extension of Kincaide's mind at times.

Flyer

"But mate with a Human?" she asked, unable to keep the disgust out of her voice. Or her mind.

Again, he shrugged.

"Just another reason that they tend to elevate Humans over many of the other species," he said. "They find us cute in a non-threatening way. A tiny, almost-cartoon version of themselves. And we are mechanically compatible."

She heard the words and listened to his emotions, shocked and appalled at the thought.

Kincaide turned to her with grimness now overtaking everything.

"On Earth, according to the legends, Humans were one of a number of related species, including monkeys, gorillas, and some of the other animals you might find in a zoo," he said, eyes boring in on her. "Humans have the largest penis, relative to body mass and size, of all of them, if I remember correctly. A Human tends to be comparable to an Alvar, that way, other than significant differences in height and mass."

"She's two heads taller than you," Odtsetseg sputtered.

His grin was back.

"And only a head taller than the tallest Human woman I've ever fucked," he answered.

Odtsetseg stepped back to visualize a woman that tall.

"Human?" she asked, intrigued.

She knew they got that tall, but that was extremely rare, even in the era of men like God, who could *make adjustments* as they desired.

Kincaide smiled and licked his lips in a way that made her blush.

"Human," he confirmed. "Redhead. Wildcat."

"So you don't find it icky, the thought of fornicating with that woman?" Odtsetseg asked.

Lost only began to describe her emotions, but this was when she understood the vast gap that existed between her and these two men.

They were Human. She was not.

She could make allowances and say more-than-Human, but the Alvar woman just brought it home. That one was possessed of some bizarre perversions, to wish to fornicate with a Human, but looking in Kincaide's mind, he saw it as a power and dominance thing, rather than sex or emotions.

"It is necessary, at this point," Kincaide replied, returning now to grim.

His aura kept bleeding back and forth between a warm salmon and harsh grays as she watched. Warm and happy. Angry and resentful.

But always controlled.

"What did you see when you looked in Ildar's mind?" Zhubin stepped close enough to speak quietly to her, derailing the conversation with Kincaide, but he wasn't apparently done speaking.

She turned to the Chairman. Grimaced.

"I once served a disgusting, evil God," she pronounced.

"Past tense?" Zhubin confirmed.

"When we are back on *Dashavatara*, I will tell you about the Chuns," Odtsetseg growled angrily.

Zhubin nodded, rather than speaking.

Why had she never seen it?

However, she knew. God had taken the woman she might have been, then warped her into a tool. A cross-bred non-Human with stripes on her face and transparent eyeballs that glowed in the dark. An adult with no curves, no chest, and no apparent sex drive at all.

She had never been touched, in any of her previous incarnations, because God had found a virgin and channeled all that energy into power instead. And then he had turned off all sorts of things in her mind to reinforce all that focus on the telekinesis she needed to lift a starship into warp-space.

She would never be a woman. Not as these men had known them in their lives.

For another instant, Odtsetseg wondered if she cared. She had not chosen this path, and could not go back and undo it.

Only Hasan Ildar had that ability. Not God. Just a megalomaniac from Tartaristan, somewhere in an imaginary, legendary Central Asia not all that far from the Gujarat that had spawned Zhubin Prakash, or the Kerala that had been the home of Kincaide's ancestors.

"You okay?" Kincaide asked.

She should have been the one to ask him. He had to go face that icky woman in some sort of physical altercation. She turned and read the concern on his face and his mind, his colors a soft green now that seemed to embrace her in mental arms.

He saw her as Human. As a friend. In spite of all the exterior things *wrong* with her.

Kincaide was making this sacrifice for her, first among all the Humans he was planning to save.

She could do no less.

CHAPTER 26

Hasan gritted his teeth, clenching his jaw in silent anger as he walked out of the conference chamber, dismissed by that bitch. As if he was nothing but another Human, so far beneath her that she barely noticed him in passing.

Worse, he could see the Administrator, a mere bureaucrat, making plans to perhaps sideline a man like Hasan Ildar in his moment of triumph.

As if Hasan Ildar wasn't going to return for them all someday. For those three, specifically. The first of many such victories that would end with a whole series of Alvar heads on spikes in his throne room, after he had ended the species entirely and taken The Gage for himself.

But he could not speak now. Merely depart with as much grace as that bitch had allowed him.

They thought that they were so suave and mysterious, but any fool could see that the bitch intended to rut with Kataragama, as if she could somehow mark him with her Alvar musk. Sway him away from Hasan's side. Perhaps convince the man to betray the great mission behind *Dashavatara*.

For an insane moment, as he entered a lift and watched the door close, Hasan wondered if perhaps that was even possible. If somehow the woman possessed some *thing* that would turn Kataragama. Did he need to identify which of the sex object designs he had created or traded for, and decant one for the Foreman, to ensure that man's loyalty?

They were late in the operation. Already, the ship should have departed, lost in space and never to be seen again. But for an unknown spawn of ideologues, he would be well on his way to creating a new colony in space where they could hide for a thousand years before returning.

Now, the damned Alvar had intruded, interfering as if their petty squabbles would be allowed to impact his life's work. Hasan wondered if they should just depart. If he could find a way to sneak aboard *Dashavatara* when the Alvar overlords were distracted, and slip out of the Glide.

Once that ship was in motion, only a Warp Voyager could threaten it. And nothing could catch his Star Flower in warp-space. *Dashavatara* was so light that it would race through the galaxy while the ponderous Alvar ships lumbered in his wake.

They would never catch him.

As the lift deposited him on the deck with the flight pods, so that he could return to his own quarters, Hasan wondered if that bitch would demand more of Kataragama's attention. The man had never been Indexed. In fact, utterly refused when offered, and had threatened to resign from the conspiracy if forced.

He would live, die, and be gone. His words.

But would the great plan be better serviced by making a copy of the man for that Alvar shrew to rut with after they were gone?

He had to hope first that Kataragama survived the experience, since the Alvar bitch might find him so bad in bed that she ordered him destroyed. If she demanded more of the man, then Hasan would need to have a frank talk with Prakash.

Kincaide Kataragama might need to be decanted, a copy left behind with key memories and perhaps personality elements left out. She could have the man's dick and his stamina, if she found it that inspirational, but Hasan needed to erase all his secrets first.

He crossed the bay and entered a flight pod, looking forward to taking his anger out on one or more of his Chuns when he got home.

CHAPTER 27

Normally, Kincaide and the others wore a simple bodysuit on duty, with the outer layer cut away at the neck to display the black of the undersuit and the yellow trim. Kincaide wore red. That was his uniform choice, when it had been necessary to distinguish himself to the crew. Most wore green. Odtsetseg wore gray. Zhubin affected Alvar blue.

Because he had flown over to deal with the Alvar on one of their stations, Kincaide had added the outermost layer today. Also red, but this one was actually rated for outer space, had he brought along a helmet. It looked like armor, with a heavy piece across his shoulders and hanging midway down his chest to hold his air controls and small tank, along with the dock where the helmet locked. Heavy gauntlets to protect his hands. The heavy pirate boots he loved as his only affectation. Pouches around his midsection and down the outside of both thighs, filled with whatever gear he might need to access when a mission took him outside the ship.

It also reminded him of the sorts of battle armor that ground troops wore when The Gage had to deal with insurrection on some world. It happened more often than they wished to admit, possibly even to themselves.

Today, he was a warrior.

Odtsetseg and Zhubin had departed. They should get home safely and quickly, and could continue the planning. Kincaide had no doubt that his own apparent willingness to deal with the old woman with a minimum of fuss had facilitated the Administrator ordering supplies be delivered to *Dashavatara* as quickly as they could be stowed.

Time had indeed run out, but they had contingency plans in place. Shortly, a message down to Boston Dome would alert Lilith and the others. With so many containers coming, it would be relatively easy for one of them to not be filled with what it appeared. The Alvar wouldn't care, if he never reported a discrepancy in his cargo stocks.

Two tall Mori guards escorted him through the facility, into a lift that took him up to one of the towers, like this was a city and the residents needed to be able to look down on the poor people below them.

Kincaide took the moment to study the two beings, because he didn't generally get this close to guards like this. Both of them were bigger than him, ranging a little over two meters in height. Normal for Mori. They had that long, squarish head that had reminded Humans of horses, with their eyes on the upper corners, where they could hunt or flee larger predators.

Except that there had been no escaping the Alvar when that kind first arrived.

One of the guards had auburn fur, and the other a darker brown. Kincaide couldn't tell the genders apart without getting them out of their uniforms, since the Mori didn't have the sexual dimorphism that Humans did.

He didn't know what to compare their smell to, except to other Mori, but Kincaide had never been a cook, nor had he spent any appreciable time in the parks that the various Domes maintained. Spicy in a not-unpleasant way.

It wasn't like there was an outdoors in that damned moon, and Humans were rarely allowed on the surface of an alien world like Al-Winoq itself. At least not rebels like him.

No, Kincaide's entire life had been spent in a Dome or on a space-born vehicle of some sort. Maybe he'd ask the Encyclopedia when he got back to *Dashavatara* what Mori smelled like that he might know. That system didn't contain nearly as much information as the Gage's Catalogue, but that was because so much was left out that wouldn't be necessary or useful to a Human colony.

Or a refugee camp containing everything EXCEPT Alvar.

Both goons were armed. He was not. Both outweighed him. He

wasn't any sort of expert at close combat, such as Zhubin practiced regularly.

Not any sort of threat to the old witch, except that he had to tread a fine line of being pleasant while not throwing up on her while he was inside the woman.

Assuming she hadn't actually brought him here to discuss the finer points of Human epistemological tendencies. Or practical tips for repairing and rebuilding worn generators. His two areas of practical expertise.

The lift doors opened and the goon on his right gestured Kincaide out. Both had hotblasters and knives. And fists, if it came to that.

He complied. Easier to get this over with and get himself home while he figured out which set of headaches he would be hauling into space when they made their run. Mori or Warednja goons would be the easiest, as a man like Prakash could take two or three of them by himself, assuming Kincaide didn't just lock them in a room and cut the air circulation to let them asphyxiate slowly.

They had arrived in an antechamber. Plain walls, at least by Alvar standards. Ornate, repeating geometric designs like a Shia mosque, but none of the baroque detailing or gothic overwork you normally found in the oh-so-superior Alvar culture. He could almost smell the headache that the next few rooms were likely to induce.

Big, double doors, even by Alvar scale. The ceiling in here was probably eight meters away from him right now. The doors themselves each looked seven tall and three wide each.

But then, when you might reach three meters tall, Kincaide supposed that you had to get kind of stupid in order to be imposing.

The doors opened and an Alvar stood there. Tall, skinny, old. Servant, by the way his tunic was on both shoulders. Important servant by the way it was perfectly tailored and crisp white rather than some color.

Taller than Kincaide, which was a given, but it also gave the man a dizzying height from which to look down his nose.

"Kataragama," he announced himself. "I have an appointment with the Noble-born."

And would probably need a shower first to meet her sensibilities, and later, to get her stink off his skin.

One step at a time.

The majordomo stepped back and to one side, like Kincaide was civilized people and didn't have to come in via the two-meter-tall servants' entrance around the side or something.

Inside, it was Alvar ornate, heavy on the blues and greens. Every surface had details Kincaide always wondered if he needed to stick his nose up against to see fully, from the bookshelf on one wall to the mural that wrapped a corner and seemed to convey the entire story of the species from discovering fire to discovering warp-space.

Useful that, leaving out the important bits where you conquered and enslaved a dozen species along the way to your current glory. He could see why they'd want to round the last half million years off as a modern era not worthy of great art.

There weren't any plants in here. *Dashavatara* had the arboretum aft, producing lots of clean air, but the lack here weirdly suggested to Kincaide that his dome up front with Odtsetseg and Zhubin needed some potted plants. He'd remember to do that when he got back.

"Follow me," the old man said as the front doors closed and the Mori servants with guns remained outside.

Kincaide considered being insulted at not even being a physical threat, but decided to let them keep underestimating him for a while yet.

He'd have the last laugh, one way or the other, as he found himself conveyed to a peculiar salon. It contained a thing his brain kept wanting to interpret as a conversation pit. Down a meter from this deck, which was an impressive waste of space on a station. Half of the pit was scaled to the lesser species, such that the short Lop, middle-sized Humans, and tall Mori might sit on the left and be comfortable, while the Alvar Lords of The Gage could array themselves on the right and just *chat*.

Hopefully, this wasn't something the old woman kept around for multi-species orgies.

"Remain here," he was instructed, so Kincaide gave the man a half bow and refrained from offering a coin as a tip.

There was being provocatory, and being an asshole.

Walls covered in formal art. Mostly oil portraits of Alvar of both genders, in a variety of costumes, some historical and some merely bad fashion. No other species present.

There was a bar off to one side that caught his attention, tall enough that he might have to climb on something to see over the top. When he walked over, Kincaide found it packed with damned near every form of inebriant a sentient being might have a hankering for, including Humans. He wondered if they had any coffee beans in the freezer that he might steal on his way home.

Humans, like Alvar, consumed ethyl alcohol in low concentrations to get loose and friendly. Or maudlin and angry as the mood struck. The blues weren't into the more interesting complex pharmacologicals that got Humans twisted sideways, but they had their own methods. But she had all the booze a man might want to try, if he was of a mind.

Kincaide located a square glass to Human scale and a bottle of good bourbon. He poured a couple of fingers and moved to the pit of doom. He was even nice and sat on the far side, opposite the steps down, on the edge where the Human scale gave way to the Alvar, in case this silly wench wanted to hold his hand or something.

He'd burn that bridge shortly.

At least the furniture was comfortable, as it adjusted itself to his back and the pointy bits of his outersuit that might have slashed real cloth. He found a button then a shelf unfolded itself for him to put the glass on.

And it left him facing the door when it opened. At least it was a simple door that retracted into the wall, and not one of those stupid, hinged statements from earlier.

Kincaide couldn't tell if he was supposed to be put at ease by the situation, or lulled to sleep.

They were all playing dangerous games here.

Roselani Thammavongsa entered. Kincaide studied the woman as she came to rest a meter inside the hatch and let it slide closed behind her. Unlike him, she had changed into something he supposed might be more comfortable, out of the one-shoulder toga that was a mark of her station.

Kincaide supposed that you could call the thing a kimono. He stood as she looked his way, at least offering some level of politeness at the start.

It was likely to get ugly and personal before it was done, but he'd be blameless. At least for now.

Certainly the new outfit was a shift away from how she'd been showing off flesh earlier, but the Alvar liked to remind the lesser species that they were a physically superior breed. Muscles, height, and rich blue skin were part of that.

Madame Thammavongsa wore a robe that would have been right at home in how the bird-like decorations painted on it strongly suggested Nihonese cultural connotations, were he in Boston Dome. Or maybe Osaka Dome would be a better comparison.

If the color patterns at her collarbones were the same, then she had on three robes, with the innermost being white, the middle a soft, dove gray, and the outermost being a steel blue that almost looked like washed out black, but he doubted it had ever actually faded, so they'd nailed that color on purpose.

Battleship was the term Humans would have used to describe that hue. And maybe the woman wearing it, if they knew enough ancient history to make such a comparison.

At least the colors looked good compared to the rich blue of her face, neck, and hands.

Like most Alvar, she had white hair. He wondered if it was still naturally that color, as hers would presumably turn orangish eventually, just as his was more than half white at this point. Hers had been pulled into a formal sideknot earlier. Now it was down, past her shoulders and framing her thin face that looked ever more like a blade.

Heirloom katana or wood ax was still open to debate.

Kincaide didn't want to contemplate the implications of *letting her hair down*, so he studied the rest of her. They might be the same relative age, across respective lifespans.

Hers had just been marked by wealth and luxury from the beginning.

Kincaide had callouses in places she probably didn't even have places.

She still looked down on him, but that was the meter difference in the floor and the half-meter in her body. He doubted she wore anything but flat sandals. That sounded too much like competing with others for approval.

"Kataragama," she nodded pleasantly. "I see you've made yourself at home."

Kincaide really didn't like those implications.

"I had no idea how long it might be before someone remembered me, Noble-born," he countered, low-balling.

Hopefully he was just a servant who needed to be yelled at for something.

A man can hope, right?

He watched her move to the bar to fix herself something. From here, he could see her feet as she moved, and the woman wasn't even wearing sandals.

Lovely.

Lacking instructions, he sat. The glass still had enough to keep him occupied, unless he needed to shoot it all at once and let the burn scour the inside of his being.

She made noises and then moved to the top of the stairs. The kimono trailed down and normally dragged on the floor when she moved, but there was a fine carpeting in here. And she grabbed a handful of cloth out of the way so she didn't trip.

No sandals. No socks. Just bare flesh that she showed off, including blue ankles.

He made a mental bet as to where she would end up. Won, too, but it had been a throw-away line in his head that had her ninety degrees away from him, when formal would have been one-fifty and seduction would have been ten.

The other bet was how she would sit. The Alvar had a variety of formalities. They could lay on one side to eat among peers. Sit upright like him, possibly crossing a leg over a knee for ceremony.

The woman ended up turned a little sideways on the couch ring, with her naked feet curled up under her robe. Kincaide had an image of Euryale. The woman would sit almost exactly the same way if she wore such robes.

Madame Thammavongsa studied him over the rim of a goblet filled with what a Human would have assumed wine. It had that rich, deep maroon and he wasn't close enough to smell it.

Her eyes smiled secretly.

Kincaide sipped his bourbon and considered greater and lesser evils.

Eventually, the glass was empty. He rose and moved to the steps on silent feet, crushing the white carpet he'd mostly ignored earlier.

Now, he had to consider naked Alvar feet as he ascended to the higher level of the room and moved to the bar. Her head tracked him like a cobra on a mongoose, but she remained perfectly silent otherwise.

He poured another two fingers, thankful that he normally consumed enough alcohol to metabolize this amount, as long as he drank this glass slowly enough.

She had not spoken. Had not moved except to watch him returning to the same spot. Kincaide sat and placed the glass back on that little personal shelf.

He turned and stared at her now. Frankly.

She waited. He eventually took a sip. She did the same.

"Most Humans lack patience," she announced in a grand, theatrical voice to an empty room, plus whoever was listening in on microphones in case the Human turned out to be rabid and needed to be put down.

Kincaide expected more Mori goons somewhere close. Maybe that punk kid Alvar from the meeting earlier, only this time with a weapon of some sort. The kind a big, tough Alvar could never imagine a Human could take away from him.

Kincaide wasn't Zhubin's equal, but that wasn't the same as harmless.

He stared at the woman, waiting for her to say something that required a response.

She smiled.

"Eventually, they must say something to fill the silence," she continued.

Kincaide shrugged theatrically back at her. He sipped his bourbon and wondered if they got Humans to make it for them in one of the Domes, or had just scanned the perfect formula into the Catalogue and could output it by the gigatank now.

It wasn't bad. A little off, but that was all his years drinking crap he and his buddies had fermented and distilled down in an engine room in their spare time.

"Human mortality comes into play then," the woman kept talking, like either he was replying, or she was giving a speech.

He continued to study her.

"Alvar lives are so much longer than Humans, that they feel they must make a mark somehow, before they are gone forever."

Kincaide discovered that he was tired of fencing with the woman.

"I'm sure you have shoes older than I am," he said simply. "Your point?"

Not quite what she'd been expecting, from the way her eyes got a little big, before they narrowed.

"What does immortality mean to a man like you, Kataragama?" she asked, wandering off on an oblique.

"Not a damned thing," he replied. "Humans are born. They grow up. They grow old like me. They die. Alvar are the same. It just takes them a hundred times as long to get there."

"You have never been Indexed," she announced.

Kincaide felt a chill in his stomach that he couldn't blame on the bourbon. That had always been his line in the sand. With anyone.

There would be no more versions of him. Ever. He was not about to let the Alvar ruin some descendant's life, let alone allowing some fucker like Hasan Ildar at his genes.

"That's right," he agreed like a dumb peasant.

"Why is that?" she pressed, shifting her body language into what he might call receptive on a Human woman. Perhaps even seductive.

"Personal choice," he smiled at her.

"You don't want to live forever?" she smiled at him now.

"We don't, Noble-born," Kincaide let his face develop a bit of a snarl now. "None of us."

Nothing serious. But certainly not pillow talk.

"No?"

"No," Kincaide replied. "I have a life that I expect will run perhaps another forty years or so if I'm lucky. If you Indexed me right now, I'd still be this age, unless you put me through the sorts of hardcore genetic manipulations that Ildar did in order to create his new Engine project. He intends to live forever. Not me."

"You wouldn't want to live as long as an Alvar?" she asked.

Nayani. But he couldn't ever say that out loud.

In four decades, perhaps sooner, he could join her in Hell and at least be with her forever. Living as long as an Alvar just meant that he'd be that much farther away from her. Maybe even start to forget her after a while. The way she breathed. The smell of her, first thing in the morning. Her laugh.

"I don't like your kind, lady," Kincaide let the bands on his anger loosen a little more.

Not much. Just a hint of a threat in the tones. Enough to keep her goons on their hooves but not to draw them from hiding.

"Anything in particular?" she asked, almost teasing the words out of him now with what he supposed would sound seductive to an Alvar.

Mating calls of rabid badgers, and all that.

"Besides conquering my homeworld, destroying most of my species, stealing the rest, and keeping us in prisons here or as arms depot munitions on forward worlds?" Kincaide asked in a perfectly flat, emotionally detached voice. "No, not really."

Alvar turned umber when they flushed with emotions. He got to see it a second time now, but still didn't know the woman well enough to tell if it was rage or embarrassment.

Hope to God themself that Kincaide never knew her well enough.

"You are of The Gage now," she retorted.

"Yes," Kincaide agreed. "And The Gage is owned in fee simple by the Alvar, however you want to dress up the pretty details, Noble-born."

"I have a name," she snapped, unaware that she was fast losing control of the conversation.

If she'd ever had it.

"And I am a lowly Human, Noble-born," Kincaide smiled, reaching for his glass and taking a sip so that he didn't tell this woman what he really thought about Gage culture.

Or Alvar.

Her recoil was faint. Probably wouldn't appear on the monitors watching, as it was mostly in her eyes and hands, rather than shoulders.

She still twitched.

Kincaide refrained from pointing out that many Alvar considered it bestiality. As did most Humans, the other direction.

The mechanics were sound. And she'd changed into something seductive and comfortable before meeting a strange Human in this multi-species orgy pit over drinks.

"You are allowed to address me as Lady Thammavongsa," she replied in a quieter voice.

"Indeed, Noble-born," Kincaide decided to make a little extra point on it. "But we are not on a personal level of relationship. I am a servant of the Colonial Dispatch office and an employee of Hasan Ildar's project to create a better Engine."

He took another sip and forced his shoulder blades to touch the back of the sofa again.

"And the Colonial Dispatch office answers to me, lowly Human," she fired back now in a voice that had a little emotion, mostly fire, under it. "So you are mine, though you might not know it yet."

"I knew it the moment you and the other Alvar joined the Administrator in the meeting with Ildar," Kincaide smiled. "So far, the only demand you've made upon me is my time in waiting upon you at your palace."

Kincaide wondered how smart this woman was. Certainly she'd been the one to initiate the verbal and emotional fencing tonight. Most Alvar were about the same intelligence as Humans. Another way that either the various Gods had decided to play a joke on everyone, or perhaps there was a particular threshold where the physics of genetics and biology hit a sweet spot?

If he had liked Ildar even a little bit, Kincaide might have asked the man. So not worth the effort for a throw-away thought.

She reached out a hand, this dangerous Lady Thammavongsa. Pressed a button to elevate her own shelf and placed the enormous wine glass on it. Brandy snifter, except maroonish purple.

Freed up both her hands. Let the woman turn her whole torso more square to him now, where she had been mostly faced inward on the conversation pit up until now.

Helped that she had her legs curled under her.

"So you acknowledge that I can give you orders?" she asked now, perhaps even a little breathless as she leaned forward. Thank Creation that the kimono was belted tight enough not to gap and show off the tops of her breasts.

Kincaide concentrated on keeping his stomach from rising. The rug was probably puke-proof, but he didn't want to test it tonight.

"You are Alvar," he replied, keeping it short and tight. "Noble-born. Of course my kind must answer to you."

"So if I did make demands upon you, you would be compelled to meet them?" she pressed.

Kincaide didn't like the way she seemed to be talking both of them into whatever the hell she had in mind, but she was Noble-born. Complying and dying were probably his options at this point.

"Yes, Lady Thammavongsa," he answered.

Her eyes lit up. Probably never met a Human willing to sass her. Certainly not in her own home, sipping her bourbon. Kincaide wondered if that was her kink, those sorts of power games.

Her skin was flushed again, but it wasn't rage or embarrassment. Her eyes had opened and those dark eyes were dilated.

She slid from the sofa and stood in the exact center of the pit, like a target on a bullseye. Except he felt like the one being shot at.

The belt got untied. Not as complicated a knot as the Nihonese did, but not a simple thing, either.

She moved slow, like there should be music to sway to in the background.

Kincaide took a sniff, but if they were pumping anything in here, it didn't have a smell or a taste over the bourbon.

She flipped the wrap onto the sofa not far from him and Kincaide wondered if kinbaku was on the menu as well as everything else. He could make a pretty good game of tying knots to imprison her in such a silk sash, given time and a low-level hatred of the woman.

Everybody gets off in their own way.

The outer robe opened like a butterfly's chrysalis now. She merely shrugged and it fell at her feet, the world's weirdest-looking python shedding.

He concentrated on her face, on the knowing smile as they made eye contact and locked. The little tilt of her head as if to ask if he was enjoying himself.

No, lady, but I'm willing to do this to protect Odtsetseg and the crew. You have no idea how far I'd go to free the Star Flower from your grasp.

He smiled back at her. This would be a grudge-fuck, if anything. How often does a mere Human get the chance to fornicate with and perhaps degrade a woman of her station?

Except that the look in her eyes promised that he wasn't the first. Just that none had done a professional enough job about it earlier.

Would she demand he be Indexed if he did this right? Give her copies of himself to keep her bed warm and the ropes handy, long after the original was dead and gone?

Immortality, wasn't that what she'd said?

The second robe fell next, leaving on the white one. It was sheer enough, tight enough, too, that it didn't leave much to the imagination. But then, neither did the toga a Noble-born wore in public.

The lesser species must be reminded of their failures.

"Stop there," Kincaide commanded in a rough voice.

She twitched for a second. Blinked once. Flushed some more. Tossed her hair like she was getting turned on.

"What do you really want?" he asked, as if it wasn't obvious.

But then, how did the old joke go?

Hurt me, says the masochist.

No, replied the sadist.

Yeah, the lines were pretty obvious, but she was going to have to play, too.

"You know," she said in a husky voice.

"You have to say it out loud, Roselani," he smiled.

She hadn't given him permission to use her personal name. He'd just taken it.

The woman's eyes filled with fire for a moment before understanding dawned.

Kincaide had taken. Would take.

Advantage. Liberties. Whatever.

She could have her fun, her abuse, but she had to ask for it. Demand it. *Suffer* for it.

He could smell her now. Humans and Alvar both had a similar musk of arousal.

She fell slowly to her knees in front of him, head bowed as if in a defeat that was only on the surface.

That head came up a moment later, eyes wicked and imploring almost at a level with his.

"I want you to take me," she whispered. "Mount me like you would a Human woman."

He reached out a hand without taking his eyes off her and found the sash. She was too tall for the seven-meter rope, and the sash wasn't that long, but he could make do with it.

Engineers learn all sorts of interesting skills when they get bored on a long delivery run, and he'd known a guy who had the same sorts of kinks as Roselani Thammavongsa. Never sexual, but just the binding had been enough for the man.

"Is this what you need?" Kincaide teased with an edge to his voice. "Bound, supine, and at my mercy?"

The surge of expectant hope on her face was almost comical.

He doubted she'd turn into an ally over this, especially not with what was coming later, but she could easily become a nemesis first if he let her.

Kincaide rose to his feet with the rope in one hand. Stepped around her and grabbed a handful of that fine, white hair with his other, pulling just hard enough to establish dominance.

She moaned mindlessly, so he knew he was on the right track.

For the hell of it, he took one end of the sash and whipped it into a quick lariat, sliding it over her surprised head and pulling it just tight enough around her neck that she turned and looked up at him with the first hint of fear.

But then, Kincaide wanted to make sure she got her money's worth out of putting him through this.

"Stand," he stepped back now, still holding the sash like a leash around her neck.

She stood. Two hundred and forty-five centimeters in bare feet to his one hundred seventy-eight plus boots. She had two heads on him, like Odtsetseg had said. Dancing might be fun, considering where that put his face, but he had other plans.

On her back or her stomach, she'd be shorter than him.

She could step away from him right now. The knot wasn't even tight enough to hold her from resisting.

But she wasn't about to resist. She *needed* this. All her body language practically screamed it in his face, including the hope he saw.

Kincaide wondered when was the last time someone else had given this Alvar woman a good orgasm.

He was probably doomed, if he did this right, but he just needed time.

Time to get back to *Dashavatara* and never leave again. Maybe blast his way out of the repair dock regardless of whether they were supplied or had Lilith and the wives.

Maybe run like hell for deep space and hope that the folks who were supposed to deliver that Eden Package got there in time, if an emergency erupted.

Because there was no way in hell he was ever going near an Indexer. Didn't matter what she thought, but he didn't need to tell her or anyone else that.

"Lead me to where I will *take* you," he ordered her in a gruff voice, layering on the ambiguities that would play the sorts of mind games that this woman seemed to need.

She stepped. He followed.

She wasn't ugly. And he would do a professional job of meeting her needs before demanding she take care of his.

Because this was just another battle in his long war.

CHAPTER 28

Odtsetseg had retreated to her cabin after they returned to the ship. Zhubin had asked a few questions on the flight, but had generally left her alone when it became clear she didn't want to talk.

Kincaide had put himself in harm's way to protect her. The entire mission, but she'd been watching his mind as the conversation went back and forth with that icky woman, and he was protecting them all.

Time and again, Odtsetseg came back to the thought that Kincaide hated everyone, but in truth he just didn't care about anyone in general. It was when they became people that he formed an opinion of them, good or bad.

The cabin door beeped twice. One of the cats wanted to come in and explore but needed her permission. Odtsetseg hadn't delved too deep into the minds of the three cats. They weren't intelligent, as people might understand. What they had were strong emotional instincts and ties. Like Kincaide they would like or loathe someone, once that person stopped being a piece of moving furniture they had to navigate.

"Enter," she called.

As last time, she was out in her little dome on the very bowsprit of *Dashavatara*. Stars and station all the way around her, as though she was flying in space. The view was even more amazing when the ship was out beyond the Glide and there was nothing around her but punctured darkness.

Somebody yarped at her sharply from the door.

"Here," she said, patting her lap because she was comfortable.

Snuggle hopped up after announcing his intentions, turning and sliding into the space between her right thigh and the armrest.

He was purring loud enough to hear almost before he stopped moving, on top of the waves of love he was sending out.

Odtsetseg rested a hand on his haunch and the purrs turned into rumbles like a badly-tuned internal combustion engine, although she'd never heard such an invention herself. Perhaps a cultural memory or something from the original woman she had inherited?

Snuggle's eyes closed after less than a minute and he seemingly fell asleep. But he did that often, the love bug lap kitty of the trio.

Her door chime sounded a second time a few minutes later.

"Enter," Odtsetseg yelled, letting the ship's systems handle things.

"Odtsetseg?" Zhubin called.

She'd left the lights mostly off in her cabin when she had passed through earlier.

"On the balcony," she replied. That was how she thought of this space.

Her balcony.

The Chairman joined her, dragging one of her chairs out to where he could sit on her left. The sleeping kitty precluded her turning her chair right now anyway.

"I figured you were still awake," he said, nodding to her other guest.

"I wanted to try an experiment," she said with a grin. "Snuggle apparently decided it was too dangerous for me to go alone."

"Oh?"

"Nobody knows how much power I have, Chairman," Odtsetseg continued. "Or what I might be able to do. God—Hasan Ildar to the rest of the universe—gave me tremendous capabilities, but even he has never mapped them sufficiently. It was enough that I could lift this ship. For the rest, I begin to wonder if I was supposed to be too pliant and stupid to try my luck."

"I wouldn't ever think of you as stupid, Star Flower," Zhubin replied. "As for pliant?"

"Unquestioning, perhaps," she offered. "Willing to accept everything he did or represented as correct, regardless. I suppose I should blame you two for what might be seen as my teenage rebellious phase."

Zhubin shrugged and smiled with a twisted mouth, but didn't speak for a moment.

"That was Kincaide mostly," he finally said. "I wouldn't have thought that a lever existed big enough to deprogram the things Ildar did to you."

She smiled fiercely.

"He gave it to me," she said. "Kincaide did. My mind, once I no longer was willing to avert my eyes."

"So what experiment did you have planned?" he asked. "Am I intruding?"

"No, but you might be bored," she smiled warmer now. "I want to see if I can reach out and find Kincaide where he is."

"You might not want to know what's happening," Zhubin warned.

"I'm an adult, Zhubin," she turned to face him without disturbing warm, kitty dreams. "This flesh has never been touched, but I'm so powerful that some days I can't tell where I end off and some of the female crew begin. I've accidentally or intentionally touched them at moments of great passion. It's a thing that is almost impossible to ignore, some days."

"I suspect that Kincaide will not have a great emotional signature," the man said in an off-hand sort of way.

"But he'll do it?" she demanded. "He'll go through with it? With that icky woman?"

"With that icky woman, yes," Zhubin nodded. "That's part of the mission."

She blew a heavy breath out. Nobody had ever asked her to undertake such a thing. At least not yet. Lifting *Dashavatara* into warp-space and carrying the ship to another star system would be an impossible task for either of these men, but one she'd been designed to handle.

Had Kincaide's entire life prepared him for the desperate touch of a greedy Alvar woman?

She shivered.

But she understood perhaps a little better.

"Please stay quiet," Odtsetseg said. "I need to concentrate."

Mostly the silence was so as to not wake Snuggles, but he didn't need to know that.

She centered herself. It felt odd that the core of her being was lower than her heart, but Humans were like that, and she was still close enough to see those sorts of things.

Down behind her navel, she who had never been born of woman. Or rather, the woman who had given birth to her had died at least five centuries ago, according to records she had seen in God's mind.

Odtsetseg drew a breath low, down into the stomach and past that, contemplating the uterus that would never give birth.

God had made sure she was one of a kind, and that only he had the power to make Engines powerful enough lift starships all by themselves.

She closed her eyes and opened her mind to the universe around her. The generators that protected the Crew Section were off right now, with the ship in dock being tweaked and loaded for the run.

Once on, the crew would be invisible to her, just as they could hide from warp-spawn in the darkness between universes.

Odtsetseg tasted them once before turning her mind outwards. Everyone here was Human.

What she needed was also Human, but not close. And it would be surrounded by Alvar taste.

There was no way to describe the process of flight, since she didn't cross the space but with her mind.

She looked and saw the station where Kincaide had remained behind. To protect her. That had been the thing she saw in his mind before they parted.

To protect her.

He had a small signature, but that was because the man was like that. Compact in his emotions, used to hiding his true self from those around him to the point that she might be the only other person alive that knew the name he had been born with.

Everything about him was compact now, so she had to draw close to find him, hidden like a needle among pieces of straw who were Alvar.

He was indeed with that icky woman, doing terrible, complicated things to her as Odtsetseg listened to his inner monologue.

Grudge fuck. Not a term she had encountered before, but it made perfect sense.

That old Alvar witch was bound. Tied up in a way that made her arousal almost painful to listen to in the mind. Tied down, perhaps, was a better term. Hands tied to ropes in turn hooked to the bedframe while she was face down on the bed. Spread-eagled.

Kincaide was doing things to the woman that looked outwardly like torture, but every blow brought the woman closer and closer to orgasm. Loudly, too, as she could hear Kincaide's commentary on the woman's moans and squeaks of pleasure.

She reached out with her mind, but Odtsetseg could not do much. She had eyes at this range, but not hands.

It took all she could do to implant just a single thought into Kincaide's mind before she withdrew back to her physical body.

Thank you.

A sound caused her eyes to spring open. Pressure on her chest.

Snuggles had woken up and climbed up into her lap, his front paws on her chest now and his nose butted up against hers.

"*Mau?*" he asked.

"Yes," she whispered to the inquisitive kitty. "I'm back. I'm safe."

"*Mau!*" he decided, rotating in place and curling up in the middle of her lap, the purrs starting up again instantly.

Zhubin was still seated there when she looked, silent and still as if studying her.

"How long was I gone?" she asked.

"Seconds," the man replied. "The cat awoke almost as soon as you left and climbed up to sniff you. Eventually, he head-butted you with his nose. You awoke."

"I was there, Chairman," she said with something like triumph in her voice.

"Where?"

"On the station," Odtsetseg nodded, one hand automatically petting the kitty in her lap. "Listening in and watching Kincaide and that icky woman."

She shuddered in spite of herself. He grimaced back and smiled in commiseration.

"How bad was it?" he asked after a moment.

Odtsetseg went looking for the right terminology. She, who had never been awakened as a sexually-mature being had to approach everything with clinical detachment.

"She's a submissive, Chairman," Odtsetseg finally said. "But her need is to be dominated by one of the lesser species. Humans work the best, because they have biological intercompatibility. Kincaide was pushing all of her buttons, with just his mind and his hand. And he hated every minute of it, wondering while I was listening if he would throw up in disgust while he was inside the woman. How could that be?"

"A Human like you or I can overcome many things in the pursuit of a greater goal," the Chairman replied.

"You or I?" she asked.

Never had she heard him use such a comparison. But then, he'd been there when God—when that fucker Hasan Ildar—had taken a simple Human, a teenage girl from the Catalogue, one with telepathic abilities, and transformed her into something else.

Something with an eight-point ray on her face to mark her alienness to any who saw her.

"We are Humans, Star Flower," Zhubin said as much with his mind as his voice. "We do this to free all future Humans from the Alvar forever."

Forever was a long time, especially when facing angry blue gods and the sorts of revenge a man like Ildar might spend decades dreaming up.

But the three of them would be dead.

She had that to look forward to. If they could escape him for long enough, everyone involved, including a semi-Human Engine at nineteen years Standard Personal, could die of old age.

Like they were supposed to.

Odtsetseg found herself looking forward to that.

She just needed to live a life first.

CHAPTER 29

Kincaide jolted up from dozing. He hadn't been asleep because his subconscious was too hyper to allow something like that right now.

He wasn't alone in the bed. That was it. The room was dim but not dark and he was in someone else's bed.

Bed. What a hell of a term. Four meters long. Three wide. He felt like a kid dumped in his parent's bunk when he'd gotten sick as a child. Didn't help to have *her* lying next to him.

At least the woman didn't snore.

She was on her back with her head elevated on two pillows, eyes closed and breathing regularly.

Compared to a Human, he didn't find her particularly beautiful, but she had regular features and proportions close enough to Human. All the same parts and pieces, in pretty much the same places, just covered over with azure skin that had geometric patterns visible when you got close enough to kiss it.

And he had.

Kincaide wasn't pleased with himself, but he'd done the thing necessary to buy them time, whatever other complications this crazy witch was likely to bring to the table later. And he'd done worse in his time.

Hopefully, she'd be lined up for him when *Dashavatara* returned from the first test jump, not realizing that it wasn't a test and he was never coming back to this system alive. Come hell or high water.

She slept nude, with the heat turned up enough in her luxurious bedroom that he had only a sheet covering. His jumpsuit and gear were piled on an Alvar chair. Her white kimono was still in the middle of the floor where she'd dropped it when he commanded her nudity.

Alvar didn't do makeup like Humans did so there was no vanity mirror in here. Alvar-sized chest of drawers he presumed held clothes. Bookshelf with the requisite knick-knacks a sentient creature accumulates if they actually have a fixed address and aren't living out of a space pack.

The bed fabric had gray and black squares printed on it. If it was possible to somehow make good flannel sheets out of silk, that's what it was.

Clock read middle of the night. Alvar used a twelve-hour clock like Humans, but broken into one hundred and twenty minutes because they were efficient like that. It wasn't tied to any planetary cycle, because they weren't. Instead, it was based on five fingers and a thumb instead of the ancient Human mythologies.

Kincaide wanted to hate himself for being here. For doing those things to the woman because she had demanded them and had the power to compel him one way or the other.

Worse, for enjoying himself then and later. Because making a woman scream her orgasms like that tended to leave you feeling like a god, so he supposed it was what it was.

She was still physical perfection for an Alvar, in spite of her age. But they didn't age like Humans did. Instead, a few centuries as a child and another few being elderly, with millennia in the middle where not much changed.

He watched her breathe now, breasts heavier than a Human woman and mostly flat laying down like this. Hair white in all places where a Human woman would have, except that the Alvar didn't have any hair on their legs, male or female.

Muscles, because she was as broad in the shoulders as he was, even though she was slightly petite for an Alvar woman. The men were just wide blocks of muscle and bone.

And attitude problem, but Kincaide didn't figure they had him beat there.

She woke from some dream. Her breathing changed as he listened.

Dark eyes opened and she returned from wherever Alvar dreams took you.

He neither knew nor cared.

Roselani rolled onto her side to stare at him.

"Will you sleep?" she asked quietly.

"No," Kincaide replied honestly. Everything had been honest with this woman, when he had actually bothered to speak. Omissions weren't lies. "I haven't slept next to someone in decades. I'll catch a nap on the pod home and then sleep depending on the ship's status."

"The ship takes precedence?" Roselani queried.

From the tone of her voice, nothing external had ever been allowed to impinge on the woman's activities or life.

"Always." Kincaide decided to remind her that he was just a lowly Human and she was Noble-born. "I am an employee of the Colonial Dispatch Administration, hired to supervise construction and then command the crew and vessel once we take flight. Even now, there are decisions either being delayed by my absence or being made by people guessing in ignorance at what I would prefer."

"So you would not stay," she mused, eyes unfocused even as he found her innocent nudity interesting.

She wasn't such a terrible person, once she forgot to be an asshole to others. He could think of a number of folks she reminded him of that way.

"I have my duty," he reminded her. Then, because his current mission in her bed demanded it, he appeared to relent a little. Relax some. Offer a suggestion he never intended to honor, but one that would distract her at the right moment. "However, I might return later, when this immediate mission is complete."

He felt like the greater of two evils. Any two evils. Even with an Alvar Noble-born lying naked next to him and needy.

But this was more than him. More than even Odtsetseg.

It was for all the marbles Humanity owned. Now or in the future.

She lit up, like he knew she would. Eyes surged with an emotion somewhere between lust and hope. Her breath caught and turned ragged as the Alvar equivalent of adrenaline surged into pounding veins.

Greater evil.

Necessary.

"You might?" she whispered.

He was already on his side, so he reached out his right hand to caress her cheek. She nuzzled into it and purred with quiet delight.

Kincaide leaned in and kissed her lightly, just to imprint the seduction so deep into her bones that she remembered him two thousand years from now. Most likely still cursing his name, but that was about as much immortality as he wanted from this woman.

Their height difference made things weird, so he slid closer and kissed her neck, letting his left hand slide under her neck and his right trail down her ribs as far as they could reach without getting acrobatic in here. She tasted different than a Human. Sweet/sour, almost like orange juice had been splashed on her and left to dry.

Roselani's hands came up and circled his head, her fingers running through his half-white hair as she purred.

At fifty-eight, he was too worn out for another round of close combat with the woman, but he had the patience to spend an hour doing things to her that nobody else would probably ever repeat.

Immortality, three thousand years from now when this woman was old and nearly gone.

That was all she was ever getting from him.

BREAKAWAY

CHAPTER 30

Lilith studied the message Staci had delivered once it had been decrypted. The other wife sat across from her desk and waited patiently as Lilith studied the note.

On the surface a simple letter from an admirer somewhere who occasionally corresponded by the archaic method of writing on paper.

Who did that? Electronic messages could fly with the speed of light and Alvar computers. They could be aggregated in datanodes and transported across the galaxy.

Actually folding up paper and franking it. Requiring a peon to carry it from place to place to be delivered. That was an anachronism.

She smiled at the thought of the amount of time someone had probably spent trying to understand this thing. It had the marks of having been opened and read in transit by postal authorities. They would have scanned it for hidden writing or tiny dots representing datachips. Everything that their paranoia could think of.

Lilith wondered if any of them had paused to actually read the words and wonder at the meaning.

A gushy letter from a fan. Someone who had worshiped at the cathedral at some point and was writing to thank her for everything she had done for the neighborhood. Even the language and grammar were somewhat nonsensical, as though written by a teenage idol-worshiper instead of an adult.

It didn't add up at all, but you had to have the key, and that wasn't any sort of code that an Alvar-supplied ultracomputer could crack.

BLAZE WARD

"Do you ever leave the cathedral and travel to other domes?"

Simple question, tucked in at the tail of a lot of other questions.

But it was the signal she had been waiting for from Prakash.

She looked up at Staci now, a smile creeping onto her face.

"It's time?" the big green woman asked.

"It is," Lilith nodded.

"How soon?" Staci asked.

"He left it up to us, once we got this message, but this has come earlier than even he was expecting, so something has changed, up in the Glide," Lilith replied. "How quickly can we move?"

"Everything is in place now," Staci said. "Two big shipping containers, customized inside for everyone to ride in comfort, regardless of shape or size. I can place a pickup call as soon as I walk out of your office if you like. They'd get here in about two hours, depending on their availability to haul."

"Close us down first," Lilith decided. "Clear the underground but leave the cathedral as normal, lacking only the confessional, and hang a sign on the door to come back in a few days. By then we'll either be away and hidden, or arrested and probably in the process of being transported to a prison planet."

"Leave late in the day today?" Staci inquired.

"Or early in the morning, if that works better," Lilith said. "Get us to the port and I'll let Prakash know when we are en route, so he can prioritize us for lift."

Staci rose and stretched, looking like a small Alvar woman now, except for green skin and tusks. Certainly the physical equal of one, and most Alvar men as well, by design.

Hopefully, they wouldn't ever need to find out.

CHAPTER 31

Hasan walked into his lab trailed by one of the nude Chuns carrying a mug of coffee and a carafe on a tray for him.

Kataragama had apparently survived his encounter with the Alvar bitch and made it back to *Dashavatara* intact. That had been the most recent risk to the project, but the man had apparently been sufficient for her sexual needs that she hadn't had him killed outright.

But a message had arrived this morning. From her.

Demanding a meeting.

With him. Here. Now.

She was already in transit, not bothering for even the courtesy of an acknowledgment from him before departing her station.

Hasan didn't even have time to fornicate with the Chun this morning, as much as she seemed to be looking forward to it from the smile on her face and the occasional sighs. No, he needed to present as a serious scientist and scholar today, rather than having just satisfied himself on a clone.

"Begone," he ordered her as he lifted his coffee mug from her tray. "Send the Alvar in when she arrives."

The Chuns had an excellent pout, but he didn't allow that to sway him.

Hasan did reward her with a resounding slap across the ass as she moved, eliciting a giggle before he turned to serious and sober thoughts.

He had not had any luck placing spies inside that woman's

household, as much as he had tried. The Administrator was subject to various lesser species watching him for Ildar's coin, but the Noble-born was too important, so remote from mere life, that all her servants in the house were Alvar.

They would not sway. Not for a mere Human.

He had no idea what thought brought that woman out from her palace to inflict herself on him.

But he would find out soon enough.

Hasan sipped at his coffee and walked to the big picture window that looked out over Al-Winoq and the Glide as the station orbited. He had seen pictures taken of Earth before the Conquest. The two worlds were similar enough from this altitude that he could understand a certain unconscious longing when Humans looked up from their Domes at the planet in the distance.

Presumably, some long-forgotten decision on the part of The Gage to taunt the Humans with what they had lost, since most of the species was trapped down on that nearby moon, rather than being allowed out onto the colonies of all the other species.

But the Humans were the newest entry in the menagerie. Some Alvar still alive presumably remembered capturing the Humans so long ago.

Perhaps his extended lifespan would have been long enough to see Humans demoted from a species to be personally degraded and instead turned into just another pet, like the others.

Pity he wouldn't be around to see it.

When he came back from the darkness, it would be at the head of fleets of destruction intent on ending the Alvar as a species entirely.

That thought warmed him considerably as he meditated on the message of the stars.

One of the Chuns appeared at the door in the reflection behind him.

"The Lady Thammavongsa," she announced in a loud tone and then fled as the woman entered.

The lab was on an Alvar station, built originally to Alvar scales. Great, vaulted ceilings were probably just tall to them, but made this place a cathedral of science and experimentation when it was just him, although it was not much to look at.

Most of Hasan's production work was done on one of the three computer workstations scattered about the wide room, to be used as the mood struck him. There was an Indexer in the corner for those few times he actually needed to input an upgrade to one of his Odtsetsegs, but normally he used the tall, glass-clear cylinder in the center of the space to decant a fresh copy after he had adjusted some setting.

The Administrator was a regular-enough visitor, since his division had funded the project, but this woman was only the second Alvar of note to have set foot in here since he had assumed control of this section of the station. Even they only sent their Mori servants most of the time.

Hasan turned and bowed formally to the woman, trying to measure his day by her appearance and mannerisms.

As normal, she wore the white toga that came to mid-thigh and hung off her left shoulder, displaying one perfectly-shaped breast like a blue grapefruit. Her hair was tied in the side knot as normal. Feet laced into simple sandals.

It was as though the ancient, Hellenic gods and goddesses had returned in cobalt.

"Madame," Hasan began, gesturing to the coffee mug in his hand. "May I get you something?"

Gods below only knew what this woman might drink, as he'd never been social with her. Never met her outside of a formal chamber surrounded by a variety of witnesses.

Hasan felt his stomach go cold at the thought.

Witnesses.

Whatever happened here today, there would be no observers except the normal automated security systems and the word of a Chun sex clone.

Nothing that a Noble-born like her couldn't override or simply ignore.

Hasan felt the first hint of true fear take hold of his soul. Up until now, he'd always managed to swim just far enough below the surface of the waters that the great powers didn't notice him.

Something had *changed.*

Citing the ancient laws of thermodynamics, there was no such thing as *good* news in the universe.

"Barratta," she said absently, looking around the space.

He nodded and moved to a room comm to tell the Chun what to do. Hopefully, he actually had the ingredients on hand to make the Alvar drink and the Chun didn't have to run elsewhere.

It wasn't coffee, but served a similar social purpose, with dried and roasted beans ground and infused. The taste was sweeter than coffee, and had much less caffeine in it, to the point that he generally considered it more of soda pop that had gone flat when he tasted it.

But it was as much a signature of the Alvar as coffee was for Humans.

Hasan turned when finished and studied the Lady from a medium distance, wondering what she saw in here. He had specifically engaged an extensive repair crew to grind, sand, polish, and repaint this entire space when he had taken it over, doing away with the ornate scrollwork everywhere, as well as the complicated murals that Alvar seemed to leave on every surface as soon as they stopped walking long enough.

Did it look raw and barbaric to her? Boring? Dangerous?

Hasan preferred the simple elegance of walls that were dark gray at the footing and faded as they reached to the ceiling, as though caught right at the very moment where the sun broke through the darkness, but hadn't yet turned the sky crimson.

But he was Human, however immortal he intended to live.

Manners were called for now, as she was still Noble-born. He gestured to a corner where a trio of chairs were set, either for him to read, or to entertain guests, such as when Administrator Sangsuriya called.

"Please, let us sit," he said, letting her lead and pick a chair.

It was not lost on him that she picked the one he normally used. It was the only one with a back to a wall, where he could not be surprised from behind by a silent visitor.

Hasan settled for the one on the left, where he could watch the Chun return.

"Your flight was comfortable, I hope?" he asked, trying to find a safe topic upon which to engage.

The Alvar tended to meander in personal conversations, but his meetings with the Administrator were usually strict presentations of progress as part of justifying budget or asking for increases.

Hasan Ildar didn't do social. Certainly not with Alvar Noble-born.

Hopefully, this one would still be alive when that fateful day arrived and he could revisit his anger on the woman personally for everything she had done to him this week.

Hasan considered designing one of his Alvar-sized Human designs and turning into a rape machine to deal with blue prisoners. Many of the oh-so-powerful-and-important Alvar would probably just break to be turned into *things*, rather than lords of the galaxy.

He smiled inquisitively at the ancient crone.

"Well," she agreed, her eyes focused on his like weevils boring into his mind for information. "And your research?"

"Excellent," Hasan replied. "I believe we are on the verge of a major galactic revolution in genetic engineering technology. And this is just the beginning, as the Odtsetseg is really more of a proof of concept at present."

"What will you do to improve her?" the woman asked, not conversational, but *intent*, for lack of a better term.

"I do not know at present, Madame," he smiled. "We have to test her extensively under field conditions to understand what she can do right now. As well as find her weak spots and address them with later models."

"And those later models?" she studied him. "What will they do?"

"Lift larger ships by herself, perhaps," he offered. "Or work in tandem with a team of others to carry truly monumental vessels through space."

"Monumental?" the crone asked.

"Something the size of this station might be within her capacity if I can scale her power sufficiently." Hasan let his smile turn sharp now.

He watched the impact of that register. Move an entire city through warp-space?

Hasan had not yet pushed the margins of the Odtsetseg design. This last year or two, while the ship was under construction, had been spent stabilizing her at a good plateau where he could test her. Refine her.

Perfect her.

"What will happen to Humans when you have a better Engine ready for sale?" Thammavongsa asked now, as though her mind was an insect innocently flittering from flower to flower.

Hasan didn't believe that for a moment.

He shrugged as politely as he could. One never knew when one might somehow manage to insult the flighty punks, after all. She'd probably never had anyone else deny her anything in her long life.

"As I understand it right now," he began carefully, "Humans are kept close to Al-Winoq to provide a steady supply of new Engines as the old ones age or are destroyed by warp-spawn. There are few colonies beyond this where Humans have been planted, and those mostly qualify as military resupply depots for the exploration fleets."

He waited for her to nod before continuing.

"Humans provide almost all of the Engines in The Gage," he said. "But they will not be as important after my improved designs become available, so presumably they will be allowed, possibly even encouraged, to migrate to other worlds and live in harmony with the other species of The Gage."

"You think so?" she asked sharply, her eyes suddenly narrowing and her voice getting sharp.

"Mere speculation," Hasan said, back-pedaling as gracefully as he could, unaware that the mere mention of such a concept would trigger such an emotional response from the woman.

What might rouse such energy?

He contemplated Kataragama. The man had made it home safe. And she had presumably almost immediately demanded to see Hasan, in his lab.

Was there a connection?

He thanked all the various gods that might listen that the Chun arrived just then with a tray. One pot of a steaming liquid so indigo as to be almost black, along with a Human-sized coffee mug that almost looked dainty as the Noble-born took it in her hand and sipped.

The Chun withdrew as though one or both of them had neural whips to goad her, which was fine. The Chuns served exactly two purposes and she had just fulfilled the only one he needed right now.

"I have concerns about this mission, Ildar," Thammavongsa finally said after sipping.

"Madame?" he asked carefully, wondering if someone's spies had penetrated the truth of the conspiracy.

Or at least deep enough that he was at risk of being put to strenuous questioning. The kind that would seal his doom quickly.

He wondered if the only thing keeping him alive right now was the possibility that the Odtsetseg model could be improved even more later.

Except that there were other gods out there who could do that work. Not all of them were even Human, as he had seen in some of his altercations and discussions on the best ways to modify the newest species in The Gage.

Hasan Ildar was not the only one seeking personal immortality. He just happened to be the only one he was aware of that was mean enough to take those centuries and build himself an army to destroy the Alvar in the process. The others were generally satisfied with their Chuns, or their Hadiyas. Sex objects of all flavors and kinds, many of them also drawing on the work of that fool Goaulda but reaching all the wrong conclusions.

They dreamed too small.

"How long will *Dashavatara* be away on the test flight?" she asked now, as if she knew something.

Hasan wondered how long until someone blew a door in and arrived to arrest him for treason to The Gage. At least the first time they tried to crack open all his personal files, everything would be destroyed, along with all the backups and in some cases the hardware itself.

The Gage didn't understand the levels of devious to which a Human might aspire. All of his systems were built with booby-traps just waiting to be triggered by fools probing where they should not go.

He would win, or he would destroy everything and those pirates would have to start over.

Nobody was allowed to betray him or outwit him.

However, that wasn't the question she sought answers to. On the surface, it was a simple enough thing.

Barring surprises and errors in the math, which he strenuously doubted, they would be gone a twelve-day at the longest, and even that presumed a random surprise where warp-spawn struck and killed the Odtsetseg, necessitating him to decant a fresh version while Prakash and Kataragama calculated where they really were and how to get home.

What was she really after? That information was in the files she had just reviewed yesterday, and even Hasan Ildar was not fool enough to think she had forgotten it.

Or was she probing him for weakness?

"The schedule calls for nine days," he reminded her carefully. "We allow a twelve-day for emergencies and unexpected complications."

Hasan leaned back now and sipped his coffee, watching her face for clues.

Flighty was not the right term, but she did not settle in any one emotional location long enough to cue him.

"I remember from the file that you intend to make a final copy of the Engine shortly, so that you have the most up-to-date backup," the woman said now, proving to him that she had been paying attention to the various briefings and reports.

Probably intent on trying to trip him up with some falsehood, as if he was an amateur at the game of deceit.

"That is correct," he nodded. "Once I hear from Chairman Prakash that he is satisfied with the completion of the loadout, I will join them aboard *Dashavatara* and take care of that chore not long before we back out of space dock."

"I think that would be a mistake," she said in a quiet tone that somehow conveyed such ominous depths that Hasan concentrated on not spilling his coffee.

He paused long enough that the first words out of his mouth weren't an obscenity, either.

"Why would that be, Madame?" he asked in what he hoped didn't sound desperate or offended.

It would be necessary to walk a thin line now, as the Noble-born's energy had returned.

"If something were to happen on that mission, it pains me to think of all the investment that might be lost," she said, those dark eyes staring at him like a hungry, deep-water creature suddenly surfacing.

Hasan found himself holding his breath in spite of himself.

"You should summon the Engine to your lab to be properly Indexed," she continued implacably. "In fact, it might be a wise investment of time to have the entire senior crew Indexed as well, so that nothing is lost if the warp-spawn do strike and the vessel is lost. That can't add more than a few days to the schedule, and might even be something that could be done in the shorter term, while they continue loading, so that nothing delays the test flight later."

The look on her face, that poised, dangerous smile, reminded Hasan that he was dealing with the Noble-born.

Not just any Alvar woman, but one of the power figures of The Gage. A woman who was probably on social terms with the Ruling Family of The Gage Empire itself.

Hasan reminded himself silently that House Phetphommasouk had been in control of the Gage for more than two hundred thousand Standard Years at this point, longer than most records suggested that Humans had been a distinct species, back on Earth.

"I will inquire with the Chairman when might be optimal to disrupt our operation, Madame," Hasan surrendered quickly on this one, nodding deep enough to almost be a bow, even seated.

She could simply order it done. And order it done today, if it were to rise to the level of pique with the woman. He must not allow that.

From the smile on her face, Hasan presumed that what she really wanted was an Icon of Kataragama that she could decant and chain to her bedroom, where the man could service all of her needs. She had that smile.

Apparently last night had been more successful than Hasan had imagined, and probably worse than Kataragama had feared.

Kataragama had made it clear that he would quit this conspiracy before he was Indexed, for reasons that had left the man threatening to quit if even *pursued* on that topic. Hasan had always assumed the Foreman was some sort of rebel with a false identity, but he had never pried.

He needed fighters who hated the Alvar.

Similarly, if Prakash was put into the machines, the Catalog would immediately alert the authorities to a match. An assassin they had decanted several times, a few even hunting the man himself, although that information had never gotten out.

Prakash had told Hasan how easy it was to outthink a twenty-four-year-old version of himself.

They would have to outwit a fifty-eight-century-old-witch now, if any of them were to survive.

She sat back now and studied his face, her own triumph evident in the way the woman smiled.

"That will be acceptable, Ildar," she pronounced, but he wasn't fooled one bit.

Time had just run out.

CHAPTER 32

Odtsetseg had awakened from a deep, lovely sleep, spending an extra ten minutes just lying there in bed under the dim light, listening to the sounds of the life support system blowing air around and the way the hull pinged as repair crews did regular maintenance.

Everything was moving now, but she had nothing to do as yet. Would have nothing to even prepare for until the ship backed out of the repair dock a second time and began to sail out of the Glide for deep space.

That would be the signal to her to begin focusing her mind towards her exercises. Toward drawing everything together against the day she had to face the darkness of warp-space alone.

Or worse, not alone as warp-spawn found her and tried to take over or burn out her mind.

She had heard the legends. The nightmarish horror stories told of things crawling on the exterior of the ship as it raced through warp-space, trying to get in.

Nobody knew the truth of the warp-spawn. Or rather, those that did lost their minds and either died or returned as burned-out husks that the Alvar quickly destroyed, possibly out of fear that the creatures of the night had managed to find themselves a vessel, a gateway into the physical world.

She would not allow such fears to overtake her. Not today. Odtsetseg felt a general joy encompass her in ways she just could not adequately describe, other than the world was *right*.

Eventually, she rose, understanding that the ship had a new emotional signature today when she carefully expanded her psychic senses to take it all in. But it was wrong. On the bridge, Reyhan Herath was emotionally loud, but not focused enough for her to follow the argument. Kincaide was there, but so subdued she almost missed him. Chairman Prakash was almost a hole in her mental image.

She wondered what had gone wrong. Something with the men did not feel right.

At the same time, someone would send for her if an issue arose that actually required her input. She had time.

Odtsetseg stripped and studied herself in the full-length projection of her bathroom. Kincaide had described her in his mind as having a twelve-year-old's body, though the words had never made it to his lips.

She had to agree.

Tall, yes, but skinny. Technically, she had breasts, but they were barely a rise from the flesh of her lean pectoral muscles. Narrow shoulders and ribs that didn't flare out into child-bearing hips just accentuated the appearance. Her ancestor was Mongolian, thus the name, so she had precious little body hair on golden skin so much lighter than the rest of the crew, and just enough pubes to again register as such.

At least she had thighs. Powerful ones that some memory of another woman's youth referred to as peasant thighs, good for hauling a plow when the oxen died. The image brought a giggle to her lips. Those thighs and the stringy black hair were about all the marks that Mongolia had left on her after so long.

Other things had left other marks.

The face was obvious, with that pattern on her skin in a bright red like a butterfly, with those four rays on each side of a red nose, however cute and upturned it was. What was not known to most people was that she had eight similar red lines radiating from her belly button, because she kept them hidden when dressed and they wrapped around her flesh pale enough to be invisible under clothing.

Not that any man or woman would willingly seek the sorts of intimacy that that icky Alvar witch had demanded of Kincaide. Even the ones that worshiped her as a goddess-made-flesh feared her at a deeply-unconscious level.

It was the eyes.

She leaned closer now, studying those orbs. No other person or creature she had ever met or studied had transparent eyeballs. Humans had opaque white orbs with black rings and colored irises, then finally the transparent hole in the soul that let light in.

Hers let a blood red light out at the same time, like a bizarre anglerfish summoning prey.

What creatures would she capture in the cold dark of warp-space?

Odtsetseg shook her head and stepped to the shower. Real water, which was apparently a luxury most Dome-bound Humans never achieved. She washed, still contemplating her physical differences, where she had only fine hairs on her arms and legs, and none beneath her arms, unlike so much of the rest of the crew.

Her hair was getting long, which she took as a personal measure of success. Kincaide had whispered at one point, in a private chat, that none of the previous versions of her had been around long enough to grow hair much past the two-centimeter buzz that emerged from the decanter.

Hers was almost to her shoulders in back now as she dried it with a cotton towel. She brushed it out of her eyes and let the natural part keep it out of her face, wondering why she had never considered even such jewelry as a hair band to keep it tamed, to say nothing of earrings.

But none of the Odtsetsegs had achieved what she had managed. None of them had moved beyond being tools. She was a woman now.

Odtsetseg was free.

God was no longer God. A god, perhaps, lower case, but not her defining deity.

He was just Hasan Ildar, the master manipulator that had been responsible for picking her out of an Engine Catalogue file and turning her into Power.

That fucker.

Before Kincaide had freed her.

Odtsetseg dressed in her gray bodysuit like a second skin, feeling almost light enough to fly as she stepped out of her cabin to make herself some tea. She generally skipped breakfast, even as Kincaide and Zhubin ate heavy early in their day against not having time later.

She had nothing but time right now. And joy at being alive, and having seen what the Alvar and God were really like.

A message chime beeped as she entered the kitchen.

"Yes?" she asked the room.

"Could you join us on the bridge, please?" Kincaide asked in a reserved voice. "Something has come up."

His tone was calm, but the words belied that. The last time something had *come up*, they had blown up part of the ship to buy time for Zhubin to save Kincaide's soul.

"Coming," she replied, tea forgotten in an instant.

She could always ask someone to make her some back on the bridge. There were a number of officers training to command this vessel, none of whom had anything really relevant to do until the ship took flight.

She exited the forward dome, traversing the airlock Ildar had hoped would keep warp-spawn at bay when all the barriers were locked. Back into the long neck connecting to the Crew Section, turning midway to climb the stairs to the bridge on the top level.

Kincaide's office overlooked the bridge, up a half-flight of stairs at the rear of the room. She entered from the starboard side to see most of the bridge crew present, just as they had been on the day *Dashavatara* first separated from the station.

The mood was somber. Sober.

Faces were hard with contained emotion, but everything in here was so bleak she nearly retreated to her cabin to escape them rather than face it. However, she had been designed to be harder, tougher than the other Humans.

And the whole wall that normally separated Kincaide's office was open, so everything was in the open, whatever it was.

What had she nearly slept through? Or had they been ongoing for some time, and then just waiting for her to emerge?

"Come," Chairman Prakash gestured when she came into sight, eliminating all chance to flee.

Kincaide was standing at his desk, a simple slab of white plastic four centimeters thick and laminated, with electronics built directly into the surface and a projector when he needed holograms. Chairman Prakash stood against the side wall, where he was out of the direct line of fire of the emotions but could see her arrive.

Reyhan stood menacingly, leaned over the desk from the front with both palms flat and a rage fit for real gods. His terrible anger had only been interrupted by her arrival, as every head in here had rotated towards her when Zhubin spoke.

But the older man stopped when his eyes focused on her. He took a deep breath and stepped back to stand perfectly upright, hands crossing behind his back, feet at shoulder width.

The posture felt military, but she didn't think he had ever been with any Gage navy forces.

Did the Resistance train that well? Kincaide had survived many years in the underground world, and known Reyhan for almost as long.

She felt meek, counting the six steps to Kincaide's level, each white laminated plastic like his desk, and backless so that she could see through beneath where things could be stored out of the way.

Odtsetseg had a hard time looking into the office. Into that stew of angry emotions that roiled around like a thunderhead. And that was another thing she had never seen. Just a cultural reference that bubbled up from one of her lifetimes.

Top step. She ground her teeth together and forced herself to rise to their level.

To face these three men, all angry in different ways now that she was close enough to feel them.

Zhubin was almost a polished steel mask when she looked at his face. Normally that helped, but today it was like facing a robot painted with flesh.

Reyhan was a god of war, but Ares, not Athena. Destruction just waiting to be called down on poor, unwitting souls.

Kincaide was—…

She had to stop and take a second look. She had been inside his soul and not just his mind, so she understood that he saw himself as an intractable failure right now. It would take her many long moments to understand why, and she would have to probe deep into his mind to do it.

That would have to wait.

Odtsetseg stepped past the little seam in the floor where the wall would extend for privacy. She flinched when she did, unconsciously expecting Kincaide to close the door on her, but all the bridge crew waited below and behind her, no longer even pretending to be doing anything but listening to these three men.

What was so critical, so utterly important that they needed her here before they could decide?

She was just an Engine at the end of the day. A semi-Human modified to lift them into warp-space and carry the ship and crew where Kincaide and Zhubin decided.

"Thank you," Kincaide said simply, so withdrawn that she had to lean forward to feel his words.

There was a chair, but she didn't think she could sit still given the emotional whirlpool raging around her, even as these three men were perfectly silent right now.

Kincaide took a deep breath. She would have said calming, but that would have been a lie.

He was tasting the bitter dregs of defeat, but she didn't know what had caused it.

"We have orders to report to Hasan Ildar's lab at the earliest convenience," Kincaide said. "All of us."

Odtsetseg gasped as the implications became clear.

She didn't have any memories of being indexed and decanted, because according to Zhubin, her asshole former-God had carefully wiped those parts of her memories each time. In fact, he generally decanted her in a state akin to inebriation, where she was mostly functional, but had no memories of the day when it happened.

She would wake back in her bed the next morning, after Zhubin had put her there, and it would all be as it had been, except that she was a new incarnation each time.

How many Odtsetsegs had Zhubin known? By his admitted count, over twenty stretching back years. None of them were her and those memories were so blurry she didn't know how many times she had met the man.

She remembered the process because he had shared it with her after she had started to break the conditioning that Ildar had put in.

And now he was calling her home. Odtsetseg wasn't supposed to understand the implications of that, because God was God and would take care of her. That was how the universe worked.

Had worked.

"Shit," she muttered distinctly. Quietly.

It still sounded like a gunshot in an empty room, so silent had things fallen.

"Indeed," Kincaide agreed with a grim smile.

"All of you?" she confirmed, looking from face to face, from Kincaide's defeat to Zhubin's quiet anger to Reyhan's terrible fury.

The silence outside made sense now. They had all been included in that same order, and not just her this time. Ildar had even summoned the two men who would move heaven and hell to resist it.

Odtsetseg turned her head to study Reyhan, the Assistant Foreman in charge of the Encyclopedia and information systems, and as close as they got to a First Officer commanding when Kincaide was unavailable.

"Tell me," she commanded the man in a hard, quiet tone.

Still, it shocked him, which was her purpose.

He had a face like a demon, with the way those mutton-chop sideburns were cut to almost look like a bull's horns on his cheeks, whereas she had been designed with the appearance of an innocent waif, a teenager who would never grow up.

Odtsetseg had an image of JM Barrie and his famous creation *Pan*. Would she truly be like this forever? How many years had Ildar given this design? And would she know anything before she fell over dead?

Odtsetseg filed that question away for another time, as she didn't need the distraction. Reyhan Herath grimaced, but it wasn't aimed at her.

"The Monsters have not arrived," he said simply. "They are in the transit process so we cannot even stop them, but the overall effort will take them days to be carried to the right ship, and then added to the correct cargo to be delivered to the repair dock so that we can get them."

She felt her entire face twist into a hard question, however unasked.

"No, they're fine in transit," he nodded like a man taking a bite out of a shark. "The problem is the delay. We can't afford it."

Odtsetseg turned back to Kincaide and his anguish was obvious now. She and Zhubin had twisted the man around his sense of honor to rescue those women. Had helped him remember his purpose on the way.

And now that fucker Hasan Ildar was about to take it away from him again.

She growled, low in her chest.

"How long will Ildar wait?" she asked sharply.

Kincaide's shrug was normally eloquence itself, a shift of body language with better command of the language than most poets. It communicated defeat now.

"I cannot imagine that he can wait that long," Kincaide replied slowly. "This isn't any part of his plan or any of the contingencies we've laid down over the last three years."

She turned to Zhubin, silent and deadly. Deadly silence.

He nodded.

"That icky woman?" Odtsetseg asked anyway.

"That makes the most sense, given the parameters of the order," he said, still a polished steel mask she could not penetrate without fighting the man.

She turned to Reyhan. Read the man's body language, so tightly compact she wondered if he could achieve fission.

"Tell me the rest," she ordered, feeling her own voice almost turn into an avatar of Zhubin's anger and Kincaide's despair.

"He wants to wait for them," Reyhan growled, one hand emerging to point at Kincaide. "Personally, I think that's stupid bordering on suicidal, but he won't budge."

"We promised them liberation, Reyhan Herath," Odtsetseg snapped at the man.

"They knew the risks," he snarled at her now, losing some of the control he'd been holding back before. That same hand pointed at the floor as though he was pounding on it. "They'll make us so late by waiting for them that Ildar's masters will grow suspicious and do something. What that might be I can't tell you, but if we give them any reason to develop paranoia, *we* might never escape, even if we blast out of here and manage to evade station guns on the Glide and local Killships or whatever Warp Voyagers might be handy."

"We promised," Odtsetseg repeated evenly.

"They aren't even Human," Herath thundered. "Why should I care?"

Odtsetseg nearly punched the man.

She didn't know what the physical manifestations of her rage were, but Reyhan staggered backwards a half step as she stepped to close the gap between them. Down on the bridge deck she saw Dinushan, Hanishka, and Tharushi did the same, mouths falling open in shock.

Only Anton, the Computer Personality of the Day, did not flinch under her gaze.

"Understand this, Reyhan Herath," Odtsetseg snarled back at the man, quiet to his thunder now. "They are all more Human than I am. All of them. You call them Monsters, but they were Wives at one time. Every one of those women is as Human as any of you. If you want your specism to come out, direct it at me. I'm the only alien that will be traveling with you. Worse, my original Icon was Mongolian, which is close enough to Chinese for some of you. I'm the enemy you hate almost as much as you hate the rest of The Gage, so do not dare tell me those women are not Human, you fucker. Do not ever tell me that or I will show you what non-Human *really looks like*."

Odtsetseg ground her teeth together before she did lash out with her fists. Her rage had carried her right into the man's face, and they were almost exactly the same height.

He had turned white.

Her breath ragged, she kept her clenched fists down at her side and stepped physically back. Her cheek muscles hurt from the rictus they had frozen into.

She turned back to Kincaide and focused on him. That man was invulnerable to her anger, which was part of the reason why she loved him.

He grounded her. Calmed her. Brought her back from homicidal fury.

"How do we defeat them?" she asked as calmly as she could manage right now, still on the verge of chewing nails.

Instead of answering, Kincaide turned to look at Zhubin.

"I have an idea, Star Flower," the Chairman said quietly.

CHAPTER 33

Kincaide still thought it was the stupidest idea he'd heard yet, but swallowing a bullet might be the alternative if this operation failed. And Zhubin thought it would work.

Right now, Kincaide was alone in a personnel pod with Odtsetseg , one of the private, four-person jobs that were either rich with interior decoration because they were available for an Alvar lord, or stripped down to raw metal and plastic for the lesser species. He'd gotten lucky and drawn a nice one today, for what it was worth.

Like last time he'd left the ship—had it only been five days ago?— he wore the overarmor additions to his body suit that would let him walk in space. Unlike last time, he had added the headpiece that would expand outwards into a helmet to let him do so. It was an awkward fit in one of his thigh pouches, but bringing along a spare messenger bag or something would look abnormal, and he needed those fuckers calm and relaxed, right up to the moment when all hell broke loose.

Then he didn't give a shit.

Odtsetseg wore her grays. Unlike him, she wasn't comfortable in the extra pieces, because this particular version of her had never spacewalked as part of her training, but it was all in there, buried deep in her memory against need.

She fidgeted today as she sat across from him, no longer even pretending to read the handheld she had brought along.

She looked up at him, studying her, and a faint blush crept up her cheeks. Mongolian cheekbones, high and sharp but then rounded down a little, like a rockface a few decades after the fall had sheared the stone sharp.

A daughter he'd never had, at least in a metaphorical sense.

"More than metaphorical," she said with a soft smile. "I'd like to be able to think of you as a better step-father than the one I actually had. Either of them."

He flinched backwards in surprise. The others had never developed that sense of inner awareness that let them see the time before she had been pulled from the Catalogue by Ildar the first time. That rat fucker had worked hard to make sure the blocks in her mind prevented it.

"What was he like?" Kincaide asked, looking for a way to distract her, and himself, as the pod carried them close to the main station.

And their destiny. One way or the other.

"I never met my biodad," Odtsetseg replied, eyes unfocused and looking at a spot over his left shoulder. "He left when I was very young. Possibly before I was born. My mother had another man she was bonded with, but that one came along when I was five, I think."

"Trouble?" Kincaide asked, from the way her breath caught.

"No, not like that," she shook her head ruefully. "He barely even registered my presence most of the time. He worked and my mother did odd jobs. I was in creche or school. In the evenings, I remember them sitting in separate chairs watching entertainment channels while eating dinner, while I was expected to play in my room or something. Just stay out of their hair as much as possible."

She shrugged and their eyes met again.

"I suppose it could have been much worse, studying some of the minds around me on the ship," she offered. "Some of the crew had terrible childhoods, didn't they?"

"Humans lack purpose," he replied. "A few get taken as Engines every year, while the rest are intended to just breed forward, with the hope that Humans will eventually birth even better Engines over time. The Alvar do not understand us as a species."

"Is that why they find people like Ildar?" she asked.

"It is," Kincaide agreed. "For a species as long-lived as they are, they are impatient to conquer the galaxy, and maybe the entire universe. So they find psychopaths like Hasan and let him experiment on his own kind, hoping that the lure of personal power and wealth will be enough to turn them into traitors to their own species. More the fools them."

"Because Ildar has a secondary plan?" Odtsetseg asked, looking at the screen overhead now.

He did the same, but they were still eight minutes from docking at this point. Just another anonymous pod approaching the land of the great ones, hat in hand.

Or something like that.

"Ildar is a megalomaniac," Kincaide reminded her. "We just want to escape, Zhubin and I. Take enough Humans with us that we can build ourselves an Eden in some forgotten corner of the galaxy. Help our descendants be strong enough to push The Gage back when they finally come that way. Ildar has a plan to conquer The Gage itself, wipe out the Alvar, and turn himself into a true god, and not just the pretend shit he is now."

"Would it be so bad, returning the favor?" she asked.

Kincaide started to say something rich and sarcastic, but the look on her face held his tongue.

She had been cross-bred with an octopus, among other things. Anything that Ildar had thought might eke out even a fraction of a percentage of additional power that he could tap.

That he could turn into a weapon designed to kill blue giants.

"I'm already going to hell, Odtsetseg," he replied instead. "But I do not wish to go before the Creator of the universe with that on my conscience. It would make us no better than them. Worse, even, because they just conquered the Humans and turned us into pets. Ildar wants to exterminate them entirely from Creation. Then he wants to go on and rule everything, just like an Alvar would."

"And you don't think they'll come after us when we do this thing?" she probed.

"I'm hoping that you'll carry us so far that they'll spent Alvar lifetimes looking," he smiled.

"But I will be able to enjoy your Eden no longer than you will," Odtsetseg pivoted emotionally now. "Why are you planning in such timeframes yourself?"

"Ildar's Catalogue Package contains only Humans he considers TrueBreed," Kincaide reminded her. "Central and South Asians of a type called Caucasian. A few North Euros. No Africans or Arabs. No East Asians at all except for one dangerous Mongolian chick I know."

He smiled as she blushed and her grin softened the hardness that had overtaken her face.

"More importantly, the only telepaths I am aware of are people like you," he continued. "They started out as Humans, but got things grafted on later. He's keen on the octopus genome because it lets you think in alien ways, but he also renders them all functionally sterile, so the Humans who serve him will never be able to challenge his power because he'll control all the telepaths and Engines."

"And you'll fix that," she stated flatly. Unbelievingly, perhaps.

"The Eden Package that Zhubin's friends have been working to assemble contains over a million Humans, representing every ethnic subtype in the Catalogue," he said. "That includes something like eleven percent telepaths of some measurable power. More importantly, all of *them* are still Human, which means that they *can* have children. They *can* breed indiscriminately with *anybody* that strikes their fancy. Presumably, in a few thousand years, there won't be ethnic variety any more, as everyone will regress to a mean that won't look all that different externally from you or I. Darker than you. Maybe lighter than me. Human. Just that."

Kincaide wasn't prepared for the tears that suddenly started rolling down her face. Or the sniffles.

What had she— ?!?

Oh, she'd been listening to his mind. Seeing his dreams for the future, after so long around men and women like Hasan Ildar or even Zhubin Prakash, who was more like Reyhan than he would ever admit out loud.

Cold and ruthless, but still something of a racist pig.

Kincaide held out a hand and she took it. He broke the contact long enough to remove a glove. She did the same a moment later and they touched flesh.

Somehow, he found this gawky teenager curled up in his lap crying quickly after that, so he held her. Like a father should do with a crying child.

They had time, so he could do this thing for her. Comfort her when fear and dread and rage overtook the woman.

Because the rest of the day was likely to get ugly.

CHAPTER 34

Kincaide already missed that transport pod and it had only been gone for about ninety seconds now. They were in a big, impersonal space with white plastic walls and a high ceiling. Empty except for the bureaucrat behind a desk that had looked up at them from whatever they had been doing when Kincaide and Odtsetseg emerged.

Ayotochtli. Humans called them armadillos behind their backs, and it was not an entirely incorrect image.

Half a head shorter than he or Odtsetseg. Broad-bodied, but light in the bones and muscle. They had armor plates across their back like the fabled nine-banded armadillos of Earth, made of something like his fingernails. Similar plates covered their arms and legs, as well as smaller ones, almost snake scales, on the face and snout. On their homeworld, it had probably been enough to protect them against large predators, but nothing could have stopped the Alvar invasion force.

Humans tended to cover themselves in clothing, just like the Alvar. Ayotochtli wore a thing like a bibbed apron that went over the head and covered the front, tying off around the back and providing pockets for tools, since they could regulate their temperature better than other species.

"Papers?" the banded bureaucrat asked as they stepped up to his desk.

Kincaide thought it was a he.

He held a reader in those weird hands: three fingers and two opposed thumbs with pale flesh that looked like weak gravy in its grayness.

This was where it got chancy. Kincaide had a pistol concealed in a pocket, but that was mostly to make sure they never took him alive, as there was no way he could get into a firefight with Station Security and expect to win.

Which was why he'd brought a bigger cannon with him. A cute, dangerous Mongolian chick he knew.

Who had mental abilities nobody had ever really tested.

Kincaide found his breath catching as his memories flittered back to Zhubin's stories of Odtsetseg *adjusting* people just before Ildar Indexed them again.

Hopefully it would work here.

He was just along today as the pretty face, getting her close, because her power was inversely squared to range. Or, as she'd said, from *Dashavatara* she had eyes but no hands.

Kincaide had a hand on her waist, almost possessively, so he felt her sway a little and clenched to keep her from face-planting onto the guy's desk.

At least they were alone in here, the three of them, so she only had to work on one person.

The Ayotochtli's eyes glazed over in the most interesting way. They had star-shaped pupils, rather than round or slitted. Both opened as far as they would go right now, before the man took a deep, bottomless breath and came back from wherever Odtsetseg had taken him.

He blinked, and those pupils closed like an airlock door sealing from five sides before opening again.

"Very good," he announced. "Approved. Wait over there and I will summon an escort."

One weird thumb pointed to a nearby bench low enough for Humans to use.

But then, the Alvar would not be held up by a servant species needing paperwork.

Odtsetseg wobbled a little, but he held onto her and guided her in the right direction, seating her carefully before he sat, and pulling her to lean on his shoulder as she breathed like a race horse crossing the finish line.

"It worked," he whispered in her ear like they were lovers, one arm around her thin shoulders to keep her seated instead of falling over.

"That hurt," she murmured back. "Alien mind so strange I could hardly find the buttons I needed. And I have no idea how long it will hold."

"Doesn't have to be long," he reminded her. "Just get us to her and out again."

Her. Even in his mind he didn't like thinking of Roselani by her given name.

It hadn't been nearly as bad as he'd feared going in. Because she was pliant and had been willing to communicate her needs in a clear manner, putting herself emotionally at his mercy. Kincaide had found that he wasn't nearly as mean and vicious as he'd been prepared to be.

Two creatures, seeking pleasure. She hadn't even been all that bad in bed, once she relaxed and let him control the pace.

What he was going to do to her today was intended to buy them a few more days. That was all he needed. Couldn't even bring Zhubin along, because that would raised too many red flags.

Lilith and her sisters were on the Glide now, with a scheduled delivery that would put them aboard *Dashavatara* in eighteen hours or so, as part of what was supposed to be the second to last major cargo drop. The last one would never be needed, because *Dashavatara* would either be gone or in the process of being dismantled by then.

A door beyond the Ayotochtli bureaucrat opened and a Mog entered.

The closest external comparison Kincaide had ever made was a puma from Earth. Tall and lean, covered over with a short, heavy fur that ranged from dark gray to true black. Short face with a flat snout, rather than a nose like Humans or Alvar. Ears on top that weren't very mobile, especially not compared to his three goofball cats back on the ship. Probably no socks either, but the woman was wearing the flowing clothes her kind generally preferred.

Loose pants he had heard called hareem that gathered at the ankle, just above leather shoes with grips at the balls. A half-kimono top that belted in way to show off four small breasts stacked in pairs. A long, swishing tail that seemed to have a mind of its own.

Slitted pupils turned and focused on them. The mouth smiled in a demure, subservient manner.

"She thinks we are important folk to visit the Noble-born," Odtsetseg whispered.

"Gotcha," he replied, rising and helping her up in a way that didn't show how much of the work was him.

The Mog woman bowed formally as they approached, and then turned and began to walk at a pace geared towards Humans, with those shorter legs relative to overall height. Even Odtsetseg didn't have the legs this woman had.

Kincaide smiled at her back then watched her turn to lead them inwards.

The Eden Package even contained Mog, so perhaps this woman's cousins would live in a universe where The Gage did not rule every facet of their lives. Everybody would be there eventually, except the Alvar.

They followed that swishing tail through corridors and into a lift he recognized, and then ascended into the tower of the Noble-born, with the Mog woman growing more and more nervous as they rose.

But she was just a servant. One of the little people who lived in fear of attracting the attention of the Lords of The Gage. His cavalier presence only reinforced that terror, because he had a role to play today that didn't involve reassuring the woman.

The doors opened into that same foyer.

Kincaide turned to the Mog and sized her up. Half a head taller than him. Maybe the same weight. Almost shaking with nerves.

"You may depart," he said in a haughty tone as he stepped out of the space, Odtsetseg trailing a step.

The doors to the lift closed and he exited the woman's life, hopefully forever. She was just a nameless cog.

He turned to his partner in crime and sized her up now. Breathing regular. Eyes bright again. Head up and hair back.

"Ayotochtli are *weird*," she emphasized, smiling with her mouth pulled to one side in the cutest manner.

"Duh," he said, stepping now to the door and locating the bell that would summon that punk-ass butler, or whatever that old fart's actual role with the Household was.

He pressed the button and came to rest. Arms crossed behind his back. Feet shoulder width apart. Balanced evenly and ready to move, without giving the outward appearance of how close the violence was to the surface.

Odtsetseg stood beside him.

As before, the audacity of the thing was its greatest strength. No one would ever imagine a Human *could* do this thing, so they would not be prepared to resist it.

But he had non-Human help today, and *nobody* had warned the Alvar what Ildar had created.

Kincaide found himself smiling and almost humming with anticipation.

The door opened.

Same old man Alvar looking forever down that stupid nose at him.

Kincaide didn't wait for the man to speak.

"I need to speak with the Noble-born," he said in a low, nervous tone, as though betraying a conspiracy and unsure who might be in on it. "It is a matter of life and death and concerns Dr. Ildar and the mission."

Odtsetseg had explained it to him, back in his office with the others at hand to offer suggestions and advice. It was easier to take a thought and twist it a little than it was to implant something cold.

Kincaide could fast-talk some victim, and she could make those little adjustments to their thinking that made them believe.

And it helped that Alvar thought processes were so similar to Humans.

He watched the man's whole face go slack for a long second. It almost looked like he would be the one to face-plant, rather than Odtsetseg, but he only wavered slightly before regaining some level of control.

"Of course," he nodded. "Come in and I will convey your message to Lady Thammavongsa."

He stepped back and gestured them over the threshold with a blue hand as big as a shovel.

Same damned headache-inducing room, with intricate details everywhere one wanted to look.

Kincaide took a deep breath now, because they were committed. Any mistakes at this point and they would be shooting their way out.

"Save two bullets," Odtsetseg whispered in his ear, which just showed that she was listening to him inside his head, but she'd said that he helped keep her sane.

Crazy as that idea was.

Two bullets. One for her first, and then one for him. Taking all their secrets to the grave with them.

The butler led them back to that damned conversation pit/orgy hall and left them there, still walking a little off as he closed the door.

Kincaide walked to the bar and poured himself some of the bourbon. The taste would take him back to that first night, when it hadn't been the nightmarish terror that it might have been, with a horny, kinky Alvar woman who had *needs*.

"Fix you something?" he turned to Odtsetseg with a tone that strongly suggested she have something in hand when the next phase occurred.

"Tea or coffee," she relented after a quick scowl.

Kincaide nodded.

"You sit while I fix it," he said. "She's likely to be a bit, as security scanners give us the once over and she tries to figure out why we're here."

He fixed himself a glass and then started poking at the bartender machine. He hadn't needed it for himself, but it was a basic coffee robot like everyone had, only with about a thousand more options built in since it was also serving various alcoholic beverages for the Lords of The Gage.

He found a tea without caffeine and told the machine to make him a pot. Better to be prepared for a wait.

Odtsetseg didn't end up far from where he'd started on that fateful night, more or less facing the door to the salon, but inwards around the ring a bit so that nobody tall could sit next to her comfortably and hold her hand.

That was his job today, so he returned to the same roost as before.

The bourbon wasn't any better or worse, but it did put him in a better mood. At least his memories of Roselani wouldn't be as negative as hers would be of him after all this was done.

They waited while house security scanned them and probably made a few calls to find out how the hell Kincaide Kataragama and Odtsetseg had gotten here without anybody knowing ahead of time.

It all depended on the bureaucrat at the landing dock. He either was still twisted and backed the story up, or was having waking nightmares and they were dead meat.

Hell of a way to live.

Or die.

He sipped and meditated inwardly on the choices that had gotten him here.

Reyhan had been right, of course, within the limited scope of his understanding of things. Better to abandon the Wives entirely to their fate than cost the entire mission. But there were wheels within wheels the man wasn't privy to.

As it should be.

Reyhan just worked here, recruited for his excellence with the Encyclopedia and all the information systems on *Dashavatara*. For Ildar, Reyhan was sufficiently specist to be hired and as Odtsetseg had noted, racist enough to fit in.

Kincaide and Zhubin were the ones seeking to save all of Humanity, in all of the various flavors of weirdness that had come up over however long.

That included risking his life for a group of women who wouldn't necessarily give him the time of day and who were intended to evoke one's worst nightmares.

But they weren't bad people. They'd just been drawn that way, to quote the ancient joke.

He turned a glance at Odtsetseg. She was holding up well. You had to know her as well as he did to see the nervousness around the edges. Mostly in the fingers twitching.

"It'll be fine," he reminded her again.

She seemed to be over the emotional breakdown they'd gone through in the pod, whatever had triggered that.

Now, he had to pull off the con job of a lifetime. Maybe for the second time, since his first night with Roselani Thammavongsa might also qualify.

The door to the room opened and she was there.

Here.

Now.

At least she hadn't taken the time to change into that damned kimono, thank the gods of hell for various small favors.

Instead, she wore the toga, showing off those muscular legs that were limber enough to wrap all the way around him like a snake, holding him in place with those cute ankles.

She had added a white half-cloak that matched the toga. Maybe he should call it a burnous, because it was that light, but it only came down to about her navel and served today to not display her left breast to everyone who wanted to look at it.

Thankfully, the hood was down and her hair was tied off in the side knot for business.

Odtsetseg wasn't prepared for any sort of sexual encounter with any being. Without seeing Ildar's files, Kincaide couldn't even be sure she was equipped for one.

Best not to find out.

Roselani stepped inside the room and allowed the door to close behind her.

"Room systems indicate you are armed, Kincaide," she smiled at him. "Is this an assassination attempt?"

At least the smile looked friendly. He held a highball glass of bourbon in one hand and took a sip, conveying *harmless* as well as he could. It was a useful talent around the Alvar.

"Dangerous world, Noble-born," he replied with equally warm tones, as if it was just the two of them in here, and not including a witness. "Dangerous people hunting me."

What Odtsetseg was to witness was best left ambiguous at this point. At least he hoped so.

The mission came first.

"So I'm safe around you?" she asked, taking another step forward.

Kincaide suddenly understood the half-cloak. He suspected that it generated a low-level force field that would stop the bullets in the pistol he had tucked into a thigh pocket.

"I have no intention of hurting you, Noble-born," he said, using her title instead of her name, since they were in public, however private the room.

Odtsetseg didn't deserve any of this.

None of them did.

She paused at the top of the stairs, showing off those legs, perhaps.

"Or should I fix myself a drink, as you two have done?" she pressed, finally acknowledging Odtsetseg as something other than a piece of furniture.

"It might be for the best," Kincaide offered. "The explanation will take some time. Might as well be comfortable in the process."

He hoped her definition of comfort didn't involve nudity or kinbaku today, but he'd burn that bridge when he got there.

He watched her turn and walk to the bar, appreciating her physical form.

Emotionally, the woman was a lonely mess. Psychologically, she was an Alvar Noble-born with all the terrible things *that* implied. But her body was pleasant enough that he just needed to have Odtsetseg adjust a few things, rather than rip pieces out and put them back together later.

Or not.

She moved with precision, fixing herself something different from the wine she'd had last week. This was blue. That was about as close as he could get without asking for a sip, and they most certainly weren't going to be on those terms today.

He hoped.

She returned, descending from the heavens to bless the merely mortal with her august presence. Except that she wasn't playing that role today, for which Kincaide appreciated her more.

Most of the Alvar were shits of the first order and he'd happily chuck them out any handy airlock in a blink and sleep like a baby later.

Roselani didn't necessarily deserve that.

Might still have to happen.

She studied him, long and perhaps even longingly, like maybe he'd come to his senses, resigned from *Dashavatara*, and was all set to spend the rest of his days servicing her sexual and emotional needs.

Hardly.

But he smiled. Politely, even.

Her eyes rotated to Odtsetseg now.

Kincaide wondered if Roselani actually remembered her name from the briefing where everything had gone sideways.

He watched her eyes, her jaw, even her hands.

Didn't look like jealousy. Like maybe Kincaide had brought his alien creature for a bizarre threesome. She also didn't necessarily look repulsed, if that was where her mind went.

Ick.

After a long appraisal, she turned back to Kincaide and drew a heavy breath.

Now, the shit got real.

He'd had to remind everyone else that everything that happened in here would be scanned and recorded. He had to spin a bullshit story that would hold up when someone went back to review the tapes later, because they would.

"So to what do I owe this honor, Kincaide Kataragama?" Roselani asked in a friendly-enough voice. "You suggested earlier that there was a problem with Dr. Ildar and the mission."

Time.

Dance for your life, Kincaide.

"We received an order from Ildar to report to his lab for a meeting," Kincaide said in a soft, quiet, even tone. The sort of thing that would lull someone to sleep eventually, if you kept at it.

Odtsetseg had explained her needs, so he was trying to hypnotize Roselani, put her into a calm, euphoric state that didn't involve earth-shaking orgasms first. If he could avoid it.

That was still Plan B, if this failed.

"I see," Roselani replied in a voice hinting that these were known secrets.

Which just confirmed to Kincaide where the order had probably arisen. Woman wanted a permanent boy-toy copy around.

Not happening.

"My suspicion is that Ildar intends to Index all of us before we depart on the test flight," Kincaide continued slowly. "Presumably insurance against something going wrong."

She didn't speak, but her tiny smile and petite nod spoke volumes for her.

Kincaide took a sip of bourbon to let tension mount. To get under her skin just a little. Maybe a little more.

"I'm on record as stating flatly that I will never be Indexed," Kincaide dropped the smallest bomb in his arsenal first. "If it is an order, then I will simply quit the entire business and retire to the ground to live out my days. *Dashavatara* can fly without me."

Technically they could. Reyhan wouldn't be as good a Foreman, but he'd be good enough at this point, and Zhubin would just have to step up and take a more active role in the day-to-day operations.

And Kincaide Kataragama would vanish back into the masses of Boston Dome, or maybe Lagos or Brasilia. Or wherever he needed to go to escape these people, including hell.

That much he could promise.

"You would quit rather than submit?" Roselani asked now, her voice soft and ever so slightly slurred in a manner that had nothing at all to do with alcohol.

She was seated just far enough away from him that they could hold hands if both reached, but not touch otherwise. He shifted across that gap into the space where only an Alvar could sit comfortably. Entering her domain, as it were, physically.

Her eyes got a little wide as he approached, but he moved slowly, giving her brain time to adjust.

And Odtsetseg time to push buttons as she needed to make certain thoughts more important and others far less.

Kincaide took her hand now, and they were close enough that his knee was touching her thigh as he turned sideways to face her. She turned as well.

"I feel very strongly about certain things," Kincaide said, understanding that he was speaking to her subconscious now as she wasn't all there. And he could use ambiguity as a weapon here. "There are things I will do, and things I won't. I would count it as a favor if you didn't ever remind Hasan Ildar about your order to Index everyone."

Her pupils were dilated. And unfocused, but she was staring at him. He wondered who she really saw. Probably some teenage crush she'd forgotten four thousand years ago.

"Favor?" she asked in a breathless voice, like a sleep-walker.

"Yes, Roselani," he confirmed, imprinting things deeper by using her given name. "A favor. When my current mission is done, I'd like to return here and repay that favor, if I could."

He was back to being the greater of any two evils. His current mission would hopefully end with his death on Eden, assuming they escaped the Alvar long enough to build such a place and live out the rest of his days.

The only way he was returning to Roselani involved being an angry ghost and haunting her to the best of his abilities. There was always that.

"Return," she repeated.

What the hell. He leaned in and kissed her, as if sealing both of their dooms. She returned it with a strange, languid fervor so his hand came up and held the back of her head to keep her close.

Kincaide broke away eventually and sat back carefully, watching her body for signs.

He'd have said she was asleep, but her eyes were open. Nipples were outlined firmly against the cloth of her half-cloak and her skin was flushed. Breathing regular but heavy.

He carefully slid back across the divide to the Human side of the pit and waited.

Hopefully, this worked and she maintained a warm, positive memory of him. At least until the moment she realized that he had betrayed and manipulated her.

Hell would have no fury equal at that point, so he'd better be fifty thousand light-years away by then.

The light came on slowly in her eyes while he watched, never once glancing over at Odtsetseg to see how she was doing. These recordings would be reviewed, and they needed to get as much mileage as they could out of Kincaide seducing Roselani with his charm and sexual prowess, rather than Ildar's Engine being strong enough to warp Alvar minds.

Hasan Ildar would be the one out the airlock when they figured that one out. Good riddance, too, assuming there was a way to destroy all his research in the process and never again make Engines like Odtsetseg.

"I look forward to you returning to me, Kincaide," Roselani said when she came back from wherever it was she'd been.

He held up his glass in toast.

"Until that day," he replied ambiguously.

"Until then," she returned it.

They drank and the woman rose to her immense height, again showing off those legs.

"You can find your way home?" she asked with a twinkle in her eyes showing just how ambiguous she could be.

Didn't he want to be a kept man here in her palace? Call it home as long as he lived, and then she would get rid of a version and print a new one?

"I can find my way home," Kincaide assured her, just as evasively.

Roselani smiled at him, ignoring Odtsetseg entirely, but that was according to plan.

The Noble-born ascended back to her level and exited, pausing just at the door to fix him with a secret smile.

Kincaide rose and shot the bourbon. He nodded Odtsetseg to her feet, noting that she was in much better shape than she had been with the Ayotochtli.

They made it to the door, turned the other way, and walked slowly to the entrance to the palace.

Once in the elevator, Odtsetseg stirred, as if to speak, but he silenced her with a glare.

Not here. Not now.

They were only halfway done, and even that just set the stage for the most dangerous part of the adventure.

CHAPTER 35

Odtsetseg caught her reflection in the monitor screen and wondered if she really looked that bad, or she was just seeing herself through the prism of her exhaustion. She felt like she should get on the scale later and weigh herself, to see if a kilogram or more of herself had just evaporated this afternoon.

And they weren't done.

"Sleep," Kincaide assured her. "I'll wake you when we get close."

He stripped a glove and held out a hand to her. She cringed inwardly for a moment and then took it, fearful of being overwhelmed again by sensory input.

The Ayotochtli's mind had been like standing in a hall of distortion mirrors filled with screaming ghosts while trying to put on makeup or something. Everywhere she had looked had been a rabbit hole wanting to suck her down into it to break an ankle.

Or worse, turn into that one fairy tale character who met the mad hare.

But Kincaide's touch calmed her. Step-father, watching over her like none of the other men in her life had ever done. Keeping her safe.

At least the Alvar mind hadn't been as bad. Almost Human, in fact.

Roselani Thammavongsa was lonely. Trapped in her ivory tower by her wealth and power. A distant, distaff cousin of The Gage Emperor himself, and all that such a connection implied.

She had been married off young in a political arrangement to another distant cousin as part of a peace treaty.

Almost five thousand years ago.

Odtsetseg recoiled at the concept of such vast time. She was supposedly nineteen years old, and had been in real-time for about twenty-eight months, if Zhubin's story was to be trusted.

Roselani's children had children, but the Alvar measured generations and millennia at similar paces.

The woman was alone, trapped in her life by enormous money, impeccable privilege, and a husband who didn't even live in the Al-Winoq system, but visited between military campaigns on a decadal scale.

Odtsetseg had been prepared to hate the woman for representing everything that was wrong with the modern galaxy. Nothing had prepared her to feel sorry for her instead.

Roselani's emotional connection to Kincaide was *need*. She had dabbled, but rarely found a Human who could rise to dominate her without turning into a bully in the process and thus earning her enmity quickly.

But Odtsetseg's step-father was a better man than that. She had been inside both minds enough to understand.

Kincaide could hate with the best of them, but he had no reason to loathe Roselani. He didn't feel sorry for her, but he didn't know anything about the woman except her need. And his purpose today to keep her distracted while he put the great plan into action finally.

Her fury would indeed be monumental when she came to understand the betrayal shaping up, but there was nothing Odtsetseg could do about it.

Just reaching into her mind and lulling her about the need for everyone to be Indexed had been nearly impossible. Actually making her forget the feel of Kincaide Kataragama's hands on her flesh would have required a dozen Engines like her, working in concert over days.

That was how deeply the man had imprinted himself on the Alvar Noble-born.

Odtsetseg wondered if she would ever feel such a need herself. Hasan Ildar had turned all those genes off, or even chopped them out so he could put other things in.

Anything for power.

She had power.

Odtsetseg wondered if she would ever find love.

CHAPTER 36

Kincaide watched the girl sleep. It had taken her a while to get there, but the pod wasn't moving with any great alacrity. And she needed it, from the dark bags under her eyes, marring the beauty of her rays.

He could almost taste her dreams through the connection of their hands, but he was awake and didn't drown in them as he had before. Didn't fall into her nightmares like when he'd seen her twist Ildar's subjects into more pliant and compatible forms before he Indexed them.

They had to strike quickly today. First Roselani, and then Ildar, lest one say something to the other and break the subtle enchantment that Odtsetseg was weaving.

There was nothing he could do about that damnable Colonial Dispatch Administrator. That fool wasn't dumb enough to let him and Odtsetseg close enough for her to work the creature over.

All Kincaide could hope was that he could buy time by twisting the two power players on the ends.

Thirty hours from now, it wouldn't matter, one way or the other. Lilith and others would be safe and *Dashavatara* could break out of the repair dock.

Clear the Glide and run like hell for the edge of the solar system.

Escape into warp-space and be gone forever.

Or die trying.

Space surrounded them as the pod crossed over to Ildar's station. Cool, calm darkness, like a cloak to hide misdeeds.

This would be even more difficult than the Ayotochtli or Roselani. Granted, Hasan Ildar was still Human enough, but she thought of the man as God, although she had apparently demoted him to just *a god* at this point.

What nobody knew was if the man had been bright enough, sneaky enough to implant any special commands in her subconscious mind that he could trigger in an emergency.

He certainly would in the next model, when all this was done.

I only have to fool you once.

Kincaide smiled and checked the timer. Close enough for her to wake and spend a few minutes just preparing.

It was only their destiny on the line here.

CHAPTER 37

Kincaide wasn't all that impressed with Ildar's lab. Plain seemed an adequate word to describe it, although he was sure the man thought he was making some grand artistic statement with the paint job.

At least it wasn't Alvar. That headache had largely faded on the flight over, and there were no optical triggers in here to worry about. Just gray walls that faded with height.

A pretty Chinese girl had escorted them from the front door to the lab. Kincaide had been all set to be impressed that Hasan Ildar could have a non-Caucasian serving him, until he met the second one and realized that the fucker had a full set of identical, Decanted clones as his house staff.

Presumably sex objects as well as maids. That fit the man's psychological profile to a T.

They had surprised him, too. Not quite caught him with his pants down in the process of doing one of his Chinese bimbos, but certainly not prepared for his orders to be followed so abruptly.

The shock on his face as he looked up spoke volumes.

"What are you doing here?" Ildar demanded angrily. "And where is Prakash?"

Kincaide stepped forward two meters into the lab, drawing eyes to him as Odtsetseg followed. That was the plan.

Distraction.

Behind them, the door to the lab closed, cutting off the Chinese girls and leaving just the three of them to have a *chat*.

"You ordered us to report for inspection," Kincaide replied in an offhand kind of tone. "We're here."

Just for the hell of it, he kept moving, walking idly towards the big picture window with the grand view of the Glide. No ships were close enough to spot, and Kincaide didn't know this portion of orbit well enough to know which stars were station, but the view was pretty.

"Now?" Ildar cried as he more or less staggered to his feet.

"Yeah, now," Kincaide smiled. "We're kinda busy these days, but I had some down time until the next set of shipping containers arrive, so I figured you'd get a two-for-one deal and I could bring your girl over with me."

If the situation wasn't so damned serious, the comicality on that man's face would have been worth it alone, but they were walking the wire today.

One slip and all hell would break loose.

At least Roselani had gone down pretty easy, but he'd seduced her.

Ain't no seductions coming today, Hasan.

"I…I'm not prepared," the fool stammered.

Kincaide fixed him with a hard eye, keeping Ildar's gaze over here so Odtsetseg could work. And maybe not remember that Zhubin hadn't come along.

"So you ordered us to report to you for a personal debriefing and then didn't even bother to plan what you wanted to talk about?" Kincaide demanded, letting his tone get a little ugly with pique.

"You should have notified me you were coming!" the man half-snarled back.

Kincaide was hoping the emotional whiplash on the fool would make it easier for Odtsetseg to do her thing.

Confronting him would do the trick. Walking towards him with anger in his eyes might do better, but it also might make the man panic and call for help.

Can't have that.

Kincaide shifted his weight back onto his left foot and held his arms out, palm up.

"We've got a little bit of time," Kincaide offered, letting emotions defuse a little. "But not all day. What do you need to do?"

He was rewarded by a wealth of angry grumbles, mostly under Ildar's breath.

Mostly.

Kincaide risked a glance over at Odtsetseg to see how she was doing.

Not good.

Oh, shit.

She'd gone white. True white, with all the blood drained out of her face to the point her rays were barely pink.

She screamed and collapsed.

Ildar was closer to the woman when they both turned to look at her. Kincaide got to her the same time the megalomaniac did.

She was out cold.

Oh, so not good.

Ildar knelt and had a hand on her neck, checking her pulse.

Kincaide figured he had about two seconds.

"Hasan?" he said just loudly enough to get those eyes turned this way.

Then he cold-cocked the son of a bitch.

CHAPTER 38

Odtsetseg was in a nightmare of fire. Everywhere she looked things were burning, including her own limbs.

Pain. Someone stabbing her with fifty million tiny needles, time and again.

She was trapped in hell, the ancient hell that Humans had brought with them to Al-Winoq from Earth. The place sinners went when they died.

Had she died? When had that happened?

Sudden sharp pain in her left hand broke through everything else and she fell upwards out of hell.

Odtsetseg opened her eyes.

Kincaide stared down at her, worry etched into his normally-calm features.

Down?

She was on the floor, looking at the ceiling.

"You okay?" he asked quietly.

He was holding her hand. Pinching still in the webbing at the base of her thumb, but he released the pressure as he saw her eyes were open and focused on him.

Were they open? Was this reality and not just a different nightmare?

Was there a difference?

She made a positive sound. Hopefully.

Kincaide nodded.

"We don't have long," he said, gesturing to his left, where God was crumpled up in a ball on the floor.

Her head hurt, but she reached out her mind to touch his.

Out cold.

What had she done?

All she remembered was pain.

"You screamed," Kincaide murmured quietly. "Then collapsed. I punched Hasan to shut him down, hoping you'd be able to do something and I didn't end up having to strangle the man and then hope we could get away afterwards."

Strangle?

Reality came back with a thud that would have rocked her back, but she was still flat on the floor.

She had reached out to touch God's mind. Started to change it, when something in her own programming rebelled. Resisted.

Fought her.

Then pain and darkness and the floor.

What had God done to her?

No, not God. That Fucker Hasan Ildar.

"Can you sit up?" Kincaide was asking.

She nodded, unwilling to trust her tongue.

His grip was firm and sure, slowly elevating her to a sitting position without any jerk to tender limbs.

What had he done to her?

Odtsetseg focused her blurry vision on the pile of brown clothes on the floor. On that stupid opera cape he wore to look like an Alvar in formal dress. Probed her own mind.

There.

Ah.

Ildar had planted more blocks in her mind. She could see him think, but could not affect him. Trying to use her powers to change him would trigger her pain receptors in proportional levels.

He had indeed foreseen his creation turning on him, and stopped her.

She would not allow that.

Too much rode on this. They would escape the terrible man and all his Alvar allies, or they would die.

Odtsetseg took a deep breath and turned her attention to Kincaide's worry.

"You were right," she whispered. "He did things to me to keep me from changing him."

"Is there anything you can do?" he asked, still kneeling and holding her up, else she might have collapsed onto the deck again. "We don't have much time."

Odtsetseg sucked a breath of clean, cool air down into her belly.

Proportionality. That was the key.

She wasn't trying to kill him, else the power might kill her as well. Maybe instead.

Just a minor tweak. An adjustment of priorities that only had to last for a few days. Forgetting that he had ordered the entire command crew to attend him in his Court. Perhaps a shift so that he saw a record of where she and Kincaide had been Indexed today and was satisfied with that.

The creature had chosen to strike her down. Had erased the possibility of Odtsetseg ever exercising free will and being a true Human.

She needed to take it back.

Odtsetseg rolled herself forward onto hands and knees with Kincaide's help and crawled closer to Hasan Ildar. Kincaide crouched at her side, hands on her hips to hold her from falling, as if he could sense something.

She had no idea how much pain she might be broadcasting right now, or how much he could pick up from touch. At least it wasn't flesh on flesh, or she might have no secrets from the man.

But he was her father. He would protect her from things that went bump in the night.

She could trust that.

"Thank you," she turned and looked up at the man.

"For?" he asked blankly.

"Everything."

Odtsetseg stripped off a glove and laid it on Hasan Ildar's face, establishing a rapport with the man while he was unconscious. That would make it easier, as Kincaide had suspected.

It would still burn.

She stepped into his mind, as she had when Kincaide first held her.

Kincaide Kataragama was Human. There was no better definition she could hone down to describe the man.

She was at best semi-Human, filled with alien genes from a half dozen species, but Kincaide still loved her like a daughter.

Hasan Ildar saw himself as the Nemesis of the Alvar. A god challenging them on equal footing on his way to a terrible jihad that would erase their taint from the galaxy.

The siren call of that devastation called her. Haunted her.

She became aware of a thing he had planted deep in her own mind that would cause her to be drawn to that revolution.

Had she no free will at all? Was everything she did the result of suggestions and commands implanted in her soul by this psychotic, rapist pig?

Odtsetseg pressed deeper and found the memories and dreams she needed.

Around her, the fire started, but only in her mind. Low, like touching a mug of tea that has steeped. Good on a cool day, but there were no seasons on a starship or in a Dome. Everything was eternal and unchanging.

The heat burned.

"You okay?" Kincaide was asking her in another universe.

A place that wasn't on fire. Wasn't blackening the flesh of her mind with Hasan Ildar's implacable commands to obey him.

"Well enough," she forced her flesh to say, lest he worry, trying to control the shaking.

She just had to slay a god right now. Nothing critical.

Odtsetseg turned back to Hasan's mind. A thought struck her and she caused him to remember the things he had done to her. Memories and imperatives he had implanted into this creature he was building.

If she survived, perhaps she could use that knowledge to unprogram herself.

If she survived.

Odtsetseg burned.

She turned to today. It was easier to cause certain memories to simply fade, as they had not been written to deep memory yet. RAM instead of Datacore, as it were.

She gritted her teeth and wiped nearly a minute from his mind as her flesh blackened with heat and pain.

There was a way. Burned skin began to flake as she took the knowledge from Hasan's mind and implanted her own commands in his psyche.

Roselani Thammavongsa had been easy to manipulate, but she'd unconsciously been willing to do anything Kincaide asked of her.

Was that love?

She filed the question for a future meditation cycle. There was much she needed to understand about Humans. About adults. This was not the time nor the place to consider.

The impact reached a crescendo at a par with the sorts of multiple screaming orgasms Hanishka Ahamed could reach with that one Information Systems Tech she invited to her cabin occasionally, except that this was pain, rather than pleasure.

But it was done.

Odtsetseg let go and would have collapsed across Hasan's unconscious form, but for Kincaide literally picking her up off the deck and moving her to a different spot on the floor.

The steel was cool on her bottom and that helped.

She wanted to pass out now. Let the darkness claim her and wash the blackened skin from her mind, but there was no time. If nothing else, the Chuns might stumble in right now and behold everything, and she would have to do it all over again.

She opened her eyes, looking up at Kincaide. There was worry there now.

Fear that he might have asked more from her than she could give.

Almost.

But only almost.

"Help me up," she commanded in a pained whisper.

He reached down under her shoulders and pulled her to her feet.

This was what drunk felt like.

She'd never consumed alcohol to incoherence, but others on the ship had, and she had touched their minds enough to know.

How much of all of her experience came from looking in on other people when they did things instead of living herself? She had known drunkenness, orgasm, and laughter, but only because someone else felt them so loudly she could not hold their minds at bay.

Odtsetseg had done precious little for herself.

Until now.

They were upright. She pointed to the Indexer machine and Kincaide staggered her in that direction.

She found the controls and brought the menu system live.

She had taken this knowledge from Hasan along with other things, but both Kincaide and Zhubin understood how to do it as well.

If she could actually form the words, she would have, but that was too much to ask.

Odtsetseg called up the Catalogue itself, that vast and seemingly-bottomless well of information that represented the sum total of Alvar knowledge and civilization.

Hasan Ildar had far greater access than any other Human she was aware of, but only within the biological folders.

She dove down into the pool of knowledge and let the water cool her.

She was in here. Many different versions of her, but not the current one. Just the woman she had been that time before when Ildar thought he had finally perfected his Engine.

Perhaps he had. Stability at a certain power level had been the goal, and it had been achieved.

Kincaide was not here. There was a version of Zhubin somewhere, but bearing a different name and only twenty-four years old. What a difference twenty-seven years made in a man.

She looked around and found an Odtsetseg file that was three versions back. It had been a short-lived model, fixing one issue and revealing three other things that had taken some work to adjust. After the introduction of genes from a Terran spider.

Ick.

Fucker.

She made a copy of the file and renamed it according to Hasan's standards, as if she had stepped into the machine and been copied today.

He could Decant her, but that Odtsetseg was less than she was, in power, in mind, in dreams.

The current Odtsetseg smiled.

She turned to the male files now. Found a Boston Dome Human of roughly the same size, color, and age as Kincaide Kataragama and made a local copy.

The wickedness of it almost made her giggle out loud. Hasan would certainly be surprised when he Decanted this new file and found himself dealing with a complete, and utterly surprised, stranger.

She looked up and found Father's face hovering close by.

"You're evil," he smiled at her, but he'd been watching over her shoulder as she worked.

His approval brought a smile to her face.

It cooled the fire that had been burning her up from the inside like a fever.

"It's done," she said, leaning back and returning the machine to standby. "He'll wake shortly, but his jaw will hurt where you punched him. What do we do?"

"You leave that to me," Kincaide said wickedly.

She could do that. He loved her.

CHAPTER 39

Kincaide knelt over this jackass and rolled him onto his side. Odtsetseg had implanted a couple more memories and compulsions at his suggestion, and now Kincaide just had to see if they would hold.

One fist was ready to crush the man's throat if he started to scream for help.

Then the shooting would begin.

He tapped Hasan Ildar on the chest with a rigid finger, a poke just short of a bruise.

"You okay?" he asked in a loud, impersonal voice.

The man on the floor stirred.

Concussion. Mild one. Someone had rung his bell pretty good and he'd be hearing weirdly for a couple of hours.

Not that Kincaide had ever done that to himself. No, sir.

"Ildar, can you hear me?" Kincaide half-yelled in the man's face.

Something centered and the eyes opened.

"Wha—what happened?" he blinked too rapidly, but Kincaide understood the feeling.

Been there. Done that.

"You tripped and clipped your chin on the counter," Kincaide said. "I was afraid you'd broken your neck, but Odtsetseg looked in your mind and everything seemed okay."

Just in case someone else went back and reviewed the tapes of the last few minutes. Hasan would hopefully follow the compulsion

Odtsetseg had implanted, to believe a certain thing in spite of what it showed, until either that memory took over, or faded.

Just give me thirty-six hours and I don't care.

Kincaide was squatting next to the man.

"Can you sit up?" he asked, offering a hand.

More eyeblinks. Sluggish mental processes.

Don't miss those days.

"Yes," Ildar managed, so Kincaide pulled him to a seat and then slid him around to lean against a nearby workstation.

"What happened?" he asked a second time, but his voice was growing stronger now. More sure.

"You had just finished Indexing me," Kincaide lied facilely, like he had learned. "We were talking about the next batch of folks to come over, in about a week, when you turned and somehow hooked one foot behind the other. Damnedest thing I ever saw and I'm sorry I laughed at you, but you went down into this table over there, chin first. Out cold. Had to make sure you hadn't bit your tongue off. Saw a guy do that once."

There. Implant a suggestion of how comical it had looked. How **Embarrassing**. Few men would want to relive that sort of accidental pratfall, so it should add to the mental walls keeping him from reviewing the tapes.

Until it was too late to matter.

Hasan Ildar was a man who lived by his projected image as a super-genius, proto-god who would eventually rule the universe. That sounded like too much work.

Kincaide was usually happy to make sure the kitchen robot got his order correct on the first try.

Hasan had a hand on his chin, right where one hell of a good bruise was already starting to form.

"What do you remember?" Kincaide asked.

Behind him, he could almost hear Odtsetseg focus her entire being on the man who had once been her god.

He'd been worried she'd kill him at one point, even if she went down with him.

Lots of twisted worship coming undone there.

"You two arrived," Ildar began hesitantly. "We were talking about the mission. Then nothing. You say I had indexed you both already?"

Big eyes. Confusion. Concern. Man who was a control freak suddenly reacting to others.

"Yup," Kincaide nodded.

"Show me." Ildar's color was coming back now. Probably a good sign.

Kincaide took his hand and pulled the man roughly to his feet, then caught him before he pitched right on over and cracked his face again.

He turned sideways to hold the man's chest and back as Ildar stabilized, then waddled the scientist to the counter and let it take his weight.

"My suggestion is that you have a medbot take a look at you," Kincaide said, trying to sound concerned. "You look like a man with a concussion. Have it give you a shot of something to handle the swelling and bruising and maybe go to bed early. Nothing major happening until we get the second set of containers in six days."

He wasn't surprised when Ildar brushed off the suggestion and staggered to the Indexer machine.

It was poor manners to have two copies of a person in existence at once. Banking was a bitch and a half because of it.

Most people would open a spare account somewhere with both their biometric information as well as a special password. Ethics demanded that you leave some money in there for a future copy of yourself, if the damned blues decided to spit out another copy of you and didn't bother giving you any cash to survive on.

They did that.

Then when you claimed the account, you took half and left the rest for another, future copy.

Banks made a nice profit, if you weren't important enough to repeat.

Right now, Kincaide was working on the hope that even an asshole like Ildar wouldn't decide to have two copies of either him or Odtsetseg. Especially not in the same room.

That was really rude, even for him.

The Alvar didn't count because those fuckers didn't have any manners to begin with.

So he watched Ildar like a hawk, however casually it appeared.

The man called up the machine from standby and checked his files. And sure enough, two new Icons were there, created in the last few minutes.

Just like the bullshit fairy tale he'd been spinning.

Ildar turned to him now with a gleam of madness in his eyes that almost had Kincaide measuring him for another punch.

"Medbot?" he asked blankly. Loudly.

"Your brain has a bruise forming," Kincaide replied. "Have it give you a shot and put you to bed until tomorrow. Best way to treat them, and you'll be right as rain."

Rain. What a weird saying.

Kincaide had never walked on the surface of a planet with weather. Just the Domes on that stupid moon where he'd been born, and ships in Al-Winoq Glide.

He looked forward to learning what real people saw. The ones that didn't live in Alvar zoos.

"Should I call for one of your maids?" Kincaide asked now, drawing Ildar's eyes up from whatever thoughts he'd been having.

Don't want the man thinking too much. Plus, the medicine a medbot would pump into him would turn the rest of the day into a hazy blur.

Hopefully, it would last long enough, that lethargy.

"Yes," Ildar nodded carefully, as if his head might fall off. "Do that."

Kincaide nodded to Odtsetseg so he could concentrate on Ildar. He heard her click the house comm.

"The Master has needs," she said in a formal cant that sounded like the sort of lifestyle this asshole lived.

One of the Chinese bimbos appeared almost by magic.

He needed to not call them bimbos, even in his head, but Kincaide had a pretty good idea what purposes these served around here, especially as he'd seen two identical versions earlier.

And he knew what kind of man Hasan Ildar really was.

"The Master fell and struck his head," Odtsetseg instructed the woman. "You will take him to the house medbot and have him inspected. My presumption is that he will be given a shot, so you will be responsible for getting him to bed and making sure he sleeps without interruption. Am I clear?"

"Yes, Mistress," the woman bowed fearfully.

"Assist him," Odtsetseg ordered. "We will depart immediately."

The choreography worked out. Kincaide found himself outside Ildar's spiderweb quickly, with Odtsetseg so brave as to be holding his hand. There were gloves separating them, but she seemed to draw strength from the contact, so he didn't mind.

This woman had just saved his ass and his life, after all.

CHAPTER 40

Zhubin stood next to Reyhan and watched on the bridge monitor as the pod approached the repair dock.

"Any increase in comm traffic?" he asked quietly.

As Chairman, he was ultimately in charge, but it had always been something of a remote relationship with this team. Kincaide had recruited most of these people, and vetted the rest personally.

"Nothing at present," Reyhan looked over with something in his eyes that might be a suggestion that the Chairman go stand up in Kincaide's office and stop bothering him.

Reyhan could be like that. But as testy as the man might get, he was also exceptional among an exceptional crew.

That was going to be tested soon, once *Dashavatara* broke out of dock off schedule and started to run away. The Glide was always busy, so they had a time scheduled when they were least likely to have to deal with Alvar patrols.

There would only be one chance at this.

Zhubin smiled at Reyhan and turned to the main screen again, ceding the man authority over the crew. Then he thought about it for a moment and turned back to the man.

"Humor me," he said simply. "What's the status with the Wives?"

The man's scowl was brief but telling. Zhubin kept his countenance serene. Reyhan would just have to get over himself and deal with their passengers on at least a formal basis. He and Kincaide could handle Lilith and the others personally, as could some of the crew, but Zhubin would be in charge, and everyone here needed to come to understand what that meant.

Reyhan keyed something and swapped the projection in the center of the square to a three-D display of orbital space, with Boston Dome, the repair dock, and one of the other stations relatively nearby in Glide space marked.

"Last check-in put them here," Reyhan said in a voice with only a hint of a growl.

The other station lit up with a red dot now.

"Schedule calls for them to be loaded onto a barge and hauled over to us later today, but I've only just seen our normal tug arrive over there, so figure they're still a couple of hours from getting their thumbs out of their asses on this one," Reyhan said. "Can't call over and yell at them to get the lead out without tipping my hand, so everything is passive sensors and estimates at this point."

Herath turned to look at Zhubin now with a little more fire in his eyes. Looked like he'd trimmed his horns to precise points this morning as well.

Must be feeling feisty.

"Supplies will become a problem rather sooner than we had originally calculated," the acknowledged Assistant Foreman stated unambiguously.

Zhubin smiled at him.

"We will outrun all news of our coming," he told the man, speaking in a voice loud enough for the others to hear as well. Hanishka and Tharushi were here. The Computer Personality of the Day was Benito.

Zhubin paused to study the computer system's face. It hadn't ever really dawned on him before now that every day was a male projection. He supposed that marked him as something of a sexist in bad ways, but there were no angels on this crew, when it came to that.

Only Kincaide seemed to be immune to -isms.

He shook his head and thought about asking someone to reprogram it later.

"When we get out into Alvar space, nobody will know we are coming," Zhubin continued, watching the faces tilt a little in his direction. As intended. "We will be able to sneak up somewhere once for certain, telling them that we have secret orders and laying in as much material as we can, while leaving behind a check certain to bounce when they tell the folks at Al-Winoq."

"That's one," Reyhan pointed out.

"Yes, and we better make it good," Zhubin nodded. "After that, the word will get out to other systems as fast as Warp Voyagers can carry it, and we will be chased off anywhere we go."

"What are the chances we could outrun such a message?" Hanishka asked. "Or will we be going in guns blazing regardless?"

She was in charge of weapon systems. Of course she would go there in her mind.

"Most Alvar stations have bigger guns than we do," Zhubin reminded her. "What they don't have is a piracy problem, since all Engines are usually Humans powering Gage vessels and they have never yet encountered another interstellar civilization."

"Piracy?" she asked. "Like Blackbeard? The old Earth Legend?"

"The same," he smiled at her. "We don't know the truth of it, because the Alvar didn't bother collecting much in the way of Human cultural artifacts when they took our ancestors, but we have the stories, the oral histories passed down and eventually written into the Catalogue. In fact, all the Humans stolen from Earth are in there somewhere, but hidden from us and everyone else."

"Could we really rescue Humans that were born on Earth?" Tharushi spoke up now, her hushed tones a little in awe in her voice. "Is that possible?"

"Possible," he agreed. "But unlikely. If I were them, I would have sectioned off that part of the Catalogue and possibly even taken it off line permanently."

"Then how do we get to it?" she asked, eyes narrowing as if she knew he was up to something, but unsure what.

"The Lords of The Gage will occasionally store an Icon file on a single chip," Zhubin told her. He held out his right hand, palm up and indicated a space a little smaller than his palm with his left. "I've seen such things. Held them in my hand in my time."

"You suppose they stored a billion Humans on chips like that?" Reyhan asked, disbelief evident. "In a warehouse or something?"

"Who knows?" Zhubin asked the man. "Remember, the entire Dome population below us is capped at about fifteen million Humans, plus another three million or so aliens. That means they never Decanted everyone they took from Earth. Barely even a fraction, to be honest."

"Which ones would they have used?" Hanishka stepped closer, her station locked for now and possibly forgotten, at least until they had to break out. "Who?"

"That is a very cogent question, Hanishka Ahamed," he replied. "One nobody knows, but many people have spent years contemplating."

"Who would you bring, if you were representing The Gage?" Reyhan asked him, eyes unfocused and staring at a distance measured in light-centuries probably.

"They wanted Engines," Zhubin said. "Humans are apparently able to function at levels of insanity far beyond the other species of The Gage, so they would have scanned all those Icons for the ones with some level of insanity and telepathic ability. Let's presume they ended up Decanting one percent of the Humans they took. Some ten million people scattered across the seventeen Domes. That's a huge breeding population to start with, but only a fraction of the total available."

"The rest get stored forever?" Hanishka asked. "Waste not, want not, since they'd gone through all the effort to capture and enslave an entire species?"

"Presumably," Reyhan interjected now. "I'd want the young adults. Old enough to care for themselves and be of prime breeding age. Leave off the elderly from that first generation, so you fill the Domes with folks twenty to maybe forty years old. Medical doctors are fine, but no scientists. Retrain everyone to life in the Domes and Gage technology, but watch them closely with a lot of security troops. Split the population into rebels and traitors to the species, and reward the latter."

"Agreed," Zhubin said. "I'd suggest you go one or two steps further, and Decant a number of copies of especially powerful telepaths, but put them all in different Domes and break up their timelines by reIndexing them and spitting them out again. Encourage them to breed with the pairings most likely to produce more powerful Engines, while working to unravel the Human genome well enough to start tinkering."

"Or hire Humans with no morals or ethics to do it for you," Tharushi sniped. "Like our buddy Ildar."

"He's just the most recent of that caste that like to think of themselves as Gods, Tharushi Sampath," Zhubin turned to the woman. "Before that, you had men like Brakiee Goaulda, the one who created the so-called Monster Wives."

"Are they always men?" she asked hotly. "Every time the subject of massive genetic engineering on Humans comes up, the tinkerer always seems to be male. A few aren't even Human, but they are men as well. Do all cultures see Human women as sex objects to be exploited?"

Zhubin didn't have a good answer to that, because that seemed to be the case. How much of that was remembered from Earth and how much came from The Gage, nobody knew.

"I will remind you that a little more than half the crew of *Dashavatara* is female, Tharushi," he said instead. "Including this command staff that you represent. We need to remember that we're building a new culture when we get there, wherever it is we're going. A better one."

That seemed to mollify her, but Zhubin came back to the Computer Personality of the Day. All males. Each day a different man responding.

How many unconscious tendencies did they need to overcome in the course of doing this?

Zhubin didn't know, but he made a mental note to start looking into it. Maybe assigning Reyhan and one of his female assistants to break things down on paper, so that as Chairman, he and Kincaide could make some changes.

Having Lilith and the others would help, as they were all female and could create an excellent example of not needing any man around.

A sound interrupted his brooding. A chime.

Reyhan turned and pressed a button on his console, turning back to smile grimly at Zhubin.

"Kincaide and the woman are docked," he said.

The woman. That was how Reyhan thought of her.

Zhubin could see where he would need to make sure they all understood that Odtsetseg wasn't just *the woman*, but was the person who would save them all.

CHAPTER 41

Kincaide took in the view as Zhubin met them at the airlock to *Dashavatara*. Getting through the repair dock itself hadn't been all that much, but he felt Odtsetseg blow out a hard breath of relief behind him as the hatch closed.

"It went well?" Zhubin asked in a casual tone at odds with his face.

Kincaide shrugged.

"Roselani wasn't bad," he said, just going ahead and using her given name. Like her, he'd be a long time forgetting. "Hasan was a bit more complicated."

"How so?"

So he spent the time explaining their little adventure as the trio walked across the aft end of the ship to where Lilith and her sisters would be moving in shortly.

All a complicated dance, as the ship was designed to take in a single Gage-standard shipping container at a time, through a dedicated airlock, pass it along rails, and then shift it sideways into a spot on one of the decks or warehouses. Ugly architectural design, but it would also give the bigger women space to walk around outside their little apartments he had assembled.

Zhubin turned to the Star Flower with new appreciation, but Kincaide could have told the man she was tougher than she looked.

"Are you ready for this?" he asked her.

"I need sleep," Odtsetseg replied.

Kincaide could hear the exhaustion in her voice, and that was after the naps she'd had on the two most recent flights.

Her power let her do those things, but the personal cost was enormous. He made a note to himself to tell the story around the crew. That would help them relax, knowing that she was only a demigoddess, and not the full deal.

She was still the only alien aboard, presuming that they could undock and run before any *helpers* from Roselani or that Colonial Dispatch Administrator showed up to *supervise* the run.

Part of Kincaide was sad that he'd never see Roselani again. The larger part of him was glad he wouldn't have to have her killed in the process. He didn't like her, but he did respect the woman, weird as that sounded in his head.

The aft cargo bay was ready to go. Nine more containers, two of which would be mostly empty when they arrived, and the ship could fly.

Kincaide found that he wanted to putter today. It was a nervous habit that involved quadruple-checking everything he had already triple-checked, but it had kept him alive this long.

"Odtsetseg, I'm going to be a while," he said, turning to the young woman and watching her closely. "Why don't you head forward and just go to sleep right now? I'll wake you up in a few hours for dinner and then put you right back to sleep after that. Maybe with a little wine."

She wanted to make a show of bravado. Tell him she didn't need a nap. But they both knew she'd be lying about it. This young woman didn't have anything to prove to him at this point.

To anyone, but most of them wouldn't believe, because they hadn't held her while she was on fire in her mind, personally slaying a god anyway.

She nodded sharply and walked away without another word, still stubborn enough to make that walk instead of maybe catching a slider forward.

Kincaide waited a long moment to make sure she didn't have any last-minute thoughts as she walked away.

"Want me to go away, too?" Zhubin asked.

"I'll bore you to tears if you stay," Kincaide grinned at the tall man. "Gonna touch every box and weld right now. Kind of a ritual thing."

"That's fine," Zhubin said. "I have a few thoughts I wanted to run by you. This is as good a time as any."

Kincaide glanced at the man once, but the Chairman was serious. He shrugged and headed towards Lilith's apartment and the block they had sacrificed to give the oversized woman space to be comfortable on a long flight.

"Shoot," Kincaide said as the man remained quiet.

"So, I've been doing a little soul-searching over the last few hours," Zhubin began, but he couldn't get any farther with Kincaide suddenly howling with laughter.

After he caught his breath, Kincaide saw the look of disdain on the man's face and started laughing all over again.

Several minutes passed. He hadn't realized how wound up he had been until it had all come unsprung.

"Are you done?" Zhubin snapped.

"Sorry," Kincaide grinned.

"I do have a soul, Kincaide," the Chairman announced archly.

Because some people might have their doubts.

Like Kincaide.

He nodded to the man to speak, rather than interrupting.

"I never really grasped the sorts of emotional detachment and even dislike that much of the crew has for Odtsetseg," Zhubin said.

"Reyhan's always been like that," Kincaide replied. "Or were you talking to someone else, too?"

"Him primarily," Zhubin nodded. "But others. And I have noted, there are a few places we need to make some changes."

Kincaide went cold and stared at the man.

"Rather late in the game, Prakash," he said in a quiet, dangerous voice.

"Not 'til we are in flight," the man reassured him. "Some of them are emotional, like reminding them that Odtsetseg just saved all their asses. And will do it again several times before we're done."

"They already know that," Kincaide said. "That's part of the resentment. That a non-Human has to be the one to rescue them. I've been asked a few times why we couldn't have done this with the standard five and one Engine arrangement, but everyone understands that the reason we're here is to test a whole new design."

"They don't see her as Human," Zhubin noted.

"Which is part of the reason I put my cabin all the way forward, next to hers," Kincaide smiled. "You did it because you're a pain in the ass who can't be seen not being tougher than anyone else in the crew."

Zhubin started to say something angry, but caught himself and grinned.

"You're the only person with the balls to say shit like that to me, you know," the Chairman stood to his full height so he could look imperiously down his nose, just like Roselani's Chief Butler.

"Oh, Reyhan will one of these days, when he knows you better," Kincaide laughed. "Tharushi will be the one who goes for your jugular, once she's comfortable. That woman knows an impossible number of dirty jokes."

They were there, so Kincaide opened Lilith's door and walked in. It wasn't much, because she was bringing some of her own furniture with her, and Kincaide would have the machine shop stepping in for interior decorating.

But only after the ship was gone.

"So what else do you want to break, after I've gotten it running just so?" Kincaide asked as he looked around and envisioned this as living quarters.

Many of the Wives could bunk forward, since they were more or less Human scale. Kali was taller than Zhubin, but would fit. Barely. Lilith, Niki, Staci, Euryale, and Serena would be largely trapped back here. A few of the others might choose to live here to be with their sisters, and maybe away from the more normal-looking Humans.

"Were you aware that the Computer Personality of the Day is always male?" Zhubin asked out of the blue.

It was Kincaide's turn to stop himself saying something tart and rude.

Shit. Really? Yes. Damn it.

"You're right," he said after a long moment. "I'd blame Reyhan, but I just hired him to run the Encyclopedia System that Ildar designed and provided for us. You aiming for a full gender-swap or just to randomize?"

"Dunno," Zhubin said.

The man was obviously relaxing, since his diction only tended to slide when he wasn't automatically trying to impress someone. Went back to the young killing machine The Gage had Decanted to hunt rebels, not realizing that the man already was one. At least this version.

What was it like to wake up in a tube and know you'd been

reconstituted from raw materials and imprinted with someone else's life?

Thank the gods that Kincaide had never gone there, but several members of his crew had. Not many, and none of the senior ones.

Otherwise, you had a risk of another Hasan Ildar Decanting a spy they had twisted around.

He wondered if he should get the whole crew together for a final pep talk and have Odtsetseg scan them all once quickly, just in case.

Oh, the tangled webs we weave.

"Reprogramming the Encyclopedia can wait until we've landed somewhere, or did you want to do it in flight from the Glide?" Kincaide turned back to look, when Zhubin stopped talking.

"Later." Zhubin apparently agreed with Kincaide's sarcastic tones, which was good.

Too many variables were still floating around right now, not the least of which were all the excess crew he was about to take aboard, and the sorts of racism and even pseudo-specism that had reared its ugly head.

But he could deal with it.

"Anything else?" he asked his boss, watching the man's body language.

"Nothing that can't wait," Zhubin said. "I'm mostly down here bothering you so I stop bothering Herath."

Kincaide laughed with the man. Reyhan could be prickly. But he was still the best there was at Information Systems.

Everyone had been the best at what they did.

Kincaide wasn't about to risk his soul for anything less.

CHAPTER 42

Odtsetseg made it to her cabin with escorts. Plural. Shadow and Blur were both insistent on accompanying her, as if they intended to curl up on the bed with her and sleep.

They'd better be quiet if they did, or she'd be kicking them right out.

Odtsetseg didn't think she had any spoons left to deal with much more than stripping and crawling into bed right now.

She got to her cabin with her two escorts and went to the bathroom to look at her face in the projection there.

Drawn. Almost haggard.

She decided not to get on the scale until after dinner. Too much fear of what she would see.

Shadow head-butted her leg as she stood there gathering wool, so Odtsetseg began stripping off her bodysuit.

Nude, she stepped into the main room and just went ahead and turned on that projector as well.

She'd always been skinny, but now she looked scrawny. Emaciated.

How much energy did it take to do the things she'd done? Or had she burned all those calories breaking free from the control blocks that Hasan Ildar had put into her mind when she wasn't looking?

Even the rays around her stomach looked faded right now.

Odtsetseg grabbed sleeping shorts and an oversized T-shirt that she'd stolen from Kincaide's laundry basket when he wasn't looking. It fit her like a tent, which was fine.

Shadow was already on the bed, standing on her pillow and watching with imperious eyes. Blur poked at her now as she stood frozen.

"*Mau?*" he asked.

"I know," she replied.

She dialed the lights down to sleep mode and crawled into bed. Shadow immediately prodded her to lay on her side, and then climbed into the hollow spot of her stomach, rumbling so loud that Odtsetseg was sure anyone standing in the room would hear. Blur hopped up and walked across her hip before settling at the bottom of the bed where he was close enough to reach out a paw and lay it on her foot.

She hadn't ever studied the ship's cats in great detail. They'd been improved at some point, but not to true sentience. However, cats were already smart, from what she remembered. Just not all that communicative with strangers.

Was she a stranger? Not anymore, if she had these two lovebugs purring at her. She wanted to probe them right now. To see what the kitties thought of her, but exhaustion claimed her and she let the darkness in.

Hopefully, she wouldn't dream.

CHAPTER 43

Lilith felt the ripples of movement as the container got detached from the tug and hopefully inserted into the loading slot aboard *Dashavatara*. With eight sensitive feet on the deck, and all those toes, she was the best suited for those sorts of tasks.

But Goaulda had intended for her to bring all the worst nightmares of a spider centaur to life, and that included a web gland and spinnerets. She hadn't actually spun a full physical web in decades. Nothing beyond just expressing web regularly.

Still, the nerves were there to sense prey that had touched one of her strands and gotten itself trapped for her to come eat.

She flashed back to the first time Goaulda had fucked her in her own web. She couldn't use any other verb to describe the act, unless rape fit better.

Except that she'd been a willing participant. As willing as possible, since he made her that way. There had been no other choice with that man. He would look at you and smile then all your mental processes shifted to pleasing him, however he decided that he needed it today.

Designing an Araneae like her, with a Human torso vertical from a spider's abdomen, had meant that she was one of the last designs perfected, but by then the man had already gone deep into his perversions and nightmares, looking for more things to abuse.

Somewhere, deep in Human cultural history, there existed a creature like her. Else Goaulda had decided to invent one so he could dominate it. There were days she was sorry that Enkya had been the one to kill the man. Lilith would have liked to try, although she doubted that she would have ever succeeded.

That programming was in her genes, however they had been twisted and spliced.

"What evil thoughts are you indulging in?" Margel asked, turned to watch her.

The shipping container was huge, but Lilith still had one end to herself and Euryale had the other, with a small forest of pipes forward to tangle herself up in. Between them, about half of the others had Human seats. Or Alvar-sized in Staci's case. Gahi had a small nesting bar, similar to Corie's, but on the deck instead of in the air.

"What makes you think I'm up to evil?" Lilith asked with a sly smile.

She could never pull one over on Margel for long. The woman was too sharp.

She'd been a significant modification from the basic Human design, inspired by the Ayotochtli and an Earth creature once called a pangolin. Individual scales like dermal scutes covered most of her body, including the cute, little spike of a tail that Goaulda had added as a handle.

He had been a predictable type as a tinkerer. Get one design perfected and then work outwards from there. Margel had been the new base for the design that became Lizab, who had been visually inspired by images of a porcupine.

Lizab didn't miss sex any more than Lilith did, because in those days, she had been utterly concentrated on not hurting the master, rarely ever enjoying herself in the process.

He'd been like that. The galaxy was a better place with him dead and never resurrected.

"Your smile gives you away," Margel laughed. "Most of the time you turn serious at the drop of a hat. You only smile when plotting."

"Thinking about the Master," Lilith said in a quieter voice, low enough that the others could ignore her if they chose.

"Oh?" Margel leaned closer. "And that made you smile?"

"One of his successors," Lilith said. "The one named Ildar behind Prakash's project. He's another one like Goaulda, but without the protection baked into our programming."

"Thinking about fucking him to death?" Margel smiled now, her face scales shifting up and out in a wide grin. "Risky prospect."

Lilith nodded. They'd all been designed to fall mindlessly into pleasure at the touch of the Master. To react to his needs as aggressively and loudly as he needed to achieve his completion.

They'd all been celibate for a long time now, not willing to risk that they might become emotionally bound to another rat turd with a penis.

"He's not coming with us," Lilith reminded her sister. "But a girl can have murder fantasies, can't she?"

Margel laughed. Next to her, Tine did the same, her unicorn horn bobbing with her suppressed giggles.

Tine's fantasies occasionally involved stabbing men like Ildar or Goaulda to death with that ivory horn, just so they understood how penetration might not be all that much fun for some people.

They had all been programmed. And none would take a risk.

But they all had dreams, and many of those dreams involved payback for decades or even centuries of rape.

The whole container jarred now, enough that people grabbed arm rests and rails, even though they'd been strapped down for zero gravity.

Gravity took hold as well, so they had docked.

If everything was going right, they were aboard *Dashavatara* finally and would be on the next leg of their escape from The Gage and men like Goaulda and Ildar.

If not, someone was about to open that door with hotblasters in hand.

CHAPTER 44

Zhubin had talked Kincaide out of joining him to greet the Wives. That was good, as there needed to be a few secrets, at least for a while yet.

Once they were all free, Kincaide could know the truth. He might even forgive Zhubin for it, but that was a little more iffy.

No man likes to be maneuvered into something like that, even when the outcome is good. Kincaide might have even done such a thing without the blackmail element involved, but the man kept his emotions close to the vest, so you never knew.

Now, Zhubin was at the storage unit where the ladies were waiting.

Hopefully it was them, and not a Gage combat team getting ready to arrest everyone and discover who he and Kincaide really were. Zhubin didn't even have anything more lethal than a knife on him right now, but this was for everything.

He pounded an open palm on the side of the container to warn them, and then began the process of unlatching all the various places to open it up. The box would need to equalize pressure from the Dome surface, so he worked slowly and got things set.

One more bang of the hand and he opened the entire short end on a hinge, unsure whose face he would greet. It took a little tugging to get it to break that last seal, and then a puff of air rushed inside and pressurized that last little bit.

Euryale was there with a sardonic smile on her face.

"Just so you didn't have any Prince Charming delusions, bucko," she grinned at him.

Not likely with these women, but it was good to know they still had a sense of humor about this whole adventure.

"I shall take it under advisement," Zhubin grinned back.

He pulled the door the rest of the way and Euryale slithered out past him into the main cargo bay. The others joined a moment later, but he was already moving to the second container. At a glance, that was the one with Niki and Serena in their tanks.

Quickly enough, Zhubin found himself surrounded by the sort of nightmarish harem that Goaulda must have had in mind. The galaxy was a better place with that rapist unresurrected.

Lilith emerged last, joining him and a few of the others close enough that the water-bound two could listen, leaning up above the edges of their tanks now that they had flipped the lids back.

Zhubin took the image in.

"Do me one favor?" he asked Lilith as he turned to face them all.

"What's that, Prakash?" she queried.

"Don't turn me into an asshole in the legends you're going to create until I've been dead and gone for a few centuries?" he smiled at her.

"Why would we make you evil, Prakash?" Lilith stepped a little closer now.

She was wearing a doublet sort of tunic over her upper torso, a dark maroon that went well with the black hairs covering her spider body and the long hair on her head.

"I'm male," he smiled at them. "And I understand what that means to you ladies. I uprooted you from your cathedral in order to drag you halfway across the galaxy and risk your lives, when The Gage might have happily ignored you for the rest of however long you were going to survive. If they ever catch us, you will likely be the only ones alive at that point with personal memories of the Alvar, assuming you don't Decant a few folks regularly just to keep the kids in line, lest they forget and desire to make peace with the elders. Finally, I used you to keep Kincaide Kataragama from falling in on himself and perhaps choosing to die instead of carrying this thing through."

"You have a high opinion of the man, Zhubin," Kali spoke up now, standing just enough in his peripheral vision that her height and blue skin made him flinch, the imaginative image of an Alvar having snuck aboard.

"He was the first person I recruited for the company, back when

Ildar finally explained what he had planned," Zhubin replied. "And one of the few that understands that we will be betraying Hasan Ildar shortly and running like hell, leaving that man holding the bag for whatever the blues want to lash out at. I've trusted Kataragama with all my lives. And all of yours."

"Has he recovered from whatever it was that made you call in your marker with us?" Kali asked. "The deep depression that was killing him faster than would complete this mission?"

"I believe so," he said, turning so all of the women could see his face. "Between saving you and rescuing Odtsetseg from slavery, he has found purpose again. I think it will carry us there."

"This Odtsetseg," Lilith queried him. "You haven't destroyed her Icon in Ildar's files, have you?"

"I have not," Zhubin acknowledged. "That would have given away too much, too soon. I cannot save future versions of her, but I can save this one. She is also special. And she spoke up for all of you with the rest of the crew, when many wanted to object to rescuing the famous Monster Wives of Boston Dome."

"She did?" Lilith seemed surprised. "Why would she do that?"

"She reminded Reyhan Herath and others that all of you were Human," Zhubin said, gesturing with one hand to encompass all of them. "Far more so than she was, in spite of her being a Human-shaped biped. With her, only her strange eyes and the red rays on her face mark her as alien, whereas all of you have some mark. But all of you are expressions of Human DNA, however far Goaulda might have taken it in his time. She declared that she was the only non-Human in the crew, or even aboard the ship, at least until such time as we reach Eden and begin Decanting the other species who are currently slaves to the Alvar."

"I would like to meet this woman in the flesh," Lilith spoke up. Several other agreed with the sentiment. "How soon until we leave?"

"If everything goes well, we'll blow the locks and begin our run in about twelve hours," Zhubin said. "Time enough for all of you to get situated in your new quarters, and for Niki and Serena to be transferred to their bigger tanks. I'll have crew back to help in a little while, but I wanted a chance to speak with you privately, in case you had questions that the crew didn't need to know the answers to."

"Will the full truth ever come out, Zhubin Prakash?" Staci asked, lurking over him with a smile probably meant to intimidate.

That might even work on a few crew members, but none of the important ones. Nothing in the galaxy had been found to intimidate Kincaide Kataragama. Or Zhubin Prakash, come to think of it.

"Once we're in warp-space, as much of it as needs to will," he acknowledged the depths of her true question. "Until then, you are refugees, same as the folks in the Eden Package we will be picking up. But unlike them, none of you exist anywhere as Icons, at least as far as I am aware, so it was necessary to rescue your bodies and not just your souls."

"Both," Staci smiled down at him.

"Both," he agreed. "If there is nothing else, I will depart and send back the cargo team to help you get moved and organized. And then the adventure will begin."

"Indeed, Prakash," Lilith nodded. "Then the adventure will begin."

They nodded and he headed forward now.

Zhubin just hoped that they would wait. Keep some of the secrets far longer than just hitting warp-space. That they left in ignorance the young copy of a man who might grow up to be Zhubin Prakash, and that that boy and his still-in-the-future-bride Aysha were able to find some measure of the happiness that had been denied him.

It had taken Zhubin decades to steal a copy of her, and he was too old for her now.

But he could give her—them—a second chance.

And himself.

That had to be good enough.

CHAPTER 45

Kincaide had the door to his office retracted. He had napped, showered, shaved, and had a shit, like the checklist covered. From here, he wouldn't leave this bridge for several days, except to run into the head for occasional bio-breaks. Food would be delivered.

The Grand Adventure, as Zhubin had called it, was about to begin. To Kincaide, it amounted to running for your life like a mouse stuck in a pantry when the cat found you.

He watched his checklist clock on the desktop in front of him count to zero, savoring these last, few moments before he was officially a fugitive again. He'd enjoyed being Kincaide Kataragama for the last several decades. Wanted to continue being the man for the rest of his life.

Then he could shed that cloak when he made it back to Nayani.

He looked up and drew a heavy breath into his lungs. All the bridge crew was there, watching him. The Computer Personality of the Day was named Daniel.

Male, always male. Kincaide looked forward to making it always female for a year or three, and then having Reyhan introduce a coin-tossing subroutine.

Even Odtsetseg was there, standing off to one side as she tended to do when he didn't need her up in the observatory overhead, staring out at the stars she was going to conquer. Kali had joined her, lurking over everyone else present, including Zhubin, however thin that margin was.

He knew about Kali. Normal height woman, with modifications added later. Extra vertebrae and a second set of collarbones and scapula to anchor a second pair of arms. Blue skin, not because of the Alvar, but going back to the Hindu Death Goddess named Kali. Black hair and dark eyes betrayed the original DNA heritage that had become this Kali.

And this version practiced a close combat dance holding four blades.

Kincaide turned off his desk system for now and pivoted away. He wouldn't be back here for a while, regardless of what happened next.

Instead, Kincaide left his cozy office and descended the six stairs to the main deck level like a god bringing fire to the little people. Or something like that. Hellenic image rather than Hindi, but he'd read all sorts of weird things when he served lower-decks on cargo transports.

He made eye contact with Zhubin and the Chairman nodded minutely.

They had arrived.

All the planning. All the details. All the *everything*.

Including the greatest triple-cross in history, as far as Kincaide was concerned.

He looked around, counting noses against his punch list. Even Blur was here, stretched out in one corner and studying everyone like the performance artist that the little furry goofball was.

Kincaide had already talked to Dr. Sewwandi Perera, back in Behavioral Medicine, and Dr. Avahan Dissanayake in Life Sciences. He was down to the end.

"Power Systems, check in," Kincaide began the final items on his list.

"All generators tuned and on-line, Foreman," Tharushi nodded, sharp as a razor right now.

Kincaide nodded.

"Weapons?" He turned to study her now.

"Unlocked and ready for combat," Hanishka replied with a grim smile.

Ready to kill the very people who had helped them build this ship over the last few years if necessary.

"Information Systems?" Kincaide turned to his Assistant Foreman, and perhaps oldest friend in the galaxy.

Nobody knew Kincaide by the name that Nayani had used, but Reyhan had been one of the first to meet Kincaide Kataragama.

"Encyclopedia backed up and nominal," Reyhan said simply.

Kincaide took one more breath and rolled the dice with his destiny.

"Helm, unlock all hardpoints, then engage thrusters," Kincaide ordered. "Ahead ten percent."

Dinushan blinked and smiled, but he'd been expecting that order. Normally, you exited the corridor of a repair dock at one percent. Maybe even just maneuvering thrusters, depending on what you were up to.

"Ahead ten," Dinushan confirmed carefully. "Stand by for free flight."

Not that he needed to, but Kincaide walked over to stand next to Reyhan and lean forward, placing both hands flat on the counter that ran around the box. It put him in line with all his other officers, and made this a group thing, rather than him as crazy Captain Ahab hunting some elusive madness.

Hopefully, Captain Ahab was an Alvar about to get a rude wakeup call, over on one of the stations nearby.

There weren't any Warp Voyagers anywhere in the Glide right now. Either one would have to come at them from one of the rim stations, or local search and rescue Killships would be tasked with running down *Dashavatara*.

Good luck with that. I have four engines aft for a reason, buddy.

Kincaide smiled as the entire hull began to rattle.

Kincaide continued down his mental checklist and opened the ship-wide comm now.

"All hands, this is your Foreman," he said in a stern, patriarchal kind of voice. "*Dashavatara* has broken free from her moorings and is about to go renegade. See to your stations and your comrades, because we are now committed."

A select few of them knew the brutal truth that Hasan Ildar wouldn't be joining them. For most, it would be a surprise, but none of them knew that man. He was just the distant, godlike being who had caused all this funding to come into being. Not someone they had known personally.

Kincaide had hired this entire crew. The only strangers left were the Wives, and he was willing to spot Prakash that one.

Nobody would be taken alive if The Gage managed to catch them.

On the screen, *Dashavatara* exited the gullet of the Repair Dock, that long tube designed to hold them in place while work crews had built a frame and then created a starship.

"Free sailing, Foreman," Dinushan announced.

"We're being hailed," Reyhan announced in a sarcastic tone. "Dock Command politely asks what the hell is going on and are we declaring an emergency?"

Kincaide considered it. Announce that they were having an engine overload and maybe were at risk of a runaway reactor event. That would certainly distract everyone for a while as they scrambled emergency units and recalled rescue vessels from all corners of the Glide to try to help.

But he found that he didn't want to do that. The truth would come out fast enough. The most such a ruse would buy right now was five minutes or so.

He wanted this to go down in Gage history books for what it was.

A prison break.

"Ignore them for now," Kincaide ordered. "I'll talk with them in a bit, but not until I'm ready."

Bodies stirred and heads came around, but nobody spoke.

He caught Odtsetseg staring at him from her corner of the dome and winked. She had learned a great deal about herself and her power over the last few weeks, so he had no doubt that she could read him now.

But Kincaide didn't have any secrets from his step-daughter.

"We are clear of the dock," Dinushan announced a few moments later. "Course for the Rim laid in."

"Bring her around," Kincaide ordered. "All sensors live and scanning forward and aft. Helm, bring us to fifty percent power. Weapons, you are free to return fire only. Do not provoke."

Hanishka nodded. Still according to plan.

But, oh, the moving violations he was racking up for this. Hell, some Gage official somewhere was probably already filing complaints to get his Master Mariner license revoked for the laws and rules *Dashavatara* was breaking.

But as Zhubin had pointed out, The Gage had no concept of space piracy, because until today they had held an exclusive on all FTL flight, anywhere in the galaxy, going back a million years or more. Every other discovered species that was developed enough to reach the industrial age had been conquered and *Incorporated*.

A few more were on the list for Gage Invasion Fleets to come back and subdue at some future point, but capturing barbarians who didn't understand indoor plumbing was generally counter-productive. Let them reach a level where they could survive in a Dome first.

Like Humans.

Except that The Gage had pounced on Humans as soon as they'd discovered what fantastic engines they made. Conquered Earth and rounded up all the survivors they could. Hauled them back to Al-Winoq and Decanted the ones that scans had shown contained some element of power.

Subjected them, and made them Engines.

Until today.

CHAPTER 46

Hasan looked up at the Chun racing into his laboratory unbidden and wondered if it was time to destroy the entire set and Decant some new sex objects. It happened. Given enough time, the conditioning he had added would break down and they would begin to develop personalities. That was the signal to throw them away and find something new.

Pity, as he had rather enjoyed this design. Maybe he'd just dump the lot and Decant new models. Might even be worth doing a little work on the design to enhance the long-term mental controls, because obviously this one was INSISTENT on interrupting his work.

He scowled mightily at the creature as she came to rest in front of him, cringing with fear.

"What?!?" he demanded in a rude, angry voice.

"The Master comes," she stuttered, shrinking in on herself in the face of his terrible wrath.

Hasan found himself growing aroused at the sudden fear emanating from the Chun. Yes, he would definitely have to do some work on the design in the future, after he had erased this batch.

"I am your Master," Hasan snapped at the woman, finding true rage now.

"I believe she refers to me," a voice intruded. Laconic, but still edged with steel.

Hasan looked up from the Chun and realized that Colonial

Dispatch Administrator Sangsuriya was standing in the doorway, having apparently followed the maid into the suite from the front door.

"Leave us," he ordered the Chun abruptly, rather than working to destroy what was left of her apparently-fragile personality.

But there would be new Chuns soon. Maybe after a quick round of Daphnes. It had been a few years since he'd had a Franco-German staff to abuse. And it would give him time to adjust the Chuns for the future.

The creature fled quickly, pausing only to curtsy properly to the Alvar gentleman who had stepped to one side so she could get by him.

Hasan took a deep breath and tamped down his anger. It was one thing for a Chun's sexual needs to intrude on his day.

Sangsuriya would not be here unannounced without a damned good reason.

Hasan hit the save icon on his screen and stepped away from the workstation, wondering what the emergency was. If someone had penetrated the grand betrayal of *Dashavatara*, they would have just pumped his suite full of gas. Whether he was taken alive or not at that point would be someone else's decision.

That the Administrator was here spoke to different problems.

Hasan smoothed down his tunic and even flipped his opera cape back over one shoulder as he approached and nodded deep enough to the man to almost be a bow.

"Administrator," Hasan greeted him. "To what do I owe the privilege of hosting you today?"

The tall man just stood there, enigmatic, for a long moment before he spoke.

"I wanted to confirm that this was the real you," Sangsuriya replied.

Hasan felt his face scrunch up in confusion.

"The real me?" he wondered aloud. "Whatever are you talking about?"

"Oh, we've consulted the records, Ildar," the bureaucrat continued. "There are no new copies of you made recently. It was the supposed copies of Kataragama and the Engine that caused some Security Officials to grow concerned today. Especially in light of what has happened."

"Happened?" Hasan repeated, utterly at a loss as to what this creature was suggesting or implying. "What has happened?"

"Your ship has suddenly broken free of the repair dock and is in the process of exiting the Glide at high speed," Sangsuriya replied with a grim smile.

"WHAT?" Hasan roared, barely managing to keep his volume low enough as to not give offense.

He found all the blood rushing out of his head, causing him to stagger slightly against a nearby counter. Hasan let the tabletop hold him up. He took a calming breath and turned back to the Alvar.

"*Dashavatara* has broken away from the depot where it was undergoing repair and resupply," Sangsuriya continued. "It had refused all communications."

Hasan found himself blinking too rapidly as he tried to calm his nerves.

Then a terrible rage caught fire in his belly.

They had left without him. After all he had done for them.

Hasan swore that he would see them all burn in whatever hell would accept such traitors to the race.

A second thought broke through.

"The copies of Kataragama and the Engine," he sputtered. "What was it you were referring to?"

"File comparisons in the Catalogue," Sangsuriya said. "The Engine was an exact copy of an older file, renamed according to the standards you use internally. Kataragama was that of a random South Asian male of roughly the correct age. Neither of them were what they purport to be."

"But I remember scanning both of them," he said, hearing his own voice take on a pleading tone.

"Do you?" the Administrator asked. "According to the logs, you did not Index anyone on the day they visited this lab. How is that possible?"

Hasan blinked at this new datum. Whatever blood was left drained out of his face to pool in his feet.

"How could she do that to me?" he hissed, almost forgetting that he had an audience as he spoke.

"That is the exact question we would like answered, Human."

CHAPTER 47

Kincaide sipped at his coffee but needed this mug to last a while. Or rather, the fewer trips to piss right now, the better, even for the fifteen seconds he might be away.

Everyone around him was a little hyper at this moment, so he needed to appear calm and in control. Regardless of the truth.

The ship had exited the Glide uneventfully, if you could call the shitstorm of radio traffic and threats from back there uneventful. With no Warp Voyagers close by and none of the Killships currently on patrol, there had been precious little those blue punks could do right now except bluster.

Trouble would come later, when *Dashavatara* got closer to the edge of the solar system. No doubt whatever Gage warships were close enough would be vectored down to intercept them, fearing what might happen if the renegade made it to one of the places where the barriers between universes was tenuous enough that *Dashavatara* could make the transition up into warp-space.

That was where the orbital fortresses would each be in a good position to try stopping him. By design, they were all placed near the softest spots in the warp-shroud. The Al-Winoq system had been blessed with a frighteningly high number of such potential portals, which was one of the reasons the Alvar had been able to conquer nearby space and forge The Gage Empire.

Other systems only had about three on average, instead of fourteen. There were places out there that only had the one in and out. Hell, some of the solar systems in the near vicinity to Al-Winoq had none at all, and those blue shits had been forced to send mechanical probes across physical space to map them.

But you could do that when you lived seven thousand years on average. So they had.

Kincaide wanted another solar system like Al-Winoq, with a number of windows he could use to escape if he needed to. One as far away as he thought they could run and still have the supplies they needed to build themselves a colony called Eden.

First he had to run the gauntlet of six-fingered fists, out there in the place where the warp-traffic could flow. That probably meant Alvar overlords in Warp Voyagers and Killships, just waiting for him, depending on how many were in-system right now and where they were located.

That had been the one thing he couldn't predict.

Dashavatara was going to live up to his name as the tenth avatar of the dread Hindi god Vishnu in a few days, but Kincaide wasn't here to do battle. No, this ship and crew were all about the other meaning of avatar, when the great God sent someone down or personally touched them in order to restore cosmic order.

For what was the Gage Conquest of Earth but a disruption of that order? And that just meant that Vishnu needed to send someone to Al-Winoq to fix this shit. Certainly wasn't a little punk rebel like Kincaide Kataragama, but the ship *Dashavatara* would be his tool.

Kincaide just got to swing that blade, hacking at Alvar in his way.

He forced his snarl to look close enough to a smile as he glanced around at his crew.

Reyhan wasn't fooled, but he also didn't try. That man had a hatred for the ages, to the point that he was willing to deal with Odtsetseg and the Monster Wives if it meant that he got to stick it to the Alvar along the way.

"Hey, boss," Reyhan suddenly spoke up from his station with an even uglier smile than he'd had a moment ago. "Got a message coming in from the Glide. You might want to see this one."

Kincaide studied the man for a long moment from under heavy brows. But Reyhan wouldn't speak lightly on such a day, so it must be good.

He nodded and Reyhan activated the console in front of Kincaide as he backed his hands from the controls to study the screen.

Slugline was Hasan Ildar. Stupid fucker was finally awake.

Reyhan had been right. Kincaide did smile at that. Broad and ugly, as it were.

He opened the file, but it was a video message rather than text transmitted across the half light-hour or so that separated them right now.

"Scanned?" he asked the species expert on Information Systems.

Humans had invented the Trojan Horse, after all.

"Nothing on my console shows a risk," Reyhan nodded. "And we're more advanced than the blues when it comes to that sort of thing."

The way he leaned on the color choice got just enough of a rise out of Kali, still standing over in her corner, but with a mug of coffee in one of her inner hands. Kincaide figured this wasn't a fight worth having right now, not least of which because he'd end up keeping the woman from beating his best friend and Assistant Foreman to a bloody pulp if she lost her temper.

He doubted that Reyhan understood what those four arms could do in close combat if she got pissed.

He nodded something of an apology to the woman instead and concentrated on the file itself. Straight video with an audio component. Nothing buried inside to trigger his systems.

"Cut all external communications channels anyway," Kincaide ordered. "Keep scanners on passive for now and we'll worry about pinging the neighborhood in a little bit. Dinushan, adjust our vector a little, mostly at random for now. We'll shift back later when targeting becomes important."

He watched the Helm nod and tweak a few things. *Dashavatara* was moving at a respectable fraction of light speed right now, nearly one percent. Any shift would change where they were to the point that anyone trying to ambush them would have to emit their own pulse and be seen.

That was the cue for combat anyway, at which point he'd be relying on Hanishka to save his ass.

All their asses.

He keyed the file and watched it unfold, wondering what this salty punk had for him today.

CHAPTER 48

Hasan had been removed from his lab. From his suite. Even his Chuns had been taken into protective custody, separated from him.

Instead, he had been taken to a different level on the station and left in a conference room designed for the masters, with everything too big. They had at least bothered to bring a single, Human-scaled seat, so he had a foot rest at the tall table, instead of just having his legs swing in the wind.

That was too close an image for comfort.

Gray room. Painted steel decorated with discreet images that suggested people being put to the question. Hasan had made the mistake of looking too closely, early on, and seen images of various creatures being put to the rack, crucified, stretched, waterboarded, and any number of other methods of torture.

Hasan had made a point to keep his eyes moving and largely unfocused after that, mostly staring down at his hands, clenched on the raw, steel tabletop that he had left for furniture, along with three Alvar chairs.

He suspected none of the lesser species would be allowed in this room. Maybe they would leak the footage later, just to keep the other gods of bioscience in line, but Hasan Ildar suspected that he was right proper fucked at this moment.

At least he would go down fighting.

There was a keyword he had programmed into his system, just in case he was arrested, although he still wasn't sure what was going on. Did they need something from him before they destroyed him?

That would make this an even sharper balancing act. One word, uttered in the presence of his systems, or even typed into a search bar, and all his records would begin altering themselves. Nothing overt. If he caused the local copies to vanish, he was certain that there were others, hidden somewhere in the Catalogue.

But if the files were merely slightly corrupted, he might have a chance to destroy those backups as well. While the Alvar were a brutal race, they were also a linear one. They hired experts to think around corners that they could not envision.

Which was why they needed the mostly-Human bio-gods in the first place.

Human insanity. Hasan Ildar was quite good at that.

The door opened. He looked up, then sprang from his seat to the floor as he recognized the person accompanying the Colonial Dispatch Administrator.

Lady Thammavongsa.

Hasan bowed rapidly and formally, wondering what terrible thing might cause that woman to involve herself. He had known, of course, about her dalliances with Kataragama. The woman's tastes for the exotic were well known, but she never kept playthings around for long.

His great fear had been that she would keep Kataragama, or destroy him. Either might have caused the man to betray the entire conspiracy out of pure spite, but he had apparently successfully navigated the woman's perversions.

However, there were no circumstances that should have her here, now.

Hasan remained standing as she entered and judged his worthiness, from the way she looked down her nose at him. She sat. The Administrator sat.

A pair of Alvar Security officers took up stations on the sides, where they were just in his peripheral vision and close enough to assault him if he provoked the two power centers on the other side of the table.

"Sit," the woman ordered.

Hasan moved carefully, aware that he had just stepped into a minefield of someone else's devising. He would have to outthink these two, as well as whatever mastermind was behind it all.

"Several have proposed putting you directly to the question, Human," she said abruptly.

The woman had a cruel voice. Cruel eyes. Hands poised like claws to rend his flesh if he did not mollify her quickly.

Hasan bowed his head and thought quiet, harmless thoughts. Better that they think him broken to whatever scheme they had in mind, than being subject to the things etched ornately into the walls around him.

Anything but that.

"I interceded, Human," Lady Thammavongsa continued in a hard, cold voice. "There are questions you will answer. If I am satisfied, then you will be given an opportunity to explain yourself, and possibly salvage the situation."

Stark. But they needed something from him, so he had some amount of value yet to the Alvar.

Whether he could manipulate these blue punks remained to be seen, as he had no idea what they wanted to know.

That shoe would be dropping shortly. Hopefully, it would miss his skull when it did.

"I exist to serve, Mistress," Hasan replied carefully, setting their expectations that he knew just how serious the situation really was.

Bad. And possibly getting worse, because he had been betrayed by Prakash and Kataragama.

Hell would not be too far to chase those two men, so they had better hope that they were dead before he caught up with their physical forms.

"The project *Dashavatara* was to create a better Engine, Human," Thammavongsa continued. "A single, modified Human capable of lifting a vessel roughly the mass of a Warp Voyager into warp-space by itself, rather than the current requirement of five plus a spare."

She paused, staring haughtily at him.

"That is correct, Mistress," Hasan agreed carefully, not taking his eyes off her face.

The others seemed to be here just to keep him in line. She brought all the anger.

"The fleeing vessel carries only Humans," she said. "There were plans to send a pair of observers along to witness this first mission, but that was not for another twelve days at the earliest, as the ship has not even completed loading supplies."

"Correct," Hasan nodded. "I was in the process of Indexing the senior crew beforehand, against the loss of the vessel to unexpected events. According to the Administrator, the files I thought I had made are not original Indexes, but copies of other files."

"How did that happen?" she bored in on him now.

Hasan took a deep breath and brought his entire intellect to bear on the problem. They had done it, so it could be done. That was axiomatic.

How?

"My memories include Kataragama and the Engine coming to my lab yesterday," he began, shifting the language from the definitive to the inquisitive. Making himself a victim, if he could. They might need him still, and not know the truth of how he had intended to betray the Alvar and The Gage, before Prakash and Kataragama had betrayed him. "I remember Indexing them, but the Administrator assures me that the files are not what I remember."

"So I have been informed," she snapped at him, but the anger was not centered his way.

Who was she angry at, if not him?

"You were treated for a medical event," Administrator Sangsuriya interrupted. "What happened?"

"Human concussion makes short-term memories unstable," Hasan replied, still careful. "According to Kataragama, I slipped and struck my head on a table in falling. After they left, I had the med-unit give me an anti-inflammatory medicine against swelling, a pain killer for the physical, and went to bed to rest until this morning."

"The security tapes show you falling to your knees, as if in agony, before Kataragama struck you with a closed fist," Sangsuriya smiled grimly. "Then the Engine laid hands upon you and did something. Is the creature powerful enough to implant false memories?"

That bitch! Had she been turned as well?

Hasan felt a terrible rage swell now, breath growing short as conclusions settled into a new pattern in his mind.

Something of it must have shown on his face.

"Tell me," Lady Thammavongsa ordered.

"I had inscribed any number of mental blocks in the creature's mind, to prevent her from doing such a thing," Hasan rasped. "She should have viewed me as a veritable god to be worshiped."

"So she can inject memories?" the woman's rage seemed to mirror his now. "If one is not wearing the sort of mind-cloaking device to prevent it?"

"I don't know, but I presume so." Hasan fell back on naked truth now. It seemed safest. "The necessary power of a telepath to carry a ship by herself suggests that she had other powers, but she should not have been able to tap them. I had designed her that way."

"So perhaps she was seduced?" Lady Thammavongsa asked now.

Hasan blinked in surprise. In shock.

Seduced? But he had carefully made sure that the creature had no sexual drive whatsoever. He had disabled any number of parts in her genetic structure when he cross-mated her genes with all the other things he had added over the last decade and a half.

How would one seduce a creature like that?

"It is possible, Mistress," Hasan stammered in a shaky tone, completely off the page from where he had expected this interrogation to go. "I would not have thought the design had such feelings in it, but I am willing to use that as a working hypothesis at this time."

"Kataragama and your Engine visited me at my palace, immediately before coming to your facility yesterday," she said. "The man seduced me, so I find it eminently possible that he did the same with your child Engine."

Hasan ranged through every profanity he knew, in every language, but only in his head.

How had Kataragama managed that feat? To seduce one of the blues?

Hasan was certain he would have thrown up in disgust at even attempting the task, let alone succeeding. Mating with such a foul creature?

And the Engine? She should not have any sexual feelings whatsoever. How would one seduce a creature with so little to offer, or even interest?

But Hasan saw a keyhole that might yet get him out of this pinch. And if he was willing to live long enough, perhaps a future generation of Alvar bureaucrats and nobles might have forgotten this little event in a few thousand years.

"Then we have both been betrayed together, Lady Thammavongsa," Hasan said carefully, studying her face for emotions. "We have that in common, as well as vengeance upon them."

"So you had no inkling that they were about to abandon you here and flee?" she asked hotly.

Oh yes, they had that in common.

"My original plan was to board the vessel when I completed the Indexing of the officers, which should have been in about a week," he said. "At that point, Gage observers and a dummy Icon Package would have been the last piece to be delivered and we would have been ready to test warp-space with my new designs."

"But you are here, and the ship is currently fleeing for one of the orbital fortresses protecting Al-Winoq from invasion or warp-spawn," she said.

The way she said the thing derailed Hasan from where his mind wanted to go.

"Warp-spawn?" he asked suddenly. "As in they might physically manifest and attack your worlds?"

He had never heard such a thing, and Hasan Ildar had been studying Alvar and Gage for seven hundred and fifty years at this point.

The quick look between the two Alvar on the other side of the table was telling.

"Tell him," Lady Thammavongsa ordered the Administrator.

Tell me? Oh, shit, what other secret conspiracies am I about to learn? Will that require my death?

"It has not happened since the early days, Human," the bureaucrat spoke evenly. "But it has happened."

"Early days?" Hasan found himself asking. "How long ago?"

"Roughly three-quarters of a million years," he said in an off-hand manner, while mentioning a date long before modern Humans emerged as a separate species. "Ships transiting warp-space would come back, but the warp-spawn had taken the crew. Replaced their minds with alien things."

Hasan blinked in shock. Those had only been fairy tales told to frighten children and superstitious fools.

Right?

The Administrator nodded. Hasan gasped.

"That is why ships have a Crew Section and an Engine Section," the being continued. "So that the crew can be shielded. And why Engines are destroyed at the first hint of problems. We keep a ready supply here and a few other places. Your project was intended to set up

258

a new Engine depot closer to the front lines of exploration, as you know."

"Part of the reason *Dashavatara* must be destroyed now is that the entire crew is at risk of being taken, if they flee Al-Winoq," Lady Thammavongsa interjected now. "We need to know what the capabilities of this Engine are, so the ships moving to engage will be prepared."

"Of course, Noble-born," Hasan agreed readily. "I have the Icon from which the current version was printed, so it will be a match, minus whatever Kataragama did to overcome her conditioning."

"Can she alter minds, Human?" the woman demanded now.

Hasan thought about it for a long moment before answering.

"Yes," he said simply, watching the woman flinch, but she'd been in a room with the Engine for a long meeting, after which the woman had summoned Kataragama to her bed chamber.

Who wanted to discover that their mind might not be their own?

"But at the same time, if they needed to assault me, knock me unconscious as you said, then her power is not sufficient unless she is close and the target completely unresisting," he continued quickly. "Otherwise, you would notice the change, as they had to subject me to a concussion that scrambled my short-term memories in order to succeed."

He watched her like a hawk for any reaction to his words. Hasan knew he was walking a thin line here, a wire strung between high-rise buildings in a wind. One word from her would be sufficient to damn him to whatever the Security officials felt necessary.

They would dig, and his computer systems would start to self-destruct, which would be all the evidence they needed to destroy him as well.

Lady Thammavongsa seemed to relax. Her eyes narrowed, but she leaned back a shade and studied him.

"After that ship is destroyed, you will have a chance to prove your loyalty to The Gage," she said simply, a bald threat so cold it took his breath away with the simplicity of it.

"What do I need to do?" he asked.

CHAPTER 49

Kincaid studied the image of Hasan Ildar as the video came live.

The bruising on the side of the man's face was almost invisible, but that might be a good medbot as much as makeup to conceal it from casual glance. Kincaide had walloped him pretty solid.

Rung his bell, as the ancient saying went.

Those dark eyes focused on the camera. Kincaide grinned, wondering if the shit thought he could reach anyone here that would listen to him. Prakash had added a few friends to the original crew, but Kincaide had interviewed everyone and watched them since. There were no spies here for The Gage.

Or Hasan Ildar.

"Greetings," the man who thought of himself as a god began. "I'm not sure what you think you will be accomplishing. Or even what you think you are doing, taking a wild joyride in my ship, but this needs to come to an end, right now. The Gage have some interesting questions they would like to ask of your officers, but I understand that the rest of the crew are simply following orders. I appreciate that, even if the Alvar are more concerned. They offer you this chance to surrender to their authority without repercussions. To come home and explain to me and to them what it is you think you think will happen when you reach the edge of the warp-shroud. Your ship is not ready. It will not be properly shielded from the warp-spawn you will encounter, if you were so foolish as to attempt it. All of you will die."

Kincaide watched the man take a heavy breath, as if committing himself to some acknowledgment of the vast conspiracy he had initiated. The duplicity he had spent at least twenty years building, like a poisoned pearl just waiting for someone to take it home with them.

The eyes looked down for a moment, breaking eye contact with the camera before he looked up again.

"There is a project file in your Encyclopedia that will spell out what will happen if you continue with this madness," he continued. "I built certain deadman switches into the system, not because I expected this betrayal, but because of my paranoia that something like today might even happen. If you command your Computer Personality of the Day to show you the contents of the *Life II* file, all will be made clear. I await your reply."

And the message ended.

Just like that. No other threats. No promises. Nothing.

Kincaide had no doubt that there were several Alvar off screen, watching the man, possibly with the threat of violence if he didn't do exactly as they wished. Ildar was a physical coward, as well as other kinds.

Did that fool really think that they would just meekly submit and shut the engines down? He knew how many of the men and women aboard *Dashavatara* wore names other than the ones they had been born with. Most Humans weren't important enough to Index, so they could get away with that, clear up until they died and it didn't matter.

Only the beautiful or powerfully telepathic were Indexed against future need.

Nobody here would be salvaged. Hasan Ildar had to know that.

Kincaide assumed that the *Life II* suggestion was a trojan horse of some sort, but he wouldn't know without doing something so stupid as to ask Daniel, hovering in the air in front of him.

Thankfully, the Computer Personality was programmed to serve, and couldn't just do things without being ordered by a crew member with prior authorization. There was even a safe in Kincaide's suite with a whole series of authentication questions that could be used by someone else if something had happened to him and Prakash had needed to promote Reyhan. Or any number of others.

When playing big, you must plan for the worst possible outcomes. Like all the bridge crew being killed in some bizarre accident and someone from the back needing to take command.

Or the Eden Package not being where it was supposed to be, and this crew having to become their own colony when they got somewhere. Again, they had plans in place, with a slight imbalance of genders towards the female by design, because you didn't need as many men if you were at that level of catastrophe.

Kincaide shut the message down and looked around.

Every eye in the room was focused on him right now.

"It's a trap," Prakash spoke up, half a beat ahead of both Kali and Odtsetseg.

"Given," he nodded. "I presume someone had a gun to his head, off camera, making him say those things."

He turned to Reyhan now, and smiled.

"So we assume that's a bomb, buried deep in your systems," Kincaide said simply. "Figure out how to isolate the file from the rest of Information Systems without triggering it, and then look for other strange files down there with similar characteristics."

"How long do I have?" Reyhan asked, all business now.

"Helm, how soon until we go into turnover for rendezvous?" Kincaide called to Dinushan. "And when will we arrive for our package?"

Dinushan checked his numbers again. And then a second time, because that was why Kincaide had hired him and then promoted him to this position. Precise, careful, and correct before he spoke.

"With the shift in vector, we'll need to turnover in about seventeen minutes," Dinushan said professionally. "Depending on various things, we should come to rest relative in about eighty minutes and be ready to intercept."

"There's your answer," Kincaide turned back to Reyhan. "I need a first approximation in eighty minutes, and potentially a plan to excise whatever the hell that rat pimp did to us before we bring aboard the Eden Package."

"On it," Reyhan replied, eyes already down on his screen and fingers dancing.

Kincaide watched for a moment, and then looked around the bridge.

"Zhubin, Kali, Odtsetseg, could you join me forward for some tea?" he asked innocently, watching the named faces recoil slightly in surprise. "Hanishka, you're in charge of the ship in case something happens while I'm forward. Shoot first and then yell for me, understood?"

"Understood," she replied, maybe with a slight gulp.

Everything had stopped being theoretical.

Today, she might be killing people.

But such folk would be aboard a Gage warship, so they already had it coming.

CHAPTER 50

Hasan blew out a heavy breath as the light on the camera went out.

"It is done," he said, emotionally exhausted by the entire affair already, and the day was still young. "Hopefully, it will be sufficient to deter them before they destroy everything we have attempted to create."

"What will happen when they access that file?" Lady Thammavongsa asked as she approached.

Hasan stepped to the side as the camera crew broke down their gear and quickly moved out of the room. They had moved him to a conference room now, rather than an interrogation suite, so he hoped that his rage at his two betrayers was seen as sufficient.

It was not faked. Only the rest was a lie.

"They will lose control of their computer system when that happens," he admitted.

It was unfortunate, in a way. This would warn the Alvar around him that he might have done similar things in his own files here on the station, but he could always place the blame on the risk of his competitors somehow breaking in and stealing his files. They were known to do such a thing, much as it maddened and confused the authorities.

But the Alvar would just wave away all crimes if it enhanced their own power within The Gage. And they did so with stunning regularity, lest one of the lesser species somehow gain a toehold into their realm.

All the more reason to destroy The Gage and them with it. But without *Dashavatara* and the Eden Package he had prepared, it might take him another ten thousand years, perhaps, so he would need to escape this day, this year, and then outlive every single one of these blue fuckers currently alive so that he could have his revenge on their children.

"Lose control?" Administrator Sangsuriya asked. "What does that mean?"

"I had planted certain commands in the system, against it being hijacked or stolen by someone," Hasan continued admitting his guilt. "The crew would have no reason to ever access those files, so it would be no risk to them. But an outsider attempting to plunder all my work would see that file and access it, thus locking themselves out until someone with the correct authorization could reset things."

"And only you have such authorization," Lady Thammavongsa focused herself on him.

He did not feel a seduction coming on, unless it involved implements of torture. Kataragama had said nothing about his time with the woman, so Hasan had no clue as to her proclivities and perversions. Except that she was blue, and thus a lesser life form.

"Indeed," he agreed, wondering again if he was going to make it out of this room alive.

However, now they knew that there were secrets buried in their own systems that they could not access without him.

"If they lose control of the ship, they will be unable to transition?" she asked, showing a great deal more understanding of the process and equipment than Hasan had given her credit for prior to this.

She had just been another Noble-born, closely related to the Ruling House but separate. Another creature of wealth, privilege, and whatever things such fools did to fill their otherwise worthless lives. Apparently, she could read, although he wouldn't have necessarily been willing to bet on that.

"That is correct, Lady Thammavongsa," Hasan agreed. "It will lock them out of certain controls and my presumption is that they will not be able to line up the correct coordinates to approach the warp-shroud."

"What happens then?" she pressed, almost hungrily.

Was she wanting Kataragama back for her perversions? Why not just annihilate the ship and be done with it? All the evidence would be destroyed at that point, and I'd be free to start over.

This creature had depths that Hasan had not recognized. Or perhaps just a low, animal cunning and the need to fornicate with whatever came along that could satisfy her.

Hasan suppressed a shudder that she might demand his attention as part of his continued existence. That she might reduce him to the level of his Chuns, just another tool to achieve orgasm.

But she had asked a question. A cogent one at that.

"If they miss their chance, the ship will continue off into deep space," Hasan replied. "If they were under acceleration at the moment, they will continue until they impact something, which is unlikely, or the ship itself runs out of fuel. Eventually, life support consumables will be exhausted and everyone will starve, asphyxiate, or freeze."

"Do you have a command that could cause the entire ship to be shut down remotely?" she smiled at him with her mouth, even though it never made it to her eyes.

Animal cunning.

Hasan wondered if the Administrator saw the direction of her logic.

"I do not," Hasan admitted. "This is part of my computer system, while the drives and other departments tend to be mechanical instead of computerized."

"Why is that?" she pressed. "Why not have a single computer that controls most of the ship autonomously?"

Yes, far too dangerous.

He could see the need for this woman to have an accident at some point. Something tragic and deniable, else he'd just dip his cock in some chemical harmless to Humans but lethal to Alvar. There were any number of such substances. It was too bad he didn't have a copy of Kataragama right now, so that Hasan could solve that problem almost immediately.

"Because the cost was prohibitive," Hasan smiled back, nodding to the bureaucrat at her side who had denied him a larger budget at the time and forced him to recruit so many apparently-untrustworthy rebels into his conspiracy.

Without that, he might not be standing here today.

They still would be, but that was their failure to imagine a species sneakier than they were, which was most of them.

The arrogance of wealth and physical size had blinded the Alvar to so much of the universe around them. Like why a man such as Hasan Ildar might be plotting their downfall.

Lady Thammavongsa gave Sangsuriya a withering look, directing at least some of her ire in other directions now, which was a relief. If everyone had to go down over this, Hasan figured he would no longer be the only scapegoat.

That was good.

"You will locate and prepare a Warp Voyager for pursuit," she announced to the Administrator in a hard, cold tone that left Hasan wondering if she intended to retrieve Kataragama's corpse so that a new copy could presumably be Decanted. It would lack the man's memories and personality if he had been dead for too long dead, but the penis would be intact and that seemed to be all she was interested in. "You will also instruct the fleet to engage the vessel and attempt to disable it first. Only destroy it if there appears to be a chance they can escape into warp-space. Am I clear?"

"Absolutely, Lady Thammavongsa," Sangsuriya replied crisply, taking the opportunity to abandon the conversation and the room, leaving Hasan to face her alone.

Well, not alone. She still had her two Alvar goons with her, willing to do her bidding presumably, which would include tearing him limb from limb if she thought it necessary.

She focused dark eyes so like his own on him, leaning down somewhat even as she stepped close enough to lurk over him.

"This feels too well prepared to be a sudden flight of fancy on their part," she hissed quietly. "I will presume that you were deeply surprised that the vessel left quite early and without you, and not pursue the possibility that you meant to be on board it as it did this thing. However, if you give me any reason to doubt you, I will find your deepest terrors and make them flesh for you to experience. Until then, you will do everything in your power to help me stop them, capture them, or destroy them, so that I have no cause to visit my retribution upon you later. Am I clear?"

She knows the truth.

Hasan had no doubts on that now. But they both had a greater problem. The Engine had broken free from his control and threatened everything he had planned. Once the Alvar understood what she was truly capable of, they would make more of her, but only after a deep understanding of the genome. And possibly some significant modifications to limit her telepathic abilities.

That might require one of the other gods to become involved.

Perhaps this blue bitch would go so far as to give them their own copies of his design Icon with rewards for the ones that could dissect it fastest. Or make a better one.

If *Dashavatara* escaped, where would he be?

But she was staring at him as he processed her words.

Waiting for Hasan Ildar to damn himself? To commit utter suicide in the most painful manner an Alvar could find to execute?

"Lady Thammavongsa, I assure you that I had no idea that this would happen," he said carefully.

It was even sincere, because he had expected the betrayal to take another form, come later, and for him to be the instigator.

He took a deep breath and committed himself to a revenge measured in millennia now.

"What do I need to do to convince you?" he asked simply.

Prakash and Kataragama were on their own. He would revisit the Odtsetseg design and reinforce all the places she had managed to break free from his control. Anything to keep the Alvar and the other bio-gods out of his files, until he could build another ship and escape, this time with a smaller crew.

He had a moment of sheer brilliance that apparently lit up his eyes, perhaps his whole soul.

"What?" she demanded, not missing the pulse of power that had passed through him.

"If they are this prepared, then they expect to succeed, in spite of Warp Voyagers and whatever else," he replied. "That must include what I've just done to them, even though it will be a surprise. They will still have days to recover and react, so you must begin preparing yourself for another eventuality."

"What is that?" she demanded hotly, leaned down almost close enough that he feared she might kiss him. Or bite him.

After all, rage, fear, and arousal weren't all that far apart, emotionally. Perhaps he needed to understand how to manipulate this creature better for his own ends, as disgusting as that might prove to be.

"Assume right now that they will somehow be successful at the warp-shroud," Hasan said quietly, drawing her into another conspiracy. "If you are wrong, nothing comes of it. But if you are right, and they escape, we will need to pursue them."

"We?" she leaned back just a bit, almost thrusting one large breast into his face as she did.

"We," he repeated, ignoring the hanging gland to study her face. "I want my revenge on those men probably more than you do. If they broke my control over the Engine, I can still Decant a new one that they have not meddled with. You presumably also wish to see them destroyed for this."

"Indeed," she said in a voice heavy with emotions, but he didn't want to know which ones right now.

Hasan needed time to steel his nerve for that sort of interaction with an Alvar woman. But it might become necessary later.

Whatever it took to get him away from their control so he could start destroying the entire species.

"So I can provide you a new Engine," Hasan said. "You could cause a new ship to be built. Either a perfect replica of *Dashavatara*, or a small Warp Voyager design that a single Odtsetseg could carry. Highly automated as you suggested. Find me a few Humans who know how to fly such a vessel and I could quickly Index and Decant a full crew for it."

"As you do with your household sex objects?" she asked, reminding him that they knew what he did with the Chuns, or the others.

"Exactly as that," he smiled up at her. "But they can also be programmed to serve me. And you. I find it useful to have a whole cadre of such creatures around to satisfy my household and personal needs."

He stressed those last words and watched her flinch. Only in the eyes, but it spoke volumes. She was besotted with Kataragama, whatever he had done to her in his time with this disgusting creature. And Hasan Ildar was an expert at creating sex objects modified to one's needs.

She thought those thoughts with eyes unfocused, and Hasan knew he had a lever on the woman. One he could use to get her to aid him.

Because he could manipulate a crew easy enough if he needed to Decant a few Humans and such to help fly it. Or just turn them all into assassins on the day he didn't need Lady Thammavongsa around anymore.

"We will see, Human," she nodded, but Hasan could see the elation in her eyes. "We will see."

CHAPTER 51

Kincaide walked into the lounge and started water boiling for a big pot of water for tea and coffee. The other three followed him in and took seats around the space.

Prakash, as normal, sat with his back to a corner. Kali did the same, leaving him and Odtsetseg to finish off a rhombus because they didn't need to have their backs away from everyone against ambush and assassination.

Hopefully, those two would get over themselves soon enough and he could get back to flying and exploring. After all, they were doing a thing no Human ever had. Or would be.

Flying through space on a ship with nobody else but Humans. Eventually, warp-space would be open to them and the entire galaxy became a place to hide.

Kincaide was looking forward to that part.

He studied the faces around him, aware that Odtsetseg was probably listening in on his mind, but he didn't have anything to hide from her except nightmares that would ruin her sleep as well.

She smiled and shook her head ruefully.

He smiled back.

"So is there a reason you wanted us all off the bridge for a while?" Kali began, looking at the other three faces.

She'd met the two men before this, but only been introduced to the woman in passing. Nothing formal like this, just strangers sailing past each other on the Glide.

"Mostly to get out of Reyhan's few remaining hairs while he works," Kincaide admitted. "The last thing he needs is for me to be breathing down his neck asking stupid questions."

"Can he solve it?" Zhubin asked.

"If he can't, then nobody can," Kincaide declared. "He was the best man I could find to handle Information Systems, and I had a lot to pick from."

"Can we just erase the file?" Odtsetseg asked. "Ignore it as a trap and move on without knowing what God had planned for us?"

"Maybe, but Ildar probably left other things, so we need to understand this one," Kincaide turned to her. "He's smart and sneaky, but we're going to amp up the paranoid to stupid levels here."

"Can we still escape, Kataragama?" Kali asked bluntly.

"Nothing has changed right now," Kincaide replied. "We're en route to pick up our new Eden Package. From there, we pivot and start our run to the warp-shroud we want to punch through, but it won't be the close one they're expecting."

"No?" the four-armed blue giantess asked.

"Hell, no, lady. Do I look stupid to you?" he asked.

She smiled slyly, but didn't take the bait. That was good, too.

"The Eden Package got dropped off here by some friends who will be staying behind," Kincaide smiled grimly. "I'll miss them, but I needed them here, and hopefully they were smart enough to Index recent copies of themselves into the package so that at least part of them escapes. I'd like to see some of my other friends live under free skies one of these days."

"And if it's not there?" Odtsetseg asked.

Kincaide shrugged and glanced at Zhubin. Plans and checklists and contingencies.

"Then the four hundred and eighty-three of us are responsible for producing a next generation of children when we do arrive, and it takes us a lot longer to produce a working colony in the middle of nowhere."

"My sisters and I will not be participating in that aspect of your planning," Kali observed with a dry, cold eye.

Kincaide nodded.

"Are you even fertile?" Odtsetseg asked suddenly.

"We are not," Kali replied in a frosty tone.

"Something else we have in common, then," Odtsetseg replied easily, knocking the blue princess a little off her perch from the way she blinked and recoiled slightly. "I was designed without even the necessary brain chemistry to be interested in the subject, let alone a willingness to participate. I understand that all of you have been celibate since your god was killed by one of his own creations?"

Not the way Kincaide would have put it, but he supposed that Odtsetseg needed to establish a working relationship with the Wives, and finding common ground would help. Weird place to look, but common ground.

"None of us have had any lovers since Goaulda was killed, no," Kali replied. Maybe still a little frosty, but for different reasons.

Kincaide wondered if Odtsetseg caught the distinction. They probably had had to settle for masturbation for several centuries now, afraid to be touched at all for fear of losing their minds, their will, and their agency.

Shitty way to live, but he could understand the logic behind it. Safer that way.

"What will you do as goddesses over a new realm?" Odtsetseg pressed, harking off on some strange side quests for information.

Kincaide wondered if she was reading the blue woman's mind for information as she did so. Kitten sniffing out treats, and about as dangerous.

At least for now.

"Goddesses?" Kali asked, genuine surprise on her face now.

"All of the rest of the crew will age and die," Odtsetseg noted. "The Wives will not. At least not for a long time. Thus, you will naturally become some level of repository for knowledge and wisdom, like a Baba Yaga. Institutional knowledge of Humanity, but immortal and aloof."

Kincaide shared another glance with Zhubin. They'd talked about the possibilities, but decided that the women had already used their extended lifetimes to do something along those lines, so continuing would be normal. And useful.

He could tell that Kali had made the mistake of seeing Odtsetseg as a nineteen-year-old girl with no chest, no hips, and an innocent-looking face, once you got past the rays. Kali, like the other Humanoid Wives, was busty, hippy, and drop-dead sexy from a physical standpoint. Designed to enter a room and dominate it, by a man who could go back and tweak things endlessly until he got it just right.

Kincaide could even see the kind of man Goaulda had been from the choices he had made in building such women. Less of a shit than Ildar, but only because he had liked to actually talk to his Wives between marathon bouts of wild sex.

Ildar had his Chuns, his Daphnes, and his Hadiyas. Nice to look at. Dumb as fence posts. Fuck and go away instead of demanding a cuddle afterwards. Or being able to tell you a really good dirty joke over breakfast.

But everybody had their preferences.

Kali was recalibrating her opinion of the young woman upwards as everybody watched, but again, necessary. She'd go off and tell Lilith and the others, and the world would be in a better place.

"What about you?" Kali countered now. "How long will you live?"

Odtsetseg shrugged. You had to know her as well as he did to see the spasm of pain in her shoulders.

"This flesh is nineteen years Standard," she replied in an offhand sort of lie. "Presuming normal lifespan and medicine, I should age at a normal rate and live another eight decades."

She paused and took in each face around her. The pain had made it as far as her eyes now.

"We should make sure to Index me now," Odtsetseg announced.

"Are you positive?" Kincaide asked quietly.

He had shared her nightmares, too, so he understood the terror that the Indexing booth held for the young woman now.

"Yes," she replied calmly. "You will need a safe backup, in case something happens to this flesh while we are in warp-space. You will want me at a point when I understand the need for it and it is my decision, rather than something you demand for the good of the tribe. And I am not Human."

"You are Human," he and Zhubin managed in perfect harmony.

"The woman who lives in this flesh is Human," Odtsetseg snapped at the two of them. "The flesh itself is not. Look at my face if you've forgotten what that fucker Ildar did to me. Did you know I have a similar mark centered on my belly button? I, who was never born of woman but bear the mark of my mother as well as the ray of my former god. An octopus reputedly lives for four years Standard before dying, on average. I've seen some of the studies Ildar referenced. Where will you be if I suddenly curl up and die in two years? Nobody knows how long Ildar designed this form to live, and we've never experimented, because my flesh is barely more than two years removed from

Decanting. And Hasan certainly won't give you an honest answer to that question right now."

Kincaide bit back his initial response. It was obvious that Odtsetseg had given this way more thought than he had, but she was also young. He was an old fart counting down the decades until he could die honorably and be reunited with Nayani.

But for this adventure, he'd already have been settling into *ennui* and entropy somewhere. Possibly on the corner bar stool as he drank his monthly income allotment away with his days.

Odtsetseg might have eighty years left to enjoy.

Or two.

Nobody knew but Hasan, and he would probably be guessing himself if pressed.

"Okay," Kincaide replied quietly.

They all understood the reasons. The cold, hard logic. The need of the tribe superseding the need of the individual.

That was what this project was about to become. A tribe.

Eventually, when they got somewhere, it would grow into a nation as they Decanted more and more people to live free. But right now they had a King, a General, an Oracle, and a Greek Chorus of immortal women to keep the tribe alive.

The water was about to boil, so he rose and made his way over. The others joined him, and everything turned into murmurs and small talk as he assembled some coffee for him and they each did their thing.

The mad energy had dissipated by the time the four of them returned to their seats. Zhubin and Kali had even gone so far as to slide their chairs closer, looking social rather than homicidal.

Not that Kincaide was going to tease them about it later.

Much.

He sipped at his coffee, aware that as Foreman, he had a personal stash reserved, but that they were no longer going to get fresh supplies delivered. Stuff out of the Decanter never tasted all that great, because the blue shit who had originally Indexed coffee as a foodstuff had chosen a batch already roasted too dark, rather than taking fresh beans and Kincaide had never cared enough to fix it. Might have to sic Reyhan on it later.

Coffee was one of the reasons the Arboretum aft had a micro-climate specifically for warm and dry planting. Agave and coffee plants would take forever to mature, but they'd have them ready to transplant when they got to Eden.

Kincaide would have things to keep him warm on cold nights, living as an old man without a dome overhead.

He was never living under a dome again. If the tribe decided to build such a thing, he'd be the crazy, religious monastic, living outside it and only coming to town for occasional supplies.

"So now what?" Kali asked, sipping on a green tea and blowing on it to cool.

"Now we wait," Kincaide replied. "That's usually the hardest part anyway. Nothing I can control right now, because I hired the right people and put them to a task. Me asking questions will just slow them down at a moment when time really is the critical factor."

"I understand patience, Kincaide," Kali shot back. "I've got several centuries more practice at it than you do. I'm one of the oldest of the wives."

"Really?" Zhubin perked up from his mocha. "I would have thought that he'd have started with a more generic design, like Tine or Olivia."

"Olivia is the oldest of us," she nodded. "The inspiration for her was an ancient piece of art that someone had remembered and replicated from the time before the Alvar came. Goaulda liked it enough to start there when he went beyond mere Human projects like Ildar usually did before Odtsetseg."

"So you are all sequential?" Odtsetseg asked.

"Each was a project that took him a decade or longer to perfect," Kali agreed. "Rather than speeding up as he got more proficient, he instead made more complicated designs. Niki and Lilith were the last, other than Enkya, but she was intended as a mass-production model, so her design was actually fairly generic, compared to the rest of us."

"How so?" Odtsetseg pressed.

"She looked like a scaled-down version of an Alvar female," Kali mused. "Three-quarters size. Roughly one hundred and eighty-three centimeters tall. Skinny like you, but with enormous breasts tacked on. Three fingers and pointed ears, following an old model for a Human fairy tale creature called an elf. Long, strawberry blond hair. She was quite beautiful, but not as smart as the rest of us."

"As you said," Kincaide said. "Mass production model. Not everyone likes smart women."

Kali smiled knowingly at him.

"Most find us quite intimidating that way," she agreed.

He nodded. Most would.

More the fools them.

The comm chirped at that moment, interrupting anything anybody might say to such a coda.

"Kincaide, need you on the bridge," Reyhan said in a voice that didn't immediately scream *Gage Warship closing*. "Think I've got it."

CHAPTER 52

Hasan had not been allowed back to his lab, much as he had been hoping otherwise. Lady Thammavongsa had brought him to her palace on another station instead. With any luck, all she wanted to do was talk, and keep an eye on him, and not leave her scent on his body.

But he still prepared for the worst possible outcome.

They were in a bizarre salon now. A circular pit one entered by walking down three steps. On one side, everything was Human sized, which meant most of the subject species could sit here comfortably, while the other had a deeper floor that allowed an Alvar to be seated roughly on a level.

So at least she was prepared to entertain Humans in her lair. Hasan didn't want to think about all the disgusting things that creature might have done on these pillows. Hopefully she had staff that knew to clean them adequately afterwards.

They had supplied him with a drink that seemed to be just slightly alcoholic. Like the fermentation had been killed quickly, leaving a citrusy/berry flavor of tartness underneath the peach coloration.

She sat across from him and drank a steaming mug of something. Possibly the Alvar equivalent of coffee, but he'd never cared enough to study their social structure.

Only the political fault lines he needed, in order to exploit their weakness. To destroy them eventually and have his revenge on the species for every little humiliation they had subjected him to over the long decades.

Hasan worked assiduously to keep his face calm and cheerful as he waited on the woman to issue orders and threats.

Long game.

She smiled to herself, but he could not read that enigmatic grin on her face, so he kept his mouth shut.

"How long will it take you to fix your little Engine so that she does not break from your control?" Lady Thammavongsa asked abruptly.

As if he hadn't just spent the last several hours asking himself that same question.

"Too long," he rasped back at her angrily. "I cannot even begin to guess what that shit Kataragama did to her, that she could do such a thing to me. I suspect it would take a month to find all the weaknesses in her programming that are obviously present, and then several more to fix them."

"Should we forgo using your Engine entirely and rely on a Warp Voyager instead?" she asked. "There will be many we can requisition."

The casual way she just tossed that out there was what frosted him the most. She was Noble-born, a cousin of some sort to the Imperial House. So wealthy and important that she could just order a Warp Voyager put at her command and expect it to happen.

On the one hand, it would let him chase Kataragama and Prakash almost immediately. Each passage through a warp-shroud left a trail. If they passed through a Gage system, there would also be records of their flight. In an empty and remote place, theirs might be the only mar in the shroud itself, which would let him trail them.

And destroy them.

On the other hand, if they waited, he could probably convince her to build him the exact ship he would need, so that he could kill her while he had a crew with something like a Chun design or three. Sex objects as sailors rather than just maids and cooks.

Hasan paused with the words on the tip of his tongue and reconsidered. The woman was too smart. Too dangerous.

He needed to play for destroying her grandchildren, rather than her.

"Let us move now," he changed his mind. "We can decant our own copy of the Odtsetseg from my files now or you can bring all my work along and we can do it aboard a Warp Voyager later. That keeps us on their trail while we still have the chance to catch them and undo all this damage. If they do escape, then I reserve the right to suggest you build a custom warship capable of being carried by an Odtsetseg and automated as much as possible."

"With a Human crew?" she asked leadingly.

"I prefer to rut with Humans, and not one of those things with fur or scales," he said honestly. "Plus, we can control a crew better if we program them all ahead of time."

"But no Alvar?" she pressed.

"One," he countered, pointing at her with his free hand. "Plus whatever staff you might need. A ship built entirely for Alvar must be much larger than one for the smaller servants. All that spare volume makes them more fragile than *Dashavatara* if it comes to combat."

"You designed a warship?" she asked, her voice going cold now.

"I designed a replacement for the Warp Voyager," he snapped at her, perhaps a little rougher than necessary. "Those are armed pleasure yachts. I had no idea what *Dashavatara* might encounter, so I built something more durable than a Voyager, but also much smaller, which makes it tougher as well."

"And you think I should just hand you over a Gage warship to hunt down your prey?" Lady Thammavongsa's voice got tart.

"I don't care what you think, madame," he said, pausing to catch himself before he crossed a line with the woman. "I'll see those two in hell for this. If you intend to help, that's wonderful and thank you. If you plan to hinder me, then they'll get away from me and do whatever it is they planned. And, I will remind you, they will do it without any Gage supervision."

Hasan took a breath and wondered if his anger at the situation and his hatred of the Alvar seated across from him had caused him to push too far. He did not understand this creature well enough to know where her breaking point might lie, but if they were going to spend any time together, Hasan was sure he would find it, soon enough.

But she smiled that enigmatic smile again. As though she knew the truth about him and had just withheld the blade for now.

Long game.

Hasan would let her die of old age and vent his wrath on her grandchildren.

She flipped open a little cover he had missed before and pushed a button.

"Noble-born?" a man's voice came back a moment later. Alvar male.

"We are departing shortly," she announced. "Prepare my yacht and tell Sangsuriya that we will need his Warp Voyager to meet us at the edge of the system where *Dashavatara* has escaped from. I and my party will transfer aboard at that point, and the Human will need access to all of his Catalogue files while we are in flight."

"As you command, Noble-born," the man said.

Lady Thammavongsa smiled coldly at him from across this circular pit.

"Understand this, Human," she said simply. "I'll see you all in hell if I have to."

CHAPTER 53

Kincaide led his merry parade back onto the bridge and studied the haggard faces looking back at him. Rough day, but they had all signed up for this and prepared as well as they could.

Now was when the bills came due.

Reyhan's eyes almost seemed to glow with an inner, demonic fire that accentuated the horns his sideburns formed. Fit the man better than anything else Kincaide had seen on him in the last decade.

The other three split off and took up their usual spots along the outer walls of the bridge dome. Witnesses, rather than crew. At least until they reached the spot where Odtsetseg became the most important person in the universe.

Reyhan smiled.

"Son of a mangy camel is good, I'll give him that," the man said. "Even accessing the file would have triggered it, if we hadn't gone in and cut out most of the system connections to that section of the Encyclopedia first."

"Honey pot?" Kincaide asked.

"More or less," Reyhan agreed. "Spun up a virtual system for it to live in and dropped a copy in there. Triggered that one and watched it play merry hell with itself, trying to rewrite all manner of files, all the way across the system. The error log it generated was fantastically huge, running into files that didn't exist. It will probably take me weeks to track down all the things it wanted to do. Serious Trojan horse, but it does solve one of your long-term problems."

"Oh?" Kincaide perked up, rather surprised.

"One of the things it does is reset the Computer Personality of the Day into a different configuration and locks it down hard," Reyhan smiled.

"Who?" Kincaide asked.

"Hasan Ildar himself, of course," the man laughed in a tone like a rusty file shaping steel.

"Then what?" Kincaide pressed.

"If I read it correctly, at that point it does nothing, because up to that point, it has already trashed Information Systems entirely and everyone is doing everything manually instead of with computer controls."

"Everything?"

"Guns have to be aimed at the weapon itself," Reyhan nodded. "Engines and generators can be controlled locally, but not from here. Dinushan is driving the ship with sails by tacking, rather than anything else, because he has to have Tharushi's team vary engine output and gyros to do everything manually. We'd be utterly fucked."

Kincaide leaned back and considered his options.

This was already a triple-cross. How much sneakier could he make it?

"Dinushan, how long?" he called out, still studying the projection named Daniel in front of him.

"Seventeen minutes, give or take," the Helmsman replied instantly. "We haven't started a hard scan yet. That was when we got to about the ten minute mark."

"Scan now," Kincaide ordered. "Find me the Eden Package."

Zhubin had detached himself from the wall and was walking closer while the two women remained at a remove for now.

"I know that look," Zhubin said as he got around the corner.

"Me, too," Reyhan echoed. "Got a good one planned?"

"Maybe," Kincaide nodded to the two men, and then the rest of the room. "Find me my package first, then we'll see about raising a false flag. Reyhan, take that error log apart right now, to the exclusion of everything else. Can we cut that file out of the real system and trigger it safely?"

"Stand by," the man replied, diving back into his screens.

Zhubin stood close, but relaxed.

"What's your scam this time?" the tall man asked.

"If they think we're disabled and coming more or less to them, are they going to chase us all that hard?" Kincaide asked. "Or would they just sit back and let inertia carry us right to them so they could board us and have their way with a band of misfit rebels that had failed?"

"The Gage are that arrogant, aren't they?" Zhubin mused.

"Plays to their species superiority, and all that," Kincaide smiled up at the giant. "Who would ever think they could out-maneuver the Alvar? Gosh, we tried and of course failed so now they'll want to hold us up as an example of failure."

Kali had left her perch along the wall, but only to move to an open spot on the square that made up the control consoles. Odtsetseg almost looked like her wingman, standing off to one side.

"Will it work?" Kali demanded.

Others wanted to ask. That was obvious from their faces. But this was still his bridge. His crew. Kali, Zhubin, and Odtsetseg were the only three that didn't answer to him.

Hopefully, they'd keep him honest.

"I don't know," he replied. "I think Reyhan is good enough. If so, we buy a lot of time and space to maneuver and plan our next steps, without the fear of a Warp Voyager lurking out here in the darkness."

"If not?" she pressed, almost angry again.

"Then we don't do it and we're back to the original plan." Kincaide worked hard to make his shrug seem natural and relaxed. "Physics is physics, so they have an edge there. We have to pick a spot and all of them have defenses. We'll have speed and a bit of maneuverability. They'll get to choose the terrain. I never promised you an easy path, but I firmly believe we can do this."

He locked eyes with the tall, blue woman for a long moment. Matched wills, perhaps, with an ancient who was already something of a goddess, just from the number of centuries she had lived.

After a moment, Kali relented. Kincaide wouldn't say she backed down, because she didn't, but she was willing to recognize that he knew what he was doing and she did not.

All the Wives were planet-bound creatures, while Kincaide Kataragama had been flying in space for two decades now. Just another one of his edges on these people.

"Scan. Contact," Hanishka announced.

With Reyhan focused, she was running many of his boards. At least until it was time to shoot something.

"Where?" Dinushan and Kincaide said simultaneously.

"Daniel, three-dee plot with reference points," she ordered the Computer Personality of the Day.

"Projected," he replied in his mild, soothing, radio-voice tones.

The space in the middle of the control box shifted into a plot of local space. They weren't that far from one of the ice giants that orbited Al-Winoq's star, but far enough that most of local space was cleared out around here, save for comets on long, elliptical paths.

And one small box responding to a ping from *Dashavatara*.

Kincaide felt something loosening in his chest. He could breathe easier.

His friends had dropped it out here months ago, launched quietly from their ship on a ballistic arc that would have eventually carried it to the edge of the system and beyond.

The gasps and little cheers around him showed just how much it meant to the crew as well.

The Eden Package.

"Helm," Kincaide felt his voice grow gruff and heavy so he paused to clear his throat and breathe. "Intercept course. Deploy the cargo waldos and prepare to bring our package aboard."

"Stand by," Dinushan replied happily.

Kincaide keyed a button on the console in front of him and waited.

"Life Sciences," Dr. Avahan Dissanayake replied after a few moments, appearing on a small screen to one side.

He was a tall man. Almost as tall as Zhubin, but rail thin, like a skeleton with parchment stretched over it, except that for as rough as his flesh was, Avahan had the softest touch of any Human Kincaide had ever met. Even more so than Sewwandi Perera, his other doctor, but she was all about Behavioral Medicine, healing minds rather than bodies.

"If you wanted to come forward, we've identified your package and are beginning maneuvers to pick it up, Doc," Kincaide smiled at the man's image.

"They really did it?" Avahan asked, breathless with shock.

"They really did," Kincaide acknowledged.

"I'll be right there," he said and cut the screen.

Kincaide leaned back and caught Odtsetseg's smile. The crew of *Dashavatara* didn't have any telepaths of particular note. All Humans had some level of power, based entirely on the Alvar selecting for it over the last few millennia. But his Star Flower was the only true telepath around.

That would change shortly, as they would be loading so many of her siblings aboard, and could carry them to Eden.

Odtsetseg would have people like her around. Not all of them would bear the mark she did, but all of them would have at least a faint echo of her power, giving Eden the ability to breed new Engines, rather than Indexing and Decanting them.

Or manipulating their genes with whatever a mad scientist dog like Ildar might decide to include in his quest to play God.

Kincaide decided to retire from the bridge now. He nodded for the others to join him up on his perch in the office. Close, but again out of the way while his people went to work.

This was just another waystation on the way to his escape.

Kincaide still had to thread a deadly needle to be free.

CHAPTER 54

Hasan had thought he was prepared for living in close quarters with the Alvar, but standing alone in the lounge aboard Lady Thammavongsa's yacht had already cured him of that misguided belief, and they had only barely broken free from the dock and begun to navigate their way across the Glide towards where *Dashavatara* was currently embarrassing The Gage fleet.

In her palace, every square centimeter of wall surface had been decorated with artwork. Murals. Etchings. Engravings. Something.

The yacht was the same, but at least in this room, every image he could bring himself to focus on seemed to be dedicated to carnal pleasures. More than half Alvar on Alvar, but perhaps even that was a bare majority. All eight of the major servant species were represented, in all manner of activities that brought home to Hasan just how vanilla his sexual existence had been up until now.

He only fornicated with all manner of beautiful and pliant Human women. The Alvar didn't seem to discriminate at all.

Anything and everything. Every kink he could imagine was portrayed here, plus many that he had never encountered before this. Ancient Hindu temples that people had depicted from memory weren't as dedicated to pleasure in their carvings.

This ship was designed for the blues, so everything was oversized. He felt like a child as he made his way to a couch and climbed up onto it, his feet sticking straight out like this was a chaise lounge. At least it was comfortable.

Hasan sat and thought back to the entry tube connected to the airlock. It had been largely functional, with just simple art. The airlock itself was a mural to the joys of space travel and exploration. The hallway just inside was similarly decorated. Art, but done with restraint.

At least as much restraint as the Alvar ever practiced.

It was just this lounge that seemed to be a focal point for so many fornicative energies.

Hasan took a deep breath and reminded himself that he had to likely face all manner of perversions in order to convince this woman that he was not a threat to her. He could do that.

Just one more thing to add to the bill.

It was a shame that the Alvar no longer Indexed themselves, leaving that as a tool for controlling the lesser species. It would have been a great joy to have a copy of Thammavongsa that he could work on. Maybe at the end, instead of killing her at the end, he could knock her unconscious and stuff her into an Indexer?

Hasan could see himself spending centuries getting those design modifications just right.

Shrink her down to barely one hundred and sixty centimeters tall. Dial up the sensitivity in a variety of locations.

Take advantage of the fact that she might live forever as his personal, sexual slave so that he could break her and watch the woman live with that knowledge. Maybe Index her again as soon as she was broken, so she could live with the knowledge forever, since he could just Decant a freshly corrupted copy if she decided to end her existence.

He made a note to add a block against just such an action on her part, just so she had to live that incredibly long life broken to his voice.

"What makes you smile so?" a voice intruded on his musings.

He looked up at Lady Thammavongsa, standing just inside the door, another Alvar male standing behind her. He recognized the man from the meeting with Prakash and Kataragama, but hadn't been introduced, so he wasn't sure of the man's role on the ship.

"Contemplating the shape of my vengeance," he replied ambiguously.

Hasan already understood that it would be much better to tell the woman simple truths, shading and omitting certain details, rather than trying to maintain a facade of lies over any length of time.

She entered and walked to a bar in the corner, taking up a spot on a stool so tall Hasan would have had to climb up onto it. The male followed and came to rest behind the bar, like a servant.

Except that he hadn't had that servile air about him then, and didn't now. Not like her butler did.

No, this one was tall and broad-shouldered. Noble-born from the way his toga only covered one shoulder and half of his chiseled musculature. Handsome in the face according to the culture those people used to measure each other.

Were the man younger, Hasan would have described him as her boy toy. Perhaps Thammavongsa brought along her gigolo to take care of her needs on a long voyage? He could hope.

Anything to keep her from making sexual demands on him. Once, Hasan thought he could handle such a request, especially with enough warning to take certain chemicals that would assist.

But not a regular diet of blue flesh.

Hasan was pretty sure he would just grab a hotblaster from somebody and begin killing Alvar until they stopped him, if it came to that.

She was watching him with careful eyes and a light smile. He had a vision of a cat playing with a trapped rodent.

He bit back any comments and watched her back.

The Alvar valued patience. After all, the species frequently lived up to eight thousand years, with much of that time spent in the perfect afternoon of adulthood. Humans didn't have a few decades to just lounge around chatting before starting their next project, so he, like the others, was constantly in motion.

Except that Hasan Ildar didn't have to be. He was already seven hundred fifty years old. Barely an adult to those people, but he had potentially forever ahead of himself, if he could just keep tweaking and correcting things as his understanding of Human genetics got better.

He could even see a day when it became possible to Decant a version of himself grown to perfection from a vat and then insert his mind into it. He'd be three and a half meters tall, along with the rest of his Human followers, and more than enough to destroy a gigolo like the bartender in close combat.

And the Alvar would fall. Kneel before him, pleading for their lives while he dispatched them one by one.

Hasan found himself growing aroused at the prospect, and had the painful realization that Thammavongsa would not have brought any of his Chuns with her.

Was that part of her plan? Leave him no outlet save herself, the bitch?

She had ordered the Colonial Dispatch Administrator to bring along his files, so eventually he might be allowed a sex object. At least he hoped so. Perhaps they would limit him to only a copy of an Odtsetseg, which would be its own brand of torture, since the child had no sexuality whatsoever.

Hasan crawled off the couch and approached the bar, interrupting the low small talk the two had been engaging in. Flirtatious, from the tone, but he had deliberately tuned as much of it out as he could, hoping to keep his lunch down for a while yet.

Apparently, the gigolo had been briefed, as he produced a glass of that same semi-fermented, tart drink Hasan had been served at the palace.

"Doctor Hasan Ildar, this is Makani Southavilay," Thammavongsa finally introduced them.

Alvar didn't shake hands like Humans did, so the man just nodded politely.

Hasan could be civilized around these creatures.

For now.

He sipped and felt the tiny lurch as the yacht engaged larger engines. Must be almost clear of the Glide and ready for deep space navigation.

Hasan didn't dare suggest a course to pursue. He would just have to be as surprised as everyone else at what Kataragama did next if he wanted to stay alive through all this.

The tall bitch smiled down at him and sipped her drink.

"We have begun," she said, holding out her glass even. "To success in our quest."

Hasan nearly gagged, but forced a smile and held his glass up to hers. The gigolo joined them a moment later with a clink.

His backbrain continued to process the words and Hasan noted that she was almost as circumspect and ambiguous as he was.

Was that a warning from her that she had seen through his games? Then why continue them, unless she was looking to him to make her a better copy of Kataragama when this was all done?

Hasan sipped and let his mind wander into a fugue of creativity.

If Kataragama was dead for only a short period of time, it would be possible to Index him cleanly. Should Hasan Decant a version with extended longevity so the bitch had her own sex object to distract her forever while Hasan went forward with his plans? He could see no other explanation for her behavior.

What other modifications would she demand, assuming that they could bring back a copy of Kataragama for her?

Female bio-gods were rare. Hasan only knew of two across the entire brotherhood of such people as the Alvar had endowed with permission to experiment on their own kind, for the hundreds of males.

Would she be satisfied with a mere sex object? Would she want Hasan Ildar to create a younger version of Kataragama for her, at least physically, so it had the greater stamina of a buck?

He smiled up at her and watched her eyes.

I will bind you to me by fulfilling your every sexual need, Alvar.

"So what happens now?" Hasan asked, letting the conversation flow on to other things.

They would be on this yacht for several days, even in a high-speed pursuit. Hopefully, that meant she would largely ignore him for now. Doubly so with her gigolo to keep her bed warm.

"*Dashavatara* has slowed significantly recently," the gigolo said, indicating that he had a brain in there.

Was the man Security then, as well?

"Have they chosen to surrender?" Hasan asked, putting on a good show for the Alvar now. "Come to rest and then return to Al-Winoq?"

"We do not believe so," the man spoke with dark eyes that constantly strayed to the blue woman across from him. "But there are several Warp Voyagers in pursuit from different angles. Normally, that would be sufficient, but Lady Thammavongsa indicates that we should prepare for the Humans to somehow be able to reach the edge of the system, evade our security forces, and escape into warp-space."

Those eyes turned back to him now, questioning, but Hasan just smiled.

If you are that stupid, I won't cure you of it. Get me a Warp Voyager where I can Decant enough crew and I'll create my own Human colony somewhere else. After I kill every single one of you first.

Except the woman. She goes into the Indexer.

Hasan blinked innocently up at the giant and sipped his drink.

"Why do you think they will be able to do such things?" Lady

Thammavongsa asked now, obviously a setup for the punk from Security who was hopefully good enough in bed to distract her.

Hasan felt his hopes falling on that score.

"I cannot imagine that they just decided overnight to do such a thing," Hasan said. "As you noted, I was apparently assaulted and my mind altered by their conspiracy, so they must have given thought to every step of whatever it is they plan."

"Oh?" the man asked, obviously intending to play a junior varsity version of bad cop with Hasan.

"There are fourteen spots at the edge of this system where the warp-shroud thins," Hasan spoke, shifting his voice to a lecturing mode. Perhaps he could convince the cop that Hasan Ildar was his intellectual superior, and gain some respect there. Whatever that might be worth. "Each has a fortress close. Each has security warships close. Killships and whatever else you maintain there. None of this is a secret."

"Indeed," the man nodded. "It is public knowledge."

"So they must think they can do something," Hasan pointed out. "I have no idea what. Or if their plans will work, but I selected intelligent, competent men to command this ship and protect what should have been my project."

"Will they fall for the trick of disabling their ship?" the man asked.

Hasan shrugged. It would never do to let the Alvar know just how sneaky Humans could be. Not if he was planning to live among them long enough to make a permanent mark.

"I have tried," he said. "Lady Thammavongsa asked for a good faith effort on my part to stop them before it became necessary for you to destroy the vessel and the crew at a complete loss. If they do trigger the trap I left, then perhaps we can salvage much of it, although I highly doubt that some of those people would allow themselves to be taken alive."

He was watching her face as he said those words, just to see what reaction he got. Hints of fear, longing, lust, and rage. About what he had expected, so Hasan turned back to the Security Gigolo of the First Rank.

"But you think we should prepare for their escape," the man said bluntly.

"Yes," Hasan spoke at him, rather than to him. "If you catch them, then all is well. If you don't, then you will need to chase them wherever they flee to. I can only imagine how easily they might have eluded you if you were not prepared to give chase in your arrogance, so I have tried to prepare you for such an outcome, however implausible it might be."

Hasan found his emotions roused now, so he finished off the glass as an excuse to break eye contact with the creature and stop short of calling them all short-sighted fools who were about to lose control of the galaxy.

Because that was exactly the risk they faced, if Kataragama and Prakash were somehow able to take *Dashavatara* and flee from Al-Winoq.

A future where Humans could meet the Alvar and their Gage minions on even footing.

Hasan didn't relish having to conquer two enemy empires when he got there.

CHAPTER 55

Kincaide watched the projection from his desk, as *Dashavatara* came up on the big container from behind and slowly matched velocity with it. Doc Avahan had taken his spot next to Reyhan and was constantly clenching and unclenching his hands with excitement, not daring to speak after the second time Dinushan had snapped angrily at the man.

Nerves were a little frazzled out there.

Dashavatara was a big ship. Tiny compared to some of the Warp Voyagers commanding the galaxy, to say nothing of the immense Starfall Landers, but still a huge mass to maneuver through space.

In the projection, the container had a slight spin, probably imparted from solar wind and unbalanced heating and cooling. Dinushan had to come right alongside on the same vector, and then slowly drift down and in, passing to starboard of the bottom drive engine so they could extend the cargo waldos aft to grasp the box and pull it into the starboard bay.

Port side was already filled with Lilith and her sisters. Plus, starboard was closer to Avahan's main laboratory.

In his office, Kincaide kept a watch on the helpful sensor pings a number of Warp Voyagers were emitting as they approached. Even at high speed, none of them would get close for more than a day, so he had no fear. Dinushan would complete his task, then they would pivot the ship and take off like a rocket in a direction he hoped nobody expected.

Space/time was dimpled by large gravity wells, but at the same time, it was only at the edges of solar systems that the warp-shroud grew thin enough to be breached, and then on the rough general plane of the system itself.

Kincaide had heard theories that the act of spinning down to create a solar system was what pulled the thread loose in the fabric of space itself, but he had no idea if that was scientifically valid or pure hokum. Didn't matter.

Everything was flat. Fourteen doors in and out of the building. All of them defended, although Kincaide had no idea against what, since The Gage was the only species in space.

Or did they have occasional rebellions within the species and just didn't like to talk about it in front of the servants? That made more sense. Imperial family who had been keeping that throne warm for epochs now. Others might grow restless.

If there was any chance of success, Kincaide might have suggested a revolution, but that would leave the same Gage in control, merely with different faces on the currency.

Fuck that. He would be free or die trying.

Closer now, Dinushan and Hanishka were dancing the ship like glass melting. Oozing slowly forward.

"Extending the arms," Hanishka called as Dinushan rode the vessel on gyros and station-keeping thrusters. Movement measured in decimeters instead of light-minutes.

Kincaide switched the view on his projection and watched the pair of spindly, mechanical arms stretching out to catch the pod. Fingers reached now and snagged a grapple bar.

Kincaide imagined that he felt the hull ripple with the contained energy, but it was just in his imagination.

The other arm swept out quickly and caught another bar. The pod came to rest, relative to *Dashavatara*.

Kincaide blew out a breath. That had been the hardest part, the risk that they would damage the transport pod or the arms and then have to suit up a team to recover it, rather than just relying on the waldos. The difference was about a six hour head start on all those punks chasing them right now.

"Solid lock achieved," Dinushan announced.

From his tone, he was just about as wrung out as Kincaide, but he'd been maneuvering the entire vessel and ordering Hanishka as she moved.

"Retrieving now," the gunner said, equally frazzled.

Zhubin stirred and Kincaide remembered that the other three were in here with him, but everybody had been so silently rapt that he'd forgotten.

Whoops.

Even Kali looked flushed with excitement.

He wondered how boring it might be to live forever. You'd run out of new things to do eventually, wouldn't you?

Kincaide could see it turning into another addiction, as you needed to up the crazy every year or decade or something, just to give yourself a reason to get out of bed. Like Goaulda and his Wives.

All the more reason to die after an appreciable time in this galaxy. See what you needed. Do what needed doing. Then go.

Nayani would be waiting for him on the other side of that veil, so hell wouldn't be all that bad.

On the projection, the pod slowly swung aft and this time the hull did rattle as Hanishka slipped the package into the airlock and everything locked down hard.

They had already scanned it, and there were no life forms inside the pod.

Well, that wasn't true. There were hundreds of thousands or more, potentially, but nobody currently drawing breath and representing a threat to *Dashavatara* and its crew.

Dinushan looked up from across the bridge and caught Kincaide's eye, but Kincaide just smiled and nodded to him to continue what he was doing.

The man deserved this moment of glory, for what they had already accomplished.

"The Eden Package has been successfully retrieved," Dinushan announced, his voice echoing across the space as well as out of Kincaide's console. "Everyone stand by for acceleration and possible abrupt maneuvering."

Kincaide nodded and smiled.

Now was when things would start to get ugly.

CHAPTER 56

Roselani watched the pitiful Human play his insipid games and wondered just how stupid he thought she was. Granted, many of her cohorts rarely rose from the *ennui* that filled their endless lives, but Ildar wasn't all that smart. Conversely, however, she hadn't had this much fun with anything in perhaps a millennium.

Maybe they needed a good threat to The Gage every once in a while, to knock everyone out of their complacency.

She couldn't prove anything with the Human. At least not without putting him to the sorts of torture that would ruin a perfectly serviceable tool if he ended up being honest after all, in spite of all the cues and subtle markers he gave off.

Roselani was certain that he had planned to be aboard that ship when it came time to depart like a thief in the night. She had warned that fool of a Colonial Dispatch Administrator that Ildar was up to no good, but the man had bent over backwards time and again to defend the Human.

Did Ildar have some bizarre blackmail on Sangsuriya? Or had he promised to make the man the perfect sex object once the Engine was perfected?

Which would have been about the time Ildar and *Dashavatara* would have disappeared, leaving Sangsuriya holding an empty bag full of promises.

She sipped her wine and considered the little man.

"Makani, show Doctor Ildar to his cabin and make sure he has everything he needs before we move to a Warp Voyager," she ordered the Security Administrator. "Then return here."

It was telling, watching the Human flinch. Unconscious fear of Alvar size and strength, but all species had that. On every one of their homeworlds, each of the servant species had cultural memories of some predatory creature this size.

For Humans, apparently the creature was known as a kodiak, although no copies had been Decanted in ages, so she could only take the word of the Archivists for that.

But Ildar was afraid of Makani's size. Hers as well, but there was also an element of lust there, cross-wired in the little man's mind when she looked in his eyes.

She had quietly studied the sex objects he kept. Parsed their similarities and differences with researchers to understand what drove a man like Hasan Ildar. She couldn't get inside his mind, but he left fingerprints everywhere around him for anyone to notice.

Power. That was the thing that drove the Human. Others of the group that called themselves bio-gods were driven by curiosity. A few by mere wealth.

Ildar wanted power over the people around him. That included her. At the same time, he feared her.

Roselani giggled to herself at the fun she might have, edging slowly closer to the man and his twisted libido, without ever quite brushing the topic. The mental anguish she could inflict on him over decades if she was careful.

He couldn't escape her on this yacht, or even on a Warp Voyager. She could violate his personal space time and again, just to stick burning slivers of wood under his fingernails, since he couldn't do anything about it.

Not if he wanted to continue living forever.

Forever.

What would a Human do with *forever*?

Kincaide had made a point of the fact that he would be dead and gone soon enough. Seemed to be looking forward to it, but no agent had been able to identify the reason. It was enough to know that forcing the man to be Indexed would provoke a terminally-hostile response.

Which was why she had done it. No Human snapped at an Alvar and lived. They acquiesced. Bided their time and then died off when one of the immortals lost track of them for a decade or two, which they commonly did.

Roselani hadn't seen her husband in nearly two hundred years now, as he was off on some campaign to pacify a few rogue colonies that had thought to reject Alvar rule. Fools.

Ildar wanted something that would take him centuries or millennia to acquire. Power, but power required many things.

She emptied her glass and reached for the bottle to refill it just as Makani returned.

"Noble-born, allow me," he said from the door, hastening to his spot across the bar from her.

She nodded and contemplated the young man.

Young? She smiled. Only three and a half millennia old. An adult at the peak of his prime. Well-endowed in all the ways she found fascinating, except for the blind spot he had towards the threat that Humans like Ildar might represent.

"When you look at Hasan Ildar, what do you see?" she asked pointedly.

He retreated into refilling his own glass for a moment before he spoke.

"Highly intelligent," Makani replied evenly, finally meeting her eyes. "Amoral and possibly unethical, depending on how you wished to parse and define such things. Willing to destroy his own kind for the promise of being elevated to some level of distinction among ours."

"Destroy?" she asked, leading him down certain paths to see what Security might have uncovered that they had not shared ere now.

"If Ildar creates a better species of Engine, what value do the rest of the Humans retain?" Makani asked seriously.

"Ah, but his little engine is sterile," Roselani countered. "We can Decant new copies of her, but she cannot be bred."

"The design cannot be that extreme," the man countered right back. "We have not interfered, as yet, because he gave us no reason to. Only your intercession has kept him from the Question up until now. Why will you not allow us to find the truth of his place in the conspiracy that had been uncovered?"

"She did something to me," Roselani replied. "That Engine. Inserted thoughts in my mind, at least once. Possibly twice, although you and I were both wearing shields that should have protected us at that last status meeting."

"And?" he asked in a carefully neutral voice.

She was still a cousin of the Emperor. Everyone walked on egg shells around her temper. That made the galaxy a better place.

Only Kincaide had ever looked at her and shrugged. But he had done his duty with sufficient verve that she would miss him, if it became necessary to destroy them all.

She had not enjoyed herself so much in bed in millennia.

And now, the Humans had enacted a conspiracy to escape The Gage. What would they do, if they thought they were free?

Yes. That was it.

"And what would the Humans do, if freed?" she asked. "What secrets or developments have they hidden from us, hoping to use them once this Human ship fled into the shadows of galactic space and hid from us? Ildar was to create a more powerful Engine, such that a single copy could carry a ship, instead of relying on five Humans or seventeen Mog. What else did he create?"

"We have all his research notes and Icons available," Makani's voice turned a little defensive.

"And you don't know, do you?" Roselani stuck the knife in just a prick, rather than eviscerating the man right now.

She still needed Security on her side. For now. Later, they might need to be purged for their failures to predict and thwart Ildar and especially Kincaide.

But only later.

"We have not brought in specialists to the case yet," he surrendered.

"Do so," she ordered, confident that her word would be taken as law now. "Bring in someone you trust. Alvar if possible, but someone we trust utterly and preferably not Human otherwise. If the Engine can manipulate the minds around her, what else can she do? More importantly, how much control is she exhibiting?"

"Noble-born?"

"She was in the room with you and I, when Ildar interviewed Prakash and Kataragama," Roselani said. "I ordered Kataragama to my bed chamber. Was that my mind or hers? Later, she and Kataragama returned and erased certain portions of my memory, but I cannot even guess what, except that they immediately went to Ildar and fooled him into thinking he had Indexed both of them. She is playing a long and dangerous game with all of us, Makani. Is she the spider at the center of this web?"

"Should we prevent Ildar from Decanting a fresh copy of his Engine?" the man asked.

"Absolutely, but do not make that obvious," Roselani ordered. "Have him dive deep into the design of the creature first, while explaining at a fairly scientific level, to one of our people we can find to follow the work. Get his attention focused on fixing all the places where she apparently broke free of his control that she could mentally assault him. We know now that he builds those blocks in. You can see it in his sex objects."

"Noble-born?" Makani asked, confused now.

"Each of them are copies that exist to maintain his household, and fornicate with him at any opportunity," Roselani replied. "They have been modified to worship him and to do anything they can to please him. I cannot imagine that he did not do something similar with the Engine, so send instructions for someone to study the design of the creatures we left behind. Perhaps even retain one or two of them when you dispose of the rest. He won't be needing them anytime soon, after all."

"It shall be as you command," Makani nodded.

"Do it now," she said.

Just like that, he was gone, leaving her to contemplate what Ildar really wanted. Or rather, what *power* would mean to a Human like that, and what steps he might take to grasp it.

And what she needed to do to thwart the man, while still keeping hold of all the threads he had spun, just so she could continue controlling things.

CHAPTER 57

Kincaide hadn't exactly *dismissed* Kali and Zhubin as suggested that they go bother someone else for a while, since nothing interesting would be happening at this time. Odtsetseg had stayed, but he suspected she just wanted the warmth of his mind around as she waited for her part in this grand performance to arrive.

"You could have gone out through one of the other warp-shrouds," she said, breaking the silence that had stretched as he studied the galactic map hanging mostly between them. "Velle might be the busiest port of entry into Al-Winoq."

"*The* busiest," Kincaide corrected her with a feral smile. "The one with the most traffic coming and going at any given time."

"Then why not head someplace like Aulil or Xyri?" she asked.

"Because every single port has the same fortress protecting it," Kincaide replied.

"That makes no sense," she said, her nose scrunched up so cute.

"It makes perfect sense," he countered. "They'll have to work three times as hard because of all the civilian traffic around there, fearing that we might slam into another Warp Voyager or a cargo transport of some sort, especially at the speed we'll be approaching."

"Stupid fast?" she asked, but now she had a smile.

"Hey, we were in the process of accelerating when something happened to kill our computer," he smirked. "Then we managed to shut down the engines, but haven't managed to flip the ship end for end so we can decelerate. We're dead meat, just floundering along, waiting for the big, bad Gage to come alongside and save us from our ineptitude."

"Until you get too close," she nodded.

"Yup," he sobered. "Suddenly roll on our side and light the engines enough to track us across the shroud itself, skidding on ice."

"How long will I have?" she asked, the fear finally present in her voice, like he had been expecting.

This would be her gig then.

"Depending on Dinushan, the current plan says we'll be in the zone for about seven seconds, even as big as it is," Kincaide said quietly. "All the engines will be shut down and everything routed into your generators at that point, so you'll be able to carry us up into warp-space and away."

"And if I fail?" she asked quietly.

"You won't," he reassured her. "I've known this version of you for long enough and I know how strong you are. How tough. You'll do fine."

"And if I fail?" she repeated, harder now. Not angry, but stressed. As expected.

"Then we're flying into deep space at high speed, on the wrong vector, with a shit-ton of inertia to kill before we can come to rest and try again. The Gage will be swarming all over us the second time and likely just blow *Dashavatara* apart rather than trying to capture us, like they'd originally planned. Odds are we all die short of the escape we'd hoped for."

For some reason, that seemed to calm the woman. But everyone had a different way to handle stress, and nobody had ever really put anything heavy on her shoulders.

Nobody but him. Which was why they paid him the big credits. Or something. This job was never going to make him rich. Zhubin and Ildar were both too cheap.

And then again, they'd offered him the one coin guaranteed to turn his head.

Sticking his finger in the Gage's eye.

"And you believe I can do this," she said, not even asking so much as observing.

"I do," Kincaide agreed. "I think you could make Zhubin look like a piker for toughness, if you wanted to. Couple of the wives would likely give you a run for the money, but not the rest of us."

"Why is that?" she asked, cocking her head in confusion now.

"I suspect partly because as you've pointed out, you aren't truly Human," Kincaide offered softly. "They are, but nobody would believe them without a gene scan, so they've had to be entirely self-sufficient since they killed that fool. Dipshit designed you to be able to carry a Warp Voyager all by yourself, instead of sharing the load with a handful of friends. That requires power, but it also requires toughness far in excess of anything most of the crew have ever had to face."

"Most?" she asked, a tease on her face now. A twinkle in those brown, Mongolian eyes.

"Zhubin and I might have spent a few decades each dancing with the Gage and the Alvar," he suggested. "With prices on our heads if our real names ever came out."

"You don't even think of yourself by any other name than Kincaide," she said. "Even in your dreams."

"I put that guy away a long time ago, Odtsetseg," he grimaced. "Until I see Nayani again, he can stay hidden and Kincaide Kataragama is the mask I'll wear."

"You believe you'll meet her in hell?" Odtsetseg asked. "Life after death or something?"

"Without that, the entire universe is just random chaos and we have no meaning we can attach to anything," he replied. "Static that seems to form patterns, but it is all a lie. An old man like me needs to find some comfort in what will come after I die."

"As opposed to the ones who intend to live forever?" Odtsetseg pressed.

"Men like Ildar live in fear that there is nothing after death except entropy," he offered. "Or worse, that they're going to go to a hell where the Dark One measures their entire life and then matches it with the sorts of retributive payback that they deserve. And he does."

"But you don't?" she asked, her head cocked again.

They'd never really gotten into the religious, philosophical discussions, but until recently she had just been a tool of Hasan Ildar. It wasn't until the woman got lost in his head that she understood she could be more.

But hey, they were all punk teenagers at one point. Kincaide didn't figure his own life was all that good of an example, except for mistakes that hadn't been terminal.

"Oh, I expect to be in hell," Kincaide corrected her. "All the bad things I've done would preclude me going to one of the heavens from a Creator who actually loved us. Given the outcomes, only the Alvar appear to have a God. Or their pantheon conquered everyone else's. And you don't even want to ask the Christians or the Muslims what they think."

"But you'll have Nayani," Odtsetseg murmured.

And he understood finally. He had someone to look forward to. Him, who had lived a largely monastic life for twenty-plus years, except for occasional stops in brothels when the need was too great.

At least he'd known that kind of a love.

Odtsetseg didn't have anything like it to look forward to. No sudden eruption of hormones that lit up all her girly bits, because Ildar had made sure to padlock them shut.

All the other people on this crew feared her. Even the ones that worshiped her as a goddess.

Everybody but him.

Kincaide reached a hand across the desk and she grabbed it like a lifesuit in a vacuum alarm.

"You got me," he murmured back, hoping it would be enough.

Step-daughter, as it were, but he could be there when she needed someone.

And maybe someone would come along one of these days and see the woman trapped inside the asexual body.

Not everything had to be about penetration, after all.

She squeezed his hand almost hard enough to hurt, but it probably pained her thin fingers even more. He'd at least been out there and done things.

She was a pretty princess locked in a castle awaiting a prince who might be too stupid to come rescue her. Kincaide wondered how many asses he needed to kick before everyone else got over themselves and saw her like he did.

"All of them," she said with a grin.

There were tears in her eyes, but not yet running down her face. He forgot that skin on skin contact let her almost step into his mind and listen to him.

But she had him.

"I have you," Odtsetseg agreed.

The moment stretched out.

"Kincaide, I might need you down here," Hanishka called in a tense voice.

He nodded to his Star Flower and they both rose. She wiped her eyes before she turned, so he was around the desk and on the platform first.

Down six steps to the bridge and looking around.

"Talk to me," he said to the crew of taut faces.

"The ones in front of us have gone into turnover," Hanishka said. "They're aiming to match us for velocity."

"Can they catch us before we get to the shroud?" Kincaide asked.

"It's going to be tight," she grimaced.

He turned to Reyhan now.

"Tell Kali and Zhubin," Kincaide began. "I think it's time to roll our Trojan horse into position."

CHAPTER 58

Roselani had rested. Alone. Makani had appeared amenable. Ildar fearful. Both left her warm with potential, but she had chosen to merely rest.

Security still believed that they had the situation under control. She might be seen as overly emotional and perhaps damage her social standing if Kincaide was taken as easily as Gage officers suggested they would, but she still suspected that he would elude all of them.

Personal morning now. The yacht was on her personal time, so everyone was in motion when she arose, despite having worked long shifts into the night as the chase unfolded. Nothing had happened that had required anyone to awaken her, which was good.

She was down on the command deck now, several floors beneath her observation deck that ran most of the length of the ship with transparent roof and walls. There were no stars down here. Just consoles and controls manned by a strictly Alvar crew. A highly competent one, too, since she could afford excellence in her employees.

The Commander was on station, standing next to a helmsman or someone that actually flew the yacht directly. Makani had slept late some, obviously, as had Ildar, so she enjoyed her time as though today was just another cruise out to enjoy herself away from her palace and her staff for a few days or weeks.

She didn't believe it for a moment, but it made a nice conceit.

"Where is *Dashavatara*?" she asked, standing to one side as everyone settled back down from jumping up as she entered the room.

"He had stopped dead in space for roughly three hours at a point with no value we have been able to identify at this time, Noble-born," her Commander replied diffidently.

She had hired the man for his ability to step from professional to invisible and back in a heartbeat. She focused her intensity on him now.

"No value?" she confirmed.

"There are no asteroids, comets, or artificial structures anywhere remotely close to those coordinates, according to the sailing log," the man nodded. Sharp. Crisp. Professional.

A little boring in bed, but she wouldn't be requiring his services on this trip. She had Makani for now. Ildar, if she wanted to torture the Human, and the crew of a Warp Voyager later if she was right about Kincaide.

And she had known that Human's touch, so Roselani did not believe for an instant that he would throw everything away on such a meaningless gesture as all this.

Kincaide had a plan. And Roselani suspected it was a good one. She had taken his measure, at least in important ways.

Kincaide Kataragama made an excellent foe for now.

"Rouse the Security Administrator and have him attend me in the lounge shortly," Roselani ordered someone within reach. Anyone would do and they were all good enough at their jobs to be hired.

She had a suspicion, but did not wish to voice it here.

"Where are they now?" she asked the Commander.

His grimace was telling. Bearer of bad news seeking the least provocative words, perhaps.

"The ship is currently accelerating madly towards the warp-shroud port for Velle," he finally just gave up and uttered baldly.

"Velle?" Roselani asked, shocked almost witless.

Was there a dumber place to try your luck than the largest concentration of Gage warships in the system?

Then a second thought struck her.

"Accelerating madly?" she confirmed.

"Essentially, Noble-born," he nodded carefully. "The ship is already running several times faster than one would expect, to the point that their ability to maneuver around obstacles is threatened. And their engines had not shut down as one would expect. Plus, they appear to have stopped emitting most signals and sensory pulses. If I didn't know better, I would have thought the ship had suffered some sort of systems failure in their primary circuitry and was right now hurtling out of control. That might prove a problem if they wish to achieve turnover to decelerate later. Also, there was a brief transmission received that seemed to suggest that Doctor Ildar, our guest, was somehow present aboard the vessel, but that has not been given any credence once we confirmed his presence here."

Shit. Had Ildar actually done it, after all?

She hadn't really believed that Kincaide would fall for such a stupid trick. Had she overestimated the man based on his bedroom skills? He had struck her as so much cooler and more prepared. Able to react to any situation. Always prepared.

Still, something just didn't ring true, though she could not place her finger on it.

Kincaide was a Human of unexpected depths, and she wondered if she had nearly fallen into the same intellectual trap as the Commander had. And this man had no knowledge of what Ildar had done, so that suggested that other officers would feel the same way. Perhaps all of Security.

"Set course for the Velle station," she decided. "Rouse Ildar and have him join Southavilay and me in the lounge immediately."

She withdrew and let her crew do their job.

Something wasn't right.

What had Kincaide done?

CHAPTER 59

Odtsetseg didn't understand everything that was going on, but trusted Kincaide. He had let her inside his mind, and wasn't just putting up a brave face before the tempest. He truly believed that they could pull it all off.

She had to trust him.

"We ready?" Kincaide asked Reyhan Herath.

She took up a spot on Kincaide's opposite side from the man with the demonic sideburns. Outwardly, it might look like Kincaide needed to protect her from the man. Or the others.

It was a silly fear, but she recognized it for what it was and smiled to herself.

"I have logically isolated everything from that section of the circuitry and backed up the entire block of code so we can restore clean copies," Herath said with a drawl that almost sounded angry as much as resigned. "Think you're being too cute, personally, but you're in charge, Kincaide."

"And I'm a mean son of a bitch," the Foreman smiled as he looked around. "This lets us throw them off. Plus, if I didn't think you couldn't undo it, I would never have asked for this, Reyhan."

She liked the way those words puffed the man's ego up a little. Odtsetseg barely understood true Humans. Most of the time, they were just rough oil paintings of swirling emotions that bled together and threatened to overwhelm her, but right now this bridge was calm and certain in ways she hadn't seen in days.

"Fine," Herath groused, but it was good-natured.

The Chairman and Kali the Four-Armed War Goddess both arrived together, so she suspected that they had gone forward to the salon to wait. Neither looked flushed, but Kali would not suffer the personal touch of anyone, lest her dormant programming kick in, so they had to have just sat and chatted about whatever.

Still, that was what it meant to live in fear.

"Whenever you're ready," Herath said with an exasperated sigh that didn't really mask his amusement at the whole situation.

She watched Kincaide turn his attention to Daniel, the computer ghost who always confused her until she remembered that he wasn't real, so she didn't have to block any emotions from the being.

"Computer, this is Foreman Kincaide Kataragama," he said firmly. "Access the *Life II* project file and display the contents here."

Odtsetseg listened as Kincaide kept his tremors inside.

Around them, the room's lights flickered strangely for a moment, but then returned to normal.

Daniel melted. It was weird watching the image go through all manner of convulsions that she didn't have to listen to. Didn't need to filter out as the man screamed silently.

A few moments later, the image returned.

This time it was Hasan Ildar.

With that stupid beret and the Van Dyke he wore as a mark of intellect. Or something.

"Good evening, Kataragama. Your Computer Personality for Today —and every day from now on—is me."

Everyone else jumped, but Kincaide seemed to mentally shrug at the projection.

"Really?" he asked in a sarcastic drawl.

"Apparently, you've discovered one of my Encyclopedia fail-safes," Ildar said with a snide superiority somehow perfectly replicated from the flesh. "But I've built in others—such as programming my consciousness into the system itself—to be triggered by your request for the nonexistent *Project Life II* file."

Odtsetseg watched the projection look around the bridge with a cruel eye as everyone held their breath.

"Obviously, you've betrayed me and left my body behind to die with those blue scum, but I will still remain with you forever," Ildar continued in a haughty tone. "My consciousness has been fully integrated into each and every one of these circuits. To get rid of me you'll have to shut down the entire system."

Kincaide just laughed now, which seemed to enrage the bald scientist ghost all the more.

"Every time you will need to access your Encyclopedia, I will be the one who will respond," Ildar snarled coldly as everyone cringed. Almost everyone.

Odtsetseg studied Kincaide and he had not budged mentally. Interestingly, nor had Reyhan.

"You cannot rid the system of my presence without destroying it," Ildar continued with a diabolical laugh. "Unless you wish to sacrifice everything. Then you will be truly doomed."

"Maybe," Kincaide said brightly. "But you seemed to have forgotten something. Not that I'm all that surprised, knowing you."

"What?" the Computer Personality of Hasan Ildar snapped angrily.

"You are now integrated into a system designed to serve this ship and its crew, Ildar," Kincaide laughed. "Computer, lower the current temperature in the bridge compartment by three tenths of a degree and hold it there for the next five hours."

Ildar's face turned into the most hideous snarl as something seemed to invisibly grab him by the neck and squeeze.

"Stand by," Ildar said in a much more professional and friendly voice than Odtsetseg could ever remember coming from the man's mouth as his face cleared. "Temperature adjustments have been completed. Please allow twenty minutes for the life support system to achieve equilibrium."

Kincaide looked around at everyone and smiled so broadly that she thought his face might crack.

"So he reskinned the Computer Personality of the Day," the Foreman laughed. "Big deal. I was going to ask Reyhan to do that anyway. Oh, I almost forgot."

She found herself drawn closer to Kincaide as he turned away from her, so she leaned forward to watch Herath's face. Another evil grin unlike the man's normal countenance.

"Okay, Reyhan, go ahead and restore most of the files, but keep Ildar in place if you can," Kincaide laughed. Around them, others unfroze from their latent panic as they came to understand what the two men had done. "Oh, and tomorrow I'd like you to gender-swap him into a female. We'll keep the look Tartar for now, but make sure she's got big tits and a low-cut top she's constantly at risk of falling out of."

"You can't do that," Ildar said, his voice started out loudly but immediately modulating down to a mere spoken word, even as hard as his face scrunched up in fury.

Kincaide turned to the projection and Odtsetseg caught her breath.

She'd been inside his mind. In his dreams even.

Seen him joyous. Depressed. Almost suicidal. Irritated. Happy. Depressed.

At Roselani Thammavongsa's palace, she had seen him triumphant. At Ildar's lab consumed with worry about her.

In many places, the warm love that kept her chin up.

She had never seen him turn to this cold, vicious, killing machine. It was like a longsword carved out of frozen nitrogen and honed down to an edge only three molecules thick.

"I can do anything I want to you, Hasan Ildar," Kincaide said in a voice like the darkness between stars. "You serve me, and always will. You chose to put yourself here, presumably expecting that we would rather destroy you and our Information Systems rather than allow you to remain in our lives."

He took a quiet breath and Odtsetseg could hear hearts beating around her in the stillness.

"I'm rather looking forward to torturing this version of you, Ildar," Kincaide concluded. "I just wish there was some way for you to communicate yourself to the real man when I was done."

The Computer Personality was designed to serve the crew. But the look of abject horror on the projection's face was telling. Ildar really had put his personality in there, but only now discovered that he was doomed to be Kincaide Kataragama's servant.

And hers.

Odtsetseg caught her breath and the two men close by turned to her with sudden concern on their faces. Even Reyhan had moved beyond his usual antagonism as he watched her.

This Ildar had to serve *her*.

God, reduced to *less* than nothing.

Odtsetseg waved a hand at the two men as they moved in her direction with concern.

"Computer," she said in a wavering voice. "Contact the forward wardroom and ask them to deliver to me some Valerian chai with organic cloves."

Ildar's face wavered in and out of a snarl for a long moment before it returned to utter calmness.

"Yes, ma'am," he said in that quiet, reserved voice that the Computer Personality of the Day did.

"You okay?" Kincaide asked quietly as she remembered to breathe.

"He's not God anymore."

CHAPTER 60

Hasan had returned to the lounge decorated in *Advanced Alvar Sexual Perversions*. At least he was still a favored guest, as someone had delivered a plate of breakfast and coffee for him just as he joined the Security Gigolo and they both awaited the blue bitch.

Hasan ate at a flipped-down side table as an excuse not to make small talk. The Gigolo sipped the Alvar equivalent of coffee and stopped asking questions after a little while.

They waited in a tense silence. Hasan took the moment to shovel food into his mouth, aware that the woman would be here soon enough and have some level of stupid demands to make on his time.

Hopefully, she was at least conscious enough to turn him loose to fixing the Engine. He had a few theories as to what those two traitors must have done to her to break the creature, but he needed to run those ideas through a whole series of tests to see if the logic tree held.

Somewhere, part of his design that he had not foreseen had gone wrong. That was never a good thing. Especially not as it exposed him to the blues at a time when he was not yet prepared to commit xenocide.

That was still coming, just much later.

Hasan hurriedly completed his breakfast and even contemplated approaching the punk in order to get some coffee from the machine behind him, but the woman's arrival interrupted. He wouldn't say *saved him*, but maybe that was close enough.

She took up her accustomed spot at the bar on the tall stool. Hasan remained in his low chair at the side table. Disengaged, but involved.

About how he would have preferred to deal with these people.

"*Dashavatara* stopped at a spot in empty space for several hours," she began without even a hello. Her eyes were focused on the gigolo, instead of Hasan, so he watched them both.

The Security agent was confused. As he should be. Those people were thugs with batons, not intellectuals.

"At this time, there are no indications that anything exists at those coordinates to give the ship any reason to pause," she continued.

"Pause?" Hasan felt compelled to ask.

"The ship is in motion again," she turned to him now with a seductive smile that threatened the breakfast he had just eaten. "Their current course aims them at Velle Station."

You people are morons. Unable to even guess that MAYBE Kataragama has a plan.

But he didn't say that out loud. Probably thought it loud enough, from the way her smile broadened.

She had gone through that line of logic already, apparently.

"The ship appears to be out of control," Lady Thammavongsa offered. "They have been accelerating beyond normal, safe cruising velocities, and all external scanners have apparently been shut down."

He must have muttered the profanity louder than he thought, as the gigolo turned this way too now.

Hasan shrugged.

"I honestly didn't believe that would work," he offered weakly. "Or rather, that they would be so incredibly stupid as to fall for such an obvious trap."

"So the chase is functionally over?" the man asked in a bright, shiny, useless kind of voice. "They are disabled and we should instead concentrate on capturing them?"

She was watching him. There was no seduction in that woman's eyes now.

Bloodlust maybe, but that was as close as it probably got to the real thing.

"So why would they stop in the middle of nowhere?" the woman asked.

She was facing him, but asking in a rhetorical type of tone that he might ignore if he chose.

However, she seemed to be weighing his fate right now. And he had the need to outlive everyone on this ship right now, even if they had to die of old age for him to accomplish that.

Besides, he knew. There could only be one answer.

He had been prepared to handle it in an entirely different manner, when the time came. One of the last containers loaded onto the ship, as part of the next round of deliveries.

Which was why they'd had to move now. Why had he not seen that?

Damn it.

"Doctor?" she asked, intruding on his rage.

"They stopped to pick something up," he growled, finally understanding the depths to which those two men had plunged. The scale of betrayal they had enacted, as well as how far back they must have been planning this. "I can hazard a few guesses, but there are not that many things valuable enough not to have smuggled them aboard the ship innocently while it was in the repair dock."

"Such as?" the Security punk asked now, his voice a little hot.

Perhaps he didn't like being shown up by a mere Human? Pity.

"They have food and consumable supplies for a long voyage," Hasan let his voice return to normal. This was not the time for rage or innuendo. Now, he needed to plan for eternity, preferably with the heads of Prakash and Kataragama flensed of flesh, sealed in enamel, and impaled on spikes in his lab as a reminder and a warning. "The one thing that the ship would need in order to be a threat would be a mini-Catalogue."

"But they have an Encyclopedia," the man countered, probably still raging inside while only a little of it leaked out.

"And an Encyclopedia is not a Catalogue, because it has no Icons," Hasan reminded the fool. "We had the hardware to Index and Decant, but not the Catalogue of people that we would be delivering to that forward arms depot. Would have been delivering. That was to be picked up at the Salou Port fortress."

"You suspect that they picked up a different package?" the woman purred at him.

Hasan shrugged again. He needed to make this load of horseshit believable.

"You asked for a theory," he replied. "Whatever it was, it has to be something of great value. Something that they didn't trust being carried on a tug in the Glide, where it might be stopped and inspected. What else might be that valuable, Noble-born?"

She nodded. Perhaps satisfied for now.

One could hope that her demands on him would be merely intellectual. He was, after all, smarter than both of them put together.

"So now the ship is careening out of control, to all appearances," she continued.

"Appearances, Noble-born?" the man asked.

Hasan wasn't fooled. She was using him, a mere Human, to make Security look stupid.

More stupid. They were already morons with billy clubs.

"The thing Doctor Ildar suggested to them would have caused the ship to shut down," she smiled at both of them. Almost tauntingly. "Does that not describe their current behavior? Accelerating madly without scanners in front of them, as though racing to their dooms? I expect them to shut the engines down soon and just coast, still aimed at the Velle Port Station. Or at least close enough that they could suddenly maneuver into the warp-shroud."

"But at those speeds, they would hardly have a chance to transition, Noble-born," the man seemed appalled now. "One must decelerate to navigational speeds before making the jump to warp-space."

"Not if you are running for your life," she said simply.

Then the bitch turned to smile at him.

"How long would it take to acquire a bootleg container of Icons, Doctor Ildar?" she asked innocently.

That question had **TRAP** in capital letters tattooed across the face of it, and he wasn't about to bite. She didn't seem to be laying the trap for him, so much as inducing him to be her co-conspirator in something else. Something aimed at undermining Security.

Not that he minded, as long as he remained free to pursue his research and his dreams of conquest.

Hasan shrugged at the woman. At this rate, he was going to be quite adept at playing the fool. Or her foil.

"You would need to tell me, Noble-born," Hasan smiled. "I have never considered how hard it might be to break into those systems and somehow download the necessary records to a portable Catalogue without alerting Security to what was going on."

Oh, hell, let's play this to the hilt. I don't like you anyway.

He turned to the gigolo and pasted an innocent smile on his face.

"So I have seen individual Icons," Hasan said to the man simply, holding out a hand palm up. "Do you ever store Humans on larger devices, such that they are off-line from the Catalogue itself? Perhaps stored physically in a warehouse somewhere, where a thief merely needed to break through a mechanical lock and bring along their own portable datacube to load up from whatever they found?"

He already knew that Alvar turned umber when they flushed. Apparently, they also turned nearly white when the situation was right. The man's face paled so far that Hasan wondered if he would pass out on his feet and fall over in a noisy lump, hopefully bashing his head against something heavy and sharp and gouging his brain out on the way down.

But that was petty.

It wasn't like Hasan hadn't just described *EXACTLY* what he had paid someone to do. Probably Kataragama and Prakash had done the same, since his package was still in transit, needing to be quietly destroyed when nobody was looking.

Security worried about the Catalogue itself. They never considered the off-line backups stored around the Al-Winoq system. Physical datasets on portable media.

It was a pleasant joy, watching Security Administrator Makani Southavilay struggle to contain his fear in front of the woman. And then rage. Finally acceptance, having passed through the entire stages of grief over the course of ten seconds or so.

She split her superior smile between Hasan as a particularly apt student and the gigolo as a fool needing a good smack upside the head.

Yes, it was his role to be the unindicted co-conspirator with this woman. So be it.

That was acceptable for now. She would get him to Prakash and Kataragama. Close enough to destroy them, anyway.

The woman ignored the punk now and turned an innocent smile on Hasan. Not that he was fooled in the slightest.

"So what might such a ship do, Doctor Ildar?" she asked. "If they had a shipping container of Humans to Decant, equipment to build and upgrade an arms depot colony, and were running for their lives from the Alvar and The Gage?"

Hasan let that question stew for a moment. He still didn't understand what this woman's game was, but she was obviously up to something. Probably petty and cruel, which was why they might be able to get along together, at least long enough to succeed at this mission.

"Assuming many things, including their ability to escape from Al-Winoq, I wonder if they could start a Human colony somewhere," Hasan offered blandly, just to watch the gigolo's eyes bulge out.

They did remain in his skull. It had looked close for a moment.

"But why would a random Human colony be such a bad thing?" Hasan asked, sticking the knife in a little deeper and twisting it a hair.

"They do have their own Engine," the woman offered innocently. "Presumably, they also have the technical capacity to build more ships later and perhaps explore and expand to more than one colony."

"Interesting," Hasan studied her, wondering what game she was playing now. This had to rate close to the top of all Alvar night terrors, after all. "A Human equivalent to The Gage, located off in some quiet corner of the galaxy?"

"Could they escape the galaxy itself?" Lady Thammavongsa asked now.

Hasan felt a tightness creep into his stomach as he finally understood why she wanted him present.

If those two could escape the galaxy itself, he'd never catch them. And in a few thousand years, they might have grown into the thing he had originally intended to rule, just about the time he would be ready to conquer The Gage and exterminate the Alvar.

A Human Star Empire that was at least as powerful as The Gage, and utterly inimical.

And he would probably be the closest equivalent to Satan in their religious upbringing.

Hasan took a deep breath to control his emotions. She might be smarter than he had imagined. With any luck, her carnal needs would overwhelm everything else eventually and he could go back to research in obscurity.

"There are two schools of thought, Noble-born," Hasan explained in a careful, wary voice. "One is that warp-space itself is a function of the way a galaxy forms. The warp-shroud gaps formed by solar systems mean that you cannot go beyond the edge of the galactic gravitational lens and escape from warp-space. At present, that is the ascendant theory among Alvar scholars."

"And the alternative?" she pressed, even going to far as to lean towards him in ways that made her naked breast sway distinctly in his direction, her nipple seeming to lengthen.

As though they should have a threesome right here in the lounge. Or perhaps just the two of them, with the gigolo forced to watch as penance for his arrogance at underestimating Hasan Ildar and the two Humans in command of *Dashavatara*.

That alone might almost make it worthwhile. He had never liked Security.

Still, ick.

"The alternative theory is that all solar systems form such rifts, Noble-born," Hasan smiled at her and her games with the other man. "That one merely has to take the immense time to cross between galaxies and you will find escape points so distant that you might never be found. You might be safe for millennia if an Alvar ship fears crossing that gulf because they might not be able to descend into real space over there."

"Are there many galaxies close?" she pressed, voice wispy, almost sounding like a groupie now. Or one of his Chuns. Innocent and breathless and hanging on his words.

It was good to know that she understood such behavior. That would make it easier later, when it was no longer her choice in the matter.

"The true galaxies are distant," Hasan lectured now. "But there are any number of smaller clusters much closer. Tens of millions of stars to pick from, rather than billions. But probably sufficient for Humans to hide and build their strength."

And then she dropped the innocent mask and turned the face of a deadly crone on the gigolo. The whiplash was so hard that Hasan nearly hurt himself recoiling.

"So all of this is merest speculation, Southavilay," she said in a cold, cruel voice. "The fugitive Humans might yet be caught like flies in your web. You will not communicate what you know to your superiors."

"Noble-born?" he squeaked.

"If I am wrong, only you will know it, Makani," she promised in a voice like death. "I do not believe that I am wrong. If they escape you at Velle station, you will tell your superiors everything that we just discussed, but only then. At that time, you will compel them to supply me with the necessary ship and support to chase the Humans to the very gates of hell itself, to keep them from eventually destroying The Gage."

"They cannot do that," the man replied, but it was a weak and fearful tone.

"Are you willing to bet the entire Empire on that?" she asked.

She turned his way and Hasan shared her smile.

The punk might have stopped breathing as the implications became clear.

But for now, Hasan let it all go.

It would take him millennia, but eventually he would be successful. This bitch was going to help.

CHAPTER 61

Kincaide studied the bridge. Everyone was still holding on well, in spite of the risks and stress. Dinushan and Hanishka had been looking a little frazzled, but they'd each been able to take a quick catnap while others watched the boards.

At this speed, there wasn't much anybody could do. Any vessel wanting to engage them in combat would have to match vectors, which was just about impossible given the limited space requirements. The ships that had been coming at them from Velle Station originally had had to go into hard turnover and decelerate in order to even have a chance, and *Dashavatara* had still gone by them like a road runner on a straightaway when they had.

It was a stern chase now, with more than a dozen Warp Voyagers and Killships strung out behind them like pearls on a string. At some point, those commanders would have to go into turnover if they didn't want to end up blowing right out past the edge of the system.

Risky flying, because out there was where you encountered comets and iceballs. Mostly slush, but at these speeds it would be like flying into a planet anyway.

The Gage officers were not generally suicidal. Just xenocidal.

Kincaide could understand. He shared that outlook at times.

Zhubin stirred from where he'd been reading a screen across the square and looked up. Kali and Odtsetseg had gone aft to eat something so they would be ready when the next phase came.

Reyhan had even slipped into Kincaide's office to take a quick nap.

Computer Personality Hasan could handle most things, and all he did was bitch and grouse under his voice while doing so. Hopefully, the Alvar chasing them had caught that brief message that suggested Hasan was in control of the ship and would leave well enough alone for now.

After all, *Dashavatara* would come barreling into range of Velle Station traffic in about six hours. No reason to try to intercept them before then, as nobody would be able to make that shift.

Easier to just wait.

"Think they fell for it?" Zhubin asked in a quiet voice as he stepped close.

"Everyone is just chasing us right now," Kincaide replied. "The ones from Aulil and Xyri stations are actually doing better than the Velle ships, but they didn't have to do anything except maintain velocity and maybe speed up a little."

"Can they catch us?" Zhubin asked, a little concerned now.

"Maybe they thought so originally," Kincaide grinned. "Dinushan was using the maneuvering thrusters randomly to introduce a little drift that's not obvious from the range they had to scan at. Nobody is hard pinging us like they would have to in order to vector down, so if a ship went silent and tried, he'd be way off-line before he realized it. At that point, vector physics works in our favor."

"Any more threats from the other Ildar?" Zhubin asked.

"No, and that's what concerns me," Kincaide said. "He was aboard a vessel that flags as Roselani's personal yacht."

"Roselani?"

"Lady Thammavongsa," Kincaide corrected himself. "Our Nemesis, if anybody over there rates that high."

"You think she does?" Zhubin turned now to face him, curiosity rather than anything else on his face.

"She's smart, Zhubin," Kincaide said. "Whatever else, there's a brain inside that pretty skull of hers and she's reacting faster than the rest of them should have. Whether that's Ildar feeding her tidbits or just the woman guessing well enough by herself, it's something to be concerned about."

"Change anything?" the Chairman asked.

"We're prepared for a long, hard run to Velle and then Gouza before we start falling off their scanners," Kincaide said. "If she's that engaged, does she have them prep a Warp Voyager with all the supplies they need to really give us a challenge? Long, hard, stern chase? Most ships aren't kept at that level of readiness because trips on a Warp Voyager are generally planned months or even years in advance. She'd a wild card and I don't like it. Plus, she's not in the mess pursuing us. I caught a beacon that indicates she's going straight to Velle Station, but not fast enough to get there before we do."

"Not part of the after-action cleanup?" Prakash pressed now.

"Not just part, maybe," Kincaide suggested. "Wonder if this is personal."

"Personal?"

"Odtsetseg and I went to her palace before we took down the good doctor," Kincaide reminded the man. "If they have him along, then they know she did something to the man, but not necessarily what. That leads back to asking what we might have done to Roselani that they need to know about."

"You use her first name," Zhubin observed.

"We didn't exactly limit things to strictly being penpals, Zhubin," Kincaide turned more towards the man and scowled. "It got a lot more personal than that."

"Regrets?" Zhubin retreated just a little, at least emotionally. Like not wanting to set him off right now.

Bit late for that, but what the hell.

"She was interesting in bed," Kincaide replied. "She had needs and approached them like a grown-up. I was able to bring her to the point she needed. She did the same for me. If we were the same species, nobody would have even commented. That should have been sufficient and we'd never see each other again after that."

"And now you have a jilted lover chasing you?" he asked.

Kincaide looked up hard, but the man was grinning.

"Even The Gage hath no fury like a woman scorned," Kincaide reminded him, also finding something of a grin. "But that one might be more dangerous than Ildar."

"How so?"

"She's Alvar, Prakash," Kincaide said. "We don't any of us know that much about the species. She's obviously powerful and rich. Now, we discover that she might be smarter than we thought. Introduces risk to an already-fraught plan."

"But she can't stop us," Zhubin said. "You said so yourself."

"Stopping us at Velle Station was never an option," Kincaide countered. "Maybe they killed us on the run in. Maybe we screwed up and missed the warp-shroud. Or Odtsetseg wasn't able to get us through. Something else. That's not the problem."

"Next month," Zhubin nodded.

"Next month," Kincaide agreed. "We were set to have time to explore some of the quieter corners of Gage Space and pick out a spot where they might not think to look for us. That's a lot harder when I have an angry Warp Voyager riding on my ass because they were able to load and launch in hours instead of days or weeks. We're still going to be faster through warp-space on account of our lower mass index, but not that much faster."

"Any chance we could kill her before we left?" Zhubin asked sincerely.

"If I had any sort of weapon that would let me fire a cloud of ball bearings into her flight path, our combined velocity would probably be enough if she's just in a pleasure yacht and not a purpose-built warship," Kincaide said. "Have considered tasking Hanishka and her crew of goofball killers with coming up with something for later. Space is huge, but if someone is chasing us, that limits the places they can fly, which means we can drop things in front of them."

"Old fashioned mines?" Zhubin smiled now. "Like maritime ships used to do?"

"Find me enough fissionables or anti-matter and tell me that a Warp Voyager sailing along with only navigational shields up wouldn't get his teeth kicked in."

"I will bring it up at the next Board of Directors meeting," the Chairman grinned. "You can make a presentation and we'll vote on resource allocation readjustments."

"Yeah, but we've got to get out of Al-Winoq first, and then get clear of Roselani after that," Kincaide grinned back, but it was forced.

"I have faith in you, Kincaide," the man said.

Kincaide wished he shared that. Roselani being involved upped the stakes considerably.

CHAPTER 62

Kali watched the Human woman eat, remembering that for all her composure, Odtsetseg was still just a teenager. She had not been exposed to the sorts of formal dining situations where one entertained the wealthy and powerful, with all the sundry small talk and linguistic games.

Still, she did not seem timid.

Reserved, perhaps.

Highly intelligent, but possessed of a raw telepathic power so great that the entire ship was supposedly a dance hall constantly filled with screaming voices.

They had eaten a subdued dinner together, and now had dessert, a kind of cream pudding covered over with a caramel sauce that the chef seemed quite pleased with. And it was exceptional, but Kali had been used to either one of her sisters cooking or someone ordering food for delivery. Nothing freshly cooked by a proper chef and plated hot.

Obviously, the crew was trying to impress her.

Thankfully, the two of them had a small room to themselves, off the main banquet room.

Odtsetseg looked up at her now over their spoons.

"You were apparently quite loud in your defense of total strangers," Kali began, watching the young woman's eyes and wondering what a telepath saw.

"I found it necessary," Odtsetseg replied, slurping at her custard.

"Necessary?"

326

The youngster took a final bite and put her spoon down. Kali still had half of hers, but she had been eating slower.

"Understand that most of this crew were selected by a trio of men best described as Human-supremacists," the telepath said. "At least originally. Hasan Ildar absolutely, then Zhubin Prakash and Kincaide in declining virulence. In addition, Ildar is a racist pig as well as a sexist. He would have personally preferred an entire crew of Central Asian Male Tartars like himself, with women only along as sex objects, if he could manage that. There aren't that many of his kind, for a variety of reasons, so he settled for genes from the Indian Subcontinent, although largely filtered through Boston Dome rather than Chennai."

"What about Tashkent?" Kali asked, intrigued.

She'd heard some of this through Kataragama's eyes, and more from Prakash, but Odtsetseg was unique. She didn't even have a last name, so she was more like the Wives that way.

"Apparently too many Siberians and Arabs were rounded up at Tashkent," Odtsetseg laughed. "He originally came from that Dome, and hated them all. Refused to ever work with anyone from Tashkent. I got the impression that if he was allowed to destroy exactly one of the Human domes by venting it to space, he would have picked Tashkent over even Tianjin."

"Then how did he end up with you?" Kali asked, intrigued now by the woman's apparent openness.

But then, the telepath could probably read her thoughts.

"Mostly I only read sentiments," the woman interrupted. "It hurts to get deep inside someone's mind. I've been watching the palette of your emotions instead."

"Hurts?" Kali was surprised.

"Most people are composed of regret at all the mistakes they have ever made," Odtsetseg said plainly. "Very few people have come to peace with themselves and decided to be happy, as opposed to suffering a daily misery."

"And Prakash and Kataragama?" Kali asked as the conversation kept meandering different, fascinating places.

But then, Goaulda had designed her to live forever, to fuck and converse, and nobody knew how long Odtsetseg might have. If she lived a normal life, she would be around long after the two men had died.

"Prakash had training to shield his mind when he served The

Gage," the telepath replied. "I find it hard to get any reading off the man at all, and even then I have to work hard at it. Kincaide is different."

"Different?" Kali pressed. "How so?"

"He has let me see all of his mind, more than once," Odtsetseg's voice fell to a whisper. "We have a relationship where he thinks of me as a step-daughter he only met as an adult. And he loves me for me."

"But you have no physical relationship with anyone?" Kali mused.

In that, she was another of the Wives. Forever celibate. Fear on Kali's case. Programming for Odtsetseg.

"And I do not miss that which I have never felt," she said. "I can see it in other minds around me, but there are few people who have found love as the poets and playwrights describe it."

"Why is that, do you suppose?" Kali cocked her head, amazed at how smart and educated this woman seemed to be.

"Being a successful rebel requires you to live a double life," Odtsetseg nodded. "Kincaide had it with Nayani, before she was killed by the Alvar, but it is extremely rare. Most people have to keep everyone at a distance, so they can have superficial love and physicality, but nothing deeper."

Kali nodded.

"We were...I was asking about Ildar and how he ended up with a Mongolian template, if he hates everyone but the Tartar so much," she circled back.

"When he started, the man had a particular design in mind," the telepath said, leaning back now to study something on the far wall instead of Kali's face.

Kali took a bite of the flan and listened with her mind to the woman's tones as she described her former god.

"When he was looking through the Catalogue, he found my template and decided that it would give him the most flexibility," Odtsetseg continued. "Plus, he already hated East Asians, so I'm sure he enjoyed torturing all the various versions of my soul in order to cross-mate me with an octopus. I became a substitute for Tashkent Dome. Then there are all the other things he inserted. It was another way he could inflict rape on me in the name of power for himself."

"Rape?"

"When a man takes something from a woman who cannot stop him, can you find a better word to describe it?" Odtsetseg cocked her head now and looked at Kali with eyes at least as old as any of the Wives.

Perhaps as ancient as life itself.

"I cannot," Kali nodded after a moment. "The Wives are all competent killers, both in mindset as well as skills and abilities, because that added an extra element of excitement to Goaulda's rape. To watch our dislike of the man melt at his touch, and him knowing that but for that programming, any of us would kill him for it."

Kali watched the young woman's eyes suddenly come to focus on her. She didn't feel anything in her mind, but she supposed that she wouldn't, unless she were also a powerful telepath.

That had been the one place Goaulda had carefully not strayed with his pets.

Nothing happened for several long, agonizing seconds, so Kali finished her custard, aware that things were about to change, but she had no way to predict how.

Hopefully, the young woman wasn't about to do something bad or stupid.

"No," Odtsetseg replied. "I would never take like that, but I wanted to look at something."

"What did you see?" Kali asked.

"Ildar programmed any number of blocks and limitations into my psyche when he rebuilt everything," the telepath replied. "I can see where he learned from someone like Goaulda to do it, comparing my mind to yours."

"And?" Kali pushed back, ever so slightly.

"And I was able to break some of mine because I am that powerful of a telepath, Kali," she said evenly.

"So?" Kali snapped. "I am not, so nothing can change."

"No," Odtsetseg said in a quiet tone. "I could break some of that programming for another, knowing how it was done in the first place."

Kali felt a chill descend on her like a cloak of shadows.

Powerful telepath. And a woman. One who understood what *rape* really was.

She shivered in spite of herself.

"To what end?" Kali found herself whispering, unable to raise her voice even to normal.

"You could know the touch of a man safely," Odtsetseg

pronounced, like Doom itself had entered the room and touched both of them.

"I'd still be a monstrosity or a fetish to any man," Kali growled, giving voice to that other fear. The secret one.

Brakiee Goaulda had created his sex objects as freaks when normal women no longer aroused him. Only a man with equal perversions would be interested, even in her, one of the closest of the Wives to so-called *normal*.

She would rather be alone.

"No, you wouldn't," Odtsetseg interjected. "Or it wouldn't hurt you so much."

Kali remembered that Odtsetseg saw her as an emotional wall, and not necessarily as a person.

"Every man sees me as a monster," Odtsetseg said sternly now. "Even the ones that worship me still fear me. If I had been programmed to have any sexual drives at all, I would be there as well with you and the others. But I know at least one man who would see you as Human."

Kataragama. The telepath couldn't be speaking of anyone else. Hadn't she mentioned that he knew what she was and still loved her as a step-daughter?

The man who had answered the demands of an Alvar noblewoman and survived.

"He did more than that," Odtsetseg said. "He treated that icky, vile woman as a woman, in spite of everything. I know because I listened in on them when he did. He saw her through the eyes she used when she saw herself."

"And you think he'd be interested in another blue freak in his bed?" Kali snapped angrily.

"I have no idea."

At least she was honest. Kali welcomed that level of honesty right now, however brutal.

"But that's not for now," Odtsetseg continued. "I merely point out that Kincaide has memories—dreams of mine I gather—where Ildar had me use my abilities to modify other people just before they were Indexed, so he could experiment with what I had done or could do. In those memories, I did things to people. Rape, even though there was nothing sexual about it. I went into their minds and changed them, and they could not stop me. I did it at the time out of love for Ildar, but

Kincaide broke me free of that man's control. I could do it for you, but only if you asked."

Kali found both of her outer hands clenching into fists, but she wasn't willing to ascribe an emotion to it. *Thwarted rage* suggested that she might have been looking forward to feeling a man's flesh pressed against her. It had been centuries and Goaulda had programmed her with desires she could not quench.

Nor could any of them.

"We will perhaps discuss this again in greater detail," Kali managed through gritted teeth.

"I understand," Odtsetseg nodded, her own voice dropping to almost nothing. "We must first survive the warp-shroud and then the risk of warp-spawn getting me."

Kali nodded and they both rose in unison, as if unconsciously acknowledging that the conversation had run its course. She would need to have a long talk with Lilith and perhaps a few of the others.

Could this little djinn with the rayed face grant three wishes?

Did they want her to?

CHAPTER 63

Kincaide noted the time and clapped his hands once, just loud enough to cut through all the murmuring.

"You've napped, eaten, and prayed to whatever appropriate deities might take pity on your sorry butts," he called to the room, turning to make sure he had everyone's attention. Dinushan, Hanishka, and Tharushi were all at their consoles with smiles.

Reyhan was here, but mostly tinkering with how he intended to warp Computer Hasan into a woman. Something about adding a full-length mirror that the projection could not escape, just so he eventually had to see himself as a Japanese babe with a big chest.

But Reyhan had his own special hatred of Ildar.

Zhubin and Kali stood along the side wall as normal, but Odtsetseg was between them now, as if the young telepath was protecting each from the other. Kincaide figured he'd get the whole story from all of them at some point, but each seemed relaxed and that was really all he needed from them at this point.

The Star Flower would be the most important person in the history of the Human species shortly. He needed to make sure she was ready for the load.

She grinned at him, so Kincaide assumed that his internal monologue was only *mostly*-private. That was fine.

Kali was watching him with different eyes than she'd had prior, but he didn't really understand any of the Wives, other than that they were

Human to the limits of their DNA and Odtsetseg had set out to personally, verbally slap anyone who suggested otherwise.

He hoped the slaps were just verbal. At least for now. Later, things might have to change, if there were a couple of dead-enders unwilling to move with the times.

Kincaide pointed to the console in front of him, where the clock continued to count down.

"In about an hour, we'll be blasting through the vicinity of the Velle Port Station," he said to everyone. "Dinushan has made sure that we won't hit any permanent outposts, so the only risk is ships too stupid to get out of our way. Here's where it gets tricky. I want us to spin end for end finally, as though we only now got control of the ship back from whatever evil thing happened to it before."

Chuckles from everyone. Quiet muttering from Computer Hasan with the pretty beret.

"Even at max engines, we cannot come to a stop anywhere close to the warp-shroud, but we need to look like we're trying,. Kincaide turned to Dinushan and got a nod from the man. Then to Hanishka. "I expect someone might try to fire on us, or possibly maneuver for boarding. Your job will be to drive them off if possible, but you're in charge of deciding when you want to cut loose with maximum firepower. Remember, we're at least as heavily armed as any of the Warp Voyagers we'll meet, and tougher because we lied about some of the internal designs. We are also playing for absolutely everything here. I will not be taken alive. Nor, I presume, will several others of you, so we have nothing to lose at this point and everything to gain. Questions?"

Again, he rotated his gaze to meet everyone's eyes.

Endgame.

Stern stuff, but he'd picked these people, sometimes over more qualified but less committed rebels. Hard eyes looked back. Snarls and smiles.

"Dinushan, take us into turnover," Kincaide said. "Remember to run your engines enough to drift us even more, but not out of the main target zone."

"And you should go teach your grandmother to suck eggs, Kincaide," the young man replied, but he had a smile almost as broad as Kincaide's.

Feisty was important now.

He turned to Odtsetseg finally. Felt all the warmth in the universe emanating from the woman.

"How long do you need to get prepared?" he asked in a quieter voice.

"I'm ready to head up now," she said in a tone he didn't want to flag as hesitant, but something.

Maybe she needed a hug to settle in. He could do that.

"Reyhan, stop playing and be in charge for a while," he said, stepping around the control square and walking towards the stairs up to Odtsetseg's mezzanine. Her loft.

Her tower.

She met him there, her longer legs carrying her faster up the steps. Plus, she was much younger. Kincaide didn't push his old knees to do stupid shit anymore.

Most of the time.

He hadn't been up here all that often.

Technically, the bridge wasn't a full dome, as it sloped up in such a way that her spot at the front of the room was at the peak.

If the ancient Romans had built the place, they would have put the oculus directly over her chair.

She climbed into the chair and began settling in. Straps. Arm rests. Water bottle close at hand. Snacks in a side pocket.

The space was about three meters across, with her centered and facing forward over the bow dome where the three of them lived. When he glanced back, the Crew Section rose like a cliff face sloped ever so slightly backwards from the neck of the forward section.

But she didn't look back. The Engine faced the future of the vessel. And the species.

It was just today where they'd be sliding backwards across the ice and into the goal.

"You'll be yelling your countdown loud enough that Lilith will hear it," Odtsetseg grinned up at him. "I won't miss the window."

Kincaide occasionally forgot that he could blush. Most people couldn't trigger it, but this was his step-daughter. He grinned back.

"So what did you need to talk about without any witnesses?" he asked, crouching down next to her and talking quietly.

She turned a serious face on him now.

"What do you think about Kali and the others?" she asked suddenly.

Kincaide rocked back on his heels, physically as well as metaphorically.

"Smart, tall, lethal, exotic, beautiful," he offered off the top of his head, unsure what question she had been *really* asking.

"But not monsters?" she pressed.

He shrugged.

"Beauty is only skin deep," he replied. "As my mother might have said it: *Ugly goes to the bone*. None of them strike me as bad people. Isolated and a little surly, but that's the pain of living forever, surrounded by fruit flies like the rest of us. Why?"

"Afterwards, I have a few questions I want to ask you," Odtsetseg said, making it clear with her eyes and the tilt of her head that she meant after warp-space.

After they escaped from The Gage.

If they did.

"Anything in particular?" he smiled at her, aware that she had to have been peeking.

But he had nothing to hide from her. That was the mistake everyone else made.

It was also why most people were all unhappy all the time. They had never decided to chuck all their mistakes out the window and start over as a happy person.

It had taken him decades, but he figured that he'd managed to finally get over himself.

In a pinch, he'd blame Odtsetseg.

"That's okay," she grinned. "It might be my fault anyway."

Kincaide shook his head and rose. He felt an eyeroll coming on, too.

"Be safe," he ordered her. "And then get us to a new homeworld."

"That's my job."

"No, that's your mission," he corrected her. "Your job is to be happy with you, because you are the most unique, special person in the galaxy, and don't let anyone tell you otherwise."

Turned out that she could blush. Cute, too, because her golden skin got red and her ray faded, as though blood flowing out to redden the tips of her ears.

He smiled and descended the steps, listening as Reyhan and the others walked the ship through a ragged, ugly turnover designed to look amateur and half-assed.

Like they still weren't in control, but unwilling to surrender yet.

Never would come before *yet*, but he wasn't about to tell Roselani or the others that.

He had a rendezvous with destiny first.

WARP-SHROUD

CHAPTER 64

Kincaide looked at the silly projected image, the one with the arrogant half beard and the pretty beret, imagining Hasan Ildar trapped forever in a funhouse mirror controlled by Reyhan Herath.

That put a genuine smile on his face.

"Hasan, what is the breakdown of the force in front of us?" he asked in a voice that—like she'd said—could be heard anywhere on the bridge.

"Unchanged, Kincaide," the electronic being replied in a polite, helpful voice. "Two Warp Voyagers and seven smaller Killships, all of different sizes, each at relative rest to the station itself. More than forty smaller vessels have moved away from the vicinity on spokes, with most of them merely coming to rest at what the station has broadcast to everyone is a safe distance. That puts them outside the effective range of most weapons."

Kincaide chuckled.

Station Administration was expecting a firefight. At least nobody here had turned and started running up to velocity to catch them if *Dashavatara* missed somehow and they ended up in the cold darkness by the time they got stopped.

But even then, they'd have to come back into the sunlight eventually, so the Security ships could afford to wait.

Or just leave *Dashavatara* out there until they froze to death when the power ran out.

"Dinushan, start your evasive maneuvering," Kincaide ordered. "I don't care that we won't move far. At this speed, they get one shot more or less, so they'll have to lay the guns and calculate where we'll be. Even a ship-width means they miss."

The helmsman subsided before he even got his mouth fully open, but they'd already gamed this out several times, including just a few hours ago as they could finally get a solid scan on the traffic they would be encountering.

Thankfully, there was a wide corridor of nothing behind the station and the warp-shroud, so they didn't risk impacting at speed.

The closest star was still more than three light-years away. They'd never get there as anything but frozen corpses if they tried.

"Hanishka, since we've got blue shift and nobody caught us from behind, start taking potshots at the forward Warp Voyagers now. Ignore anybody else, because Killships can't pursue us through warp-space unless a Voyager carries them. Same with the station, although feel free to rattle their cages just a little if you want to."

She smiled wickedly, so he had a pretty good idea of what was coming.

Everyone had energy shielding sufficient for the amount of time that they would be in range of one another. This was just poking someone with a stick to make him flinch.

Calm people don't make as many mistakes as riled up ones do, after all.

Kincaide took a deep breath and watched the scanner readout in front of him. They were moving at nearly three percent the speed of light right now, so nothing was visible. And would be past them almost too fast to notice.

He blew out the breath and said a little prayer of thanks to Vishnu, or whomever, that The Gage hadn't decided to park a couple of freighters across his flight path and then order the crews to maneuver for impact.

At these speeds, there wouldn't be anything left but atomic debris expanding in a cloud so hot it might take seconds to cool enough to be visible to the naked eye.

"Tharushi, stand by to cut all the engines and route everything to the generators," he said. Again loudly. Everyone needed to know what was coming.

The young engineer nodded, her hands poised over the controls that would take all the power this mighty ship was capable of generating and turn it into a field that Odtsetseg could manipulate.

They hadn't tried this before, for all the obvious reasons. If they had, someone might have asked why they needed to, when the first trip was still in the future. *That* would be when they tested everything. Controlled circumstances and careful planning.

Not blasting through the parking lot racking up fines from just about every section of the book.

Somebody was certainly going to revoke his Master Mariner's Certificate over this.

Maybe even before they executed him for treason.

"Dinushan, when you're ready," Tharushi said in a quiet voice.

Hanishka had a whole set of generators that would keep the main beams firing, but again, they'd really only get a couple of shots. It would all be up to Odtsetseg instead.

Kincaide watched the room as everyone was poised.

It almost felt like all of Human history was on the cusp of something.

But then, *Dashavatara* was intended as something like the literal Tenth Avatar of Vishnu, come to set the world right.

Now, he just had to pull it off.

"Thrust is set to zero," Dinushan called, checking his boards one last time with a hint of regret in his voice.

But they all had that. Wasn't there one more thing they could have done to tip the balance a little more in their favor?

"Stand by, Odtsetseg," Tharushi called out as her hands began to dance now.

Kincaide leaned forward enough to put both hands flat on the console itself, as though he might merge himself with the ship that carried the rest of them to safety.

Kincaide felt a rattle transmit itself through his hands. He turned to Hanishka. She smiled grimly.

"Counter fire," she said. "They're letting loose with everything they've got right now. Not all that accurate, but a whole lot of it."

"We at risk?" he asked, concerned now.

"I don't think so," was all she had to say.

All any of them could guess.

If he had to die to get them over the line, now would be as good a time as any, because he had brought them all to the edge of infinity.

CHAPTER 65

Her name meant *Star Flower* in the ancient language of Mongolian. Odtsetseg didn't know if Ildar had picked it up at some point and embedded it in his new project's mind, or if that had been her real name, back in a previous lifetime.

She had almost no memories of anything before being Decanted the first time. Just a scrawny sixteen-year-old wondering what was wrong with her that she hadn't developed like other girls did.

Now she knew the truth. There were no other girls like her.

Odtsetseg, who had no last name, was unique.

Around her, *Dashavatara* hummed with powerful energy, but it was silent for the first time on the mental plane where she was used to raucous noise constantly. Someone had turned on the shielding for the Crew Section behind her, blocking all those minds away.

She listened to the men and women below her as they went through their final preparations. Heard Kincaide's voice calling orders and the other chattering.

"Stand by, Odtsetseg," Tharushi's voice rang off the dome overhead.

It was time.

Odtsetseg had a set of screens in front of her identical to everyone else's, showing the scanner reports and locations of various ships ahead of them as they barreled madly forward.

Careened might be a better term, since the bow where she was pointed was turned one hundred and forty degrees to the right, down nearly thirty degrees, and rolled onto its left ear compared to how everyone else was sailing today.

Not that there was any true down in space. But Odtsetseg felt like someone rolling down a hill on a planet that she had never visited. Inside an avalanche, except that everything was utterly silent now. Not even the blowers registered.

All those ships, set to stop them today, or perhaps chase them next week. Except that the icky woman somehow knew too much and was coming for them.

Had Odtsetseg accidentally left clues in the Alvar woman's mind when she rooted around and turned some ideas off? She would need to meditate on that and perhaps work on refining her power. Especially if one of the Wives took her seriously enough to ask for help.

Odtsetseg smiled at that. The oldest crew members asking the youngest to do something that was outside their power.

The station crept closer on the screen, along with all the ships. Vibrations in the hull traveled up her bottom and spine into her mind, telling her that every ship with a gun was trying to hurt them right now.

Odtsetseg wished there was something she could do to stop them, but at this range she only had eyes to watch. Not hands to adjust.

And then the entire weight of the ship settled on her shoulders, pressing her mind down into the chair that had been designed for comfort.

"Odtsetseg, all engines and generators are now in-line and ready for you," Tharushi yelled up the stairs. "As you bear."

As you bear.

It was out of Tharushi's hands now. Out of Kincaide's. Even Chairman Prakash was powerless.

Only the Star Flower had the power to do this.

She watched the nearest edge of the warp-shroud come onto the screen, far enough away from the station that traffic had space to maneuver safely, but still close enough to make the journey relatively short.

However, ships weren't supposed to be going this fast around here.

They would blow by the station in about five seconds, entering the nearest edge of the warp-shroud less than a second after that. Dinushan had absolutely bullseyed the target, as *Dashavatara* would pass through the thickest part of the warp-shroud before exiting back into mundane space and leave them drifting between the stars.

She would have less than four seconds to do all of this.

Odtsetseg stepped inside her head, like she had done that first time to keep watch over Kincaide when he was trapped with the icky woman. Fortunately, none of the cats had come along. Perhaps they were smart enough to understand that now was not the time for distraction, but Odtsetseg suspected that she might find all three curled up on her bed right now, waiting for her to return.

The ancient Hellenes had a tale of one of the older gods, imprisoned after losing a war, and forced to hold up the entire sky on his shoulders. That was what this felt like. All of the mass of *Dashavatara* that needed to be lifted.

She could do this.

Most telekinetics could perhaps move an orange across a room by themselves. On a good day.

She had frightened and surprised herself while cooking and jumped her body entirely out of the kitchen and back to her cabin before she even realized what it was she was doing, so Odtsetseg reached down into those memories and replayed them, her mind so sped up right now that she felt as though she could take a long, refreshing nap between heartbeats.

Around her, above her, a whirlpool swirled, threatening to pull her into the sky. Except that she needed to carry *Dashavatara* with her when she did so.

Other ships carried a team of Engines. Some old and veteran. Some new. But the newbies could learn from the old farts how it was done. Plus, Warp Voyagers moved with calm deliberation when they sailed between stars, so as to not disturb the *Very Important People* back in the crew section.

Her Important people were just a few meters away, outside the Crew Section shielding and sharing all the risks with her, even going so far as to sleep in the same, dangerous waters.

Odtsetseg went deeper into the maelstrom of power. Touched it. Tasted it. Watched colors emerge, as both she and the plasma itself seemed to have escaped the ship to swirl around outside, but it was all in her mind.

The plasma was real, though. Contained in immense magnetic fields inside the shields, where her mind swam in it. Felt it coursing over her body.

Felt it burn.

She was deep enough now that the sensation was heat and pain, as though she was back in that fucker Ildar's lab, trying to make him forget that he owned her soul.

Odtsetseg had thought that she might die from that pain, and had even considered if she wanted to, but not as much as she wanted to be free. Free of Ildar's fingers in her mind. Free to find out what it meant to be non-Human. Even as the crew was Human, there were almost all of the other species stored as Icons that could be Decanted later.

Eden would be a paradise for all the victims of the Alvar, and not just the Humans.

A stray thought wondered if someone might create powerful engines from one of the other species. None of them were as natively powerful as Humans, which was why the Alvar had pounced on the planet and greedily taken every Human they could grab, however few they actually used later.

Most of her mind was consumed by fire. Heat. Pain. It was as though someone was driving spikes made of pure fire into her skull and somehow not killing her.

Odtsetseg growled like she had defeating Ildar and demanded that the plasma behave.

And then it did.

She gasped as the pain vanished and the field of energy seemed to settle on her shoulders as a cloak, rather than all the sky.

She reached out with her mind and spotted the onrushing weak spot in the very fabric of the universe. *Dashavatara* had almost entered it.

It had felt like less than an eyeblink, but at least five seconds had passed while she fought for control. She had only a few seconds to lift the ship.

Odtsetseg knew the instant they crossed into the warp-shroud. The air around her turned so cold that it took her breath away and she expected frost to form on the inside of the dome overhead.

Except that all the ice was in her mind.

She commanded the plasma, and it rose up, turning now into wings of fire around her like the ancient bird the First Nations had venerated.

The cold melted as quickly as it had formed and Odtsetseg studied her new limbs. That was *Dashavatara*. All the power that Tharushi had supplied her, turned into majestic wings that would flap as she needed them to.

Already, Odtsetseg felt lighter, like she could just step off this deck and vanish into warp-space.

Just before she did, she understood the seductive trap for what it was. *SHE* could step into warp-space easily. But she needed to carry the ship with her if she wanted to survive.

What would it be like to just fall into another universe? Would it be like walking out of an airlock here, where she would freeze and asphyxiate?

Except that warp-spawn survived in that space. Supposedly flew in between those stars, where they could prey on travelers using warp-space as a shortcut to the limitations of light-speed.

Odtsetseg reached down with feet transformed into talons, grabbing the physical being known as *Dashavatara* and lifting.

It refused, content to remain within its own universe, where the laws made sense.

Odtsetseg glanced at the far edge of the warp-shroud, rushing towards her impossibly fast.

She had one more chance to do this, or they were all doomed. Every one of her friends, including the Wives who would eventually turn into her sisters as well.

Odtsetseg snarled her defiance at all the warp-spawn in the universe and lifted. Something snarled back at her, but she was too focused on *Dashavatara* right now to hear what it said.

The ship refused, but she willed it. Reluctantly, it began to transition, fading and becoming lighter with every meter they crossed.

Odtsetseg howled once as the edge of the warp-shroud reached for her.

And then they were through.

CHAPTER 66

Roselani studied the woman who was a Paramount of the Second Rank and—currently—responsible for all security at the Velle Station Port. Roselani had already made it clear to the Paramount of the First Rank who was the Station's Executor that she was not willing to be deflected.

Makani Southavilay had just finished his explanation of the conversation that had occurred aboard her yacht.

Paramount Phoumsavanh watched her in turn with concern in those eyes. She was young to be in such a senior post, which spoke to her abilities.

Nobody had warned the woman about Kincaide Kataragama. Including Roselani or Southavilay.

"I do not believe that we would have ignored your suggestions, Noble-born," Phoumsavanh began carefully, obviously working hard not to give any offense to a cousin of the Emperor. "However, my writ runs to the station itself, so I would not have been able to give orders to the Commanders of the various vessels stationed here. That would have had to come from Gage Fleet Headquarters, in the Al-Winoq Glide. Such orders would have likely taken more days to be delivered than we possessed."

"And you didn't believe that the Humans would be able to succeed," Roselani said without any fire behind her words.

The Paramount bowed her head in silent acknowledgment.

"I am unaware of any Warp Voyager ever attempting something

similar," she agreed evasively. "Most are barely moving when they enter the warp-shroud, and only accelerate later, after they have transitioned."

"Which is why I am not calling for political or social repercussions," Roselani said, dangling that out there as both bait and threat. "But I will be pursuing *Dashavatara* through warp-space. You will identify the vessel best suited to a long pursuit that presumably eventually moves through uninhabited systems as soon as the renegades are able to do so. All non-essential passengers will be removed except for scientific missions. I will probably need that assistance. Then you will place the vessel at my command and I will chase the Humans down and destroy them. Questions, Paramount?"

The woman paused, lips pursed as she sought to frame her response in a manner helpful and honest, without being provocative or career-ending.

"Again, I lack the authority to issue such orders, Noble-born," she began instead. "I will conduct the research, and there will be nearly twenty Warp Voyagers in the vicinity once everyone has decelerated and docked. I can ask the Executor to send such a message to Gage Fleet Headquarters, but perhaps you would consider also signing the note? If not doing so yourself independent of Velle Port Station authority?"

"You still do not believe the Humans are a threat," Roselani observed dryly. From the corner of her eye, she caught Makani's flinch.

"They are a single ship," Phoumsavanh replied, trying to understand. "Lacking drydock or servicing facilities. They will be declared renegades as soon as a message can cross The Gage, so no station or ship will trade or resupply them. The crew cannot be more than a few hundred. Why should they be considered a threat?"

"My pet Human, back aboard my yacht, suggests that they stopped dead in space to pick up a package of Icons that they could Decant later," Roselani said slowly, sticking her knife into the woman, at least metaphorically for now. "The ship was constructed with the express purpose of building a forward arms depot colony of Humans, closer to the Line of Exploration to save time."

"Mistress?" the Paramount replied carefully, obviously still not connecting the dots.

"So they have the potential to create a viable pool of Humans outside of Gage control, Paramount," Roselani said. "With, I might remind you, their own Engines. That means that they could become a threat to The Gage itself. There are no other interstellar species that the Alvar have encountered in the last million years. We have now touched more than half of the galaxy, so there may not be any. Until now."

"So you think the Humans are a threat to us?"

"They are short-lived, Paramount," Roselani noted. "That makes them aggressive, hungry, and perhaps harboring something of a grudge against the species that destroyed their homeworld. I will also remind you that they only discovered metallurgy itself in the lifetime of our parents, so they can develop quite rapidly given the chance. They are an infection that we cannot risk ignoring in the hopes that it would just go away. Instead, we face a cancer that must be excised, and done now, before it grows dangerous. Am I clear?"

Roselani leaned back, aware of how loud and angry her voice had grown over the course of her speech. But it must be said, and said now. The Alvar were notorious for spending decades even considering a solution to any given problem, because they had centuries to work at something.

Kincaide Kataragama and Zhubin Prakash would only require years to accomplish whatever they had planned. Based on hints and suggestions Ildar had unwittingly let slip over the last week, that one had possibly been planning on making his own version of Humans who were the physical equals of Alvar.

Did he mean to topple them within The Gage? Or simply destroy The Gage itself? Roselani didn't know, but she did know that Hasan Ildar was thinking in Alvar time scales now to do things, so he could be considered an ally of convenience for the time being. She could always have him killed later, if the need arose.

Certainly, if Ildar wanted to conquer The Gage, it would be better not to also have to face a hostile Human star empire as well on that day.

So she would watch him for now, and allow him to guide her thinking about how to handle Prakash and especially Kataragama.

"How long do you expect the pursuit to continue, Noble-born?" the Paramount asked.

"Years. Perhaps decades, but that will require resupply and perhaps a larger fleet of searchers than one Warp Voyager," Roselani replied. "They will flee me as though a Human devil was on their tail, because that will be closer to any truth than they will wish to discuss."

"With your permission, I will depart, Noble-born," Phoumsavanh said quietly. "I will inform the Executor and ask him to communicate your needs to the people able to issue such orders. In the meantime, I will prepare an inventory of Warp Voyagers against those orders arriving."

The Paramount bowed again and Roselani nodded.

At least the woman was willing concede defeat quickly and cleanly, so Roselani was not required to use her birth rank to make an ugly and unnecessary point. Makani had laid out the entire conversation, including how and why Velle Port Station would fail, so everyone would finally be aware that only Roselani Thammavongsa had been willing to take the Humans serious as a potential threat.

Now she just needed to chase Kincaide down.

She had questions for the man, and nobody but him could answer them.

CHAPTER 67

Kincaide had never been in warp-space before. Only Warp Voyagers or similar Gage ships did such things, and his new identity as Kincaide Kataragama would not stand up to the biological checks necessary for him to serve the Masters so closely.

Hell, Prakash had had to finesse a number of things just to be able to hire him as Foreman, but the Chairman had all manner of connections and abilities. He had been a Gage assassin several times in his various youths, after all.

Warp-space was the color Humans called pearlescent. Made of the same hue as the inside of an oyster he had seen in the Encyclopedia, dark cream colors shot through with the entire rainbow in a way that was almost the exact opposite of life outside the warp.

Black spots in the distance apparently represented stars, somehow dimpling space/time in this universe. Or perhaps all universes were overlain on each other like layers of a cake.

Of course, that suggested that warp-spawn might just be the ghosts of every creature who had ever died in the place Kincaide was born. Fortunately, he didn't have the theological background to delve into such things.

Nor did he give much of a shit.

They had made it. Ass-backwards, tumbling slightly, and almost missed, but they had done it.

Correction: she had done it. Everything was because Odtsetseg had done the impossible.

No ship had transferred into warp-space with only a single Engine powering it in something like one million years. Back when the first Alvar explorers had suggested the method, and then built a machine to try.

Those first vessels had been tiny. Not much larger than this bridge, and carrying only one crew in the early days, and later barely any crew, because the upper mass limit was a hard-set thing, and every person you carried with you was that much less cargo you could carry to a new colony.

Thus the machines to Index a living thing and then Decant it later as a perfect copy. How better to colonize the galaxy than to convert most of your colonists to electronic records you carried, instead of having to haul them and all their life support supplies?

And then the Alvar had discovered the Mori and conquered them. Mori Engines became the standard for carrying ships, and you could hide the important Alvar behind shields to keep the warp-spawn from getting them, as long as you carried spare Engines and could Decant more later as you needed to replace the ones destroyed along the way.

Kincaide still had a deep and abiding hatred of the Alvar, not counting Roselani. But she was a person, not a thing. The Alvar was a thing.

And now, a Human warship flew through interstellar space for the first time ever. And he was the Foreman. Pretty good as far as immortality went.

He looked around the bridge one last time and nodded to the exhausted faces.

"All hands stand down," he announced. "Computer Hasan, you will keep watch on all sensors and alert the command crew if you encounter an issue beyond one standard deviation."

"Understood, Kincaide," Hasan replied in a pleasant voice, no matter how hard he scowled in his projection.

"I'll maintain the first watch," Kincaide continued. "So someone remember to have the wardroom send me forward some food in a few hours. The rest of you sleep. Or whatever."

He didn't care, as long as everyone took some time to decompress. The last several days had been more insane than anything he'd ever done.

"You sure?" Reyhan asked. "You've gotten less sleep than anyone."

"Scoot, you lazy camel," Kincaide smiled at him. "And don't let me hear about you staying up late to tinker with Information Systems. It can wait until next week. Or next month."

Reyhan grinned like a kid with a hand in the wrong cookie jar, but nodded and turned towards the stairs. Everyone else flowed around him except Tharushi.

"Do we trust everything?" she asked, always the paranoid engineer.

"You sleep," Kincaide ordered. "Take something if you have to, because if your team can't handle it, I need to fire the lot of you."

She laughed and trailed Zhubin down the stairs.

What they did with their down time, and who they did it with, was none of his concern, as long as everyone kept their edge.

Kali emerged from the shadows of a pillar where she had drifted when nobody was looking and stared at him. Blue-skinned, dark-eyed, beautiful goddess of destruction with four arms and a pretty laugh, once she relaxed.

"Do you and the Wives actually need sleep?" he asked, genuinely curious now.

"Less than most Humans," she replied.

Kincaide caught the suggestion that she was as Human as he was. And she was, two extra arms and a head of height notwithstanding.

"Would you like company?" Kali asked in an off-hand manner that didn't fool him.

"As long as it's not anything complicated," he replied. "I really am that tired, but everybody else needs the downtime more than I do. I'm here for Odtsetseg, in case she needs anything."

"How is she?" Kali asked, walking slowly around the command square now to stand *close*.

Kincaide slid a little to one side and gestured to the screen he was monitoring.

"Heart rate elevated but within tolerance," he said. "Brain scan looks like REM sleep, but I have her design specifications and she's not pushing that hard right now. Adrenaline went off the charts, right there before the jump, but I put that down to learning a shit-ton of new things in a very short timeframe, while someone holds a gun to your head, ya know?"

"I do," she said.

Kincaide wondered if she was close enough to smell that he'd gone too long without a shower and a shave. Maybe also a haircut while he was at it, as he ran a spare hand through the gray parts above his ears and back.

He also wondered what the hell this woman was up to. Didn't feel professional, although she'd been the one Lilith selected to monitor the bridge during the crazy bits. Several of the others were just as technically-minded, but Kali looked the most Human, even with two extra arms.

She wouldn't do personal. Lilith and the others had all made it clear how they felt about *men* in general. Gelding knifes and hot pokers were hinted at in those conversations.

"You still plan to die soon?" she asked, as if reading something deeper into his face than was there.

"Never planned to die," Kincaide countered. "Had a pretty good depressive cycle there for a time, but I got over it. Wouldn't have *objected* to dying, just never set out for it. Besides, compared to you I'll be dead soon enough anyway and you ladies can deal with the kids coming up. Tharushi and Odtsetseg are young enough to be thorns in your side for a while. And vice versa."

"And you will never be Indexed, Kincaide Kataragama?" Kali asked.

"Never," he agreed. "Got a pistol hidden in my office to ensure it. Got another one in my cabin and a few others stashed around the ship, in case I got cut off aft somehow. They are never taking me alive. Why?"

"Well…"

Whatever she was going to say got cut short by a whole series of alarms going off on his console.

Computer Hasan manifested, but Kincaide waved him to silence and started silencing things.

"What is it?" Kali asked.

He'd already forgotten the tall woman was standing next to him. Behind him now and looking down over his shoulder as he typed furiously and studied readouts.

"Something's happening to Odtsetseg."

CHAPTER 68

She dreamed of star flowers, drinking in the darkness of the night sky on an endless field of grass.

Home. At least an ancestral one, as the person she had been built from had been born in a dome on an alien moon.

The Mongolian steppe was in her genes. It called her now.

She could see lights in the distance as she walked towards them, wondering if those were stars where Gage colonies had been set. Ildar had told her stories of how a group of Engines would create a shared visual delusion to handle their movement, with the strongest and oldest training and flavoring the youngest.

Here, she was alone. And had no one upon which to draw.

Other lights appeared in the night sky above her, but they were not stars. Each felt like a nightbird, circling above her like a vulture riding on invisible thermals.

The breeze lost the scent of flowers that she had been smelling and took on a darker tone now. Death and decay, perhaps.

The one vulture had turned into a half dozen, flying a ring above her at a great enough height as to be shadows rather than birds.

Odtsetseg studied them for a long moment, and then decided that this was her vision, so she changed the sky to morning.

Each bird turned a gray so dark as to be almost black, flecked with red beaks and heads, with yellow talons and feathers down the sides of the torso under the wings, almost like flames licked at them.

She had not seen another living creature on this plain, so she was at a loss to who these might be.

One turned a baleful eye on her now and swooped. It pulled back while still meters above her, cawing harshly like laughter as it flew up to join its mates.

Another did the same.

Odtsetseg found herself pivoting quickly in place as they circled her, one by one flying closer with each pass until she was certain that one would try to rake her with those sharp talons.

warp-spawn.

They could hurt her here, because she had ascended into their realm, carrying a starship and a crew of her friends.

And the dreams of all Humanity.

The first bird seemed to be the leader. It squawked at her now and dove.

Odtsetseg raised a hand, unsure what she could do to stop these demons, as she had no weapon.

Looking down, she was even nude in this place, although she had not realized it until now. She saw the way the rays on her stomach glowed with inner fire.

Leaderbird flew close, talons suddenly forward like he would grasp at her hair and carry her off, but he was no larger than a vulture, with a wingspan only as wide as her own.

Still, she stumbled and went to one knee.

With a triumphant cry, the others fell out of the sky, seeking to swarm her and perhaps bleed her to death from a thousand cuts. To feed on her flesh because she had had the temerity to invade their realm.

To walk the warp.

Odtsetseg understood now how Engines were lost. How young ones came to just die while they were in warp-space.

The warp-spawn came for them.

But she was more than a mere Engine. More than Human. Perhaps a goddess, waiting to be born.

She held up both hands and howled her rage at these creatures, these things that raped.

They *took*.

That was what it meant to be warp-spawn.

Demons from some dank, ugly abyss that preyed on the living.

Her cry seemed to fill the air with a wave of energy that drove them back.

One came close and she swatted at him with her hand, connecting with a slap that knocked him to the ground in surprise.

Odtsetseg stepped back and continued to pivot, that none could swoop on her from behind.

The grounded bird staggered to uncertain feet and stared at her with malevolent eyes. She had an image of a demonic goose, intent on attacking her with long wings that could break a leg on the unwary.

She took a step back and it hissed, striding towards her.

Odtsetseg planted and snapped quickly back at the bird.

"Back!" she yelled in its face, waving both hands just as he did.

Surprise overtoppled it onto its back again with a squawk of terror.

The others answered now, crying at her, but she could taste the fear on their voices.

Odtsetseg slid away to one side, eyes on the downed bird, eyes on the swarmers overhead.

"Leave me alone!" she snarled at them, waving her hands upward.

She was a telekinetic, as well as a telepath. She had more power than any creature ever born or Decanted.

Odtsetseg reached out and brushed them all out of the sky like a net.

Angry, surprised warp-spawn fell at her feet and thrashed about in the crushed grass before they could right themselves. She had a vision of penguins on sand, lost and trying to maneuver.

"Begone!" Odtsetseg commanded them.

Rather than fly off, the warp-spawn faded from existence, leaving her to wonder if they had ever been there. Except that she found a sharp pain on her left arm.

Looking down, someone had cut her with a talon. Barely a centimeter long and little more than one might do with a sharp razor, but it had not been there before.

And it hurt as a drop of blood welled up and began to run down her shoulder.

Odtsetseg concentrated on it with her power and wondered if she could will the cut sides to merge and heal. It stopped bleeding after a moment and she smiled.

"Odtsetseg, are you okay?" a voice seemed to emanate from the heavens themselves.

She paused and looked around, but there were only those lights on the horizons and the places where the grass had been trampled down.

"Odtsetseg?" he asked again.

Kincaide.

He was not here. He was back in the realm where *Dashavatara* flew through warp-space. But then, where did that leave her? What was this plain?

She had a frightening image of many such universes stacked one atop the other. Humans and Gage could reach warp-space with organic Engines that had sufficient mental power, but the warp-spawn themselves did not live here. Were not native.

Where did they come from? And could they be defeated? Could warp-space be made safe for Human ships to travel, without monster birds emerging from the night to take their souls?

She wondered, but Kincaide needed her, so she released her hold on this place and opened her physical eyes instead.

CHAPTER 69

Kincaide had watched all the numbers, but he had no idea what was happening to Odtsetseg. Once she settled some, he headed upstairs to see her personally, Kali dragging along in his wake.

She was in her chair. Buckled safely in and sweating a little.

He called out to her, but she just moaned in some dream.

Finally, her eyes opened and one hand came up to her left arm and she hissed in pain when she touched it.

Her eyes locked onto him and something Human finally settled in them, but he wasn't sure what had been there before. All the stories of warp-spawn suggested that they just killed Engines that came across their domain, but Gage Warp Voyager designs included the ability to vent an entire Engine compartment to open space as a way to kill everyone in the room. As though flooding a compartment with poisonous gas might not be sufficient.

But he recognized the smile in her eyes, and Kincaide figured he probably knew her better than anyone.

"You okay?" he asked as she rubbed at the spot. "Do I need to get the medpack?"

"Maybe?" she said. "I had a strange dream, except that I don't think it was a dream."

"What happened?" Kali asked, stepping around to the other side of the chair and squatting down while Kincaide rooted around for the box with the red crescent on the side.

"I think I met my first warp-spawn," he heard Odtsetseg explaining as he opened the box and rifled around. "They attacked me and I drove them off, except that one of them cut me."

"Cut you?" Kincaide looked up at her now as she unbuckled herself and began stripping the top part of her bodysuit off.

He had never seen her nude. Even half-nude was strange, as the young woman had no breasts to speak of, even though his unconscious mind kept expecting them. Any bump other than her pectoral muscles and nipples, but she had almost none.

He had heard her mention the rays on her stomach that was revealed now. They were identical to the ones on her face in design, scaled up to perhaps three times the size.

There was fresh blood on her arm when she got the top of her bodysuit off, but he couldn't find a cut. Only a scar that looked red and freshly healed.

Had she done that to herself?

Kincaide grabbed some wipes and cleaned up the skin, noting how sensitive she was to Human touch right now from the way goosebumps rose everywhere immediately and her flinch at his hand holding her wrist.

But she calmed quickly and started breathing normally again.

"Well, you had something," he noted, tracing the apparently-new scar with a fingertip. "Not much blood and healed now. You'll want to change shirts."

"I have a spare," she said, reaching with her other hand under the large chair.

Kali found a bundle wrapped in plastic and opened it, pulling out a new bodysuit and handing Odtsetseg the top. Kincaide flipped the bloodied one over his shoulder. He could toss it into the laundry later.

"So what did you see?" he asked as she moved to stand and pulled the shirt over her head.

"They presented as birds," Odtsetseg said.

With both women standing now, he was the shortest person here. Maybe he should call Zhubin to just finish it off?

"Birds?" Kali was asking as he watched the two women talk.

Kincaide was fine with listening, and apparently the two of them had come to some sort of neutral ground or even the beginnings of a friendship over the last few days.

"Large hawks, though they felt more like vultures," Odtsetseg explained, describing them in detail.

Weird coloration, but they were all in warp-space now, and he had never heard of anything like that Mongolian plain where she had apparently fought them.

"And they attacked you?" Kincaide asked.

"Swooped and swarmed," she nodded. "One after another, until they got worked up and then all of them came at me at once. Somewhere in that mess, once of them hit me with a talon, and I think that's when I stepped up and chased them off."

"How?" Kali asked, astonishment in her voice. "Weren't those warp-spawn?"

Kincaide nearly laughed when Odtsetseg squared her shoulders and looked up at the taller woman like a mouse giving attitude to a cat.

"That fucker Ildar designed and built me to be the most powerful Engine ever known," Odtsetseg said in a voice too dry to be angry, but nowhere close to pleasant. "The most powerful telekinetic known, but I am also the most powerful telepath I am aware of, Kali. I just had to use that power against them."

It was educational, watching a deadly creature like Kali back down and maybe even pale just a little bit under that azure skin. Kincaide wondered if anyone had ever frightened a woman like Kali before today, but those were the seeds he saw taking root.

The Wives had apparently never considered just what the implications of Odtsetseg's design were.

"Will they come back?" he asked, drawing both pairs of eyes this way now and defusing that confrontation a little bit.

At least until another day.

"They will," Odtsetseg said. "But I know that I don't have to be afraid of them now. Just keep them at bay long enough and drive them off when they get obnoxious."

Kincaide was amazed. What would the galaxy be like if the warp-spawn weren't such a great threat? What if they didn't kill so many Engines that ships had to carry spares and then be ready to Decant replacements regularly?

What if Humans could be people instead of just *tools*?

He found himself holding Odtsetseg's hand after she had put on her shirt and went to drop it, but she gripped him tighter so he held on.

"What do you need?" he asked.

"Human touch," she said quietly, one hand snaking and snagging Kali's bottom right hand before the woman could withdraw it.

"Nothing more. The ship will fly itself fine for a while, so I don't need to do any piloting until later. I just want to be back in this world for a while."

He nodded and gestured all of them towards the stairs. His office was close enough in case Computer Hasan detected anything, and he could get tea delivered with food.

It would be a long night, but they had all the time in the universe to do this thing.

Odtsetseg looked like she needed a nap almost as bad as he did.

CHAPTER 70

Roselani would miss her yacht, but she did have to say that a Warp Voyager would not be that great of a trial. Being installed in an Ambassadorial Suite helped, as this space was almost as spacious as her palace at the station had been. And while the staff were mostly Mori with a few Mog and Warednja instead of Alvar, they also displayed proper understanding of etiquette around her.

Makani and Doctor Ildar got installed in flats nearby, commensurate with being senior advisers, although neither came with their own staffs to handle things for them. On the one hand, having a large staff would be useful. On the other, every extra mouth required resources that would have to be transported with them, thereby cutting into the time they had to continue the hot pursuit after Kincaide.

Roselani settled for a few personal staff, and made arrangements to eat most of her meals with the senior staff in the officer's wardroom, so as to reduce the load and stress on others.

As a cousin of the Emperor, she was within her rights to make extravagant demands, and everyone aboard both knew it and would fall all over themselves to comply, but she wanted answers. Explanations that only Kincaide could provide.

She would chase that man to the ends of the universe, if that was what it took to get them.

A knock at the door and one of her Mori housekeepers opened it to admit the vessel's commander.

Noma Genevong was short for an Alvar woman, being barely five centimeters taller than Roselani. But instead of being petite, the woman was squat and broad, massing nearly two hundred kilograms, all of it muscles and strength. No fat, so the woman must work with weights on a regular basis.

Humans like Kincaide would have called her a bulldog. Roselani had seen the species in pictures, but Alvar didn't tend to keep tamed animals in their households.

"Commander?"

Roselani had been seated in the lounge area at the front of her suite. The salon for entertaining guests or having informal meetings. She gestured Genevong to join her.

Gage naval uniforms looked more like what the other species wore in public, tending to cover most of the body, while Roselani wore the half-toga of her station anywhere that the weather could be expected to be pleasant enough. She had longer gowns that she could wear if necessary, and even could cover her chest when it got cold enough.

Genevong looked more like Kincaide in his normal uniform. The Gage Navy wore white, at least the officers. Roselani could see where Kincaide had generally kept the uniform pattern and changed the colors. And he had added those tall boots he called *pirate*.

This was pure white, with the piece that covered the shoulders and draped front and back being gold. Her belt and trim were blue, and her bodysuit had that same tunic feel, coming far enough past her waist to cover the flare of her hips.

On Roselani, such a uniform would have made her look even more slender, but Genevong almost looked like a short male with the way her muscles stretched everything.

"Noble-born," the commander nodded as she sat.

Tea was delivered quickly, but the staff were getting used to her needs and had learned how to please her.

"You are wondering if you have somehow drawn a punishment detail, Commander Genevong," Roselani began.

The woman did not nod, but it was there in her eyes.

"No," Roselani said emphatically. "I asked for a list of Warp Voyagers that could make a long journey easiest. From that list, I inquired about crews. Yours came with the best reputation."

"I see," Genevong said carefully. "And our mission is to track that one, Human ship until we can locate it, corner it, and destroy it?"

"It will not be an easy chore, Commander," Roselani confided.

"They have obviously spent a long time planning how they would accomplish this task. In addition, they may have done things to the vessel *Dashavatara* that we are not aware of, so you should consider them at least as powerful as your ship."

"As *Vanechon*?" the woman asked derisively.

Genevong wanted to argue more. It was there in the back of her eyes, but she did a remarkable job of hiding it as she sipped her tea instead.

"My pet Human thinks that the smaller size works in their favor," Roselani said. "I reserve my judgment, but we are in the process of packing as much material as we can, and we will notify every system we transit, and have them notify others. Eventually, *Dashavatara* will not be able to get supplies from a Gage station. At that point, they have to find a planet and begin producing it on their own."

"I am given to understand that they will attempt to create a Human colony?" Genevong said. "A forward arms depot, as it were?"

"Without Gage supervision, Commander," Roselani pointed out. "A Human warship sailing warp-space, when we have had a monopoly on it longer than most of these species have existed. They are a threat to the Gage itself, to say nothing of the Alvar they hate."

"We will see them destroyed, Noble-born," Genevong replied crisply.

"Good," Roselani nodded. "Let me tell you about your foe, Kincaide Kataragama..."

CHAPTER 71

Hasan minded his manners as best he could. Back at the station in the Al-Winoq Glide, he had generally been left to his own devices, and was able to surround himself with his Chuns, a model that barely came up to his chin. Here, he was the lone Human on the crew, not counting the Engines forward with whom he had no reason to ever interact.

Most of the rest were Mori, with a declining number of Mog, Warednja, and the rest. Mori and Mog were both tall, as a rule, compared to Humans, so he was almost forever the shortest person in the room, at least while he was trapped aboard the Warp Voyager *Vanechon*.

Worse, he had to spend much of his time associating with the gigolo from Security, Southavilay. The man was a moron, obviously chosen because he could keep that bitch's bed warm. At least in that he had some useful purpose. For the rest of the time, he seemed intent on being annoying.

Hasan was in his new lab, if you could call it that. Most of the scientific crew had been removed to a different part of the ship, leaving him a space not much larger than his bedroom back home, but at least it was private and he could work.

If not for this moron seated across the desk from him.

"So what do you think allowed the renegades to break your control over the Engine?" the gigolo asked. Again. It was a regular occurrence.

"Without a copy of her current brain scans, I can only guess," Hasan fumed. "There were any number of blocks designed into the creature's psyche that should have prevented her from assaulting me. I was designed to be her god."

"Aren't Humans historically somewhat culturally in favor of deicide?" the man asked.

Hasan glowered at him. In addition to everything else, apparently the man knew Human history.

Possibly too well.

"It has been a recurrent theme of your literature," Southavilay continued with a helpful smile.

"She should have been immune," Hasan explained. Again. "The Engine lacks the secondary sexual characteristics, both physical as well as mental, that would allow her to bond with a Human psychologically. That is the most common method by which such a psychological change might occur. That was part of the reason I did that to her."

"Pair bonding?" the gigolo asked, as though the Alvar did something similar.

Hasan had never heard of such a thing among the blues, but he had also never cared enough to dig deeply into their culture to find out.

Trust Gage Security to send an expert in Human affairs on this mission. Just one more reason to keep the man distracted.

Hasan wondered if he might arrange an accident or something that would permanently disable the gigolo. Maybe leaving his penis intact so he could keep servicing the woman's needs, but stop him from sniffing around at what Hasan was up to.

There was probably no way to hide some of the things he would like to do, short of just waiting a decade to start over.

"Pair bonding is one way to look at Human mating interactions," Hasan felt a lecture coming on, but he had a victim he didn't like, so maybe he needed to spend several days torturing the man's mind by filling it with useless trivia. "Two people find themselves attracted at the physical, emotional, and social levels. In successful instances, they will choose to *become* someone else. Someone better suited to a long-term relationship with the other. When both do such a thing, you have the basis for a lifetime union."

"But the Engine was designed to remain juvenile both physically as well as emotionally, correct?" the man pressed. "More easily manipulated, because she lacked certain adult characteristics?"

"That is correct," Hasan allowed, wondering where this fool was following his logic.

"I am interested in Human familial structures, Doctor Ildar," the Security agent said. "If you were designed into her psyche as a god, would she have interpreted that following the standard patriarchal model?"

"I'm not sure I understand what you are asking," Hasan replied, grumbly that he had to admit any shortcomings in front of this blue scum.

"Could she have found another god?" the man asked. "Could Kataragama or Prakash have displaced you in her theological hierarchy?"

Hasan started to snap angrily at the man but stopped himself. Kataragama had brought her to his lab, where the two of them had assaulted him. Broken part of his mind and left a fuzzy blankness that had not cleared.

She could not be doing it out of sexual love, because she was incapable of such a thing. Could he have somehow become a father figure to the creature?

Kataragama?

The man was known to hate anyone and everyone. Prakash had recruited him from among other options based on a reputation of disdain for all the other species, and Odtsetseg wasn't even remotely Human. Hasan had added the visual cues to her face and body specifically to call attention to her alienness.

Prakash, however.

How much of the crew had Prakash recruited? How much of all of this was his fault? Obviously, the Chairman had betrayed him. How deep was the treachery? How far back did it go?

Had he and Kataragama been in cahoots from the very beginning? Had Prakash been intent on leaving him behind from day one?

Had all of this been a sham?

Certainly, this iteration of the Engine had been in existence for close to two years now. Was that long enough to work on her in such a way that Kataragama became her god?

How was that ever possible?

"You see something," Southavilay accused, leaning forward now.

"I see a hint of a possibility," Hasan countered. "I will need to explore certain sequences in her genetic code and run a whole battery of tests to see if I can find a way to break the control channels I built in."

"Will you need to Decant a fresh version?" the man asked.

There was something in his voice, but Hasan could not place it. Worry? Intention to thwart Hasan from having his own dangerous telepath?

Ah, yes. That might be a concern, if the Human had a creature capable of exerting mind control on the Alvar around here.

Could he use her to turn them all his way?

What a lovely option!

Hasan smiled and leaned forward.

"No, it is far too early to actually produce a living specimen," Hasan informed him. "These tests will take time. And from there, all I will know is how they broke her conditioning. I would then need to design new ways to reinforce it so that she exhibits complete loyalty to the Gage and the mission."

The man leaned back and relaxed, presumably confident now that the crazed Human scientist wasn't about to unleash any sort of trouble.

Hasan leaned back as well and considered his near future.

He knew that the current design was stable enough to work. And had been loyal for most of her time, so they had only managed to break her at the end.

Had the terrorist incident been a ploy to buy time because they had not gotten her fully deprogrammed? Hasan hadn't considered that the explosion might be an inside job. That Prakash might have done it out of sudden fear that Hasan would be ready to depart.

How deep did this conspiracy go?

But he had time to contemplate that.

"So how long will your research take, Doctor?" the Security Gigolo asked.

Hasan shrugged easily, trying not to let triumph into his eyes now.

"Months," he replied. "We will be hunting that ship for a while, and *Vanechon* has its own Engines, so nobody will need my design to replace them at the present. Plus, we need to be sure that a new Odtsetseg remains under full control at all times."

The man nodded too hard, revealing some aspect of the Alvar fear.

They were not great scientists, compared to the servant species, which was why they relied on bio-gods like Hasan Ildar to advance their technology. They needed Humans, but would never trust them. Especially not as long as anyone remembered Kincaide Kataragama and *Dashavatara*.

"Then I will leave you to your work, Doctor Ildar," the man said, rising with a nod of something. Encouragement? Camaraderie?

From an Alvar?

Hasan rose and nodded back, eager to get that fool out of his lair.

When he was alone, Hasan relaxed so much he almost preened.

Yes, he needed to create a test variant of the Odtsetseg model, but one that would never be needed to fly a ship.

He would taper off the telekinesis significantly, which had always been the hardest element. Instead, he would create a model that emphasized telepathy.

What could he do, if he had his own Warp Voyager, with a crew of Noble-born Alvar lords in command doing his bidding because his Engine told them to?

Hasan smiled at the possibilities. At what he could do to that blue bitch responsible for all his recent problems?

She would pay, but he had other things in mind first. And time to pursue them.

I'm still coming for you, Prakash.

CHAPTER 72

Zhubin had called the meeting. He wanted to do this on his terms, one of the rare times that he actually exercised his executive authority as Chairman, rather than answering questions off-hand and on the fly as things came up. He had recruited a good team, specifically so he didn't have to micromanage things, but there still needed to be *those* meetings.

Kincaide was here, as Foreman of the crew. Reyhan had been elected representative for the general crew. Doctors Avahan Dissanayake and Sewwandi Perera were here to speak for Life Sciences and Behavioral Medicine respectively. Odtsetseg, because everything that happened from here on out was due to her.

Zhubin had originally expected Lilith to send Kali again, but apparently the woman had decided that she wanted to speak directly for the Wives, rather than relying even on her closest friends.

Zhubin could appreciate that sentiment. Normally, he let Kincaide speak, but not today.

As a result, they had convened aft, in the converted cargo section where Lilith would be comfortable. She could only get around some of the ship. It just took a long time and a significant amount of pain with some of the internal hatchways.

Not necessary today, other than all the other Wives had been asked to remain in their cabins or forward, those that were close enough to Human size that they had been able to join the regular crew.

Until he added a large enough aquarium for some of the piscine designs he only had as Icons right now, Niki and Serena were kind of stuck. But that day was coming.

"So we have done the impossible," Zhubin looked around the group. They had taken over one of the conference rooms Kincaide had built back here for Lilith, but as it was intended for many more people, they rattled around a bit in here. "A Human warship has escaped Gage control and is now flying free in warp-space on the way to our first transit point at Velle itself. It is time to lay out and organize some of our priorities, people."

Smiles turned to frowns, but he was expecting that.

Other than him and Kincaide, most of the folks had probably been expecting to be caught or destroyed before now.

Lilith smiled, but this version of him, the one known as Zhubin Prakash, had known her for close to twenty years now, so maybe she believed in him.

"Life Sciences, what is the word from your arboretum?" Zhubin turned to Avahan now.

Food would be the first problem they ran into. It was possible to Decant things, but eventually the ship would run out of raw materials, and they could not maintain a perfectly closed system. Inputs would be needed.

"We have a variety of fruit and vegetable crops coming in over the next month, as well as the usual hydroponics outputs," Avahan replied with a smile that only hinted at grimness. "As not everyone on the crew are vegetarians by nature, at some point in the next six months we will need to begin a colony, giving it time for herbivores to get established before we later introduce a crop of predators to balance everything."

"How long will such cultivation take, Avahan?" Zhubin asked.

"Two years would be optimal," he said uneasily. "I presume that in the meantime you would be loading chemicals and organic supplies aboard the ship and breaking them down for the Decanters and such."

"Indeed, Doctor," Zhubin nodded. "At present, we cannot rely on having escaped the Gage well enough to colonize somewhere, but we could deposit food animals somewhere at the same time that we seeded a planet, with the goal of coming back later to harvest and place secondary and tertiary animals."

"So what do we do in the meantime?" Reyhan spoke up now. "We are eating more than the hydroponics facilities can supply, and our food stocks are finite. Terraforming a habitable planet is the long-term goal, I appreciate, but we can't rely on that."

Zhubin saw Kincaide's eyes light up, so he nodded to the man. Let the rest of the crew finally understand why Kincaide Kataragama had been the perfect choice for this job.

"We'll take them from the Gage directly," Kincaide said.

Zhubin noted the surprise on most of the faces. Again, Lilith seemed serene, but the others were caught off guard, including Odtsetseg, who apparently hadn't looked close enough at the man before now.

"Take them," Reyhan echoed sarcastically.

Everyone forgot that one element of sartorial splendor that Kincaide affected, over and above his red bodysuit that mimicked the Gage in fashion, but not color.

Those pirate boots that came up to his knees and folded over. Straight out of a history book that Kincaide had shown him, early on when Zhubin had asked.

Pirate. Corsair. Buccaneer. Whatever term you wanted to use to describe a brigand with a warship.

The ancient Americans had a hero named Robin Hood that also fit, except that he was arboreal, instead of maritime.

"Take," Kincaide nodded. "We are running ahead of news of our rebellion. That means we can sail right up to a station with a cock and bull story about a secret mission, demanding that they provide food and resupply while we do whatever it was we were up to when we found them. Perhaps we had a problem with our Engine and had to limp to the nearest station, but we're okay now, save for needing food because we spent so much time in real space before we could Decant a new Engine to get us home. The Alvar are not that bright, especially as you get farther away from Al-Winoq."

"They'll fall for it?" Reyhan's eyebrows went up.

"At least once," Kincaide smiled. "Depending on how quickly the Gage chase us, and how many ships they send out, we might get to do it a few times, but I wouldn't want to push my luck, because a station could let us come alongside and then open up with cannons big enough to destroy *Dashavatara*. But once, certainly. Maybe twice if we run hard enough, which I would like to do anyway."

"What is our destination?" Odtsetseg asked in a voice filled with curious wonder rather than the hard-headed stubbornness of most of the rest of the room.

"Aways," Kincaide said, nodding back in his direction for Zhubin to speak.

He was Chairman, after all.

"The Gage have physically surveyed less than half of this galaxy to some extent," Zhubin said. "We have no expectation that we will find another space-traveling species beyond their current Line of Exploration, but that just means that we can go places they have not."

"What about Earth?" Odtsetseg asked, causing Reyhan and Lilith to stir. "Could we go home?"

"We don't know where it is," Zhubin replied. "That is one of the great secrets the Alvar have kept from us."

"Somebody has to know," Odtsetseg perked up and smiled.

Zhubin stared to retort acidly, and then realized that she could read their minds, if he got her close enough. Just like she had done when Kincaide had spent the evening with that *icky woman*.

Everyone fell silent as the implications settled in.

Earth would be the perfect world for Humans, because they had originally come from there. It would have wild animals that they could eat and all manner of grains and vegetables that could be picked and eaten without any processing to remove toxins.

He had never considered it, because nobody would tell him where the planetary system was.

What if they didn't have to? What if the Star Flower could take it from them?

What could the Humans do then?

"Would they guard our ancestral homeworld?" Lilith asked, crashing them all back down to earth with such a simple question while reminding them that they were all Human, external shell be damned. "We know they invaded and destroyed much of it, before capturing as many Humans as they could, most of whom were never Decanted again. Would they want to keep others from finding the place and perhaps gaining their own Engines?"

"There are no others," Kincaide spoke up in a hard, angry tone. "No other species has ever risen to warp-space, that they might threaten The Gage and the Alvar's ultimate control of the galaxy, and possibly the entire universe. With this ship, we represent the first successful rebellion to Gage control in the history of the Empire, going all the way back to *Conquering* the Mori."

Zhubin watched faces fall just as fast as they had risen. Then a thought occurred.

"So why would they need to guard the remains of the planet?" he asked. "If nobody else can get to warp-space, then nobody needs Human Engines, right?"

"If I were a right, paranoid shit…" Reyhan started to say, before being interrupted by a wave of laughter so loud that even he smiled after a bit and waited for the rest to quiet down. "As I was saying, if I were paranoid, I might want to send a ship or two to Earth right now, just to stop the crazy, renegade Humans. Maybe even build a base there, if they hadn't before this."

Sewwandi leaned forward now. She was as short as Avahan was tall. Curvy with skin even darker than Kincaide's southern heritage. Her hair was long, and generally curled tightly up in a bun on the back of her head, with a stylus holding it in place. Her face was almost square, which should have looked masculine, but she was every bit feminine, when she wasn't intently focused on her work.

Physically, she was a rather plain woman, at least in Zhubin's eyes, but she was a brilliant, multi-disciplinary genius. And hated the Alvar almost as much as he did.

She was also in charge of Behavioral Medicine, which went beyond taking care of colds and sniffles and went to the heart of healing their souls.

"Sewwandi?" Zhubin asked quietly, drawing all eyes down onto the small woman.

"Perhaps that needs to be added to the mission, Prakash," she said in a low, enthralling voice. "A quest to find Earth, and perhaps repopulate it. That would give us more than just escaping with our lives."

"That was Ildar's vision," Kincaide said sourly. "Destroying The Gage and xenociding the Alvar."

"And while I did not see eye to eye with Hasan on many things, I do not necessarily think he was wrong in this instance, Kincaide," Sewwandi snapped back. "At some point, either The Gage expand and conquer the entire galaxy, and as you noted, perhaps the universe, or they are stopped. I do not see them stopping of their own accord, so someone will have to prevent them from conquering other species to add as slaves to The Gage. Right now, as you also pointed out, that is us. Only *Dashavatara* has the potential to stop them. Us. Here. Now."

"And how would you do that, Sewwandi?" Kincaide asked.

"I'm not in command, Kincaide," she smiled sweet and evil in equal amounts with just the perfect amount of head tilt. "I am merely in charge of the well-being of the Human crew, just as Avahan will focus on all things botanical and related to Decanting and colonizing. The warriors will have to show us how. I merely point out that as a rallying cry for stopping the Alvar, Earth has a very potent symbolism, especially if we were to bring it up to Gage levels of technology."

"You expect to find anyone alive after all this time?" Zhubin asked, almost in spite of himself.

Sewwandi shrugged.

"It takes two Humans and time to create a third one," she smiled. "There have been several thousand years since then, so perhaps a few survivors escaped the original Conquest and were able to hold on. My expectation would be that they would have been able to mine the existing infrastructure for metals and materials, so they should have retained some level of culture. We won't know what until we get there."

Zhubin looked around at the others, noting the way that everyone seemed a bit in shock. But she had hit the heart of the thing.

They had set a mission to escape and form a new, secret colony, well away from the Alvar such that they could survive. Earth might only be a symbol for a generation while they did so.

However, it would provide a rallying cry for those future children. To retake what had been taken from them. To perhaps actually see the place that had given Boston Dome its name. Or Osaka. Lagos. Chennai. Makassar.

Earth.

Dare they dream?

CHAPTER 73

Kincaide looked around the command square at the smiling faces. Odtsetseg was upstairs, but he had a screen in front of him with her face. His step-daughter appeared to be in a deep, relaxed sleep right now. One she would wake from soon enough.

Kali was off to one side, standing with her shoulder blades finally touching the wall behind her. Zhubin was perhaps a top arm length to her right, also apparently relaxed.

Everyone was loose.

Kincaide knew how much of a sham that was, but he didn't want to call anyone out and disturb their false bravado at this point.

"Approaching the warp-shroud, Kincaide," Odtsetseg said in a dreamy voice, her eyes never opening.

Supposedly, she was back on that Mongolian plain, risking vultures as she sailed the ship to the first harbor on this voyage.

Dashavatara had entered warp-space with much greater velocity than was appropriate, at least according to Gage records, but speed in warp-space was unrelated. You moved as fast as your Engine could throw you. Odtsetseg was far more powerful than any other single Human, but by herself she was only a pretty good match for a normal Warp Voyager team of five.

If there was any ethical way to have a second person with her same power helping, Kincaide could only imagine how fast they could fly, but it would need to be a different person entirely, and not just another copy of the same woman.

Odtsetseg deserved better than that.

They were coming out of warp-space now. Speed was again a bizarrely relative thing, so the ship would emerge with whatever push Odtsetseg could give them at the transition.

"Helm, light your engines and prepare to bring them up hard when you have a universe to push against," Kincaide ordered. "Weapons, you are to return fire only. Am I clear?"

"You are," Hanishka replied in a tight voice. "All guns unlocked. All sensors active but listening like a polite little Warp Voyager dropping into system."

Kincaide nodded to the woman. She would factor in later, when he went pirate, but for now they needed to sneak through the Velle system as quietly as possible.

"Power Systems, we're going for a sustained burn." Kincaide turned to Tharushi now. "Emergency Gage orders for some distant station, so we won't stay around to chat. Everything solid?"

"Perfectly on the beam," she smiled back. "Eventually, I won't be able to say that, but not today."

"Good enough." Kincaide looked around. He opened the public address system now. "All hands, stand by for arrival at Velle. Warp-transition shortly."

He cut the line and took a deep breath. Reyhan looked over and smiled demonically, but he probably practiced that look in the mirror. Certainly, he trimmed those sideburns into horns with mathematical precision each morning.

But he was the man for the job. And had promised a fun surprise today, so that meant that he thought he had cracked the visual controls on the Computer Personality of the Day, however forever it might be Hasan Ildar.

At least until the man's face pissed Kincaide off enough that he ordered a hard reset on the system from the backups that had been stored safely.

Kincaide considered leaving Hasan a note as they crossed the system, but decided that it would probably blow their cover, as much fun as it might be.

One of these days.

Warp-transition…

Everything turned inside out for the eternity of an eyeblink before it turned back. Colors inverted. Black to white. Gray to blue. Red to green. Kincaide thought he smelled roses in the air, but it was gone just as quickly as it appeared, so maybe he imagined it.

Or the transition also did things inside his head, messing with all his senses.

The transparent walls of the bridge dome were back to the deep space darkness he'd lived with for so long.

"We have exited," Odtsetseg announced unnecessarily.

Kincaide looked down at his screen and her eyes were open. Maybe a little glassy right now, but she'd done it again. For her, another first. After this, entering and exiting would be old hat and that was good.

"Course laid in and confirmed," Dinushan announced in a shaky voice, like he was also recovering from the crossover.

"All ahead," Kincaide ordered. "Standard burn for now, but we'll be exceeding speed regulations again. Let me know when our bow wave triggers a response from any of the stations or nearby ships."

On his screen, Odtsetseg was stirring, so he nodded at Zhubin to assist her. Everything would be a learning experience for her for a while, as powerful as the young woman was. She needed to know that everyone supported her.

"Station query," Hanishka announced. "Automated only, requesting navigation updates."

"Give them the story we worked out," Kincaide responded. "Destination Emhax on a priority run from Al-Winoq, under Gage Fleet authority. If someone live comes on the line and asks, we are a courier. Obviously a Warp Voyager, however small. Let me know if they demand to talk to the commander."

"I can do it, you know," Reyhan murmured just loud enough for Kincaide to hear him and just quiet enough to ignore if he chose. "Make you look like an Alvar on a transmission line, with little enough delay that it appears natural."

"Pretty sure you're right," Kincaide muttered back. "Rather not test it until much later. Every day we can run and not be outlaws is that much farther we can get from the Alvar."

"Still think she'll chase you?" Reyhan asked.

There was no doubt who he was referring to. None.

"At least this far," Kincaide said, letting go a tiny sigh. "And more, but I don't know how much more. That's part of the reason we're running hard and fast now. At some point, someone will jerk her chain short. As the old saying goes, I only have to run faster scared than she can chase me angry."

"I had an ex-wife who was like that," Reyhan nodded. "Pretty sure the far side of the galaxy wouldn't be sufficient with that woman."

Around them, the bridge buzzed with low conversations as the others talked or opened channels aft to their subordinates. Outside, things had returned to normal.

Zhubin met Odtsetseg halfway down the stairs, offering a hand she initially resisted, until it became obvious from her face how tired she was. Then she leaned on him.

However, she had done the impossible. No ship in hundreds of thousands of years had crossed warp-space with a single Engine, let alone something as big as *Dashavatara*.

"Station acknowledges our flight path and reminds us of acceptable flight regulations in their space," Hanishka announced in a light voice.

"They can put the fines on my account," Zhubin called back. "I promise to pay them off next time I come through Velle."

That got a round of laughter, however tinged with hysteria it might be from the stress.

One down. Dozens, perhaps hundreds more to go, but at some point, there wouldn't be a fortress guarding the warp-shroud. Eventually, there wouldn't even be Gage vessels or automated beacons when they came into a system.

Then they would truly be free.

REBELS

CHAPTER 74

Lilith surveyed the faces around her. The Wives didn't gather as a single group all that often. After this many centuries, there were old rivalries and personality issues that would explode if they did this too frequently. At the same time, they were all dedicated to a new mission.

As Zhubin had pointed out, they would all be goddesses at some point. Immortal beings while the mayflies around them came and went.

"How do we shape Human culture, once we are on a planet?" Lilith began, smiling at them.

"Should we even limit ourselves to a single planet?" Serena asked, perched up on the side of her tank with her chest pressed against the glass in a manner that looked like it should be uncomfortable, so she had a point she wanted to make that strenuously. "Should we instead cause Prakash and the others to build us a ship to our scale and needs?"

"We would need Humans to fly it," Lizab pointed out from a corner where her porcupine spines wouldn't poke anyone. "Did you think to extend the cult or start a new one? Or would it be an exploration vessel we used and recruited widely?"

Lilith noted the eyes turning to face the woman, but Lizab didn't speak up much, so she had surprised everyone.

"Would Odtsetseg join us?" Gahi spoke up now from the other corner.

If Lizab was reserved, Gahi was almost monastic, rarely ever speaking, even in the privacy of their old home. But she was also the least Human-looking of the lot, which was saying something.

Even Lilith—for all that her abdomen and eight legs reminded people of a giant spider—had a torso that was Human enough. Woman enough.

Gahi was a roadrunner.

Goaulda had specialized in top half/bottom half designs. Lilith as a spider centaur. Niki with her lower half as an eight-legged octopus.

Goaulda had started with Corie's design of a harpy from ancient legend, with flattened, feathered arms and legs that hinged backwards like a chicken and ended in talon. But he had pushed Gahi's design further, to that of a ground cuckoo.

Gahi had a beak and headcrest, with most of her feathers in lavender tones. Wings like Corie, but shorter, to the point that she couldn't even glide, unlike her harpy sister. She had a long neck that let her turn her head almost backwards, like owls once had, and a tongue like a woodpecker.

Goaulda had given her speed in those legs, at the cost of overall strength, so her design had the endurance of a ground bird, to the point that the thug had fucked her for hours and hours, once upon a nightmare.

She rarely spoke of much of anything, so she must have strong opinions.

Lilith started to answer, but Kali caught her eye, so Lilith nodded to the war goddess in blue.

"She might, but she was not designed to be immortal," Kali said to the room. "Odtsetseg specifically asked Prakash to Index her before the first flight, so that they had a copy of her in the current form, at a time when she had made up her mind that it was in everyone's best interest to do so."

"She was Indexed?" Gahi asked with a gasp. "Voluntarily?"

All of them had seen the inside of an Indexer. And been Decanted any number of times, at least while that fucker Goaulda had been perfecting his designs.

All those records had been wiped, the morning after he ended up dead.

"She was," Kali acknowledged. "She walked into the machine to be destroyed and reborn, because she knew Kincaide needed her."

"Do we know how long she will survive, then?" Euryale asked, coiled up in the center back, directly across from Lilith.

"We do not," Kali shrugged. "Her octopus genes might mean she has only a few years. Or she might live a full, Human lifespan and be around for another eighty years. I doubt that Ildar would have given her great age, just because a man like that wouldn't see her as a person. According to both Prakash and Kataragama, he kept sex slaves that were clones of a single, modified Human, so he would see Odtsetseg as a tool. Because he had a Decanter, he could use her up and create a new version whenever he needed one. I presume that we will not be following suit?"

Lilith smiled as everyone recoiled at the thought of *'Just Decant a new Engine'* when the old one died off.

The Alvar saw Humans as a disposable resource. The Wives needed to see them as an embryo of a galaxy-spanning culture that would force the Alvar to behave. Or be destroyed.

Not everyone agreed with Kataragama that the Alvar could be broken of their arrogance. He was, in fact, part of a small minority in that regard.

"So does that imply two kinds of Humans, over the long term?" Niki spoke up from her tank next to Serena. "One culture planetary in nature, and one permanently space-borne? Planetary Humans would not need Engines, as long as they could trade with their cousins, who would. At some point, evolutionary pressures perhaps create a new Human species that is entirely telepathic and telekinetic, rather than the traces common in most today."

"It would be more pronounced if we had records of ancient Humans, taken after the Conquest," Ancen spoke up, her faun ears twitching with emotion.

But she was an emotional creature. A faun done in the old top-half/bottom-half design, with a female torso covered in fine fur and legs hinged like a Mori or the ancient Human beast known as a minotaur, ending in hooves.

And a cute, white tail that was as emotive as her ears when she went nude. At least today she was wearing a long dress and a loose top, both in a faded mustard color.

"How so?" Lilith asked Ancen.

"They grabbed something like a billion survivors, according to the legends," the faun said in an excited voice. "But the Domes could only hold twenty million people. Thus, they selected hard for a very specific type of Human. Mental abilities that perhaps were not that common, but helped the Alvar drive their ships. Then you have thousands of years of tinkering since by jackasses like Goaulda and Ildar, pushing even further. I wonder how Human any of us really are, compared to the natives of the planet that we might meet someday."

That caused a stir. All the more so because Ancen was known to be flighty, rather than intellectual. But none of the Wives were stupid.

Goaulda had wanted all of his victims to be keenly cognizant of what he was doing to them, and to understand just how little control they had over their own bodies and minds, may he rot forever in the worst of the available hells.

"Should we avoid the homeworld, then?" Kali asked. "The rest of the crew seem to be embracing that as an eventual goal."

"Perhaps not avoid," Ancen tilted her head back and forth in thought. "But they will need to be prepared to be seen as aliens if we do return. Contemplate the evolutionary pressures that produced men like Kincaide, versus what the survivors of an extinction-level event like the Conquest would have faced. We may need to steal some of the ancients, if we could find such records, just so a competent biologist could compare them."

"I will make sure that we have a conversation with Zhubin and Kincaide at some point," Lilith made a note. "That might be a worthwhile task in the current generation, as we seed various worlds secretly against an Alvar future."

"Speaking of futures," Megaera spoke up, her eyes glowing especially brightly today and her devil's tail twitching almost as much as Ancen's ears. "What of the other species we carry? The Mori? The Ayotochtli? The Mop? What will their place in this future be? I know that much of the crew of the vessel was originally selected for a certain specism and even racism within Humanity. How will they handle it when aliens are their neighbors?"

"I think that is one of the places where we will need to step in as goddesses," Lilith spoke firmly now, drawing all their eyes forward. "As you have noted, we will outlive everyone on this ship, assuming we don't get killed stupidly. We understand what it means to be an underclass, so we should look to protect the others. It cannot be allowed for the Humans to oppress the Mori, else they turn into just another version of The Gage."

"Have you read Human history?" Megaera laughed uproariously. "All of it is a case study in one group identifying a useful way to oppress minorities, usually on the basis of externalities. Even Hasan

Ildar had intended to only carry Tartars, until he found out how few there were across all the Domes. That forced him to extend cousinhood to South Asians and a few Caucasians that were dark enough. The man hates Arabs and Chinese so virulently that I was surprised he never spontaneously combusted."

"Will laws be enough?" Ghost asked from her spot. She wore a cloak today with the hood down, but they were all used to her—as her namesake—haunting quiet places. "Kincaide can force a legal structure into place, even over the objections of others. What should we help him create?"

"It will be enough for now," Megaera replied. "But you have the Founders Problem to solve. Or will, in a few generations, when the great-grandchildren forget."

"Thus, they will need us," Lilith stated. "All of them. All of us. We will not forget. Whatever the rest of Humanity does, we will need to remind them what was founded and why."

"And when they turn on us?" Euryale asked. "They still call us the *Monster Wives*, even though Kincaide has taken to issuing fines to anyone he catches. We represent their nightmares, *because Goaulda designed us that way*."

Serena laughed, cutting off all other comments.

"Which takes us right back to where we began," she said harshly. "Should we have our own ship? Perhaps our own fleet of ships that could carry us away from the generation that decides they don't want gods? It is not a problem we have to solve today, but we should begin planting the right seeds in the right minds. Nobody else will live to rest in the shade of such trees, but we might need them to build walls to protect us later. However much later."

Lilith cut off conversation with a quick clap.

"Megaera, you do the research on political and social structures that can provide the greatest stability over time," she said. "I seem to remember North America before the Conquest managed to accept people from all ethnic groups and somehow make it work. At least better than most places with a visible minority. Assume a plurality model, as Humans will not necessarily be anything but the largest single group, as opposed to a dominant majority."

"How do we enforce that?" Serena asked.

"That's your assignment, Serena," Lilith replied. "Find me an answer to that question. Niki, should we stay on one planet or remain mobile for the next thousand years? Staci, how do we build cultural structures for the non-Humans that will belong to Human civilization?"

She paused to study the women facing her.

"Goaulda created us with brains," she reminded them. "Everything else was for his benefit, but we have the greatest understanding of what Human civilization will need today, next year, and a generation or a millennia hence. And we will be able to shape it, by doing little things today that will not bear fruit in the lifetimes of this crew. Let us make sure that what we create is something we will be proud to own when everyone else is dead and forgotten, shall we?"

CHAPTER 75

Roselani made it a point to be on the bridge of *Vanechon* when the ship emerged in the Velle system. Kincaide had come through here, but nobody had any idea how fast he could have made either the run across warp-space or the subsequent burn to cross this system.

Or where he had gone to next.

How long could she chase him?

Commander Genevong stood at the peak of her command oval, with her officers standing down both sides. The Computer Personality of the Day was a Mori named Suul, which she found a little disconcerting, but only about half of this bridge crew were Alvar, with Mori, Mog, and even an Ayotochtli present, all dressed in the white and gold of Gage officers.

Roselani didn't travel great distances often. Thinking back, it had been something like seven hundred years since she had last entered warp-space, on a vacation to a spa world.

She had forgotten how bizarre the warp-transition was. It took her several seconds before everything was the right color again, but she didn't appear to be the only person present suffering, so she found that acceptable.

"Contact the station immediately and have them provide scanner logs of *Dashavatara*," Genevong called out brusquely, still shaking her own head a little. "Light speed lag on communications is fine for now. I don't need to talk to anyone until we get closer."

The Ayotochtli on the right, standing at a station lowered for her shorter stature, nodded and began to type quickly on her keyboard.

Roselani stood off to one side, but it was obvious that the bridge was designed with an Ambassadorial presence in mind. There was a chair that could be deployed down from the wall, as well as places to rest drinks or a handheld, letting *Someone Important* be present, but still out of the crew's immediate way.

She understood that her mission was going to cause this crew to miss shore leave and anything else they might have planned, but they served The Gage. That came with costs that they should have all come to grips with a long time ago, so she made it a point to smile in a friendly manner at everyone she dealt with.

Roselani knew she would be cursed, but she could at least not be a complete, flaming bitch to the crew in the process. Let the lower classes be petty.

Time passed as the officers busied themselves with the esoteric magic of being a Warp Voyager in Gage service.

"We're getting a report back from the station," the Ayotochtli woman called. She sputtered incomprehensibly for a moment before she spoke again. "Records show they departed via the Jeirolul Port Station six days ago."

"How is that possible?" Genevong demanded angrily. "They have one Engine, not five."

"Calculating now, Commander," the woman replied without looking up.

Roselani had been standing well back. She took a step closer to the Commander now, drifting to her right to appear in the woman's peripheral vision, where she could still be ignored if necessary, but seeking answers when some were available.

"Based on records at both ends of warp-space, *Dashavatara* was a little more than five percent faster through warp-space," the Ayotochtli woman said aloud, still not looking up, but speaking with a measured, professional tone. "Upon arrival, they did a hard burn across the system, violating navigational standards and telling everyone that they were on a priority run to Emhax."

"Where?" Genevong asked.

"Records show it as a Survey Base currently serving Sector Twenty-Nine on the Line of Exploration, Commander," the Ayotochtli woman replied, finally looking up. "About eight light-millennia forward on the clockwise side of the galactic core."

Genevong turned to Roselani now, her face hard with malice.

"Do we believe them?" the Commander asked, sounding more polite than the fire in her eyes might lead one to believe.

"Not in the least," Roselani replied with a shake of her head. "Liars, rogues, and renegades. But I presume that it would cause the locals to perhaps not question them moving faster than normal?"

"It would," Genevong said sourly. She turned to the Comm Officer. "Plot it on my station for myself and the Noble-born to view."

A nod drew Roselani closer to the Commander, where she could see a small projection appear in the air before them. None of it made any sense to Roselani, but she wasn't a sailor. That was what she had this crew for.

The solar system was centered on the star, with irregular bright spots presumably indicating the warp-shrouds, as both *Dashavatara* and *Vanechon* appeared at one and *Dashavatara* traced a path across the system. Numbers appeared and Commander Genevong cursed quietly before turning to Roselani.

There was new respect in the woman's eyes.

"They are running hard and fast," Genevong announced in a voice quiet enough for just the two of them. "Accelerated across the system faster than *Vanechon* can safely do. They also went into turnover much later than regulations call for, so that they were still at a relatively high speed when hitting the warp-shroud to Jeirolul, at least compared to what a Warp Voyager normally does."

"Can you match them?" Roselani asked quietly. "They can stop someplace to draw supplies from a station that doesn't know any better, but they will not do so until they are sure we are too far behind them to catch them at rest."

Genevong nodded and turned to the rest of her crew, cautiously watching the exchange out of the corners of their eyes.

"Notify all stations and vessels that *Dashavatara* is a rogue vessel," Genevong ordered. "Armed and dangerous, to be destroyed on sight under Gage Fleet Authority. Sign my name to it."

She glanced sideways for approval, but Roselani stepped up and raised her voice.

"Sign it under my name and mark the message with *Imperial Authority*," she ordered the woman with a warm smile. "Let all the questions and complaints come to me instead of the Commander. I am happy to discuss this with anyone feeling especially obstinate."

Snickers under breaths, but nobody spoke up. The Ayotochtli woman nodded and started typing again.

"Thank you," Genevong murmured quietly.

"You should only bear the success of this mission, Commander," Roselani said, turning to her. "All the failures will be mine, for any of a number of mistakes I have made along the way. It is even possible that I will need to change chariots at some point, simply because you will have chased that man farther than you were originally willing, and I will not rest until he is dead."

Genevong started to say something but caught herself short and nodded crisply instead.

Her face cleared and she turned into The Commander again.

"Helm, plot a matching course and burn to get us to Jeirolul Port Station," she ordered in a loud, strong voice. "Comm, order them to send a messenger ahead to Jeirolul itself to prepare for us to take on supplies there. We will be slow on the near side of warp-space when we emerge, so they are to depot all the supplies we will be low on and container it in place for us to pick up in motion. We will not dock, so a tug will carry everything into a safe corridor and bring it up to speed for us to overtake. Questions?"

An Alvar male and the Ayotochtli female repeated the orders back crisply and Genevong nodded, turning back to Roselani.

"Thank you, Commander," Roselani said. "I will retire to my suite now and let you run your ship. Let me know if anything interesting comes up before we transit again, but otherwise I will join you for dinner as normal."

"I will, Noble-born," the woman said.

Roselani exited the bridge and rode a lift down two decks to her level.

Kincaide was pushing. Even harder than Genevong or the others had originally anticipated. Did he know she was going to be chasing him?

That brought a smile to her face.

CHAPTER 76

Kincaide reviewed the logs with Reyhan, both of them seated up in his office with the walls deployed to give them some privacy.

"Nine systems," Kincaide said, listing them from Al-Winoq to Velle to Jeirolul, all the way down to Sextantis, coming up in a few days.

"Still think we could have tried our luck at Mohghin," Reyhan replied. "Eight is a long ways from home."

"That's the joy of this job, Reyhan," Kincaide smiled tiredly at the man. "We have no idea how fast they are coming up behind us, other than we've been pushing as hard as I dared and Gage Warp Voyagers don't tend to do that. Certainly, everywhere we've crossed so far will be pissed at us for speeding, until someone tells them we're pirates. Not that it will make it any better."

"So, we're finally far enough?" the man asked with a shark-like countenance.

"Yeah," Kincaide agreed. "We ought to be able to land and then try our bluff with the far side Port Station."

"Prakash will be thrilled," Reyhan laughed. "Should we send Odtsetseg along?"

"Normally, I'd love to, but if something happens to her, we'd need to Decant a fresh copy and bring her up to speed," Kincaide countered. "And I don't want to have to put her into the Indexer right now unless I absolutely have to. Know what it does to the woman, even when she understands it and approves."

Reyhan nodded, but didn't speak. Kincaide classed that as a win. The man had come around over the last several months, no longer seeing her as an alien to be disdained. Even the Wives didn't seem to get his hackles up, most of the time, but Reyhan rarely dealt with any of them other than Kali, since none of the women had the training or expertise to take a job in Information Systems.

Probably reminded them of the bad days. A couple of them had hinted that they understood the Indexing and Decanting machinery better than Avahan, but Kincaide wasn't going to take them up on it.

"So I have to ask the rude question now," Reyhan sighed and leaned back in his chair. One hand ran back over the few hairs on top of his head, but that was more of a nervous tic than anything. "Do we need to maybe create another Odtsetseg? Not a copy of the woman, but someone else with that same level of power? I appreciate your position about having two copies of the woman at the same time, but do her telepathic abilities make her so valuable that we should have someone who can twist minds when we encounter a station or a ship?"

"She has to be almost close enough to touch someone, if she wants to really affect them." Kincaide leaned back as well. As Reyhan had said, they'd had this conversation over rotgut aft a few times, but never done more than circle aimlessly around it. "You'd almost need to create a telepath from scratch. I'm guessing that if you dialed back the telekinesis you might free up some space, since I remember her mentioning that moving objects was the hardest thing for their kind."

"We've got experts available," Reyhan scowled.

"Who?" Kincaide asked, a little perplexed. Avahan was more an old country doctor than a mad scientist like Ildar. And Sewwandi took her Hippocratic Oath way too seriously to experiment on people.

"The Wives," Reyhan said, looking as though such an admission pained him.

It probably did, even more so than thinking of them as Human.

"The Wives?"

"They all got designed, tweaked, and rebuilt however many times by that first freak," Reyhan said. "Some of the older ones probably know the theory and practicum pretty good if you asked."

"Why the hell would we do that?" Kincaide asked, exasperated now. "And who the hell are you to propose it? What have you done with Reyhan Herath, you imposter."

That brought a smile to the man's face.

"He'dsa fugitive from Gage justice, fleeing in a stolen warship with a band of illegal revolutionaries," Reyhan replied with a tight grin that reminded Kincaide of the old days together. "I'm looking at every edge I can get to put one over on those blue fuckers, Kincaide. We're going to have to push somewhere."

"And who would you trust with that ability?" he asked his oldest friend still alive. "Who do you gift with the power to twist minds if they felt the need? That's where we stop being freedom fighters and turn into full-on evil."

"Yeah, I know," Reyhan replied. "Except I don't know. Nobody of the current folk. They all have axes to grind pretty fierce. I'd like to say you, but I understand that you'd have to get Indexed and then be stuck in a machine for a while as somebody took your brain apart and put it back together. You'd never go for it and we need you in command here when The Gage finally catch wise to us and we have to start getting sneaky. Same goes for Prakash. Pity we couldn't make a different copy of Odtsetseg and call them both sisters or something."

"Again, evil," Kincaide stated in a hard voice. "We're doing this so that people like the Alvar and Hasan Ildar don't have the power to just experiment on the *lesser species* as they desire."

"Any way we could boost Odtsetseg's power?" Reyhan tossed that out there. "Turn on enough generators, but instead of having her power us up into warp-space, maybe she uses that to extend her telepathic reach?"

Kincaide was struck dumb. He opened his mouth, but nothing came out.

Reyhan turned a little pale as the implications of his words hit.

"Shit, could we?" the man asked in a scared voice.

Kincaide reached out and triggered the door wall to slide open.

"Tharushi," he called, catching the woman's eye. "Join us for a bit?"

She cocked her head at him, as if she could smell the trouble the two of them had been stirring up.

He had to remind himself how young she was when she looked at him with such deadly maturity in her eyes. Barely older than Odtsetseg. Hell, Hanishka could be her mother, but the two got along too well.

Her black hair had gotten long, kept back in a tail these days. Tharushi had rich, dark skin that sometimes got mistaken for African genes and a slender face.

Not just smart. Brilliant.

She touched something on her keyboard and nodded to one of her assistants, currently facing her from across the Command Square, before ascending the stair warily.

She nearly jumped out of her skin when Kincaide slid the wall shut behind her as soon as she crossed the threshold.

"Sit," he commanded, pointing at the middle chair.

Kincaide had added a third chair, since he so often had Kali, Odtsetseg, and Zhubin in here for things.

"What have I done now?" she asked, nervous.

"Nothing, yet," Kincaide assured her. "Got a technical question and figured I should start with my expert."

"Okay?" she said warily, still expecting a bear trap to close around her ankle from the look in her eyes.

"Me and this troublemaker were talking about options," Kincaide pointed at Reyhan, who was innocence itself right now. "We know that you fire up all the generators and switch all the engines over to provide Odtsetseg a field of power that she used to push the ship into and out of warp-space."

Tharushi nodded slowly, but her shoulder blades still hadn't touched the back of the chair yet.

"If we were at rest, say, docked to a station, could you do something similar?" Kincaide asked.

"Wouldn't do any good," she replied instantly. "Stations are always a safe distance from the edge of the warp-shroud. And that's in populous places. Pretty soon, we're going to reach planetary systems that aren't important enough for more than one port station, so they'll put it in orbit of the main inhabited planet."

"Not aiming for a jump," Kincaide explained. "If we were there, could you generate all that power?"

"Sure," she said. "Why? We don't need that much for shields and weapons, and there's no way we could take fire from a station at close range without getting pummeled pretty quickly."

"Trojan Horse," Reyhan spoke up now.

But he was Information Systems. Kincaide had no idea what the man was talking about. Tharushi did, though, so the two of them nerded out while Kincaide ignored them and clicked on his call box.

Computer Hasan appeared in response to the summons. Kincaide supposed you could call the projection Hasan still.

The features hadn't changed that much. Softer eyes and forehead. Less jawline and more cheeks. Poutier lips and a more aquiline face, drawn forward. And Reyhan had been experimenting with her body. At least the visible parts from about the hips up. Hasan was female now. Slender and without those impossible, gravity defying breasts teenage boys drew when they first learned pencil art or graphics programs. Computer Hasan's breasts were merely impressive, for what it was worth, rather than bursting out of his green crew uniform. But Reyhan was still a juvenile delinquent in some ways.

"Yes, Foreman?" he asked in the same male voice he'd always had, which was just weird, but Kincaide was getting used to it.

At least he had that same scowl, as if Hasan had a full-length mirror in front of him to see what Reyhan had done today. The beret was even there, but he had long, wavy hair now, like Tharushi's would be if she had any body to it.

Altogether an attractive woman. But it was still Hasan Ildar inside there, his electronic soul being tortured by a man like Reyhan Herath. And maybe Kincaide Kataragama.

The two nerds fell silent.

"Could you locate Odtsetseg and ask if she's free to join us, please?" Kincaide asked the projection.

Reyhan commanded the wo/man projection without such niceties as "please," but he had a particular dislike of Ildar that hadn't faded just because the real one wasn't here.

Kincaide tried to always remember to be at least polite.

He'd beaten the son of a bitch, after all.

Kincaide waited. The other two watched.

"She acknowledges and will join you momentarily," Hasan said in that reserved, upper-crust accent he got going when he was fulfilling his function as Computer Personality of the Day.

Whatever s/he might think of their new appearance.

Kincaide cut the line so she didn't distract him.

He opened the slider and just let the ambient noise of the bridge fill the air. Folks looked up long enough to confirm that no emergencies or orders were forthcoming, and then went back to ignoring him. Just like they should.

Odtsetseg climbed into view a few moments later.

Her hair was getting long, like Tharushi's. And several other people, come to think of it, but most of the crew no longer needed to keep their hair buzzed short for EVA in a suit. Kincaide had gotten his cut every ten days for so long that he wouldn't know how to grow it long. Or shave it all off.

But the galaxy was changing, so he supposed that his crew could change with it. Wasn't like they were Gage Fleet, with rules about every damned thing.

She smiled as she climbed the stairs and slid into the empty chair.

Kincaide closed them back up and returned the smile.

He didn't feel her touching his mind, but Kincaide knew it was second nature now, so he just pointed at Reyhan.

"All his fault," Kincaide said blandly, just to watch the man flinch.

"Excuse me?"

So Kincaide explained, letting the two nerds fill in technical details when they thought he was skipping over the interesting bits, but they'd have been hours if he let them talk.

Finally, he wound down and studied her face.

"Are we completely insane?" he asked her.

Nothing so prosaic as "Will it work?" for this group. Oh no. Go for the gusto here.

"I don't think anybody has ever even considered it, Kincaide," she replied after a long, thoughtful pause. "Certainly Ildar was more about either tweaking his various sex objects or building me to lift starships. Until I did it to him, I doubt he put a lot of thought into what I could really do, since the few times he had me adjust someone's mind was right before he put them into the Indexer, where he could have a clean copy to work from. But that was one person, in controlled circumstances. Or the time you and I went at Lady Thammavongsa in her palace. I have never tried to go after more than one person."

"But you could?" Reyhan asked.

Odtsetseg shrugged, but Kincaide was expecting that. They wouldn't know until they actually did it.

Before they could start up again, Kincaide opened the hatch and waved them away.

"Take it somewhere else," he ordered them gruffly, but he wasn't even sure they heard him, as the threesome was talking ninety meters a second right now as they descended the steps.

Kincaide called up Computer Babe Hasan and stared at her for a long moment.

"Tell Zhubin I need to see him, please."

CHAPTER 77

Hasan studied the readout and tried to contain the scream of triumph that wanted to erupt from his lips. Nobody was physically present, but that didn't mean he wasn't being watched.

Someone was always looking over his shoulder.

Fortunately, there was nobody on this crew capable of even understanding what he'd just done, let alone explaining it to that bitch.

Seriously, there were only a few thousand people Hasan knew of, out of the trillions that made up The Gage, who could look at the screen in front of him and decipher it. And most of those wouldn't *believe*.

He might not even have to wait a thousand years for his revenge.

Hasan missed his Chuns. Now would be the perfect moment to have one of them bent over a workstation to service him. He had no way to celebrate his achievement.

At the same time, he could not allow one hint of what he'd accomplished to become evident.

Not if he wanted to survive.

That blue bitch only kept him around because she thought she controlled him. Owned him. Perhaps wanted to torture him for a few centuries by dangling power and possibility in front of him, at least until she grew bored and forgetful, as her kind did.

If you were going to live more than seven thousand years, it behooved you to use them effectively, but the Alvar were as bad as the average Human, wasting their lives in front of a screen being passively entertained.

Which was why they would allow him to destroy them all.

Hasan made sure the current configuration was saved and then went ahead and told the system to generate an Icon as well. That would go into cold storage against future need, and prevent those silly turds from meddling in his affairs.

At least when they crowned him Emperor of The Gage, he'd be able to point to this date and laugh as he had them all hauled out front and shot in the parking lot of his palace.

He leaned back and sighed almost orgasmically. Checking the time, he noted that it was late in the afternoon for ship time. Hasan had modified himself early on to only need three to five hours of sleep, giving himself almost an extra week each month in which to work.

Use every moment.

He closed the machine down and slid it to the desk, letting the remaining hard, cold planes settle him back down into something so prosaic as living aboard a Gage Warp Destroyer in pursuit of the never-to-be-sufficiently-damned Zhubin Prakash.

Idly, Hasan wondered about the contents of the Eden package they must have picked up once they left the Al-Winoq Glide, back as part of their original flight. There was no way to determine if his same suppliers had put together a second package for them, as he had been in Alvar custody before he was even aware that there was a problem to address.

Prakash and the others had been selected for their racial purity. No East Asians in their genetic history. No Africans or First Nations. All the Arabs and Siberians had been carefully eliminated, leaving him with an arc of geography ranging from Sri Lanka north and west until he emerged on the verge of Western Europe.

Pure. Untainted by lesser breeds.

Had Prakash maintained that, or allowed a wider range of Humanity to escape their oppressors?

Hasan found himself cursing, again silently and internally, at the thought of how he might have to start over from scratch.

But if this worked, he would own the Warp Voyager *Vanechon* outright. They maintained Human Engines and backups, so he had genetic records to work from, although he had never bothered looking them up.

Never give your enemy any clue as to your plans.

But he also knew that the bitch thought they were slowly catching up with *Dashavatara*. Certainly, Prakash had not stopped in any of the systems he had crossed in order to pick up supplies. This vessel had been able to radio ahead and have supply containers deployed in space where *Vanechon* could pick them up without having to dock.

Whittling away the lead Prakash had built.

One of these days, *Vanechon* would catch them. If she took long enough, Hasan might even be in command when they did.

Then he would be in a position to take *Dashavatara* as well, and have all those Humans to work with. First, he would Index the ones he wanted to use, then out the airlocks with the rest. Then into their Eden Package and he'd probably end up deleting at least half the records, unless he wanted to work on a whole new range of sex objects to keep himself entertained.

Certainly, the new Engine variant he had designed would be no more useful on that front than the old one. Certainly, she would serve him, but the boyish figure would never excite him.

He needed someone to abuse.

Hasan sighed again and reached out a hand to key the comm, flipping quickly through the list to find Southavilay. The man wasn't really Thammavongsa's gigolo, although Hasan still presumed that he was keeping her from interrupting Hasan's work. However he did it.

Hasan shuddered at the thought of having to fuck the woman.

Maybe he'd Index her anyway, and then shrink a copy down to Human scales, just so he could dominate her aggressively. Hasan didn't think he could achieve orgasm that way, but sometimes it was an act of power, not sexuality, and he owed that woman for many things.

Having a copy of her, bound to him and cognizantly subservient, might be the greatest thing in the galaxy, to get him through the next few millennia.

Hasan pressed the button and waited.

Southavilay appeared on the tiny screen.

"Doctor Ildar?" he asked pleasantly.

From the background, the man was in an office similar to Hasan's lab, but they didn't allow their pet Human to range the enormous vessel beyond the three corridors connecting him to his cabin, his lab, and a dining hall. And even then, more often than not he had them deliver a plate so he could work uninterrupted.

"I believe I have done it, Administrator," Hasan said in a tired voice, trying to sound even now as a man tirelessly dedicated to saving The Gage from the renegades.

"I will join you shortly and we can go over the details," the man replied with a nod and cut the line.

Brusque. Most people would probably find that offensive, but it just meant that Hasan didn't have to spend stupid time entertaining such idiots when he could be working instead. There was nothing left to accomplish at this point, at least until he convinced them to Decant his improved design and he could get to work taking over this vessel.

Hasan could relax.

The Security Gigolo did not take long to arrive, opening the hatch and spying him at the desk. The tall Alvar moved to sit and had a smile on his face.

But then, Hasan supposed that a new Engine design, reinforced against any rebellious thoughts, would be another breakthrough. They had already determined that the one Odtsetseg carrying *Dashavatara* was a slight improvement over the five Humans moving *Vanechon* through warp-space.

But hadn't they lost one recently? Warp-spawn or something had caused one of the Engines to start frothing madly, but they'd been able to kill it before the man infected the others, so they'd only been slowed for a brief time while the sixth got brought into line and a replacement was Decanted.

Still, Odtsetseg by herself was at least four times as powerful, kilo for kilo.

A team of them might make it possible to sail to the far edge of the galaxy in less than ten years, even if you had to stop and survey each warp-shroud.

The Gage could possibly complete their conquest of this galaxy in the current generation and start thinking about surrounding galactic clusters next.

"Good news, I hope?" Southavilay asked.

"I believe so," Hasan said in a weary voice. "It was necessary to change certain design elements, once I located places where control could be ruptured. Weaknesses in the genetic structure itself, so I made changes to the model's physicality as well."

"Oh?"

"She will still be similar to the Odtsetseg model with which you are familiar," Hasan reassured the man. "But I made her more of a blond Siberian, rather than pure Mongolian, so that everyone can tell them apart. As a result, we will call this model Altantsetseg, which means Golden Flower."

"What other changes were necessary, Doctor?" the creature asked, eyes bright with interest.

"I increased her emotional stability and dialed down her intellectual capacity some," Hasan replied. "Odtsetseg was smarter than average for a Human. Altantsetseg is a regression to the mean of the species. Like the Odtsetseg model, she will present with no secondary sexual characteristics, and will have the rays marking her abilities on her face. As I noted, the hair will be golden blond instead of black, and her eyes are now blue, but that is a physical cue to me that I am working with the advanced model."

"Why is that a concern?" the creature asked, reminding Hasan that Southavilay was a Security Administrator of the First Rank, and not just a gigolo.

"They have an Odtsetseg model, Administrator," Hasan said darkly. "It and Kataragama were able to walk into my lab and mentally assault me. Lady Thammavongsa suffered a similar indignity. They will not be able to do anything remotely like that when we are expecting an Altantsetseg model instead."

"I see," the man leaned back in his chair. "And you expect such a thing?"

"I expect this ship to chase *Dashavatara* to the ends of the universe, Southavilay," Hasan snapped. "I cannot imagine Lady Thammavongsa being satisfied with just blowing their vessel up. No, she will want to look Kataragama in the eyes before she kills him. We must be prepared for whatever they think an Odtsetseg model can do to stop you at that moment, yes?"

"I agree," the Gigolo nodded. He paused for a moment in thought. "I take it you would like permission to Decant a new Altantsetseg model for your next round of experiments?"

"There is only so much I can do with theory, Administrator," Hasan reminded him. "With Odtsetseg, I Decanted nearly two hundred versions as I worked through issues over the course of ten years. Altantsetseg will be much more stable at the start, but I have had to make any number of changes to her design, and even the best computers will not predict everything. I need to have her in front of me, answering questions, before I am confident that everything is working as it should."

"I will relay your request to Lady Thammavongsa," the man said, rising now to that stupid, impossible height of an Alvar male.

He left, and Hasan blew out a heavy breath.

If those fools fell for this, they were all doomed.

Hasan smiled, but only inside.

CHAPTER 78

Zhubin stared at the airlock hatch and waited for it to open. In the back of his head, he heard the clock ticking, but it would be doing that regardless of what he was up to.

Somewhere, a Gage Voyager would be chasing them still. Maybe more than one.

That nobody had shown up on their scanners before they had escaped each system before now didn't mean anything at all. Zhubin had no doubt he had gravely angered the Alvar with this stunt.

But he'd been planning something like this for nearly thirty years in this incarnation. Maybe other ones as well, because he'd always been something of a rebel. The Alvar had noted that and channeled it into aggression, turning him into a killer before one of his copies had gone rogue.

Occasionally, he wondered how many other times he had. Zhubin had killed two younger versions of himself that The Gage had sent, one of whom had originally killed Aysha when his shot missed the target and he never got a second one off.

Nobody had managed to find him in a long time, but he suspected that the old records of Zhubin Prakash were getting a much closer review these days. They might even find his real name.

But not at Sextantis. Not this far away from Al-Winoq where the first surge of colonization, so long ago, had more or less petered out, about the time Humans were considering evolving into a separate species from the other hominids.

This was the last place he and Kincaide thought that they would encounter a system big enough to resupply *Dashavatara* without asking too many questions.

Zhubin just had to bluff his way through the locals.

Oh, and not die in the process.

Like Kincaide, there were no backups of his current life. Just that dumb kid, two years from meeting Aysha, and her, a year after they'd been married and happy. His safe had instructions for Kincaide or whoever was in command if something happened to him.

At least those kids would get their chance.

The hatch began to move, parting in the center and sliding backwards into the walls with a slight puff of pressure equalization.

Zhubin appeared to be alone in the airlock, but there was a team of killers back and hidden. Even Kali had joined in, holding a hotblaster pistol in each of four hands. Frightening, if she was that multi-dextrous.

Beyond, he could see a gray uniform in front, and two black uniforms behind it. The light on the other side was dim, compared to *Dashavatara*'s side.

It resolved into a Lop Customs officer. Male. A head and a half shorter, so maybe one hundred and fifty-five centimeters tall at most. Peach fur on the face and hands. Ears that stood upright and moved like the ship's three cats, but taller and thinner.

To Humans, the first Lop had reminded them of rabbits. Bipedal. Omnivorous. But still rabbit-like, especially the way they tended to move up and down as they walked, rather than the smooth forward motion of a Human.

The Mori and Mog security goons behind the man were just to make him look official. Even at fifty-two, Zhubin could kill all three before they knew what had happened, but that would only compound his problems.

"Chairman Prakash?" the Lop officer asked as he looked up.

"That is correct."

"I will convey you to the Station Executor, sir," the man said, turning and walking immediately.

The two soldiers slid away to the wall and pivoted inwards, where they would form something of an escort or honor guard, depending.

Zhubin felt a bead of sweat form at the exact center of his back, right between his shoulder blades, and slowly ooze downward as he walked, even though outwardly he appeared to be another bored bureaucrat, come to explain everything to the person in charge of the station because the security level of his mission was too high to even commit things to radio waves.

It helped that Sextantis was a backwater. There might only be a handful of Alvar on this entire station, depending, as the system didn't produce any particularly valuable exports.

It would be him against all of them. And if anything went wrong, he would likely die here.

Hopefully, the Star Flower could protect him.

Or at least get the rest of them to safety afterwards.

CHAPTER 79

Odtsetseg sat in her piloting chair, above the bridge, and tried to breathe normally. She'd asked Kincaide to join her, so he'd brought a chair up and rested it next to her facing backwards, so she could hold his hand and he could watch her while she slept.

Except that she wouldn't be asleep. She wouldn't dream.

She was going to try something nobody had ever done before, if all the Alvar and Gage propaganda was to be believed. After all, against most telepaths those little necklace shields they wore were sufficient armor against a Human's mental invasion.

She hadn't corrected them then, either.

She took another heavy breath.

"You'll be fine," Kincaide said calmly.

"Easy for you to say," she smiled at the man. "You don't have anything to do here."

"I have to worry about you," he said, a serious look coming over his face.

That suddenly removed a load from her shoulders that Odtsetseg had not even realized she was carrying. He would watch out for her. Worry about her.

Love her.

She could do this.

"Tharushi, where are we at for power?" she asked, turning to look at the face of the Power Systems expert on a screen by her right hand.

"All the power reactors are running at normal power," the woman said after a quick glance down. "The engines are currently on standby, but I can bring them inline in about eight seconds if you need that much extra drive."

"Let's try just this," Odtsetseg replied.

She took a third breath.

"You've got this," Kincaide announced.

Odtsetseg smiled and closed her eyes, grateful for his hand holding hers as she went inside herself.

Just like that night he had been with the icky woman, Roselani Thammavongsa, she stepped up and out.

Dashavatara was a tiny beetle on the side of a flattened grapefruit, docked next to the station. Unlike Port Stations at more important places, this was shaped as a simple disk, bulging in the middle and flat at the top and bottom.

Velle Port Station, in Al-Winoq, had eight arms coming off it like a snowflake, each separating into smaller fingers to provide the most places where ships could dock to transfer people and cargo. Sextantis was a third-class system.

Around her, she felt part of *Dashavatara* go dark as Tharushi brought the warp-shields up around the Crew Section aft. They weren't in warp, but it would block off the minds of her crew from being a distraction as Odtsetseg listened to the other lives and minds around her.

The power the ship was generating was like a river of mercury flowing next to her, but Odtsetseg didn't try to grasp it yet.

She was back to that night, so she stepped onto the station and listened for the taste of Zhubin Prakash against the background.

There were few Humans on this station. It was rare to find one valued as anything other than Engines or bio-gods by the Alvar, so they were not free to live normal lives. There were supposedly six trillion Mori serving The Gage in one form or another across the galaxy, but only the fifteen million Humans under Domes or being Engines on Warp Voyagers.

Zhubin was easy enough to find.

She watched him walk through dim corridors in the presence of three alien minds, a ghost floating behind them.

After all the wealth in the Al-Winoq Glide, this station struck her as poor and grungy. Like Maintenance was losing the battle against entropy and didn't even care enough to fight all that much.

She tasted hallways where the air had gone stale because the filters had not been cleaned in too long. Smelled lubricant gone old and dry. Felt the spike of old wiring shorting inside conduits.

Odtsetseg was tempted to be insulted, but she knew that such *ennui* worked in their favor, as it reflected a crew that was not purely dedicated to their Alvar overlords.

Zhubin rode a lift up to a tower looming over the vast plain of the top deck. It reminded her of that steppe where she went to carry *Dashavatara*, always watchful for the vultures, but they only circled in the distance these days, never getting too close.

As if they had learned to fear her. It was good.

The lift door opened and she watched Zhubin focus his mind on a single Alvar officer.

Female. Older. Tired and heavyset. Starting to get squishy, in spite of the genes that selected against such things.

Lazy.

Odtsetseg followed the others into the large chamber and looked around once. Mori, Mog, and Lop underlings and staff surrounded the woman. Odtsetseg listened elsewhere and saw no other Alvar minds.

The planet below them had Alvar. Probably factory managers and plantation overseers, as their presence was a light film across the tops of the culture she could taste.

Odtsetseg reached back now and dangled a hand in the river of mercury, feeling it climb up her arm and across her body until she glowed with a radiance she felt should have lit the physical room, even when she was only a ghost here.

Perhaps she would try to manifest herself sometime, just because Odtsetseg could think of no greater way to terrorize a group of Alvar than to confront them with angry Human ghosts.

She stepped into the Executor's mind.

Zhubin appeared now, through other's eyes. Short, when the man was taller than Odtsetseg, but she was Alvar now. The Human was another mayfly, here briefly and then vanishing into old age and death, as so many of her underlings did.

The lesser species were constantly dying off on her, just when she had them trained properly. She considered asking if they could be adjusted to live longer lives, but understood that Gage Fleet and especially the Noble-born would never allow it, even if Humans were apparently so easy to modify.

"Chairman, you are here," Odtsetseg felt herself saying to the man. "What was so secretive that you could not broadcast it?"

Odtsetseg took a silver hand and touched the woman's mind. She had done something similar with Roselani, once upon a time.

Roselani? When had she started to think of her as someone other than that *icky woman?*

But then she understood. Kincaide was with her in spirit, even though he could not be here as another ghost. He didn't hate the woman. Respected her, in spite of everything she had done.

Odtsetseg saw them all with new eyes, opened by having Kincaide inside her, just as she was inside this Executor.

She watched Zhubin turn carefully, looking at all the staff around them, any of whom might be spies.

Odtsetseg whispered in her ear.

"Clear the room," the Executor ordered in a suddenly-firm and commanding voice. "I will speak with the Human alone."

The smell around them turned to surprise, tinged even with excitement for a moment before it lagged down into entropic decay again. People transferred operational control to other command centers then rose and departed. Even the Customs guards moved, although their officer took several moments to process that he was being evicted as well.

The punk had a twinge of shock as he was suddenly *little people*.

Odtsetseg reached out and reinforced that feeling, just because he felt like a bad man and maybe he could be less of an asshole to everyone in the future.

Quickly, only the three of them remained: an Alvar, a Human, and a ghost.

Odtsetseg whispered again, a bit awed at how easily the woman took her suggestions as gospel. But looking around the inside of her mind, this was not another Roselani. Just a sad, tired bureaucrat who really didn't give much of a shit about anything anymore.

"I understand that you have a top-secret mission from Gage Fleet Headquarters, Zhubin," the woman said now.

Odtsetseg watched the man's eyes flare just a little with excitement as he recognized what she had done.

"That is correct, Executor," he replied with a more-than-necessary bow. "I would like to draw supplies from this station, but we are in a hurry to get forward to the Line of Exploration, so you would need to expedite everything."

The Executor stirred within herself, as though to argue, but Odtsetseg found a lever she could pull and the woman subsided just as quickly. Another dial seemed to be marked Military Duty so Odtsetseg turned it up several notches.

It wasn't like they would be around when the woman suddenly rediscovered her purpose. She'd have to take it out on her staff.

Odtsetseg wondered if anybody would react badly enough to assassinate the woman and make it look like a terrible accident. Perhaps she could implant some suggestions before she left, like seeds put into the dirt in spring.

"Your mission is critical, Chairman Prakash," the woman spoke now, standing firmer and taller. "I will issue orders to my staff immediately. Is there anything else we can do to help?"

"Just your authority will be sufficient, Executor," he replied firmly. "I will make it a point to tell the authorities how helpful you and your station have been, when I have a chance to report in again."

Odtsetseg felt the woman preen like a bird at the words, so she pushed a little. Not much. Enough to see what she could do, with that river of mercury to guide her.

She drove the woman to her desk and opened a console. Whispered the words into her ear and watched them get typed into the system.

She leaned into the woman now, to get her to push the button that would transmit them to everyone on the station, and every ship in system, but the woman stopped, her finger just a centimeter above the key that would send it.

Odtsetseg pushed harder now, but the woman would not budge. Something in her mind had suddenly woken up to what she was doing and rebelled. Odtsetseg felt her control slip.

"I need more power," she whispered to herself, trying to wrap her arms around that mind before it slipped away from her, an eel wriggling away.

Kincaide Kataragama suddenly appeared next to her, like another silver ghost, but this was a much younger version of the man. Perhaps him at twenty-five years old, rather than the tired and angry fifty-eight-year-old he was now.

He smiled at her.

"Here," he said, suddenly holding out a box that she took.

The box was smaller than her head, but large enough. Odtsetseg opened it and white-hot power poured out, almost burning her as she reached a hand into this new river and grabbed just a handhold.

The Executor had turned around inside her mind now, staring at her —at the two of them—in absolute terror.

Odtsetseg grasped her mind and twisted it back to the front, using silver nails like railroad spikes now to hold it in place. Another spike drove the hand down on the keyboard, sending the message.

Odtsetseg relaxed and looked around, but Kincaide was gone. The river of solar fury remained, so she took another handful and spread it like butter across the woman's mind, softening things and making adjustments.

She would remember the message. Remember the importance of what she had ordered, but eventually would remember this battle as well.

Not until long after *Dashavatara* was gone and there was nothing she could do about it.

Odtsetseg let go of the woman after turning to Zhubin.

"It is done," she said.

Odtsetseg opened her eyes and felt the immense exhaustion roll over her like a tide.

"What did you do?" she gasped.

"You asked," he said. "I yelled at Tharushi to bring the engines up, and then leaned in and whispered into your ear. What did you see?"

She smiled at him, but everything went black as she fell asleep in his arms.

CHAPTER 80

Kincaide was aft supervising, mostly because he did three dimensional puzzles better than just about anybody else on his crew, and they weren't going anywhere until all those empty containers were swapped out for full ones.

Already, two teams had emptied the bay and pushed everything out the back cargo airlock, like a giant goose laying eggs in the spring. He was surrounded by nothing. A cathedral of space that almost reminded him of the place nearby where the Wives had taken up residence.

Lilith appearing around a corridor and aiming at him from across the way just reinforced that perception. But this was the one part of the ship where she could move around easily. Even walk up walls and across ceilings if she wanted, because the scale here was standard cargo containers, which were big to Alvar.

Both work crews found reasons to be busy across the space, where Kincaide would have to walk over or yell. He wondered if the woman had made arrangements with them earlier for a private conversation and nobody had bothered to inform him.

Kincaide hated surprise birthday parties.

But it was Lilith. Leader of the Wives by consensus, and one of the smartest folks on the ship, even if she would never serve as an officer.

Maybe he *should* build his next ship big enough for the Wives. Be interesting to see Euryale or Lilith at a bridge station. Both had the brains for it.

Kincaide checked his wrist chron, but the teams would still be moving empty containers clear of the hull for a bit yet, before they started wrestling a full one around with tugs.

He turned to Lilith and watched her skitter closer, a quiet patter of spider toes on the deck. Black hair on her head and long, spiky black hairs on the parts he could see, just like a spider. She wore a top somewhere between a bustier and a corset around her torso, made of vertical straps of something rigid in alternating gold and bronze metals. Her hair was pulled back and held in place by a kind of face crown, around her head like a tiara, but with vertical pieces that hung down and accentuated her lovely cheekbones.

Pale skin and bright red lips, but Goaulda had been experimenting equally with nightmares and kinks, so an undead creature from the darkest depths of hell was probably his goal.

She was still beautiful, just in a frightening way. Normally as tall as an Alvar when she walked on those eight long legs. At least the design hadn't included mandibles. Apparently after he had finished Gahi the Roadrunner babe, Goaulda had decided that he wanted upper bodies to be much closer to normal for a Human woman. Something about breasts to enjoy, necks to nibble on, ears to nuzzle, and lips for kissing.

Shame none of them dared risk intercourse. It would suck to have to consider centuries and perhaps millennia of celibacy. At least he'd be dead in a few decades and had already slowed down some from his crazy days as a newly-widowed rowdy on the docks and whorehouses.

She returned his smile and came to rest just far enough away that he could not reach out a hand and touch the front of her abdomen, where it pivoted up into the Human part of her torso.

Idly, Kincaide wondered if she had a belly button under there.

Lilith surprised him by lowering herself to the deck, like a Human kneeling, except that it put her eyes at about the same level as Zhubin or Kali when she did that. Tall, but not towering.

Kincaide made a point of looking around, obviously noting that everyone else seemed awfully busy right now. He smiled up at her.

"Am I in trouble?" he asked in a teasing voice.

"Perhaps," she replied, equally light, her head tilted just enough to call attention to her eyes.

Usually, blacked hellpits, but today they just seemed dark, like his.

"To what do I owe the pleasure?" Kincaide smiled, gesturing around them. "Obviously, you wanted something private without a lot of warning."

"Just to talk, Kincaide," she nodded. "Two of us, well-met strangers in a bar, except that you don't do that sort of thing much and I didn't feel like squeezing myself into painful contortions, just to come forward to the lounge you share with the others."

"You could have asked," he said.

"More fun this way," she said, growing a shade more serious. "Neutral ground, as it were."

"That, young lady, is what frightens me," Kincaide replied.

"Young?" she asked, rising up just a little by straightening her spine to grow another couple of centimeters. "I'm five hundred years older than you are, Kincaide."

"And you look barely five years older than Odtsetseg," Kincaide countered. "Plus, I'm a cranky old man and all of you will be around long after I'm gone."

Again, she cocked her head at him. Studied him silently as he watched her, careful not to scowl at the woman. She'd done nothing to justify it. He just wasn't a people person.

"I've had a number of conversations with Kali since we left Al-Winoq," Lilith said abruptly. "Contemplating our future since, as both you and Zhubin have noted, the Wives will outlive the rest of you and the entire crew."

He nodded and watched the woman, unsure where she was headed.

"How do you feel about Odtsetseg?" she asked, slamming him pretty good with an emotional whiplash.

Kincaide rocked back on his heels a little and then shifted his weight onto his right leg, kind of scrunching over to view the woman in a new light.

"Do you trust her?" Lilith added quickly.

"Implicitly," Kincaide said. "As to the woman herself, I see her as something of a step-daughter I inherited late in life, where she was already an adult, but willing to treat with me that way. Ildar twisted her genetic structure when he built her, so in some ways she's still a twelve-year-old, emotionally as well as physically. She doesn't understand wide swaths of Human emotion because she's never had them, and probably never will. Do you remember being that age?"

"I do not," Lilith replied softly. "I'm certain that Goaulda wiped those parts of our memories away in the process of reprogramming us. I came into existence like Athena, the Hellenic Goddess of War and Wisdom, sprung from the head of Zeus."

Kincaide nodded.

"She never went through all that crazy shit that occurs at puberty," he said. "Never had the fights, the worries, or the insecurities. Not sure she ever will, either, but I'm a guy, so I don't know if that's a good thing or not."

"I could not answer that either, Kincaide," she nodded. "Perhaps we should ask Tharushi or Hanishka sometime. Perhaps it would even be appropriate, moving forward."

Kincaide went a little cold. Nothing about her set off all his sensors, but the air in this bay had just changed. He wasn't sure he liked it.

"Appropriate?" he repeated the word slowly.

"Odtsetseg raised an interesting question with Kali, early in our flight to freedom," Lilith continued.

"Did she now?" Kincaide let the words drawl out, wondering if he was about to be fighting for his life with this Monster Wife. There was a gleam in her eyes that had not been there a moment ago.

He measured her for the best place to strike, wondering if he should climb atop her abdomen like a rider, in order to get at her neck, once she stood up.

"Not like that," Lilith said hastily, arms coming up defensively as she apparently saw something in his eyes.

Like, maybe, death?

"Like what, then?" Kincaide demanded in a harsher rasp than previously.

"Odtsetseg told Kali that it might be possible for the woman to reach into the minds of one of the Wives and change things," Lilith said in a rushed tone. "To alter us in ways that nobody else could do, short of another bio-god Indexing us and making changes before Decanting a fresh copy."

The panic in her voice caused Kincaide to relax. She might have size and reach, but he doubted that the woman had ever killed someone. As far as he knew, only one of the Wives had ever done so, and the victim had been Goaulda himself. The one who did it had self-terminated afterwards, unable to live after deicide.

Kincaide was just fine with killing gods.

"Go on," he prompted, relaxing his hands and sliding back off the balls of his feet now.

"When we got to this station, she was apparently able to reach into the mind of the Alvar in charge and shift patterns around," Lilith said.

"Yes," Kincaide agreed. "She has telepathy, but not on a scale with her telekinesis. Tharushi was able to route all the generators and provide her with extra power, just like when we enter warp. Still needed the main engines when the Executor started to resist."

"We wouldn't be resisting," Lilith said enigmatically.

"You want Odtsetseg to modify your brain?" Kincaide asked, completely gobsmacked now. "All of you?"

"One, for now," Lilith said. "As an experiment. According to what she told Kali, those changes don't necessarily last, but nobody has actually experimented with it, except Ildar."

Kincaide took a deep breath and considered it. There was an ancient saying about opening a can of worms. He'd actually had to look worms up in the Catalogue to understand the reference, although he still wasn't entirely sure what the phrase meant, except that the linguistic implication was that once opened, all the worms could never be stuffed back into that can again.

Angry djinn and brass lamps was perhaps a better euphemism.

He wondered how long the Wives had been kicking this one around. Like the Alvar, they had a tendency to see things in such long windows of time that they talked but rarely acted.

"Fine," Kincaide announced, still unsure what the hell this woman was about. "And?"

"And we need help," Lilith said, her head turned just enough sideways that he perked up now. "Your help possibly."

"Mine," he repeated, wondering who was going to catch hell for whatever they thought they had maneuvered him into this time.

"Yours," Lilith said. "It gets complicated."

"Gets," he assaulted the word with an extra layer of sarcasm on top like frosting.

He fell silent and watched. If she wanted something, she was going to have to come right out and ask, whatever the hell it was.

She seemed to glom on to that point fairly quickly.

"Odtsetseg should be able to reach into a mind and turn things around," Lilith said. "At least for the short term. Maybe longer, or perhaps she can go back later as she learns the techniques."

He nodded, unwilling to trust that his voice would sound even remotely friendly at this point.

Kincaide didn't like setups, and that's what this kept feeling more and more like.

"We have not approached her yet, because she is still a relative stranger to the Wives," Lilith continued. "I decided that you and Zhubin would be the best ones to ask, but especially you because the two of you have a closer relationship. Step-daughter, as you said. That suggests a protectiveness, both ways, which in turn means that we might be able to trust her."

Kincaide cocked his head as a way of prompting her. Waving his hands to speed her up felt like it might yet be a little rude.

Apparently, Lilith was still seeking the right words, which made him feel better, because that meant he wasn't likely to have to get utterly stupid today.

Today.

"So she can do a thing." Lilith's evasions continued, circling without ever drawing closer from what he could tell. An uncertain shark in calm waters. "But what she can do is only half the issue. We will need someone else's help. From her conversation with Kali, it seems that you might be the most promising candidate to help us."

He caught himself short of making a rude noise at the woman.

Barely.

"How about you ask, instead of dancing around whatever the hell it is?" Kincaide growled at her finally, when it looked like she'd run herself out of words.

Lilith took a deep breath. For a moment, he saw pain in her eyes, which surprised him even more than everything else so far.

He probably wasn't going to like it.

"Brakiee Goaulda built each of us as sex objects, Kincaide," she finally said, probably about the point where she should have started earlier, but he wasn't going to snap at her now. "Much like your old comrade Hasan Ildar had his clones, except that we were Goaulda's exclusive property, built to his needs and specifications."

Kincaide nodded, more friendly now. They were finally making progress.

If you could call it that.

"Each of us is wired in such a way that when Goaulda touched us in any manner, certain programming kicked in and overrode everything else." She was spitting the words out now. Raw rage he could appreciate as she bit off each syllable. "We stopped being able to think for ourselves, and became hopelessly indentured to that man's sexual needs. Since Enkya killed him, none of us have dared allow another man to touch any of us, for fear that such programming wasn't just confined to Goaulda, but would cause us to become emotionally bound to whatever man it was. For as long as he lived."

Fucker. Good thing Goaulda was dead and beyond Kincaide's reach about now.

He hadn't considered that in great enough detail to appreciate that these women were built specifically for sex, and then forever denied even Human touch.

And going to possibly live forever.

Might make a woman a little grumpy.

He blinked as he considered what Odtsetseg might be able to do to help these women, if she had the power to reach inside and break that programming, much like she had done to herself to reduce Ildar from a god to a punk.

Then they would be free to...

Kincaide growled. Probably louder than he thought because Lilith flinched away from him. Not much, but enough. Telling, as it were.

Lilith could know fear of a Human.

What had Odtsetseg said? Every person in the crew feared her, even the ones that lusted after her or considered her a goddess?

Except for one.

Except for him.

He didn't fear Odtsetseg. Didn't lust after her. Didn't view her as a goddess. Just a young woman without any friends or role models, so he had adopted her as a step-daughter so she had someone.

Kincaide felt his head tilt forward until he was looking at this woman from under hooded brows.

Somewhere, Odtsetseg might have just tasted his rage, wafting telepathically across the ship like the scent of fresh shit.

Lilith had turned shy and skittish, like maybe he was the monster here and her the innocent about to become prey to some terror coming out of the darkness.

He licked his suddenly-dry lips once as an excuse not to say anything.

"So Odtsetseg thinks that she might be able to break that particular bit of conditioning?" he asked slowly. Angrily.

Lilith nodded just enough that her head actually moved, looking more like a kid and less like a mature woman however many centuries old.

"And you'd be free to…whatever?" he continued, fighting to keep the rage from turning his eyes red.

Again, the nod.

"But you'd need to test it, wouldn't you?" he asked. He tried not to sneer or snarl, but to be an adult about it.

Maybe.

"And you don't know who you might be able to recruit, since all the Wives were designed by Goaulda to be frightening monsters that played on the darkest bits of the Human psyche, yes?" he pressed.

"Yes," she whispered, eyes fiercely locked on his now.

He ground his teeth hard enough that he might spall chunks of enamel off shortly.

"I have a particular reputation, you know," he offered grumpily.

"And according to Odtsetseg, it is largely a sham," Lilith replied with just a little more heat as her chin finally came up. A little more volume in her voice. Her confidence growing with each word. "You don't really hate anyone, but use that as a mask to keep people at bay so you don't have to deal with them. That you aren't anywhere near as virulent in your racism or specism as even the next closest standard Human on this crew, to say nothing of men like Zhubin Prakash or Reyhan Herath."

He scowled, but she suddenly seemed immune. Kincaide had been afraid that would be the case.

Her flinch had turned to almost a smile now. He kept the profanities inside his head where only his step-daughter might be privy to them, if she was listening in right now.

Step-daughter.

Had she maneuvered this as some bizarre thing to get herself a new step-mother as well? Suddenly, he wondered if he'd been accurate in his assessment of the woman as being a preteen in more ways than he'd thought.

Was this her way to get him over Nayani? That wasn't possible, but he'd been functionally alone for over twenty years, not counting occasional professionals paid for their time and faux enthusiasm.

He didn't know who to be angry at, so he settled for taking it out on himself. If that was the case, Odtsetseg meant well. She'd been inside his mind and his dreams enough to know whatever truths he might have suppressed along the way.

Kincaide took a deep breath and stepped sideways in his mind, trying to see this like an adult, washing all the emotion off the table and letting the cold, rational light of morning come in the window.

Hangovers were a bitch. Doubly so when you woke up next to a snoring stranger and couldn't find your shoes. Been a while, but that wasn't the same as saying it had never happened.

He studied Lilith now in that new light of morning, wondering how many people were involved in this little conspiracy. At least three, with Kali acting as interlocutor of some sort.

Lilith hadn't moved.

"You're nuts, you know," he stated unequivocally, the rage gone from his voice like dew melting in sunlight.

"We all are, Kincaide," she replied with a simple nod that turned into a pretty smile. "That's what makes us Human."

Human?

He supposed so. She was as Human as he was, just in a form that had eight legs instead of two, but Niki was the same way, once you realized those eight legs were tentacles. And just as Human as all of them.

Even the one that wasn't really completely Human at the genetic level, but she was his daughter, and she meant well. Wanted to ease some of the pain she'd seen in his soul, apparently.

"So if I'm to be your victim here, who is the one taking all the risks on your side?" he asked tartly.

He hadn't agreed to anything yet, but he hadn't stormed out of the bay screaming curses and profanities at anyone and everyone he met, either.

"As I said earlier, it gets complicated," Lilith said, turning deadly serious now. "Not all the Wives are convinced that it will work, so many of them don't want to take any risks. Others think that because you aren't Goaulda, that the programming won't kick in, or that Odtsetseg can make the necessary changes, at least for now."

"And if it fails, I'll be dead in a few decades anyway, so they'd eventually be free," Kincaide replied without much sneer to his voice.

"Eventually, yes," Lilith agreed. "So if you are prepared to risk it, several of us are prepared to step up."

"Us?"

"Yes," she said. "I lead the Wives, so it should be something I'm willing to face, if I intend to ask any of them to."

Kincaide blinked. He studied the woman, unsure.

Unsettled.

"How?" he asked, confused now.

Derailed might be a better term, as he'd gone completely off whatever rails they might have been following.

At least she smiled at him.

"Goaulda designed all of us for his pleasure, but he also wired our brains to enjoy the experience," she said. "For all the man was scum, he at least let us achieve orgasm. Big, loud, long ones, too, which was part of what helped him over the top. Perhaps he had some measure of empathy left over when he was done being a god."

"I meant the structural mechanics of the thing," Kincaide corrected himself.

"My vagina is at the rear of my abdomen, Kincaide," she said, gesturing back over a shoulder. "Rather than the bottom of my torso. The spider's spinnerets are actually dual-purpose, in that I can spin and lay web, but they are also correctly placed to hold him against me during the act of coitus. He would stand, with a hand on each of my rear knees, and I would hold him in place like a normal woman would with her legs. Even my clitoris was placed at the top so that it would be properly stimulated. My upper spine is flexible enough that I can lay back flat and look up at him, if he wished to play with my breasts instead."

"Huh." That seemed to be about the limit of his vocabulary right now.

She watched him.

How does one negotiate with a goddess who has the ability to apparently grant wishes as easily as she might destroy you?

"Huh," he repeated. "Who else?"

Mostly idle curiosity at this point. He still had not agreed to anything.

Might not.

Might.

Fuck only knew.

"Kali," she said. "Staci. Theodosia. Noor. Ghost offered, but did not seem that enthusiastic, since you would not know what she looked like and that seemed to factor into her thinking."

"In the dark, all women look alike, Lilith," Kincaide countered. "All women. Even you."

Spider centaur. Four-armed midget Alvar. Orque. Puma. Leotaur. And maybe a completely normal woman, if you were to explore her with your fingertips and your tongue instead of your eyes.

Lilith nodded.

"And I do not expect any answer now," she continued. "Unless it was to be a flat denial and refusal to discuss further, but that does not seem to be the case?"

"I don't know," Kincaide replied.

Truthfully, he didn't. Roselani had expected something other than what she got. What, he didn't know, but he doubted that she would have been on that ship chasing him to the first Port Station if there was no emotion involved.

Now Lilith and the Wives were asking for something from him. And knew that he didn't hate them with the sorts of rage and fear that someone like Reyhan might.

But they were just people, once you got past the skin. Even Roselani had been a person, however wealthy, powerful, and Noble-born she was. Whatever kinks she had needed to exercise.

Or exorcise.

Kincaide wondered if he gave off a particular scent that women could identify, or something.

"I will leave you alone with your thoughts," Lilith said now.

She rose from her crouch and did a complicated thing with her legs that turned into a formal curtsy involving her entire body, before she backed away, smiled, and turned to leave.

Kincaide found himself alone on the field of battle, having won by default merely because he was the only one left around here, Lilith having fled. Or maybe she'd won and left him to suffer.

Maybe.

Something.

Fuck.

In the distance, the cargo airlock rattled and banged, indicating that the first container had arrived.

Hopefully, that would give him something else to think about for a while.

CHAPTER 81

Kincaide stood at his usual spot next to Reyhan along the square counter that made up the bridge of *Dashavatara*. Unlike the others, he hadn't raised the console to a comfortable height, because he had nothing to do but listen to questions and issue orders.

Computer Hasan had the appearance of a native of South America today. Female still, because Reyhan probably wasn't ever letting him have a penis again, even electronically. Flat face with big cheekbones and a cute button of a nose. Felt tiny, but she was never Human sized for comparison. Straight black hair worn loose past her shoulders.

Hasan's eyes looking out. Kincaide detected a hint of acceptance, as though Reyhan was getting better at tweaking the personality circuits underneath and not just the easier presentation layer. Be interesting when Herath finally mastered the Personality programming enough to either pull the man out, or whatever evil Reyhan had planned.

Kincaide grinned over at Reyhan. Man was slowly losing the few hairs left on top, but still brushed the strays back every morning. Sides were extra bushy this morning. Horns cut with a laser maybe.

Evil grin.

The others were just as poised when Kincaide looked around the room. Odtsetseg was upstairs in her station, half-asleep and listening to the woman in charge of the station with all the generators backing her up and Tharushi ready to flood the ether with every bit of power she had in a pinch.

Backing away from this station would be the most dangerous maneuver they ever pulled. After this, it would be piracy or predatory, but today they needed to act like good little citizens on the local Glide. No speeding tickets or traffic infractions.

Nothing that might suggest to the station authorities that they needed to open fire with the massive turrets on the top and bottom decks. The kind that could smash *Dashavatara* into rubble and shards.

"Stand by for detachment," Kincaide said unnecessarily.

Everyone was ready. Had been. He'd taken a little extra time just to refill the water tanks full, and then every container they had that could hold water. The Arboretum smelled like a swamp right now, but it would dry out in a few days. Spring rains, as it were.

"Helm, release all locks with the station," Kincaide said firmly. By the numbers. "Power Systems, prepare to cut engines over to thrust. Station-keeping thrusters begin pushing us away from the station."

Right now, the power they unleashed could give Odtsetseg godhead, apparently, but using that power was inversely cubed to distance, so the Alvar commander over there would break free soon. Hopefully, the right seeds had been planted.

That or a good optical migraine that would send that Alvar woman to her bunk for a day or two, leaving the rest of the station a little headless.

Odtsetseg had described the emotional and intellectual decay that had overtaken the place.

Dashavatara rattled as various waldo arms aft let go. Then, they were floating in space. Thrusters wouldn't move them far, but would get the ship drifting in the right direction.

"Helm, ahead at one percent acceleration," Kincaide nodded to Dinushan. "Slow and polite."

"Ahead one percent," the man grinned.

Dashavatara began moving away from the last Gage station where they would ever be welcome. From this point on, Kincaide Kataragama intended to become a pirate, living up to the worst legends of old Earth, men and women still revered today, however many thousands of years later or light-centuries away.

"Odtsetseg, how is everything behind us?" Kincaide asked in a louder voice.

"Calm, Kincaide," she answered in a voice just this side of waking.

He nodded and watched the plot on Reyhan's screen. So far, so good.

"Reaching the first marker buoy," Dinushan called after a few minutes.

"Accelerate to one quarter," Kincaide answered.

"Warning," Computer Hasan Babe said with concern in his voice. "I am detecting transmissions from a Gage Warp Voyager, directed at the station. They identify *Dashavatara* as an enemy vessel and order the station's gunners to open fire."

Not quite the worst possible time to catch up, but damned close.

"Odtsetseg, do whatever you can to buy us time," Kincaide yelled. "Dinushan, max acceleration right now. Sensors, find me that ship."

Maybe he could have skipped the extra half-day to refill all the water tanks to capacity. Maybe he could have sped other tasks up.

At the same time, pushing the station crew might have caused them to rebel a little, or even ask why everything had to be in a hurry. Which might have led them to demand to speak with the Commander of *Dashavatara*, who wouldn't have fooled them as an Alvar, whatever Reyhan thought he could do.

Walking a wire.

Worse, *Dashavatara* was full and heavy right now, so their acceleration was cut significantly from what it had been at Al-Winoq and other places. Maybe enough that a standard Warp Voyager chasing them from home might be faster.

"*Vanechon*," Hanishka said after a moment. "They were at Velle Port Station when we left, but not one of the ships that shot at us, being out of position to engage. They are a couple of hours out of the warp-shroud we came from and headed this direction at high speed."

"Have they seen us?" Kincaide rasped.

"I don't think so," she replied. "Or rather, they saw us on sensors, but they were about half a light-day out and send the message ahead of themselves. Light-speed lag means we'll be in motion before they see where we went."

"Only three options out of here," Kincaide reminded the woman. "Sextantis was the end of formal stations and the beginning of wild space. Helm, go for hard burn. Use up all the water you need to get us speed. We can always find more in a comet somewhere else."

"Moving," Dinushan replied tightly.

"Odtsetseg?" Kincaide called.

"I've bought us time," she yelled back. "The Executor just suffered a medical event that will hopefully distract them until we are out of range. Nobody is in charge right now."

Medical event?

Kincaide wasn't sure he wanted to know what his step-daughter had done to the woman. Or what she could do, with that much power behind her.

Still, all was fair in love and war, and this was definitely the latter.

The Gage had finally caught up with them.

VANECHON

CHAPTER 82

Roselani was on the bridge of *Vanechon*, in her accustomed Ambassadorial seat off to one side. The crew in here had relaxed considerably about having her near them, which was good, because she didn't want to impinge upon their efficiency, but there was no way in the six hells that she would be willing to remain in her cabin while this occurred.

Warp-transition.

As jarring as always. At least she had learned to have tea in her stomach and nothing else. That helped.

Sextantis. According to the Catalogue, the first of the planetary systems in this direction with only a single Port Station, located centrally over the planet, rather than at each of the warp-shrouds. The middle of nowhere, to a woman used to the Al-Winoq Glide, where there were almost more stations and ships around than stars in the skies.

This system was almost bereft. One station. No permanent Gage Warp Voyagers assigned. A few cargo haulers that came through on a regular circuit from more important worlds, bringing supplies and manufactured goods in and hauling foodstuffs and minerals away.

Nothing at all to mark it valuable, other than it was on the path to the dark side of the galaxy, beyond the Line of Exploration.

A place where feral Humans might turn into a threat and engage the entire Gage one of these days, even without Hasan Ildar to guide them.

Roselani watched the crew work and wondered if perhaps it was time to have her pet Human killed. He was forever scheming, however much he thought he was being sneaky. Humans didn't have the patience to play political games with Alvar Noble-born.

Still, it was useful to keep him at arm's length, if only to watch him suddenly think of new ideas about what the rebels might be up to. He'd had a surprising accuracy rate with his prognostications to date.

Like perhaps he'd already planned all this, and was just pissed at his fellows for leaving him behind?

Roselani smiled.

Commander Genevong turned this way and had a look of triumph on her face.

Roselani was on her feet before she realized it.

Genevong nodded.

"Scanners had identified the Human Warp Voyager *Dashavatara* docked with the station," Genevong said. "Presumably, they are drawing supplies, just as you suspected."

Roselani nodded and took the credit, rather than explain that Ildar had told her which of three systems to expect the ship to attempt it.

How had they convinced the station's Executor to do so, without even basic signed orders, to say nothing of an Alvar in command to communicate? Or had they taken their Engine aboard the station to manipulate folks at close range?

Risky, if something went wrong. Decant a spare copy, perhaps, just in case?

Except that Kincaide didn't strike her as that callous of a person, even if he was Human. It would be a rudeness she didn't expect from him to do so.

One more mystery to solve. Or another crime to lay at his feet when she caught the man.

"Can we catch them?" Roselani asked simply.

Genevong's face lit up, but fell a moment later.

"Most likely not, Noble-born," she said. "We are perhaps three days travel to the station from here. Less if we push. They will have likely undocked and begun to run in that time, but we can give chase."

"Order the station to open fire on the ship and destroy it," Roselani said after a long moment to consider her options. "They can take prisoners if possible, but they must do something right now."

"You are certain, Noble-born?" Genevong asked. "We have caught up to them across eight warp-space jumps."

"Only because we could have supplies staged ahead for us as we emerged in the next system," Roselani reminded her. "From here, there will be no more stations arranged in that manner. If they have just resupplied, it is possible that they could run farther than we can reasonably give chase, if we give Kincaide another chance to escape."

Genevong started to say something but caught herself. A question, perhaps.

Roselani had called him Kincaide, rather than referring to *Dashavatara* or the Humans.

"This is personal, Commander," Roselani confirmed with the woman. "My honor, as well as that of The Gage and that Alvar. I will see them destroyed."

"I will issue the orders, Noble-born," she replied in a subdued voice. "Hopefully they will arrive before the man has a chance to escape again, but we will be able to identify which warp-shroud they intend to use and redirect our burn to chase them down if they do flee. *Dashavatara* will not be able to escape us, either way."

"I would not bet heavily on that, Commander," Roselani said. "Kincaide is a man of hidden talents and abundant resources. But you do my will here. I will retire to my quarters for now. Send a messenger if anything important happens."

The woman bowed and Roselani turned to depart. She paused long enough to fix the image on the projection into her mind.

There were questions she wanted that man to answer, but if she had to go to her grave in ignorance in another twenty-five centuries or so, Roselani would not lose any sleep.

CHAPTER 83

Zhubin was off to one side of the Command Square, in the place that had apparently been reserved for him and Kali to keep watch on the crew's business without interfering. She had joined him just a few moments ago, apparently jogging forward from her cabin in the Crew Section, given the way her breath was a little ragged.

In the distance, Sextantis Port Station continued to fire at them with a variety of beam weapons, but from the wild inaccuracy involved, it was obvious that none of them had been calibrated in years. *Dashavatara* had been struck exactly once as they fled.

Zhubin was beginning to wonder if that had been accidental, considering the other attempts.

Would Mog and Mori gunners in Gage service be as committed as the Alvar in destroying a Warp Voyager in the process of going rogue? Did any of them retain some level of wistfulness that they had been taken by the Alvar?

The Gage was supposedly an egalitarian place, according to all their propaganda, but Zhubin knew better. Gage vessels were commanded by Alvar, and flown by Human Engines. Humans were contained on Al-Winoq's moon, a few forward depots closer to the Line of Exploration, and pitifully rare elsewhere. Everywhere you went, the blues were in charge, and that was never going to change until Humans forced it.

Zhubin looked forward to watching the galactic change unfold, even if he'd be in hell before then. There'd still be a good view, he suspected.

Kali had ended up a little closer than normal when he glanced over. Almost touching his shoulder with her top one, the one that stuck out the farthest. She had a man's width of shoulders, but that was because her lower pair of arms were tucked in close to a wasp waist.

"Are we at risk?" she whispered.

He turned enough to note the confusion on her face. Nodded.

"They do not appear to be that dangerous," he agreed. "I was contemplating if they actually wanted to hit us right now."

"Why would they not?"

"We're doing the thing that perhaps many of them always wished they could do," Zhubin said. "Mere speculation. They might merely be that incompetent. If so, I suspect new orders will go out to increase weapons training everywhere."

"Ah," Kali grunted. "And the other ship?"

"That's where it gets risky," Zhubin said. "You were not here to catch the signatory on the orders to destroy us that were issued by *Vanechon*."

Kali turned herself sideways now, facing him with her whole body in a way that reminded him that many would see her as a tiny Alvar, except that the inspiration, the Hindi goddess Kali-ma, predated the Conquest by thousands of years.

"Who?" she asked.

"Roselani Thammavongsa," he replied.

Her look was confusion.

"The Alvar Noble-born that invited Kincaide to her palace for a night of amorous escapades before all this began," he explained. "Apparently, she's aboard that vessel, and invoking Imperial Authority, which she can do as a distant cousin of the Gage Emperor."

Kali snickered quietly, drawing his head fully around. Zhubin's body came with it, and now they were facing each other, almost close enough to dance. She was a couple of centimeters taller than he was, which was rare in a Human woman. But there was no doubt she was Human, even with the extra arms.

She even smelled Human, which the Alvar did not.

"So, Lilith had a particular conversation with Kincaide while we were docked," Kali explained with a wry smile on her face.

"About?" he asked, wondering what sorts of trouble these two women had gotten up to.

Zhubin was still an assassin, even in his 50s. Did he need to do something to the Wives to protect his crew?

"I have been talking with Odtsetseg," Kali replied. "She thinks that she can break some of the psychological programming Goaulda left us."

"Programming?" Zhubin asked, confused now, though still slightly relieved. The woman was not a danger.

Not to him or the mission, at least.

"The sex-drive overrides he implanted in all of us," she said, her voice growing a little grim now. "We might actually be free, if she can succeed."

"And you were asking for Kincaide's permission?" he pressed, still not sure where the conversation was headed.

"She asked him to be a guinea pig," Kali smiled. "If Odtsetseg could do it, we would need someone to test the results."

"Oh," he said, shocked out of his rationality now. "Oh!"

Zhubin had never stopped to consider them as females, now that he thought back. He had known Lilith for almost two decades now, but usually saw her as a relic of Alvar arrogance. A thing that had been built, and then had survived long past the point when it had served its purpose.

Monster Wives, with an emphasis on monstrosity, rather than femininity.

However, they were technically all women. Madonna figures, to use the Western thinking, since Hindi lands really didn't have an equivalent. After all, the *Kama Sutra* had been a thing from his own Indian culture.

And Kincaide might conceivably fornicate with such creatures? Willingly? Zhubin suppressed his shudder of revulsion. They had not asked him to make such a sacrifice, after all. Let Kincaide be their victim.

"So why were you chuckling then?" he asked as he worked his painful way through the logic of this conversation.

It would be difficult, reassessing them as real women. Human, even. Females with needs. He saw them all as aliens, which had been Goaulda's entire point, once upon a time. Figures to frighten people, when that man had needed some level of perversion to achieve release, apparently.

And Kincaide might participate? They would not have broached so delicate a topic without asking Odtsetseg, who knew that man better than anyone else in the crew, possibly including Herath.

The mind boggled.

"The Alvar Noble-born aboard *Vanechon*," Kali said. "Roselani Thammavongsa."

He blinked up at Kali for a moment before he saw the connection. Yet another alien lover, chasing across the galaxy after Kataragama.

His mouth fell open in appalled silence.

Kali chuckled.

"Yes," she agreed. "It makes you wonder if there really are gods out there, and what kind of a sense of humor they might have."

She turned back to the room now, planting both shoulder blades against the dome. He did the same, noting that the two of them didn't —quite—touch this way. Zhubin focused on his breathing, wondering if he had just become a spectator in a game of alien women chasing a rabbit named Kincaide Kataragama.

And who would win.

CHAPTER 84

Odtsetseg opened her eyes and tried to keep them uncrossed. The light was stabby and the sound of the fans moving air around grated on her skin.

But she'd apparently been successful. Maybe.

Only one shot had actually hit the rear shields, and that one only after they had gotten some distance and it had not been enough to even threaten the energy barriers back there.

After screaming into the mind of the Executor of Sextantis Port Station, she had moved on to the gunners, but there had been so many of them. As the distance increased, she had just projected a generalized fear at them, hoping to make those people flinch when they focused their aim.

It helped that the station had no Crew Section shields against her mental powers. Why would they need it, when they never crossed over into warp-space?

But Gods, did her head hurt right now. It felt like a covey of ducks (herd? something?) was beating at the inside of her skull with their beaks, trying to get out.

She squinted and focused on breathing.

Tharushi had routed all the energy she could to thrust and shields, not bothering to try shooting back. There had been a little left over, and Odtsetseg had used it.

Most of it had come out of her own head, though. And her soul.

She wanted to curl up and sleep for twelve hours right now, but her mind wouldn't let her.

The station had finally stopped firing at them. She had one last thing she wanted to try.

"Tharushi," she called into the open comm line beside her.

"Go ahead," the Power Systems genius replied in a tight voice.

"Can you route some of the generators back to my control for a bit?" Odtsetseg asked. "I need to boost my range for something I want to try."

"Stand by," the woman said.

There was a longer than expected lag. Probably looking over at Kincaide and getting his permission. It was his ship. His command. His genius that had saved them.

"Okay," Tharushi said after a moment. "Go ahead."

Odtsetseg took a deeper breath and closed her squinty eyes the rest of the way.

She fell into herself and spent a long time composing her mind from the chaotic leftovers of her first battle.

This would need focus. Precision. Range.

Odtsetseg opened her mind to the cosmos and let everything drift for a long moment. They were too far away to even see from here, except by watching sunlight reflect off a metal hull and then washing the signal through a whole series of computers to isolate the one thing that didn't belong.

Vanechon.

Gage Warp Voyager.

She had no idea what the ship tasted like. Or even sounded like. It would be impossible to find at this distance.

She didn't need that.

Roselani Thammavongsa was aboard.

That *icky woman* who had done things with Kincaide. To Kincaide. For Kincaide.

Odtsetseg knew what her mind tasted like. She reached out and found the woman.

For a moment, Odtsetseg blinked in surprised terror and nearly lost herself.

God was there as well.

That fucker Hasan Ildar was aboard the ship that was chasing them? Serving the Gage? Or at least the Noble-born woman at the heart of their problems?

Odtsetseg contained her rage and tried to ignore Ildar as best she could. At least for now.

Roselani was her target.

She had seen the inside of that woman's mind before. Several times, now, when she thought about it. Why was that woman here now?

The distance was so great that Odtsetseg could barely touch her, but she didn't need to change anything.

Just to read the words from here.

Rage. That was to be expected. The woman had never been thwarted before, let alone by a Human, however awesome Kincaide was as a person.

Lust. Odtsetseg tried to slide past the *ickiness* of the things the woman still wanted Kincaide to do to her, down in the depths of her mind.

Ew.

Curiosity, if you could boil off all the anger that flavored it. Why had he done the things he had done? What had it meant to him, to have taken her that night as he had? What did he think of her now?

Odtsetseg saw her as a person now, and not just an angry Alvar. A woman, in ways that a ray-faced half-Human could never be, because God had cut those parts out of her soul in his quest to give her power.

She would never feel this thing she found down in Roselani's heart. It might be called love, but Odtsetseg wasn't sure. She might have to show these memories to Kincaide and ask him, but that was already necessary.

Kincaide and the crew knew who was chasing them.

But more importantly, they needed to know why.

She let go and fell back into herself with a hard shudder that was almost pain.

Sleep was necessary, but she had one thing left to do.

"Tharushi, I'm done," she said. "You can cut all the generators now."

"You sound exhausted," the woman replied.

"I touched *Vanechon*," Odtsetseg explained in a ragged voice.

"Sleep now."

Kincaide was suddenly standing there. She held out a hand and he lifted her to her feet, but she blacked out for a moment.

When she opened her eyes, he was carrying her in his arms, opening the airlock to the forward dome.

Odtsetseg started to say something, but he shushed her with a kiss on the forehead, so she snuggled into his warmth.

She woke in darkness. Three balls of furry love purred around her in her bed. The clock said she had slept for several hours.

It was good.

CHAPTER 85

Kincaide had the slider doors open. There was nothing that was going to be said in his office that he needed to hide from the crew. All their lives depended on what happened next.

Odtsetseg had slept, recovered, and joined them. She still looked like someone had pulled her backwards through a knothole, but she was awake and even broadcasting a radiant joy that put a smile on his face when he looked at her.

Zhubin was going to play the role of Angry War God, apparently, but whatever. He was just the Chairman.

Kali represented the Wives. Kincaide suspected that in a way she had also become something of an icon or mascot for the rest of the crew, in spite of Reyhan standing opposite Zhubin in the other corner.

Still, the symmetry was pleasing, with the two women seated and the two men standing back and away.

"Simple gravitational geometry," Reyhan answered the original question. "We are aimed at a particular warp-shroud and accelerating right now. At some point, we'll undergo turnover and slow down to hit our target more accurately. They can cut directly across from their position, and are out-accelerating us, but not enough to catch up before we slip through, assuming nothing breaks and sticks us on this side."

"How much of a lead do we have?" Kincaide asked the man.

He appreciated that Reyhan leaned out far enough to look down the stairs at Dinushan, standing at his station and actually flying the ship right now.

"Dee?"

"Maybe six hours," the Helmsman replied. "Assuming we maintain current values and they don't do anything silly."

Reyhan returned to his corner.

"Six hours," he repeated. "If we're lucky. My original plot an hour ago suggested that it was more like four hours, but we'll be able to refine that much better in another day as everyone gets down into endgame."

"Do we know that they won't try the same stunt we did at Al-Winoq?" Zhubin spoke up. "Go for a late turnover and hit the warp-shroud at high speed, just so they can maybe get a few shots off at us before we can escape?"

"We do not," Kincaide replied flatly. "Again, final calculations await, once they begin decelerating. I'm willing to drive this rig faster than we are right now, if that's what it takes. I have a much higher confidence in Odtsetseg than they probably do in six faceless Engines of unknown provenance."

"So we escape," Kali said. "Assume we slip into warp-space and get away from them. Won't they be right on top of us when we reach the other side?"

"Not necessarily," Kincaide replied. "Odtsetseg should be able to carry us through to the next warp-shroud faster than their team can, so we gain a certain amount of breathing room on the other side."

"What's there?" she asked. "Who will stand witness to this final confrontation?"

"Gemaharn," Zhubin said. "According to the original plan, that would be where we could disappear from Gage eyes, because the system itself has never been colonized. No planets worth exploiting and no particular value, other than five warp-shrouds leading off into a variety of places, some of which are cultural dead ends."

"Cultural?" Kali rotated her head back to look at the man now.

"No Gage presence," Kincaide said loud enough to pull her attention back to him. "They were explored, hundreds of thousands of years ago, but there were more interesting systems in other directions, so the Line of Exploration passed through, but never rated this sector worth pursuing."

"In hundreds of thousands of years?" she asked sarcastically.

"Not that many Alvar generations, regardless of what it might mean to Humans," he grinned. "They don't breed that fast, and certainly don't want to leave colonies out there unsupervised. Imagine what might happen if you left Humans alone for even one thousand years."

"Revolution," Kali nodded.

"And most of the Alvar alive today would be there to witness it, with memories of the docile, little creatures that had fled into the underbrush."

"Are they smart enough to realize that at an intellectual level?" Kali asked. "Not just instinctual?"

"They are," Odtsetseg leaned forward and put her hands on her knees, looking much older and more mature now.

For all she was a kid.

They shared a quick smile.

"I have touched *Vanechon*," Odtsetseg began. "Roselani Thammavongsa is aboard, but you already knew that from the orders she had sent to the station. Hasan Ildar is there as well."

Kincaide watched the other three faces around them stir uncomfortably at that news. She had whispered it to him, half-asleep, so he was not surprised.

Kincaide felt his eyes pulled to the Computer Personality of the Day, always and forever Computer Babe Hasan because that idiot had tried to out-maneuver Kincaide Kataragama and Reyhan Herath.

Fool.

Reyhan was having fun adjusting the visualization every day even though the voice never changed. Today, she was an African woman, supposedly from the central western jungles, according to Reyhan. Darker skin than his, a brown verging onto black, with full lips, wideset eyes, and kinky hair in a large halo. And great big tits, just to frost her some.

Kincaide wondered if he should finally give Reyhan the time to disassemble the system and pull out all the threads that were Computer Hasan, just so they could go back to a random rotation of semi-faceless helpers. He had said it would take several days of work, when everyone was locked out of the system, so Kincaide had let it slide.

Eventually, they'd find a planet where they could slip quietly into orbit and begin surveying. Reyhan would go to work.

They just had to escape *Vanechon* first. And Roselani.

His staff was settling, so Kincaide nodded to Odtsetseg to continue.

"Roselani understands the implications of us escaping," Odtsetseg said.

Kincaide noted that, unlike the others, she called the Noble-born woman by her given name. Had she picked that up from him?

"If we get away, we will do exactly what she fears, which is build up another space-faring culture that will eventually challenge The Gage for control of the universe," Odtsetseg continued. "And because we grow so much faster than they do, we are a true threat."

Kincaide nodded. What was a century to an Alvar who might see eighty of them? It was like him burning a year in a monastery finding himself, except that he'd never gone through with it. Too much work focused on becoming a better person, when he'd really wanted to just kill Alvar.

He'd found other ways to survive and cope.

"And it is only the one ship?" Reyhan asked now.

"Correct," Odtsetseg nodded. "I read enough of her mind to see that."

Kincaide wasn't surprised that his step-daughter was staring right at him, even as she was speaking to Reyhan. Must have seen something she didn't want to broach in front of company.

"How dangerous is one Warp Voyager?" Kali asked the group, leaning back to look around.

"Pretty evenly matched," Zhubin interjected. "Depending on the model. Some are larger. Some smaller. If I was her, I would have gone for a medium-sized cruiser unit with great range."

"She did, if I read her mind correctly," Odtsetseg nodded. "Her thinking was very similar to yours."

"Then we should have a slight edge," Zhubin nodded. "More compact construction. Larger and more powerful generators. Probably the same number of beam turrets."

"Can we win?" Kali asked. "We're a renegade now, so we can't just sail into any Station Port for repairs like they can. Any damage that they do to us hampers our ability to escape, and you've just said that she was likely to chase us to the ends of the galaxy."

"We just resupplied," Kincaide smiled wickedly. "They haven't, so we should be in a better position for supplies as we run. Sextantis is the end of the line, as far as truck stops go, unless they follow the entire loop around to one of the main trade routes on the far side, where they'll pick up Gage stations again. We're on equal footing then, if they didn't bring a second ship that they could use for scouting and resupply."

"Was this your original plan?" she asked, looking around.

Kincaide shrugged.

"Not Plan Number One," he agreed. "But it had been on the list of contingencies we prepared for. Nobody ever assumed that The Gage would just wave merrily at us as we sailed into the darkness."

"So what are we doing next?" Kali asked.

"I have some ideas," Kincaide replied simply. "We'll see what happens when things get closer."

CHAPTER 86

Hasan looked up a the hatch to his laboratory opened. He missed having the autonomy to lock his own doors from the inside, but that was just going to be the price he would have to pay for still being here.

Later, he had to live forever, but first, he had to help the worthless blues hunt down his betrayers, and then there was making it home alive so he could lull them to sleep again. Let the dragon snooze for a few centuries while he worked, a quiet, assiduous little mouse in the cupboard.

Doors opening without a bell first just spelled out how little control he had over his own existence. For the time being.

And then she stepped into the room.

For once, the Gigolo didn't accompany the woman, not that she needed him. Even a small, slender, Alvar woman was more than his equal physically. That was how they'd managed to conquer half the galaxy, *en route* to the rest of the universe.

Hasan saved his current work files and closed the console down. It was obvious from her face that she had something she felt was important enough to interrupt his work, without even summoning him to her space.

No, she had to inflict her smell on him.

Hasan made a mental note to kick the fans up a notch after she left, to try to clear the air out. It wouldn't eliminate the smell of Alvar, that odd, rich musk unlike anything else he could match it to, but maybe he could draw in some of the scent of the other species. He didn't like them any more, but anything to mask blue.

Lady Thammavongsa came to rest just inside the door as it slid closed, one ample breast hanging out of her half-toga like a mockery of a real woman. Thighs like pillars ended in sandals laced up her ankles. White hair pulled up over the naked right breast in the sideknot of her social class.

Hasan pasted a brittle smile on his face and stepped towards the lounge area where there was one chair for a Human and two for Alvar.

"Lady Thammavongsa," he nodded politely, gesturing her to please sit and make herself at home.

IN HIS LABORATORY!

"Should I have servants bring wine or tea?" he asked as she settled, hovering close by but not sitting until she nodded for him to.

Lesser species and all that.

"That will not be necessary," she shook her head. "Sit. I wish to ask questions of your expertise."

Hasan forcibly kept his mouth from falling open in shock at her words. Alvar never admitted to shortcomings, even when they were idiots. He wondered what had gone so badly wrong with the world outside his lab.

But he sat. Poised and relaxed, as though on call to perform for his supper.

Not entirely inaccurate, considering.

One of these days he would keep an entire line of Alvar women. The only question was whether he shrank them down to Chun size, or scaled himself up to bed them in their native form. Had he escaped with *Dashavatara*, Hasan might have just resized himself and lived out the rest of his existence three and a half meters tall.

Much more complicated now.

She studied his face, as if she might learn something, but if she could, they would have already executed him long before now.

Hasan smiled blandly and waited.

"We have arrived at a system called Sextantis," she said, watching for a reaction.

"I am unfamiliar with that place," he replied after a moment, wondering if she presumed that Prakash was following the same plan Hasan Ildar had originally worked out.

Except that they would have simply vanished during a test flight to

Aulil. That had already been worked out. Just keep flying, but by the time anyone caught on, they would have had a month or more of a head start. After long enough, even the warp-shrouds stopping showing ripples indicating that a ship had passed.

Apparently, his ignorance was communicated sufficiently, as she nodded at some internal conversation.

"*Dashavatara* has been spotted in-system," she continued, staring at him. "They have fled the Port Station and are currently running flat out for one of the warp-shrouds at the edge of the system. We are in pursuit."

Hasan didn't try to hide his surprise, nor the spike of triumph that surged through him. Had Prakash underestimated how quickly the Alvar might give chase? Could they all be destroyed, right here, right now, and head back to Al-Winoq with this bitch unaware of his secondary plans?

He licked his lips, almost biting them with excitement.

"You would like to see your old friends again?" she asked, more of a purr now than anything.

"Only to confirm that we have all of them before you destroy every one of those fuckers," he growled back, unconcerned about her interpretation of his rage.

He would see Prakash and Kataragama pay for everything they had done to him.

"And then what?" she inquired, her face tilting just a little away from him now.

Hasan blinked, suddenly aware of the trap opening at his feet. He sought the correct words with great care.

"I have used my time aboard to improve the Engine design," he said cautiously. "She is more stable and less likely to be won over from my control. Your control, once you take charge of her."

"You think your Engine will still have value after this?" she asked.

"One of her has done at least as well as the five you have flying this Warp Voyager," Hasan reminded the woman. "Her power is without question. Everything else is always about control, isn't it?"

Something flickered in her eyes, but it was gone before Hasan more than registered its passing, so he wasn't sure what had drawn her interest.

"And you are a man used to being in control, aren't you, Ildar?"

she probed, her voice taking on a different flavor now, one he could not identify.

He leaned back now, biting back his first arrogant reply, lest she take exception to him.

The dragon must be lulled back to sleep.

"Until this," he gestured to the ship around them, and by extension everything else, "I had absolute control of my world. This disruption is necessary, but unwelcome. I look forward to returning to my lab and finding more and better ways to serve the future of The Gage."

"What would you do next?" she asked. Something had vanished from her voice, notable now only by absence, but he needed to assuage this creature's concerns. Distract her from his true plans until it was far too late to stop him from doing the thing Prakash was doing now.

Escaping in a Warp Voyager and disappearing forever, with all his research and his hunger to destroy the Alvar.

"What does the Gage need?" he asked, pushing the conversation carefully out of the personal and onto the neutral ground where they might talk as something appearing to be equals, whatever the truth might be.

"Could you create better Humans?" she asked, without any color to her voice to suggest what *better* might entail.

"Yes," he replied flatly. "The Odtsetseg Engine was a vast and radical improvement unlike anything the galaxy has ever seen. The Altantsetseg Engine enhances that. Neither will breed true, but that is a small thing in the hands of the Alvar, as you can just Index them and continue to Decant fresh copies as you need."

"Could you make them breedable?" Her face was turned back and focused on him now.

Hasan found such attention a little frightening. She might learn too much.

"No," he said in a gamble. "The design sacrifices certain parts of their genetic code around reproduction. To bring those elements back would cost significant power. If you wished such a design, they would be probably about twice as useful as your current Engines."

"So only a doubling of power, while still representing a viable species?" The bitch smiled.

"New species," he corrected. "They could not breed true with existing Humans, although hybridization might be possible. I would have to complete a few and then test their genetic patterns with a significant amount of computer time in order to determine. Is that a project worth pursuing when we return home?"

He struck hard on the last two words, watching her eyes for some sign about the creature's intentions, but she gave nothing away.

"It might," she replied. "There will be many changes to how things are done when we return to Al-Winoq. As you said, The Gage needs to be improved. Perhaps a new breed of Humans will need to be created, but obviously the Colonial Dispatch Office will have to spend significant time doing cost/risk/benefit analysis patterns. How long will you live, Ildar?"

The question took him aback. Humans were mayflies. Here today and gone tomorrow, while the Alvar lived forever.

But again, this witch probably held his fate in the palm of her blue hand. He would need her as an ally for a while. Or at least not an enemy.

"At least another millennium," he said vaguely, unwilling to suggest that he intended to be the first being to achieve true immortality and live forever.

If nothing else, eventually he would find a way to transfer his mind and memories into a younger body, so that each might live ten thousand years before transferring on again.

She nodded, as if she knew the truth, but if that were the case, then she was already a co-conspirator, for having overlooked many of the things she might have taken exception to ere now. The crimes that didn't break Gage law, but easily could have annoyed an Alvar Noble-born enough to have him imprisoned or possibly destroyed.

"No person aboard *Dashavatara* will be alive in another century, even if they did escape us," the woman said simply. "It is the threat they represent that is the problem. The dream. However, the very act of dreaming so tells me that The Gage needs to change. Needs to find a way to bring the Humans out from their domes and incorporate them into the broader empire."

Hasan felt his mouth fall open anyway.

Even hints of such things, whispered in the darkness on the Al-Winoq Glide, would probably be sufficient to have one disappeared by men like that Security Gigolo. Had this Noble-born bitch suddenly developed self-awareness? Had she discovered that The Gage kept Humans like pets—slaves—to power their ships?

All seven of the other major species were aligned as second-class citizens of the Gage Empire. Only Humans were third.

Did she mean to free them? Or was she willing to have him create a new breed of slave by improving Humans and then letting the rest either fade out or rejoin The Gage?

She smiled and rose before he could speak. Turned and walked to the door, pausing only to glance back and smile again, a knowing, conspiratorial sort of thing as the door opened and she vanished.

What the hell had just happened?

CHAPTER 87

Odtsetseg had asked Zhubin to remain in his cabin after dinner, so that she might have the lounge to herself and Kincaide. While all of them had personal space built out to entertain, she wanted a more neutral ground.

She didn't understand all the emotions, but knew that they would be too big to contain.

Kincaide was seated. Comfortable. Almost rumpled, though she knew the man showered daily. Fastidiously. Today felt like the last day of a vacation up in the mountains, if she understood the implications of low-tech isolation.

The language contained so many euphemisms and references to a planet none of them had ever seen, that it confused and confounded things.

Had it been worth retaining such things in the face of the Alvar Conquest, rather than allowing themselves to be absorbed?

Kincaide laughed, cutting off her train of thought. She stared at him, puzzled.

"You're muttering under your breath," he said simply. "Yes, it was absolutely worth it. That's what makes us Human."

"Am I not Human, then?" she inquired, uncertain.

"Not an adult," he corrected her. "Completely Human, but I'm sorry, but that's one of the places where the other side of puberty changes your outlook. That stubbornness is one of the main reasons why the Alvar wanted us, above and beyond being another industrial society that might have eventually found the tools to challenge them. We can carry their ships better than any of the other species. You are just an improvement on that, but Ildar didn't strip out any of our native intractability when he upgraded your design."

"Oh."

"So what did you see on *Vanechon* that caused so much emotional turmoil?" Kincaide asked.

She blinked.

"I know you better than anyone else," he said, turning serious now. "Even Ildar. I know you saw something."

Odtsetseg considered his words.

"Roselani was there," she said simply.

"Not *that icky woman*, as you've described her?" He smiled with a tease in his eyes.

"I studied her mind this time," Odtsetseg replied. "Tharushi gave me the generators and I have learned many things after what I did to that fucker Ildar and then to the Executor of Sextantis Port Station."

"Oh?"

"I still only have eyes at that range, and not hands," she tried to explain it. "But I was able to look deep inside the woman, at least for a brief period of time."

"What did she show you?" Kincaide asked.

Odtsetseg started and shook her head at his turn of phrase. Then she understood.

"She hates you," Odtsetseg acknowledged. "And there is a fair bit of lust as well, for what you did to her that one night, better than anyone she remembers. But I went deeper."

"Deeper," he echoed.

"She respects your mind," Odtsetseg continued. "Your cunning. Even your brilliance at what you have accomplished. If I didn't know better, I would call it love, what she feels for you, mixed with a rage at the circumstances that separate you and requires her to kill you."

"Requires her to try, perhaps," Kincaide said. "I don't have to destroy the woman. Just escape her. Then I'm gone forever and she won't ever find me again."

"And that pains her incredibly," Odtsetseg said, pleadingly. "Why would she feel that? What would cause all that rage to turn into tenderness and sorrow?"

"You have it backwards, daughter," he said in a soothing voice. "The tenderness and sorrow have turned into the rage. I gave her something nobody else had in a long time. Perhaps ever. Now, she knows what she was missing and knows that nobody will ever be able to do that for her again."

"You fornicated," Odtsetseg stated. She felt confusion threaten to overwhelm her, and she knew she lacked the experience to understand.

"That, too," Kincaide smiled. She tasted the rue emanating off of him now like a cologne. "But the act itself didn't take that long. Wasn't that impressive, in and of itself. It was the two hours leading up to that moment. And the hour of cuddling afterwards. I doubt Roselani had ever experienced something like that in her life. Alvar culture still retains all the ancient warrior trappings. Or found them again in modernity."

"I don't understand," Odtsetseg whispered.

"Alvar men and women tend to live separate lives, especially at that level of wealth and power," Kincaide explained. "Circles of friends of the same gender, but husband and wife do not spend all that much time together. I think I heard her mention that her husband has been away for several centuries, off doing Gage things."

"And you gave her something she had never had?" Odtsetseg asked.

"Tenderness," he mused, eyes not seeing her as he looked into some indescribable distance. Memory, perhaps. "But also the domination she needed."

"Domination?"

"She's a submissive, Odtsetseg," Kincaide explained, projecting images into the air that she could taste. "She achieves arousal by being dominated by someone else. Told what to do. Allowed. Ordered. Submissive. No other Alvar is going to be a good dominant to her."

"Why not?"

"Either they are a lower socio-economic rank, and thus would approach the situation with fear and trepidation, or they are something of an asshole, and don't know when to dial it back. How to calibrate things. So she has to turn to Humans. We're the most like them physically, and her kinks don't require a Mori's physicality. Or a Mog's."

"What does she need, then?" Odtsetseg asked, lost. These were the parts Ildar had cut out of her. The ability to experience these sorts of emotions herself, rather than listening to others and trying to understand what they were seeing and doing.

"She needs someone who is a lesser. A servant," he nodded. "But one that will step right up and not give a shit that she's a princess. Or whatever the title is. Princess is a description, not a rank."

"And that would be you?"

Kincaide shrugged. He did that a lot. This was not a man to have an opinion, just for the sake of hearing his voice. Odtsetseg had heard others use such terms to describe him. Usually females. Usually in glowing terms.

She had the correct plumbing, but not the wiring.

"You are not the only person to point out that I don't give two shits about a lot of things," Kincaide continued. "That I didn't worship you. Or fear you. Or anything else."

Odtsetseg nodded, suddenly warm all over as she remembered falling asleep with his arms around her. Yes, the only man on this ship she could do that with.

Had Roselani recognized that, as well? He didn't fear the woman. Or worship her. Or even particularly lust after her body.

Alvar were built like Humans, after all. But taller. Much broader. More perfect, in many ways. She wore the half-toga of her station that displayed one enormous, but apparently perfect, mammary gland. And the thighs that were long and powerful, where Odtsetseg's were merely long.

"So she could fall in love with you?" Odtsetseg pressed.

"I doubt it." He surprised her by chuckling now. "She's probably only remembering the good bits and has forgotten the rest. I might have become a blank slate upon which she would ascribe things. She might have fallen in love with the image she has of me, rather than the memories."

"Is that good or bad?"

"Probably both," he agreed. "On the one hand, she wants to pursue us—maybe me—in order to get me back. On the other hand, it has driven her to chase us fast enough to actually catch up, when our original plan called for a more leisurely pursuit by the Gage, taking weeks to even send a ship after us, and that ship taking their time in the hunt. You understand how hard and fast *Vanechon* had to be running in order to catch us at Sextantis, Odtsetseg."

It was her turn to nod. And shrug. Another Earth turn of phrase, to chase someone right up to the gates of Hell and beyond.

Was Sextantis hell? She didn't know.

"So now what?" Odtsetseg felt compelled to ask. "How do we stop her?"

"I'm not sure we can," Kincaide replied. "They will pursue us for as long as it takes, I suspect."

"And we can't escape them?" she pressed. "Her?"

"Didn't say that," he smiled now. "If there was a way I could separate her from that ship and add her to the crew over here, we might even be able to have a conversation that resolved things. I did talk with Lilith."

"I know," Odtsetseg nodded. "Kali told me."

"You three are nuts."

She smiled. Beamed. It felt good.

"And you're the sane, rational one here?" she teased the man. Her step-father. Her friend.

"Fair point," he agreed. "But if you look at her in the same light as a Lilith, or a Kali, or a Staci, then you see that all of that exists on a spectrum, with quiet, nerdy people like Hanishka at one end and Roselani somewhere closer to the other."

"Hanishka is not quiet," Odtsetseg scowled lightly at him. "There is a botanist that occasionally visits her quarters. Some nights I have considered asking someone to put up the Crew Section shields just so I don't have to listen to the woman's orgasms."

He blinked in surprise. Probably thought that the older woman had moved past those things, but Odtsetseg didn't feel like explaining some of the things she heard, sitting forward here alone with her thoughts. And those of the rest of the crew.

She occasionally wondered if Hanishka was just broadcasting on the right mental frequencies, or if the others hadn't learned to enjoy themselves like that, since most of them were closer to her age than Kincaide's.

Still, she did understand that perhaps Roselani had felt such a thing once before losing it and only recently discovered that she had forgotten about it.

That was the sort of thing that might drive her to the gates of hell. Odtsetseg had never felt such a thing for herself, but she could live it vicariously through others, and they seemed to enjoy it.

459

Both had fallen silent. She looked up and Kincaide was studying her closely.

"Can we win?" she asked simply.

"We're going to try," he nodded.

CHAPTER 88

Roselani entered the bridge of *Vanechon* and studied the body language of all the officers and crew present. Not just Genevong, but also that Ayotochtli female who handled scanners and communications, and the Mori male at the helm. She already knew that the Alvar male handling the forward weapons array was angry enough to kill the renegades without mercy.

Dashavatara was a new thing. A Human warship, rather than Gage. Fleeing madly ahead of them and likely to slip into the warp-shroud before *Vanechon* could catch them. Renegades who represented an existential threat to Alvar civilization itself.

Roselani didn't think that anybody else felt that in their bones. To most of them, it was an intellectual thing. Of the mind rather than of the soul.

Or perhaps The Gage had been infected by Alvar lassitude. Why jump on something immediately if it will still be there next decade? Or could it wait a century?

She could see where the mayflies had to do things differently. *Now*, regardless of completeness or beauty, because they only had so many years in which to live, moving one hundred times faster than the Alvar.

Normally, that cultural stability worked in everybody's favor, keeping things level and smooth. But stepping outside of one's self took effort.

The Grand Gage, Emperor Kapono Phetphommasouk, had

ascended to the throne about the same time that Humans had mastered metallurgy. Ruling House Phetphommasouk had been the dynasty possibly longer than Humans had existed as a separate species on their homeworld, depending on which scholars you believed.

They had to move quickly to accomplish anything, and that was why they were such a threat.

Commander Genevong turned to her with inquisitive eyes.

"Noble-born?" she asked simply, arms crossed behind her in a relaxed position.

"Can we catch them?" Roselani asked simply.

A few officers glanced up in shock and then buried themselves in their work, hoping she hadn't noticed them. Alvar social culture did not do *direct*. It spent much time inquiring as to various mundanities and irrelevancies before moving on to the important meat of a conversation.

Why move now when you had so many years ahead of you needing to be filled with *something* other than entropy and *ennui*?

Because your enemy is Human, and possibly the most dangerous creature ever born, at least to The Gage.

Even Genevong gasped but covered it quickly.

"I do not feel comfortable attempting it, Noble-born," the Commander said after a moment.

Even that represented a radical change from the hard professional Roselani had met on boarding. On that day, Noma Genevong would have damned the risks and charged headlong into battle, but she had come to appreciate that *Dashavatara* needed to be run down. Any risk that let them get away possibly doomed The Gage itself.

What would Kincaide do with a thousand years in which to hide?

So Roselani nodded to the Commander and glided over to rest not far from the woman.

If they made a mistake now and Kincaide got away, his progeny might return while she was still alive to see it.

Roselani shuddered once and then drew a calming breath. They would approach this with Alvar patience. That would be sufficient for now.

"What are the current circumstances?" Roselani asked.

"They escaped the station without damage," Genevong replied. "From there, a high-speed burn has them aimed at the warp-shroud to Gemaharn. *Dashavatara* has undergone turnover and is decelerating, but not such that they would come to rest before entering. We have also rotated and are approaching them now in deceleration. At present, we expect them to enter the warp-shroud roughly five hours ahead of us. Depending, that might give them as much as a ten hour lead on the far side. Sufficient to evade our weapons, but not our scanners. They cannot run anywhere that we cannot pursue at this point."

Roselani nodded. It was as Ildar had suggested when she last engaged his intellect.

That Human was also a renegade, but had come to appreciate that he had to help her destroy Kincaide Kataragama or she would destroy him right now.

That she intended to destroy Hasan Ildar after *Dashavatara* was stopped was inconsequential at this point. He would pour all of his vitriol into the chase, under the false impression that she intended to let him have a thousand years hiding within the Al-Winoq Glide. Perhaps he saw himself as a tick, quietly sucking blood from his host while he got stronger. Until such time as he could return to this particular field of battle, somehow either conning the Colonial Dispatch Authority into building him another Warp Voyager or giving him a crew he could somehow suborn.

She would not have it.

But Roselani Thammavongsa had to save The Gage today by stopping Kincaide. Ildar was tomorrow's problem and she would deal with him when the time came.

"How are we for supplies?" Roselani asked. "I presume that Sextantis restocked *Dashavatara* while they were there."

"They did, Noble-born," Genevong replied sourly.

The two of them had turned outward now and were looking down the Command Oval, watching all the Commander's people studiously not looking this direction and keeping all conversation to a minimum.

"*Vanechon* was designed for long cruising," the Commander spoke, seemingly addressing her words to the room instead of Roselani. "We stripped the vessel of all non-essential crew at the beginning, and have worked to overload ourselves with supplies at every opportunity. However, there is a concern, going forward."

Roselani turned only her head to look and nod at the woman to continue.

"Gemaharn is not an inhabited system," the Commander continued. "Nor are any of the systems you can reach from there, save Sextantis.

Dashavatara has an arboretum aboard, so presumably they have the ability to grow crops and thus achieve some level of food independence from standard resupply. *Vanechon* cannot."

Ah.

Roselani considered the hydroponics section that supplied fresh air and clean water to the ship, but understood from Genevong's terms that it could not feed more than a few people consistently. Fresh vegetables for herself and occasional treats in the Officer's Wardroom, but the rest of the crew would be eating from dried stocks and freezers.

When those ran out…

"We will continue to pursue," Roselani said in a quieter voice. "But notify me when we begin to approach the point at which we must turn away from the hunt and race to a station ere we starve."

"As you command, Noble-born."

"Non-essential crew?" Roselani asked.

"Noble-born?"

"You mentioned that the vessel had been stripped of non-essential crew."

"That is correct," Genevong nodded.

"If we Indexed more of the crew right now, that would stretch our supplies some?" Roselani asked.

After all, Indexing had originally been invented so that Alvar colonists could be carried across the cosmos, back before modern technology made it a rapid and safe journey. That the process was generally reserved for the servant species didn't change anything.

Most of the crew weren't Alvar.

Genevong did an exceptional job of hiding her horror, keeping it away from everywhere except her eyes. Those gave her away.

"I would need to consult my Life Sciences department, Noble-born," she said in an obvious deflection that Roselani allowed for now.

Could they strip the crew down even more? Cut back on standard maintenance for a while, slowing such work and thereby stretching their leash?

Because that's what it had become. A leash around her neck.

Slack yet, and not a fine silk sash held in Kincaide's strong hands, but an absolute limit to how far she could chase.

"I will be interested in their review, Commander," Roselani said. "You will also notify me in time to rejoin you here when *Dashavatara* makes the transition. I wish to witness it with my own eyes."

"It shall be as you command, Noble-born," Genevong replied more firmly, back on safer, military ground and away from the insane demands of a cousin of the Emperor.

Roselani swiveled and began to return to her quarters.

The chase was approaching its climax.

CHAPTER 89

Kincaide sat in his office and breathed a sigh of relief.

"You're certain?" he yelled back down to the rest of the bridge.

"Affirmative," Hanishka called back. "I have been pinging him, and he us, so we both knew exactly where the other was. We will hit the warp-transition with about five hours head start on *Vanechon*."

Kincaide turned back to Zhubin and nodded grimly.

Zhubin made a gesture for him to close the office, so Kincaide waved at everyone and locked the doors.

"So now what?" the Chairman asked. "We have a small advantage at this moment, but it's not enough. What do we do?"

"We get crazy," Kincaide smiled at the man. "You could have hired someone rational and sane as your Foreman."

"That describes most of the candidates for the job, you know," Zhubin smiled back.

"Most," Kincaide agreed. "But none of them would have been crazy enough to get you this far."

"So I think I'm hearing that you have a plan?" Zhubin asked.

"I have an idea, at least," Kincaide replied. "It's insane and possibly stupid. Some might even call it suicidal."

"Gosh, I like it already," Zhubin said sarcastically. "Why now?"

"Because we control the gameboard for a very short time," Kincaide turned serious. "We know where everyone is and what they will do next. I can't guarantee that in the future, so we should take advantage of it while we can. I figure we'll only get one chance to pull a stunt like this. Whether or not we survive is a different discussion, but you've heard Odtsetseg's story. Lady Thammavongsa and Ildar are after us, angry, and probably relentless right now."

"Can't we just outrun them?" Zhubin asked. "At some point, this ship's design gives us an edge in supplies, so we can go farther from a base than they can. They'll have to turn back to restock the larder, or they risk starvation. We don't because as soon as we lose them, we can find a planet or even a comet, mine it for raw materials, and eat out of the Encyclopedia and the Decanters for a while as the arboretum continues to produce food. Isn't that enough to win?"

"It limits us, Zhubin," Kincaide growled. "We're in a pocket right now. Seventy-five or ninety stars, depending on how you want to classify them, before we drop back onto the main communications corridors leading to the Line of Exploration."

"And?"

"And the door is closed behind us, Mr. Chairman," Kincaide reminded him. "Those systems will be ordered to shoot on sight and telling everyone else the same. If *Vanechon* breaks off, pretty soon they are better off cutting sideways or even forward to run to a base. Maybe someplace like Arblemar or T'panik. They tell those people and cut us off there as well. It forms a net that traps us. I'd rather not end up circumnavigating the edge of the galaxy to get where we want to go. That will take years and maybe decades."

"So confrontation?" Zhubin pressed.

"Times to run, times to fight," Kincaide agreed. "We've been running. With any luck those fools will ask themselves the same questions and start wondering what they need to do to extend their range to stay after us. Chase us down like a hare in the high grass. They'll forget that we have teeth."

He watched the Chairman. Looked like the Stages of Death going on over there, but the man was an assassin by training. Hell, his new name supposedly meant *spear* in some ancient language from Earth, so he wasn't going to be a shrinking violet here.

"And then what?" the man finally asked. "What do we do after we surprise them?"

"Then we run like hell," Kincaide assured him. "Get as gone as we can go and don't ever look back. Right now, Reyhan can tell you exactly how far forward the message about us should have gotten, traveling at the speed of the fastest Warp Voyagers. They can move faster than we can, but not everyone will immediately echo it on or resupply the messenger to keep running, so it slows over time. Function of entropy and friction, because the Alvar have never had to face a situation like this."

"As long as you're sure about that part," Zhubin begrudged.

"Forward of the Line of Exploration is blank canvas, Zhubin," Kincaide replied. "Hell, even behind it there are blank places in the maps we stole. Whether those weren't worth exploring or they found something to avoid, I have no idea, but we have places to hide."

"Found something?" the Chairman perked up. "What are you talking about?"

Kincaide grimaced a little. He'd let his emotion get the better of him and spoken out of turn. But the cat was kind of out of the bag. Zhubin Prakash wouldn't let something like that slide.

He reached out a hand and keyed the doors open.

"Reyhan, can you join us?" Kincaide called at the faces that looked his way.

Herath nodded to Hanishka and set off up the stairs. Weirdly, Blur chose that moment to go all performance artist, racing up the stairs ahead of the man and into Kincaide's office.

Once there, he looked around for a moment, announced his presence, and jumped up on Kincaide's desk.

"Really?" Kincaide asked the goofball cat standing there.

"*Mau!*"

"Okay, fine," Kincaide surrendered.

Then the silly little shit walked over and hopped down into Kincaide's lap, curled up, and started to purr.

Seriously?

Kincaide put a warm hand on someone's butt and left it there.

Reyhan was apparently stifling the giggles at the scene as he entered and took one of the chairs. Kincaide slid the door shut again.

"What's up?" the man asked, looking back and forth.

"I opened my mouth," Kincaide said.

Which just caused Reyhan's mirth to spill over into uproarious laughter. When he was done, Kincaide turned serious.

At least as serious as a man can with a purring kitty in his lap.

"Tell Zhubin about that patch of darkness you found," Kincaide told the man.

Reyhan recoiled. His mouth opened, but nothing emerged, so he closed it again.

"Speak," Kincaide ordered him.

"I might be imagining things, Kincaide," Reyhan snapped.

"And you might not," Kincaide said. "We're moving to a new phase of the game and it is now time to start figuring out where we go from here."

"You're nuts."

"So many people have told me," Kincaide agreed. "Talk."

He leaned back now and watched the two men. Zhubin had turned to watch Herath. Reyhan swallowed once and then took a deep breath.

"We have a copy of the standard navigational reference," Reyhan began. "All Warp Voyagers have it."

He paused, as if looking for the words, but nodded to himself before either of the others needed to goad him.

"I was studying all the information as we continue to plot our path forward," Reyhan continued. "Then I came across something written in an archaic version of Alvar and have been translating it as best I can, but we didn't bring those sections of the Catalogue along when we built the Encyclopedia. Limited storage capacity and nothing like this would have made my top one thousand list."

"Go on," Zhubin said in a quiet voice.

"The records say something that kind of reads along the lines of 'No Trespassing' around a set of systems," Reyhan turned to face the Chairman. He'd already told Kincaide what he'd seen and his theories.

"*No Trespassing*?" Zhubin asked, worry evident in his voice.

"It's about as close a translation as I can manage," Reyhan said. "It's a dialect of Alvar that might be eight hundred thousand years old at this point. At least some of the references date back that far."

"*No trespassing* suggests that you would be encroaching on someone else's territory," Zhubin said carefully. "As opposed to encountering some sort of dangerous natural phenomenon."

"Yup," Kincaide agreed. "That was my impression as well, but the zone marked that way isn't on our current path, or even remotely accessible right now, whatever else happens in the next two weeks."

"Then why are you telling me this?" Zhubin demanded quietly.

"Because it is on this side of the Line of Exploration," Kincaide said. "The Gage and the Alvar marked an area no-go on their charts, without explanation. But we're the first vessel ever not to be commanded by an Alvar. Not to have already been taught what to fear there."

"Fear?"

"The Alvar see it as their mission to conquer the galaxy, and then move on to the rest of the visible universe, Zhubin," Kincaide growled irritably at the man. "What Reyhan found suggests that maybe they found something in there. Or someone, and decided to leave them alone."

"And we shouldn't?"

"Can you think of a better place to hide than one that even the Alvar are afraid of?"

The room fell silent. He'd already gone through this with Reyhan and come to terms with the potential for things that go bump in the galactic night.

The Alvar had been exploring space for over a million years, but the galaxy was billions of years old. Who knew what might have come along and disappeared during the time that dinosaurs walked the Earth and the Alvar were just thinking about inventing metallurgy?

What might those people fear?

CHAPTER 90

Odtsetseg clenched her jaw and lifted *Dashavatara* into warp-space.

The transitions had gotten easier with time and practice. It was like diving into a pool of warm, still water now.

Another woman's memories she had stolen, as Odtsetseg had no memory of swimming in her current incarnation. But she seemed to know how. Had apparently learned in a previous lifetime.

Or Ildar had stolen part of someone's mind that knew those things and had welded it into her head.

Odtsetseg looked forward to someday becoming her own person, with enough memories that she could perhaps forget other women. If that was possible.

For now, they had escaped. Fled into the serenity of warp-space: that vast, endlessly rolling plain of Mongolia and Siberia that her ancestors had traversed more than once when setting out to conquer the rest of the world. Kincaide's people had known her kind. As had Ildar's.

None had been able to stand before the Horde. Odtsetseg needed that surety. Kincaide had asked her to do something that her soul raged against. But this was war, and morality had to give way to necessity. Practicality, even.

She stared at the morning sky above her and saw those predator birds in the distance, circling lazily on invisible thermals as they sought prey. Only a few of them, rather than the massive flocks she had encountered a few times early on in their flight.

It was as though those creatures were drawn to corridors where the Warp Voyagers flew. Did they feed on the living? Odtsetseg didn't know how else to describe the difference between her and them, save living and dead.

An alternative would mean invaders like her and locals defending their lives and their crops. It would be as if she were a Mongol Horsewoman, coming for them.

No story or legend she had ever encountered made the warp-spawn seem anything other than demons, but what if she were created as The Destroyer?

But they left her alone now. Odtsetseg didn't know if they were the same creatures she had fought that first time, or if there existed a network that let them call to one another, like hunting birds, warning their comrades of which minds were too dangerous to approach.

Hasan Ildar had succeeded in making her *Power* itself.

Dashavatara glided through warp-space now, cutting a fine, thin wake that would fade, but not fast enough to be invisible before *Vanechon* or another vessel might scan it and know her path. The disturbance was still too great.

But Odtsetseg had already learned new things about herself that she had never imagined. She suspected that Ildar had never dreamed of the things she might do. Perhaps she had needed to free herself first, in order to become a person and not just a particularly-bright hammer?

She smothered the profanities before they slipped out, but one of the birds seemed to notice. It turned a head her way and started to fly towards her, before another cried out and it withdrew.

That behavior surprised her. Were they intelligent creatures? Everyone presumed them monsters come to feed, because Humans were tossed into their midst while most of the ship was shielded against them. Even *Dashavatara* was shielded, though the bridge was open to warp-space.

But Kincaide relied on her to protect them, something no Alvar had ever done.

Trust. And love.

The first bird returned to the circling flock, keeping such a vast distance of safety that they appeared as moving Ms against the morning sky.

Could she communicate with them? Her rage at Ildar had caught someone's attention.

Odtsetseg *considered*.

After a long moment, she looked all around her to confirm the emptiness of the nearby sky, and focused her mind on that distant flock.

Could she call them? Dare she?

If one killed her right now, Kincaide would have time to Decant a fresh copy, but one she had taken early in the flight, before she knew what she did now.

Should she call him and warn him what she planned? Or would he stop her?

Who could she tell?

Odtsetseg looked back into the other world just enough to note who was on the bridge right now.

Yes, that would do.

Kali, could you join me? she pulsed a thought at the woman.

The woman nearly jumped out of her skin in surprise, but then turned and began ascending the stairs to Odtsetseg's mezzanine.

Rather than lose sight of the flock, Odtsetseg held out a hand and felt the woman take it in both of her right hands. Odd, but comforting.

She reached out to the tall, blue woman with her mind and tried to share her vision. She hadn't done this before, but Kali had turned into another unexpected friend on this flight and that made it easier.

A ghost appeared next to her on that Siberian plain. Thin and almost invisible, but present.

Odtsetseg felt the gasp pass through the woman's frame.

This is what you see? Kali asked.

For me, Odtsetseg replied. *Others might have a different vision because they followed those who taught them. I had no teacher.*

What are those birds?

warp-spawn. I mean to see if I can talk to one, but needed someone here in case something went wrong.

Can they hurt us?

They could kill, if I let them. That first time I was cut by such a bird. Humans without my power would have been killed. Possibly taken, such that a warp-spawn might control my body in the real world. Alvar ships are designed to kill all their Engines immediately rather than risk infection.

Wow.

Indeed, Odtsetseg pressed a smile at the woman.

She reached out now with her mind and called softly. Several of the birds turned her way for a moment, but most kept flying in their circle.

One slid closer. Studied her from about midway between the two groups, almost hovering as it flapped strong black wings.

It called like a bird, a resonant caw that seemed to be more than animal inflections, but Odtsetseg could not decipher the tones.

"We are visitors," Odtsetseg let her voice carry to the creature, watching it as well as glancing around lest another sneak up on her like before, but the others kept a great distance.

The bird chirped something back, suddenly banking over onto one wing and turning its flight into a grand orbit, all the way around Odtsetseg and Kali once, but from a distance that might have been two hundred meters. Or twenty light-years.

Still, it was a mindful flight, and not just a hunter seeking mice in the grass. The bird kept his head turned inward, all the way around as Odtsetseg rotated in place with it.

After one perfect orbit, it hovered again and stared at her. Called in its voice.

"We pass through, using your world to move more quickly through ours," Odtsetseg said.

It was like talking to the three cats. Each were smart enough to understand her, but lacked the vocal chords to speak. Instead, you had to focus on interpretive dance and the way the tail and butt wiggled to see what they were trying to say.

Was it possible to speak with the warp-spawn as equals, rather than fight them as predators and prey? Why had the Alvar never done such a thing?

Because they were Masters, and kept slaves. Human slaves today, but Mori, Lop, Boomer, and Ayotochtli in the past, when the weaker telepaths were all the Alvar had.

Had a Human Engine ever contacted a warp-spawn? Spoken with it? Returned to the other world and tried to communicate with the Alvar?

She could see the masters immediately destroying such a creature in fear. Much of what they did was predicated on preventing the lesser species from rising up and threatening their control of The Gage.

And one Human would only be a sixth as powerful as she was in this realm. Easy prey for a bird with razor-sharp claws. Humans who lived in mortal terror of the warp-spawn.

Odtsetseg studied the creature hovering and cawing.

She nodded to it and bowed now.

"We will speak again," she said.

Odtsetseg let go and fell back into *Dashavatara*.

Kali was there when she opened her eyes, face drawn and so pale she might be periwinkle today rather than her normal rich azure. They still held hands, one of hers in two of Kali's.

Kincaide was close, standing in front of her and just watching. She tasted concern on his mind, but not fear. Trust. And Love.

It warmed her.

"I spoke with them, but we do not have a common language yet," Odtsetseg told him.

"Who?"

"The warp-spawn," she smiled. "They always appear as vultures in that place, circling, but have learned to keep their distance from me now. But I called one closer and tried to speak with it. It tried to speak with me. We will get there, eventually."

Kincaide turned to Kali, but Odtsetseg wasn't offended. Every Commander lived in terror of his Engines being taken by the warp-spawn. That was one of the underlying assumptions of warp-space and The Gage.

They lived in fear. She would not.

"It's true," Kali breathed the words heavily.

Both of the blue woman's hands were cold, so maybe all her blood had flooded into her belly. It was a fight or flight thing with Humans, but Odtsetseg had known what she was doing. Not if it would work, but what she needed to do.

"And?" Kincaide rasped heavily.

"And we will see if they are willing to communicate," she replied. "From there, can we?"

"Don't do anything risky or crazy, okay?" he smiled now. "We're close to a critical juncture. I promise that after we get away you can try, but not yet. Maybe when I let Reyhan rebuild the Information System to strip out Hasan permanently."

She smiled and began unbuckling various things holding her in place. Kali rose to stand next to Kincaide, towering over him by nearly twenty centimeters. Odtsetseg rose as well, feeling a little woozy, but Kincaide caught her with a hand.

"Food first," he ordered, but that was his usual response to her overextending herself.

Good food, some tea, and maybe a long soak in a tub of warm water to loosen everything seemed to cure most ails. She needed it.

Because she might be able to solve the problem of the warp-spawn.

But she had to fight *Vanechon* first.

CHAPTER 91

Hasan had been summoned. There wasn't a better verb to describe it, but he was a servant here. Nothing more. Certainly not valued as a bio-god capable of creating new species and better Engines.

Just a servant at beck and call.

He kept his opinions to himself.

Dashavatara had escaped, for the moment. Slipped away into warp-space on the shoulders of their Odtsetseg Engine and were currently racing across warp-space at Faster-Than-Light relative velocities, with *Vanechon* in hot pursuit, headed towards a system marked as Gemaharn.

Unpopulated. Irrelevant. A vast nothingness of no value to the Alvar, save that it might witness a war with the ancient Hindu demon Raktabija. The original battle that had necessitated the first Kali-ma in legend.

Hasan entered the lounge, even as the Mop crew woman who had summoned him remained outside and closed the hatch.

Hasan tried not to blink in furious surprise. He had been expecting just the bitch. And the gigolo.

The woman Commander of the vessel was an unwelcome addition. It spoke of extra complexities in an already messy conspiracy.

He nodded more than the situation demanded, almost a bow, and joined them in the seating area, noting that a Human-sized overstuffed chair had been added, so he was not required to sit next to the bitch, his feet dangling off the edge like a child.

A glass of wine had even been deployed for him as Lady Thammavongsa gestured for him to sit.

Hasan kept his thoughts to himself.

"You have met Commander Genevong, at least in passing," the blue bitch began, indicating the other woman.

If you could call her a woman. She was built like a male. Broad and muscular. Alvar women had little in the way of a waist, tending to simply come down from broad shoulders to narrower hips. But for the breasts under the uniform, he might have been hard-pressed to gender this creature.

The other one left no doubt, but she never covered both breasts at once. Alvar Noble-born, and all that superior tripe.

Hasan nodded again.

"In passing," he agreed carefully.

"I have asked you to join us so that you could talk to her about Zhubin Prakash and Kincaide Kataragama," she said.

Asked. Of course. Not even your language recognizes the commands of the wealthy and powerful to make everyone else jump when you snap your fingers.

Hasan turned to the other woman and smiled. It kept him from scowling in general at the situation.

"How may I serve?" he asked, hoping that the situation wasn't some sort of bizarre and disgusting orgy in disguise.

Two Alvar females and the gigolo. Alvar enjoyed Human males because they were sexually compatible. While there existed enough alcohol to get him that drunk, having consumed it beforehand Hasan would be unable to perform, having fallen into a coma from the poisoning.

Might not be the worst outcome, assuming the doctors on this vessel were at least halfway competent.

"How dangerous are those two men?" the Commander asked, sounding more like a professional and less like a bimbo. For what it was worth. "How smart? How canny?"

"I needed extreme competence to build *Dashavatara*," he replied, picking his way through the minefield of vocabularies here. "It was an entirely new thing. So I also needed men capable of thinking outside of the normal channels that The Gage prefer. Creative problem solvers who would not be limited by a shortcoming of rules or procedures. On top of that, they were crafty enough to betray me, steal my ship, seduce the Engine with whatever promises were necessary to break my control of her, and then flee Al-Winoq without me realizing what they were up to. From there, they have made it across several Gage systems, and even somehow convinced the Executor at Sextantis Port Station to resupply them fully. Oh, and then get away when the station opened fire at what should have been a lethal range for their weapons."

He paused and fixed a terrible eye on the woman.

"Competent enough for Humans," he continued, unable to resist the chance to take a dig at the Alvar superiority that had allowed this situation to occur.

And fester so.

"Lady Thammavongsa believes that they can outrun us right now," the woman replied. "That they have sufficient supplies and hydroponics to force us to give up the chase and return to a Gage Port Station somewhere, from which other vessels can spread the word of the renegade vessel and either help track it if they do emerge from the nearby darkness, or bottle them into this sector until such time as sufficient forces can trap them somewhere and destroy the ship."

"That might be sufficient," Hasan allowed. He paused and considered something that had eluded the great noble blue shits around him. It was a secret that had been part of his long-term plan. But he needed them in pursuit of Kataragama. If *Dashavatara* got away right now, they would never be found again by the Alvar, save by the slimmest of luck.

"But?" the blue bitch asked, perhaps catching something in his voice that the others had missed.

"Warp-shrouds represent the shortest, most-direct means of sailing from system to system," Hasan said, rolling the dice that they would continue to need his genius. Certainly, these three were all morons, but that wasn't a rare thing among the blues. "The safest. There are alternatives."

"Such as?" the Commander asked, almost angrily.

"If you know where a system is, and where the warp itself grows thin, you can long-sail between two points not normally on a sailing corridor," Hasan said, staring flatly at the tall woman and challenging her to gainsay him.

She fell silent.

"Is this true?" Thammavongsa asked now. From her tone, it was an unwelcome surprise.

"The risk is exceptional, Noble-born."

"Is it true?"

Yes, angry now. Surprised, perhaps. Possibly thwarted.

And yes, risky, but so was getting out of bed in the morning or deciding to take one of your Chuns right there in the lab, with a mug of hot coffee in one hand.

Were the rewards commensurate?

"It can be done," the woman allowed. "But the risk of warp-spawn destroying your Engines goes up for every day you are in warp. Long-sailing means that they might be eliminated at the very time you need them. Gage Warp Voyagers do not do it for that reason. I would be surprised to see the Human vessel attempt it, as they only have the one Engine."

Hasan felt eyes on him. The Security Gigolo. Southavilay. Studying closely, but that creature had been the one assigned to play good cop, so the two of them had something of a professional relationship that wasn't entirely stupid.

"They have Indexing and Decanting capabilities aboard that ship," Hasan reminded them. "The whole point of *Dashavatara* originally was to be able to establish a new forward arms depot close the current Line of Exploration. I would be surprised if those men weren't crafty enough to have Indexed their Odtsetseg against risk. I would have. Granted, if I were aboard that vessel, we would have already been sailing in the correct direction, and I would have been improving the design, much as I have done with the Altantsetseg model."

Hasan liked the look of pain that flickered across the man's eyes.

Obviously, these people were morons who needed an adult to hold their hands as they frittered away their lives.

"So you would consider it necessary to chase them down, in spite of the various risks, rather than to assume that The Gage fleet is up to the task of bottling them in somewhere?" Southavilay asked.

"Having caught up with them, they must now flee us," Hasan agreed. "Up until now, they have been flying like a normal Warp Voyager, perhaps a bit too fast across systems, but for obvious reasons. Now, they are threatened. Would you trust that every Port Station can be notified of their existence and intent, faster than they could get there? Sextantis just gave them whatever they asked for, without any orders from Al-Winoq. If you are content in trusting the system, then there is no reason not to just break off pursuit now and race ahead of them, bringing warning."

Hasan turned to the bitch in charge.

"You can out-think them, right?" he asked sourly.

Her resulting scowl made this entire journey worth it, just to witness.

"We can out-last them," she replied, speaking as if they were the only two people left in the galaxy. "But they must be destroyed now, for exactly those reasons. If we let them escape us, there is no telling when we might catch up with them again. If ever."

"Agreed," he nodded, appreciating that this creature was at least smart enough to realize that Kataragama and Prakash were smarter than she was.

As was he.

They both turned to the Commander in a delightful unison of purpose, but Hasan refrained from commenting.

"Assume they will emerge from warp-space and be running as hard as they dare to escape us," she said in a dread, implacable voice. "That we must take exceptional risks to stay in pursuit of that vessel, until such time as we have to break off and find a friendly system that we can reach, spreading the word to destroy them on sight."

Hasan felt a small burst of joy surge through him at the thought that Kataragama and Prakash would be destroyed shortly. He had already begun planting the seeds that would lull the dragon to sleep when they got back to Al-Winoq, buying him half a millennium or more to work in semi-secrecy as he continued to improve things.

"It shall be as you command, Noble-born," the Commander nodded compactly.

She rose from her chair and immediately departed. Southavilay did as well, leaving Hasan alone with the bitch.

At least she was growing used to listening to his advice and acting on it. Idly, he wondered if there was a way to put her on the throne, just so that maybe the Alvar might turn The Gage into something useful, but it wouldn't matter.

Hasan Ildar still intended to build a better Human. Alvar sized but not blue. Racially pure. Intent on wiping the stain of Alvar blood from the face of the cosmos. Let the other species fade into irrelevance or continue to serve. He didn't care.

She was studying him. Smiling in a way that Hasan found disquieting.

Almost icky. As if she was about to proposition him into sexual activity.

He rose to forestall.

"If you have no further need of me, I will return to my lab, Noble-born," he said quickly, sliding away from the woman lest an arm come out and snag him, dragging him back to that disgusting, naked bosom.

"Go," she finally said after a moment.

Hasan fled as if he were aboard *Dashavatara* and this woman was on his trail.

CHAPTER 92

Kincaide was on the bridge today. Normally, he could sit up in his office with the door open, remote but accessible, letting the secondary triumvirate of Hanishka, Dinushan, and Tharushi handle things, with Reyhan as Kincaide's alternate. He had an exceptional crew.

Today demanded more.

Zhubin and Kali were at hand, off to one side in their normal place. Kincaide had been paying attention to body language over the last six months, enough to note that they were barely ten centimeters apart today, both leaning against the wall, rather than the meter or more that had once been the case.

He doubted that Zhubin had been approached by Lilith. The Chairman was much closer to Ildar on that axis of thought. He would see them as monsters first, immortals seconds, and only as beautiful women a distant third.

But Zhubin Prakash was his own kind of fool. Who was Kincaide to judge?

Reyhan had things in hand, but he normally did, a generation older than Hanishka and two for the other two. A Grandfatherly figure, just one that knew almost as many dirty jokes as Tharushi did.

"We are approaching the warp-shroud," Odtsetseg said in that sleepy voice that said she was still in that other space, watching those birds fly.

"All stations come to combat readiness," Kincaide ordered. "Stand by to overload shields in all directions as soon as the load comes off the engines. Prepare to fire on any vessel within range, before you identify it."

Risky, but Gemaharn was unoccupied. There wouldn't be any innocent bystanders just happening to be anywhere close. Anything they saw would be *Vanechon*, and should be hammered as fast as Hanishka could manage.

If the gods had chosen to make him annihilate someone innocent, that would just be one more crime on his printout when he got to hell, and probably not even in the top ten, all things considered.

Kincaide looked around and nodded to everyone.

Hell or glory time.

"Stand by," Odtsetseg called.

Warp-transition.

Gods, he hated that feeling of falling through the entire universe faster than he could feel it. Hot and then cold, cycling infinitely back and forth in an eyeblink.

And then they were through.

Kincaide held his breath as the people around him went to work.

All the training came down to them being able to react correctly right now, without needing to ask him anything. He had given them parameters for engagement and expected them to carry it off.

Kill, or be killed.

However, apparently, nobody needed to die today. Nearby space was empty.

Small victories on a larger battleground.

"All scanners empty," Hanishka announced unnecessarily a few moments later.

All hell would have already broken out otherwise.

"Station-keeping," Kincaide ordered.

"Already in place," Dinushan answered grimly. "Calculating our location now."

Rather than sling them out of warp-space as hard as she could, Odtsetseg had opened a portal and just dropped them, like a rubber duck floating on the surface of her bath.

Where in the hell had that image come from?

Kincaide shook his head once to clear it. She might not have any sexuality, but she was still naked in that vision, and he was seeing her as she saw herself.

Weird.

"We're just a little off center," Hanishka said a few moments later. "High and a little clockwise, but just about dead center."

"Back us down to the original target." Kincaide took in all three of his crazies in one glance. It helped that they tended to be across the square and one corner these day, where they could look up from their station and make eye contact with him when he was back and up at his desk.

Reyhan standing at his station would be directly in that line of sight as well.

"How long?" Kincaide asked after a few moments of people staring at their screens.

"Take about an hour," Hanishka spoke, after a quick glance at Dinushan, who nodded.

"Too long," Kincaide decided. "Use the engines and the gyros right now to get us there faster. We should be able to compensate later, or react faster than whoever is in command of *Vanechon*."

They nodded, both a little pale, but he was ordering them to do crazy things.

Crazier things.

Like have *Dashavatara* at a dead stop, sitting inside the physical coordinates of the warp-shroud itself, but in this universe. Back on the short side, though, so that when *Vanechon* came through at high speed, the chances of a collision should be right up there with all fifty million of the Hindi gods deciding to play a practical joke on Vishnu and his Tenth Incarnation, the *Dashavatara* itself.

"Odtsetseg, how are you doing?" Kincaide said in a voice loud enough to carry.

She didn't answer for a moment, but he figured she was somewhere else anyway.

Preparing for battle her own way.

"I'm fine," she said. "Pushing my mind up and out to try to give you some warning that *Vanechon* is coming, but I'm not sure I'll be able to."

"As long as you can do what you need to when they get here," he reminded her.

There wasn't all that much that *Dashavatara* could do to *Vanechon* directly, even with absolute, bloody surprise. He would need her to pull a dirty stunt. While the others were raising a ruckus.

If it worked, he might gain enough time to lose *Vanechon* forever, although that would be asking too much.

Several days head start again would have to be enough.

Because if this didn't work, he was probably a dead man.

CHAPTER 93

Roselani had given much thought to the final moves of this terrible game. At least she hoped they were coming to conclusion.

If Kincaide truly made his escape now, that might quietly signal the end of the Gage Empire as it had been known. That fall might not occur for millennia, but she might yet be young enough to witness it.

Humans, returning from the darkness like some terrible armed plague, set to avenge themselves on the Alvar for what had been done to their homeworld.

To all homeworlds. The Humans were only special in that theirs had been the most recent world added to The Gage. Others would follow. Some worlds had already been identified with intelligent, tool-using life on them, but The Gage preferred slaves from an industrial base. Easier to fit them into modern civilization if you weren't literally seen as evil demons sent by the gods as punishment.

However accurate that assessment might be.

She had summoned Southavilay this evening. Not to warm her bed, but to still her racing thoughts with his logical assessment of probabilities. The hatch chimed and opened.

"Your guest, Noble-born," the Mori at the door announced quietly, bowed, and withdrew.

Makani entered, bowing gracefully as he stepped to the center of her small lounge. Roselani was in a comfortable chair. He moved to the couch and settled.

They waited in a companionable silence.

Time passed.

"What happens tomorrow?" she asked.

It was not a new question. He would not have any new answers. That didn't matter. It was her nerves that needed a balm.

Makani Southavilay had initially been resistant to her ideas. Hesitant to suggest that she might have seen a scenario worse than was actually within the reach of the renegade Humans.

Time spent watching Hasan Ildar at her command had cured his doubts.

Each day, more and more of the crew apparently whispered similar questions.

Had The Gage already fallen, and was just a shambling corpse that would continue for a time before failing? Humans had broken the hold that The Gage had on their minds.

Shown them *doubt*.

Could other species find a way to escape Alvar domination? Each had been raised from perhaps mere industrial technology to galactic, but it had come at a price.

Alvar control of their lives.

Until today.

"We will emerge from the warp-shroud and give chase," Makani replied simply. "They cannot escape us at this point, unless we choose to allow it."

"Could they point at a different system and long-sail it?" she asked in a tiny, almost fearful voice, worried that *Vanechon* had already lost this race.

"It is possible," he shrugged compactly. "But they entered the warp-shroud on this vector. If they chose another, I do not know what we could do on arrival, except to note that they had not appeared where expected. Presumably, Commander Genevong would wait for a time, and then turn to run hard for the nearest Port Station to spread the alarm and perhaps summon more vessels that could be used to chase them down. Eventually, they have to come to rest somewhere. We will find them."

"We will find them," she echoed his words with far less conviction.

When would they find them? Him?

She would not admit to herself feelings of betrayal beyond The Gage. That she wanted to look Kincaide in the eyes one last time to ask him the most pertinent question.

Why?

"What else could they do, Noble-born?" he asked.

They were alone in here, and she had given the man permission to use her personal name, but this was not a personal conversation, so he had fallen back on formality and duty.

What, indeed?

"Could they stand?" she asked. "Ambush us as we came out and attempt to damage this vessel so badly that we cannot pursue them anymore?"

"From what I have seen of the design records of that ship, they might believe that they could try, but the two sides are too evenly matched to succeed."

She nodded. Old answers to old questions.

Had Kincaide truly run out of options? Reached into his bag of tricks one time too many and come up empty? Already, the man had done the impossible more times than any Alvar was going to be comfortable admitting. Al-Winoq. Velle. Gouza. All the way to Sextantis.

And it would end at Gemaharn.

Wouldn't it?

Or had Kincaide lulled them all to sleep, much like Hasan Ildar seemed intent on trying to do with her?

She had wondered if the man's rage and energy might make him an interesting bed-mate. Certainly his arrogance had threatened to bring her desires to the surface more than once, but he could not get past himself and his hatred of all things non-Human.

Not like Kincaide, who could dominate her like a jeweler cutting diamonds, with exact precision to accomplish the task and not stray one bit.

No, Ildar would see them all fall. Roselani had no doubts that it had been a triple-cross, where Kincaide and Prakash had indeed betrayed Ildar, but only in that he was originally supposed to have been aboard that vessel when they left.

Why else had they taken such enormous risks then? Blasting out of the spacedock. Racing across the system to pick up what everyone now assumed was a replacement Indexing Package. Charging headlong into battle to reach the safety of the Velle Port Station, and then fleeing madly across the empire.

And it would all end at Gemaharn.

She didn't believe it for a moment.

"He's up to something," Roselani murmured.

"Noble-born?"

"Does this look like a man to be so easily cornered?" she asked. "So simply thwarted?"

Makani kept his own counsel, which was probably wisest.

"You expect a surprise?" he finally asked.

"Kincaide is nothing but surprises, Makani," she retorted. "Layers of an endless onion that you might continue to peel without ever reaching the center."

"What message should I deliver to Commander Genevong?" he asked now, earnest in his intent.

"I do not believe that any message would bring her to a higher state of readiness than she already anticipates," Roselani replied. "You will simply mark my words that Kincaide has something terrible planned for us when we emerge from the warp-shroud, so that when others begin to doubt, you may remind them that I was right. Again."

"Again, Noble-born," he agreed. "This entire quest has succeeded to date because you were right when others doubted. Myself included."

"It is not too late to save The Gage, Makani." She stared at the man. "But tomorrow we will discover the costs that must be borne."

He nodded now and rose, as though dismissed. In that, he was probably correct, as they had reached a vast emotional peak and it would now recede. Intercourse at this point would be a tawdry afterthought.

Better to end on such a note.

Roselani hope that she was wrong about tomorrow.

That it would, indeed, all end at Gemaharn.

GEMAHARN

CHAPTER 94

Kincaide heard the call and it practically levitated him out of his chair. Rather than fight it, he just kept moving, up and across the room to the door.

"They're here," Odtsetseg had called in that weird, distant voice of hers.

The one that suggested she was in another realm, talking with her ghosts. Or those birds.

There had been no successful communication thus far, but that didn't mean anything. She was six times as powerful as any other Human Engine that ever existed. And it was her current existence on the line here as well.

Because *Vanechon* had arrived.

Kincaide went down the stairs in two bounds and let the Command Square stop him as he slid to a halt next to Reyhan and looked at the map that the Computer Hasan was projecting.

Reyhan must be in a particularly foul frame of mind today, as Hasan looked exactly like one of his Chuns, down to the apron he wore to protect his breasts and stomach and nothing else.

Kincaide looked forward to returning to a less provocative Information Systems functioning. Even if he did have to slap Reyhan a few times to get the man to agree.

Enough was enough.

The four officers had all remained close, taking breaks in staggered rotation but not actually leaving this deck so they weren't too far away when it happened.

How she had managed to see them through the warp-shroud was another question Kincaide would ask her later. If they survived.

"All power to shields, weapons, and Odtsetseg," Kincaide said unnecessarily.

Tharushi was already there. Had been. They had maintained everything at a safe level just short of red-lining things, and done so for several hours now.

It was time.

Kincaide keyed a switch on the console and heard the system chime in every chamber.

"All hands, stand by for combat," he announced.

They didn't need more than that. Everyone was at whatever damage control station they needed to be, save for the cooks who would continue to make food and stewards who would deliver it to folks that were tied to a console for however long.

And then *Vanechon* appeared, shimmering into existence as it parted the warp-shroud and entered their universe again.

Dinushan and Hanishka had nailed his placement perfect. It helped that Gage crews were as by-the-book as you could get in this galaxy.

Vanechon appeared dead center of the warp-shroud laterally, just a little closer to the star than the exact center of the chaotic spherical shape that the shroud itself took when it intruded onto this space.

And going away from them.

Or rather, blasting hell-for-leather for the center of the solar system, on the expectation that *Dashavatara* was running for all they were worth with a five and a half hour head start.

Because those people thought inside the box.

Never colored outside the lines.

Never expected this...

"Fire," Kincaide ordered, about a half heartbeat after the first beam flickered out and licked the ass end of the other Warp Voyager.

Kincaide had learned something interesting in his studies of naval architecture, when he was hired to build this vessel. The Gage had a lot of beam emplacements on their ships, but focused them all forward, like a swordsman in an arena.

Dashavatara had been intended from Day One to be running away, so most of his guns were arrayed in such a way that they could come to bear on somebody dead aft, as well as dead forward, with good coverage up both wings, like a bird in flight.

One of Odtsetseg's vultures, perhaps.

Dashavatara had come to rest facing back the way he came. Dinushan was already using maneuvering thrusters and gyros to slew the bow around, but not much.

They had caught *Vanechon* from behind. Almost bow on stern.

And at a range where Kincaide wondered if he could have thrown rocks at the other guy.

Technically not, as the distance was already thousands of kilometers and growing every second, but even on a Glide, distances were enormous.

And they'd caught him off guard.

Dashavatara lashed out again and again. *Vanechon* was nothing but a flicker of silver in the distance, if you were relying on eyes, but Kincaide had ordered a couple of satellite probes be deployed, just to provide extra parallax on scanners.

He could watch representations of beams splashing and cutting, based on those scans.

Better, he watched a section of energy shielding start to leak, with shots striking raw hull metal and blasting chunks off then punching holes in the skin.

Kincaide refrained from commentary at this point. Dinushan, Hanishka, and Tharushi had trained for this and gamed it out extensively over the last few days. Nothing he could add would help.

Might detract, if only by distracting.

He shut up and watched in awe.

Like every kid, he'd played those immersive computer games where you flew ships against each other in virtual combat, but it was nothing like this.

Vanechon had been caught with his pants down, and *Dashavatara* was pounding away with everything Hanishka could throw.

He felt a moment of sadness, but only a moment, as he'd always known it was going to come down to something like this.

He nodded.

"Odtsetseg," he yelled. "Phase Three."

CHAPTER 95

Odtsetseg listened with half an ear, waiting for Kincaide. He had a plan. Brutal. Rude. Possibly vindictive, but nobody else had been able to come up with a better one.

"Odtsetseg," Kincaide called to her. "Phase Three."

Because nobody else could do *this*.

She sprang from herself and sought out that icky woman, pausing only to reach out a hand and dip it into the river of mercury flowing nearby.

Except that Roselani wasn't icky. She was a complete woman, with needs, fears, and dreams.

Things Odtsetseg wanted for herself, once she figured out how to be a Human.

Then Roselani was there. Easy to pick out against the background of other minds. It allowed Odtsetseg to pace *Vanechon* and watch them.

Like a vulture circling above that Mongolia steppe, looking for victims.

There. Six of them.

Theoretically, her match, except that they were individuals, and not a gestalt entity. They lifted the ship on their shoulders like pall bearers at a funeral, each taking part of the load, while she could carry it all in her arms.

Odtsetseg moved at the speed of thought and studied the group. Four females, including the alternate. Two males, one of whom was older than Kincaide and really should have been allowed to retire and live out his days in Maputo Dome.

She considered that what she was doing would at least free his soul for a time, before those Alvar shits dragged it back to this world and enslaved it again. He would have a brief taste of liberty.

And maybe the Alvar would learn fear.

Odtsetseg insinuated her mind into his, brushing him politely aside as he was distracted by the effort of recovering from the warp-transition.

All of them were tired. The Alvar didn't think of them as people, to be treated well. No, they were merely Engines. Use them up until you had to Decant a new one from the Catalogue. Recycle the old body into raw materials.

Trap the soul here forever, when it really wanted to fly above a Mongolian steppe on thermals and sunshine.

Eobasa. That was the man's name. Odtsetseg took a moment and scribed it into her deep memory so she didn't forget it later.

You should always remember and honor the people you kill.

She sucked in a deep breath and took control of his body away from him.

CHAPTER 96

Roselani had rested as well as her mind would allow without giving in to temptation for narcotic or soporific. She was as calm as she could manage, outwardly as though nothing interesting would happen today.

She did not believe it for a moment, but knew that she needed to project such an image to the crew around her. Even Commander Genevong needed to believe that the Noble-born was emotionally detached from this as they closed on the warp-shroud and prepared to end Kincaide's life.

The others were simply collateral damage. Without Kincaide Kataragama, they would not have managed even half as much as they actually had. Probably would have been destroyed in Al-Winoq.

Or perhaps they would have carried Hasan Ildar off to his dreams of Human militaristic glory.

Kincaide had made all the difference. It had taken Roselani this long to appreciate that he was a special case, and not just a particularly bright Human.

He was *dangerous*.

She felt a thrill course through her as the call came.

"Stand by for warp-transition," the Ayotochtli Sensors officer said loudly.

Roselani had never learned the woman's name, and realized that it might be important. They all existed to serve her will, and Roselani Thammavongsa found that she had been securely wrapped in the cocoon of her wealth and privilege for so long that she had taken everyone around her for granted.

Tomorrow, she would take each of them aside and begin to treat them like people, and not cogs. They had all earned that level of compassion and trust.

However, she wasn't sure she would ever forgive Kincaide for impacting her so. For puncturing the veil of arrogance that had surrounded her like a cloak for so many centuries.

He had changed her. A Human, no less.

Roselani took a deep breath and blew it out as she felt the transition take hold.

Inside out. Infinite cycles of hot and cold, bright and dark.

The deck under her feet lurched, throwing her into Genevong before she could get her feet under her. The woman caught her and held Roselani up with a shocked look on her face.

Again.

Roselani fell the other way. Stations occasionally lost gravitational control, but she had not felt such a thing accidentally in millennia.

Sound intruded now. Genevong issuing orders loudly and others answering.

"Where are they?"

"We're taking beam fire!"

"Damage control to deck six."

"Stand by medical."

"*Dashavatara!*"

That caught her attention as Roselani threw herself into the chair and hooked the straps to hold her in place.

Kincaide was here. And had sprung some sort of ambush on them.

She had been right. Damn him!

Was there any sentient creature who was a match for Kincaide Kataragama? She began to entertain doubts.

Her inner ear wobbled as the vessel staggered, at least as the gravity under her feet hiccupped.

Lights came on and off randomly, as though someone couldn't find the switch they wanted and were trying all of them randomly.

Alarms bounced off the walls around her and the bodies. The everyday chatter of a competent bridge crew grew loud and restive, men and women of several species yelling over each other and the sound of sirens.

Plus the terrible, thumping crash as something happened to the ship around her.

Roselani wondered if she should make her way to the escape pod that weekly training mandated she be familiar with.

Would Kincaide rescue her if he managed to kill *Vanechon*? Or would he send hunters after her specifically for ruining his plans?

A screamed profanity from the far end of the bridge oval brought her head around with a snap.

"Repeat that!" Genevong roared, temporarily drowning out the rest of the noise.

"warp-spawn," a Mori officer looked up from his station, his eyes showing whites as they bulged with panic.

"Where?" Genevong screamed, terror starting to take hold of her voice now.

Roselani felt it infect the others around her, but she didn't understand. Or perhaps it was an intellectual fear, where all the men and women around her felt it viscerally.

"Main Engine compartment," the Mori replied. "We have infestation. One of the Engines has been compromised by a warp-spawn."

Roselani felt her blood go cold.

She had heard the sailors' tales of the things that lived in the darkness between stars. In that other realm where Gage vessels plied in order to move at hundreds of times the speed of light, relative to this place.

She was safe. She understood that *Vanechon* kept their six Engines in a special compartment outside the warp shielding that protected the rest of the crew. Those six were vulnerable, but not everyone else.

They could be eaten by demons from the depths of warp, while a Noble-born woman from Al-Winoq could live a life of comfort and lassitude.

Roselani Thammavongsa would never have to pay that price. She had Humans for it.

Damn you Kincaide for making me understand that.

She watched Genevong hesitate for a long moment before the woman turned to look this direction.

Around them, the sirens continued to wail and mourn. The deck lurched and other officers reacted by turns calm and hysterical, depending. Voices raised and formed a solid wall of noise so great that Roselani felt like she could taste it.

But what she was really tasting was fear. She did not enjoy the flavor.

Roselani wondered if she would ever get the scent out of her toga, or if she would end up needing to ritually burn it somewhere as a mechanism of purification.

Genevong started to speak, but stopped. Slammed her mouth shut hard enough that Roselani might have heard it above the noise.

Or felt it as an earthquake through the deck plates.

The Gage Empire had just changed. *Irrevocably*.

"Blow the compartment," Genevong ordered in a voice clear even through the impossible din.

"Main Engines?" the Mori yelled back, as they always seemed to do when the orders were complicated.

Or dangerous.

"Vent them to space," Genevong commanded. "Alert Life Sciences that we will need new Engines as soon as they can manage."

The Commander looked over at Roselani with hard, bitter eyes. She had been there with Ildar and heard that Roselani thought that there would be an ambush here. How he had done it, she couldn't be sure, but Roselani was utterly certain that an infestation at this moment, even as *Dashavatara* was shooting at them, could not be happenstance.

Again, the Noble-born had been right. Kincaide was more dangerous than anyone but Roselani had been willing to grant the Human.

Humans were more dangerous than anyone else was willing to admit.

Genevong nodded to her. It was so tight, so compact, that anyone else would have missed it, but it spoke volumes now.

Roselani had been right. They would listen to her in the future.

Believe her.

The Mori officer slammed a broad hand down on a glowing red control disk on his console. Another alarm wailed in fury now, overtaking all the damage control signals and whatever else was making the racket in her.

"Cut all alarms," Genevong howled in a terrible rage.

In a moment, the room fell to silence, save for the ringing that was more a thing in your ankles than your ears.

"Maintain all ahead full and begin evasive maneuvering," Genevong called in a voice suddenly too loud for the quiet. "Get me away from his guns and bring new shields up before he kills anything else important."

"Thrusters to full burn," the Helmsman nodded, voice sounding like it had yesterday.

Yesterday.

A lost era when The Gage were going to rule the galaxy unchallenged.

Before Kincaide Kataragama and *Dashavatara*.

"All weapons engage and prepare to turn a wing to him," Genevong continued. "Sensors, let me know when he's gone."

"Gone, Commander?" the woman looked up and her jaw fell slack. Ears flickered forward like a questing tongue.

Genevong looked over this direction and Roselani saw fear take root in the woman's eyes.

"That's right," Genevong said to the Ayotochtli, even as she locked eyes with the Noble-born. "Gone."

And Roselani finally understood what that man had done.

CHAPTER 97

Kincaide watched and waited, everything out of his hands.

However, he had a good team. The best set of people he could have envisioned right now, doing their utmost for him.

The Command Square had gotten so quiet he was almost afraid to breathe, as the three of them—four with Reyhan's occasional comment —went about their jobs with whispers and murmurs, when Kincaide was pretty sure he'd be way too loud for the room.

Vanechon was punch drunk in a bar brawl by now. And it had been barely forty seconds of dancing, which made it all the weirder. But Kincaide wasn't complaining.

"There," Hanishka said louder. "Hasan, confirm that scan."

Computer Hasan as Bimbo-Chun closed their eyes for a long moment and then opened them again.

"That is correct, Hanishka," the said in Hasan's voice. "*Vanechon* has vented their Engine compartment to deep space. I confirm six bodies being jettisoned in their ejection seats. None were dead before this. All are in the process of dying now."

Cold. Brutal. Honest.

Computer Hasan, for all the real man was an asshole, was simply a projection when he was being asked to work.

Hanishka turned tired eyes Kincaide's direction and nodded.

Kincaide took a breath and promised some level of evil retribution on the Gage Warp Voyager *Vanechon*, but it wasn't happening today.

Didn't have to. He'd just won.

Well, not won, but burned those fuckers hard and solid.

"Odtsetseg," he leaned back and called up the stairs. "Take us out."

Kali stirred from her designated docking station along the wall, almost but not quite close enough to Zhubin to touch shoulders.

"Just like that?" she asked as the room fell silent.

Hanishka was still hard at work, but she'd keep firing everything she had until they exited the universe. Like him, she owed The Gage a few things, and had never once in her life been in a position to pay those mangy camels back.

Nayani would have liked Hanishka. Maybe Kali, too, although Lilith would have squicked her right out. Spiders did that. Had done that.

"Just like that," Kincaide agreed in a tired, fifty-eight-year-old voice.

Warp-transition.

Smoother than the rest had been, but he'd had Odtsetseg flying crazy from the beginning, rather than taking her time to slip in and out of warp-space in a comfortable way.

Like say, sitting perfectly still in the middle of the warp-shroud and not having to compensate for movement as you parted the veils?

He could get used to this, but he doubted that they'd have much of a chance. Maybe once they got far enough, they might actually fly like sane people, but he'd always be looking over his shoulder for Hasan and Roselani.

They hadn't been destroyed, after all. Just thwarted in the best way Kincaide could think of to do it.

He keyed the ship-wide open.

"All hands, we have transitioned to warp-space," Kincaide said in a normal-enough voice. "Stand down and return to normal rotations."

He closed it and nodded as Kali drew closer, Zhubin trailing in her wake.

"They can Decant a new set of Engines, sure," Kincaide smiled tiredly at her. "But that takes time. A simple Warp Voyager like that probably only has one Decanter aboard, unlike *Dashavatara*. But we're a colony ship, so we can spit out one hundred simultaneously in a pinch. They'll be three days minimum Decanting themselves six new Engines. Maybe longer depending on how prepared they were when this happened."

"While we're getting away," Kali completed the thought.

"Even with new Engines, it will take them time to get everything ready for warp-space," Zhubin said as he stepped up next to the woman.

Again, not touching. But not not-touching by all that much. Kincaide grinned for a flash of an instant.

"How long?" Kali asked.

Kincaide shrugged.

"If everything else was perfect, probably only a couple of days testing," he spoke. "Then you push up and into the warp carefully, so everyone can get used to it. I have no idea how skilled their six Engines are, or how recently they were Indexed."

"Only one veteran," Odtsetseg said as she began to descend the steps to join the mere mortals on the bridge. "The others were much younger, and had not been Indexed in a considerable amount of time. Plus, they won't want to trust the oldest Engine, so they might settle for a different model. He was the one I possessed."

"Possessed?" Kali gasped.

"It had to look like a warp-spawn had taken one of them and was about to infect the whole ship," Kincaide interrupted before his step-daughter could speak. "So I told her to go after the strongest one. Make him go nuts on their ship. Maybe we can infect them with a little panic. But standard Gage procedure in such an extreme case as a manifestation is to kill all the Engines immediately. Open the compartment to space and send all six to a quick death by explosive decompression followed by turning into another set of miniature comets floating in space around here."

"Meanwhile, *Dashavatara* slips up into the warp-shroud and disappears back to Sextantis, except that we're pushing now," Zhubin completed the thought.

"They'll still be able to tell *Vanechon* which shroud we took next time," Kali pointed out.

"We wouldn't have ever gotten this big a lead on them again," Kincaide said. "Plus, all this assumes that their ship itself is in perfect shape. Hanishka also pounded the living shit out of him in the minute we engaged."

He turned to her and smiled.

"What's their status?" he asked.

"They are right on the edge," Hanishka nodded with a grim smile. "Maybe they need dry-dock. Maybe they can chase us some more. I expect that they will take the safe path and dock at Sextantis instead of immediately coming after us. I would, given the sorts of damage to their thrusters and power systems."

"So they'll settle for now with sending messages every direction, warning everyone where they think we've gone, but again, we have at a dead minimum a full week head start and I intend to be a brutal taskmaster to everyone, to make up as much distance as we can."

Odtsetseg joined them now, having listened. Kincaide pulled her close and wrapped an arm around her waist. She felt cold, but that was just him running hot with adrenaline and emotion right now.

And maybe she had just killed someone for the first time in her life. He remembered his first, and all the emotional processing he'd had to do afterwards. And his victim had deserved it.

Odtsetseg had just killed six innocents for no better reason than they were in Kincaide's way. And he had asked.

"And we needed their sacrifice," she whispered, tilting her head towards his so she could lay it on his shoulder. "I hope I brought them a little peace, at least until those necromancers bring them back."

Kincaide glanced at her in surprise. Necromancer wasn't a term he'd heard used to describe the Alvar all that often, but it really did fit in this instance. Those six Engines were dead, but only until someone summoned their souls back for more service.

Djinn, maybe.

That was one of the big reasons Kincaide had never been Indexed. He would die and be gone, and nobody could drag him back to the land of the living.

"So we have a little time," Kincaide said. "Not enough to let Reyhan take the Computer Personality apart and remove Hasan. Not enough for a lot of the things we want to do, but enough that we should celebrate a little."

He looked around at the frowns.

"You people have just defeated a Gage Warp Voyager," he said louder. "Understand? That has never been done, as far as I am aware, so add one more thing to the revolution that *Dashavatara* represents. They will have to chase us across the entire damned galaxy from here, and pretty soon they'll run out of places where they have maps, so we'll have an even greater edge. So good job. I know I don't say that enough, but you've done the impossible yet again and I'm proud of you."

Odtsetseg almost seemed asleep on her feet, from the way her weight settled more and more on him. The others also had a haggard look going.

"Dinushan, you've had the least to do since we parked," Kincaide picked out the face that looked the least tired. "You're in charge for a while. Everyone else go off duty and take a nap. Eat a meal. Stand in the shower until you prune. Something to relax."

Groans and sighs greeted him as he turned Odtsetseg towards the stairs.

"We're back to normal in six hours, so you've been warned, but consider this shore leave," he hollered at them and guided his step-daughter forward.

Kali caught his eye and Kincaide nodded.

He had only delayed the next issue.

He still had to deal with the Wives.

EPILOGUES

EPILOGUE - ROSELANI

Roselani stood on the supposedly-safer deck of Sextantis Port Station. Safer in this instance only because Kincaide hadn't bothered firing back when he had fled the place, drawing *Vanechon* into his wake.

Laying a trap.

It was a measure of how far she had traveled from Al-Winoq that there was only one station in this entire solar system, in spite of the four warp-shrouds present. One to Gemaharn. One back to Xyri. One spare.

And the one *Dashavatara* had taken to flee. She was not surprised that it seemed to point out towards the very edge of the galaxy, where the stars got thin. Kincaide wanted to hide from her.

From the rest of The Gage, true, but also from her. She had no doubts about that now. He knew it was her, although she couldn't tell anyone why she felt such certainty.

But it was certainty.

Roselani followed Lukadia Gereben, the Ayotochtli Sensors officer from *Vanechon*, as they progressed deeper into the station. Lukadia had no specific duties while the ship was being repaired, so Roselani had asked that she be detached to serve as an aide for now.

It gave Roselani a chance to practice being polite and friendly with someone who wasn't Alvar. After all, the only other Alvar in this system besides those on *Vanechon* was the Executor of the station, and she had already been arrested by Security officers under Makani's authority.

Whether or not she was found guilty of treason later would be irrelevant. She had aided the renegades in their escape, and needed to be punished for it.

Roselani had filed a report about the level of mental control that the Odtsetseg model seemed to be capable of. That might mitigate. And it might necessitate that the woman be destroyed before she could tell others what the Humans could do.

Others besides Hasan Ildar might decide to create god-slaying weapons.

Lukadia paused at a closed door and turned to look up at her, those wide-set Ayotochtli eyes locked in and her ears forward in nervousness.

"Your suite, Noble-born," she said in a quiet voice.

"Join me for tea," Roselani said, possibly confirming the woman's worst fears.

But she keyed the door open and Roselani followed her into an Ambassadorial suite comparable-enough to what she had on *Vanechon*. Mostly. Perhaps three-quarters as fine as the ship, which was only half as good as her palace.

But it would do. She was off the ship and out of Genevong's hair while that worthy commander put her ship back together.

Losing the Engine compartment was a known risk on a Warp Voyager. Things happened to your Engines and you had to kill them and Decant new ones.

But this had happened in the middle of a battle. Kincaide had somehow *summoned* the warp-spawn and set them on *Vanechon*, as though the demons of the night would ally themselves with the Humans against The Gage. Or at least the Alvar.

How had he done it? Or was she seeing bogeymen under every rock at this point because of him? And how did she get the rest of The Gage to move past their inertia and act?

Could it get any worse?

Roselani found a comm and keyed it.

She started to speak and caught herself before the phrase began "*I will require…*"

"Would someone please deliver tea and service to my suite?" she asked instead.

Damn you, Kincaide.

"Sit," she gestured to Lukadia.

Most of the furniture in here was scaled to the smaller woman, Alvar being rare so far from home. And the locals probably expected an Ambassador like her to remain on her ship.

Roselani just wanted a change of scenery for a short time.

Vanechon would be her chariot for a long time at this rate.

She smiled at the Ayotochtli woman as she sat. Noted how the long face, covered with scutes to protect her nose, seemed to point an arrow in this direction.

"I made a mistake," Roselani began, just to watch Lukadia's eyes open wide and her whole body flinch in surprise. "I warned everyone that Kincaide was competent, but even I didn't realize just how dangerous one Human could be, Lukadia."

"Mistress?"

"He drew us in and came exceptionally close to crippling us at Gemaharn," Roselani clarified. "Commander Genevong has told me that two shots penetrated the hull in such a way that we nearly lost all of Power Systems, venting those chambers to space and requiring us to Decant a whole new engineering crew and not just new Engines. That was why it was necessary to limp to Sextantis and repair things, giving them several weeks head start on us."

"He cannot escape The Gage," Lukadia ventured carefully, turning suddenly as a hatch opened and a Mog in a steward's uniform rolled a cart into the room, bearing tea and various edibles.

Rolled. How utterly quaint. And perhaps a mark of poverty in this system, that they didn't have repulsors, even to serve a visiting Ambassador.

Roselani added one more thing as a strike against her kind, that only the Alvar in the important systems were able to live such decadent lives. Noble-born like her, when the rest had to make do in much more primitive conditions.

But then, as she watched the steward place everything within reach and withdraw, only the Alvar rated.

Damn you, Kincaide.

She could see that becoming a common refrain.

Lukadia stirred to serve them, but Roselani waved her back.

"You sit," she ordered. "I will serve us."

Again, the woman's mouth fell open. Her ears might hurt from straining so far forward for so long, ere this day was done.

But it had become necessary. Kincaide had proven to be more than a match for *Vanechon*. He himself might be a match for the entire Gage.

Roselani poured out tea into two mugs and handed one to Lukadia. Various sweetbreads accompanied, and Roselani snagged one for herself as a reward for surviving Sextantis Port Station.

They sipped the hot brew in companionable silence, mostly to give the Ayotochtli woman time to find her equilibrium again. From a serving officer on a little-known Warp Voyager to perhaps a Lady-in-Waiting to the Lady Thammavongsa herself was something of a step up, but Lukadia had impressed Roselani with intellect and competence. All the more so for not being Alvar.

That needed to be rewarded. Especially now.

The Gage had changed.

Like that warp-spawn manifesting and threatening the entire vessel, *Vanechon*'s story would get out and eventually infect the entire empire with *change*. Her kind would have the worst of it, as their generational changes were measured in millennia, while the woman across from her saw things in mere decades.

Kincaide could not get away from them or The Gage was doomed.

"What happens next?" Lukadia asked tentatively.

Roselani nodded to the woman as she found the right words. An Ayotochtli would not understand someone willing to spend one hundred years on a task, when her kind didn't live that long.

Millennia. Decades.

"Messages will be sent out from Sextantis, warning all stations that *Dashavatara* is to be destroyed on sight," Roselani replied carefully. "Eventually, we may need to assemble an armada of Warp Voyagers to give chase. Had we such resources available at Gemaharn, that battle might have turned out differently."

"Might have, Noble-born?"

"Kincaide Kataragama is dangerous, Lukadia," Roselani studied the woman. "Everything that has happened can be laid at his feet."

She saw a question come into Lukadia's eyes and hang there, unvoiced.

"Ask," Roselani said firmly. "We are alone and I will not take offense. You need to learn new things, just as I do."

The gasp was tiny, but telling.

Do we live such lies that even a small truth disturbs us?

"There are suggestions that you have lain with Kataragama, Noble-born," Lukadia hesitated, flinching as though expecting a blow.

"And they are truth," Roselani nodded. Smiled. "I have not had that many orgasms, nor that intense, in longer than I wish to consider. He was amazing in bed."

Apparently, an Ayotochtli blushed by flaring the ears straight out sideways while the eyes bulged in a manner similar to Alvar. Or Humans.

"Humans have a very large penis compared to their overall body size, Lukadia," Roselani explained. "Comparable to Alvar in absolute terms, so fornication between the two species is generally a pleasurable event, regardless of the genders of the participants. I ordered Kincaide into my bed and enjoyed myself. And him. He used that time to measure me and perhaps all the Alvar, but he did his duty and then fled into deep space."

"Is this vengeance?" Lukadia asked, then nearly jumped as she clapped a hand over her mouth and snout.

"At the beginning, perhaps," Roselani agreed. "But nobody took Kincaide seriously then. They expected him to fail. Kept expecting him to fail. Gemaharn had hopefully taught Commander Genevong an important, if painful, truth. She will communicate that to the others of her kind."

"A truth, Noble-born?"

"Humans could bring down The Gage, Lukadia," Roselani said simply. "Destroy everything we have spent nearly a million years building. And do it in the blink of an eye to my kind."

"Oh."

"Yes," Roselani agreed. "We must work exceptionally hard right now to save the Empire, lest an army of angry Humans descend on us like a plague of hornets."

"Can we succeed?" Lukadia asked.

"I don't know."

EPILOGUE - KINCAIDE

Kincaide was aft, in the space where Lilith and the others lived. Most of them weren't trapped back here, technically, but couldn't necessarily get around easily. Lilith and Staci, for example. Niki and Serena could travel in tanks small enough to be rolled or repulsored around if they felt the need, but the Wives were used to living an isolated existence. Thus, Kincaide had let his crew know that they were safe to interact with.

So some enterprising wag in the aft kitchen had apparently gotten Reyhan to approve opening a new lounge back here, taking up an empty space after they broke down four shipping containers for volume, so now there was a bar that had a limited menu and soft music playing in the background.

Kincaide pretended that he didn't see any of the things around him and concentrated on the folks at the table with him.

Normally, he would have had an exceptionally private conversation, but that wasn't going to be possible yet. Maybe later. Maybe not.

Nature of being in command around here, and all the other folks with claims on his time and his mind.

Odtsetseg and Kali sat side by side, like sisters or something, leaning on one another and occasionally whispering and giggling at some joke. He most certainly didn't want to know.

Zhubin was on Kali's far side, but that wasn't a personal thing. He had fallen into the habit of being next to the woman, particularly when the two of them were on the bridge.

Reyhan reclined beyond that, going around the circle, which put him uncomfortably close to Lilith, crouched down with her legs arranged more like a sphinx than anything. But he was Assistant Foreman of this ship and this crew, so he needed to be here to speak. Or take over if something went insanely wrong.

Hanishka was on the other side of Lilith and looking far more comfortable. Kincaide had wanted a woman officer present as well, because Reyhan was a something of a sexist pig on top of his other failings. Hadn't been an issue three years ago when Kincaide recruited him, but the galaxy had changed a wee dram since then.

Noor sat between Hanishka and Kincaide, close enough that he could smell the odd musk of her fur. Leotaur. At least that was the term Lilith had taught him to describe the woman. Top half was a woman like many of them, covered with a fine fur like Theodosia, only golden instead of black. Bottom half, starting where a normal woman would have hips, she had a tiger body, with four legs ending in clawed feet.

The ship's cats had apparently freaked out the first time they had encountered Noor, and then adopted her as something of a goddess later on. Another goddess, as at least one of them seemed to be forward near Odtsetseg anytime Kincaide went looking for his step-daughter.

Noor smelled like sunshine, coming through a Dome sky on a nice day when the overlords had decided to shift the sunlight to spring. Nothing floral about her, but he kept expecting her to have a scent like roses that have just opened. Her smile held a similar promise.

He leaned back, finished his highball glass of bourbon and sat it noisily down on the big round table as a way to bring this meeting more or less to order. All of them had been waiting on him anyway, but Kincaide had needed those few moments to get his shit together.

Or at least as close to together as he was going to manage today.

It helped that the rest of the room was largely ignoring them, although Kincaide could see every single one of the Wives present, some talking to crew and some separated. Even Niki and Serena.

Dashavatara had escaped *Vanechon* for the time being.

Now, for the hard, *weird* parts.

He circled the ring of faces again, left to right this time, starting with Noor and ending with Odtsetseg.

"So, there is a motion on the table," he said, trying to act businesslike, even as the rest of the room seemed to fade to silence around them.

No keeping this a secret, even if he'd thought it possible.

The smiles around him didn't help his state of mind. He focused on Odtsetseg.

"You have been approached to participate in a scientific experiment," Kincaide stated. "Explain."

Because why the hell not treat it thus?

Odtsetseg smiled at him, but she was probably touching his mind enough to see what he was actually feeling. It was good to know she worried about him almost as much as he worried about her.

"I have learned many new things about my abilities," Odtsetseg said in a bright, firm voice audible beyond just this table, since the rest seemed to have quieted. "Some of them Hasan Ildar never intended. Some were expressions he had left dormant in my design, although I don't know if that was intentional or merely an expression of genes he had to include for other reasons."

Kincaide nodded. He scowled at the waiter delivering another glass of bourbon, but didn't reject it.

He wouldn't need to be drunk right now, but maybe a little more relaxed would be in everyone's best interest.

"With power from *Dashavatara*, I can reach into a mind and make some changes," Odtsetseg continued. "It is possible to override someone fighting me, but not for long and it likely leaves damage and scars over the longer term. But in this instance, I have been assured of a willingness by the person being affected."

Willingness. A pretty way to put it, but he didn't know how any of The Wives were really mentally wired. How many of them might just be horny and unable to risk anything. How many wanted to become someone beyond what Goaulda had originally built.

He nodded as his step-daughter paused, studying his face and maybe listening to his internal commentary. She needed to know that he trusted her.

She smiled. And blushed.

"So once a candidate has been identified and approved, I can work with her to see if it is possible to make the necessary changes over the short term, as well as how they might become permanent," Odtsetseg spoke in a voice that blushed as well.

She didn't have the mental wiring to understand *need*. She could experience it in another's mind, but Kincaide didn't think that such a thing would ever arise in the woman herself, unless she managed to figure how to trigger it in her own genetic structure. Could she?

Would she? was another question entirely.

Kincaide turned to Lilith now and studied the woman. Like Noor, perfectly Human in shape from the belly button up. Both women were covered with a light fur that would make an interesting textural experience. All of Noor, but only the sides and back of Lilith's torso. Breasts larger than average on both but not subject to age and sag. Lilith's raven-black hair was shoulder length and curly, while Noor kept her wavy blond locks shorter.

Women. Monsters as Goaulda had designed them, but women.

"So Odtsetseg thinks she can break things in your minds," Kincaide spoke to Lilith as if they were alone, rather than the whole lounge and maybe the whole ship listening. "What about you, Lilith? What happens if she can't? Or if they revert later and you develop... *attachments*?"

Lipstick on a pig, but he might as well try to pretty his language up right now. Everyone was listening.

"I step down as leader of the Wives," Lilith replied calmly. Professionally. "Kali or Noor step in. One of the others is elected to speak for us, and I'm discounted until such time as either the connection can be broken by Odtsetseg, or you die of old age and I spend another decade in mourning recovering my mind, like happened last time."

He'd never really thought that closely about how the Wives must have been devastated.

Their former God and master had built himself a new sex object. To test it, he had taken several drugs designed to greatly amplify and extend his endurance. Like, stupid long amounts.

One bad interaction and the man had been found dead on the floor of a heart attack. Or something.

Hell of a stupid way to die. Probably still made the galaxy a better place as a result. But they had all been emotionally bound to him while he was alive. And apparently it had taken them a decade or more to recover.

He could appreciate that, since he was three decades beyond Nayani and still mourning.

Too bad that fucker Ildar had escaped Kincaide's idea of justice.

"So you, Kali, Noor, Theodosia, Staci, and possibly Ghost, but you aren't sure about her," Kincaide named the women who had apparently provided at least a semi-positive response. At least to the experimentation phase.

Or whatever you wanted to call it.

"Correct," Lilith agreed. "But you haven't assented to such a thing yet, Kincaide."

He scowled, but she was right. He'd merely not thrown a tantrum when approached. Not irrevocably said no.

However, he hadn't said yes, either.

Three of the Wives were here at the table, representing all nineteen of the survivors he could see by turning his head. Three that might want to *experiment* with a mayfly. Three of his officers as well, counting Zhubin in that mess.

Plus his step-daughter.

He turned to Odtsetseg and focused on her dark eyes. In many ways a preteen daughter, possibly trying to find herself a new step-mother, from the way the whole thing had seemed to play out. A way for her step-father to stop being sad about Nayani, perhaps.

He would always love his wife, but he tended to agree that he got a little too wrapped up in himself at times, and ignored or discounted the people around him. Easier to hide behind a wall of gruff rudeness and not have to deal with others on a personal level.

Odtsetseg held out a hand now and he took it. Human touch, even though she considered herself even more alien than the Wives around her, alien in appearance for all their DNA was Human.

He drew a breath and released it, finding Lilith's eyes. He hadn't really paid that close of attention to them before now. They were dark, like everyone's, but there was a blue underneath, where his were brown.

"Yes," he said simply. "I will participate in this experiment. I will provide whatever assistance is needed to see it to conclusion."

"And who would you select as your partner?" Lilith asked quietly, again as if they were alone in the chamber.

Kincaide flashed back to that damned conversation pit in Roselani's palace. That night. Doing things at the time because it had been a grudge-fuck in his mind, but the woman had had needs and kinks and apparently never been able to find the person capable of handling them.

Of scratching that particular itch.

Ghost was probably the closest to Human, at least from the blurs he could remember. But every woman looks alike in the dark, when you are seeing her with your fingertips and your tongue.

Kali would be next, in terms of basic Human morphology, once you got past four arms she could be doing things with at the same time.

Staci was built like an Alvar, just green and with cute, little tusks sticking up. Almost exactly Roselani's height, but heavier with muscles and broader shoulders. But he'd already climbed an Alvar mountain.

Theodosia would be almost like bedding a Mog again. Her puma design was even apparently inspired by that species, but the Mog had different mating equipment, and Goaulda had been just as much a specist shit as Ildar, at the end of the day, so his slave was Human under that black fur.

But all of them could more or less pass for Human women in the dark. Get a little drunk first so you didn't notice fur where there should be skin, claws on the tips of fingers, extra equipment that made docking procedures a complicated choreography of intercourse.

Lilith seemed to quail a little as he stared at her, but then her chin came up. She was wearing a blue tunic today, so maybe that was what brought out the blue of her eyes. It looked like silk and hung loose in some places but tight across her breasts, almost outlining things.

Or perhaps she was a little cold right now. Kincaide was warm.

"Are you still willing?" he asked her, as if they were the last two Humans in the universe.

It would be completely different from anything anyone could imagine, but Goaulda had been after a certain range of kinks.

The rest of the crew would fear her, even the ones that worshiped her. Like someone else he knew.

Odtsetseg squeezed his hand just a little. Step-daughter, trying to make her father happy.

Weird, because he'd been on his own for three decades now, but he had a family of sorts. People who relied on him, and worse, looked to him for examples.

He should set a good one.

Lilith's face flushed a little. Her pupils dilated as he watched. Kincaide thought he picked up a new muskiness that competed with Noor's spring smell.

"I am," she said, barely a whisper.

"Then you and I need to talk, without the rest of the crew listening and watching, Lilith," Kincaide concluded.

Zhubin nodded like a man who had just won a long-shot bet, but Kincaide wasn't really surprised. Some things were as much political as social and personal, and an undertaking like this had wide-ranging implications. The Chairman had been an assassin in his youth, after all.

"Should I clear the room?" he asked now, gesturing compactly with one hand.

"No," Kincaide replied. "The rest of you stay and enjoy yourselves. We'll go elsewhere."

"Should I accompany you?" Odtsetseg asked as he dropped her hand and rose.

"No," Kincaide said again, smiling down at her. "Not tonight. But soon."

He stepped away from the table and considered holding out a hand for her to take, but Lilith was already skittish as she stepped back and stood up.

Kincaide felt like a kid, since she was so much taller, but then again, Roselani had been as well, and he'd made that work out.

However, this was going to be much more complicated.

EPILOGUE - HASAN

Hasan watched the woman enter his laboratory and held his commentary. Polite body language.

She was still an Alvar Noble-born woman, and had the power to have him executed on a whim.

Commander Genevong followed behind her, surprising him, and then Makani Southavilay joined the little conspiracy as the door closed and was locked with the controls.

"We need to talk," Thammavongsa announced.

Hasan felt the air turn frigid, but that was just him, all the blood in his body pooling behind his navel as adrenaline suddenly began pumping everywhere else.

Fight or flight, when he was the only Human in the room, against three Alvar.

He concentrated on his breathing, pausing only to save his current notes and close the lid of his console so it didn't distract him.

Rather than speak in a voice he didn't trust, Hasan moved to the lounge area and sat, gesturing the others to join him. Genevong scowled. Southavilay nodded.

Thammavongsa had a secret grin as she followed the other two invisibly.

It did not bring any warmth to Hasan's world.

"*Dashavatara* docked at Sextantis station for several days," the woman began. "Picking up supplies and interacting with the Executor of the station personally and directly."

He wanted to still hate her, but even Hasan had to admit to a grudging respect for Lady Thammavongsa. She had been right about Kataragama and Prakash when everyone else had guessed wrong, including himself if Hasan wanted to be honest.

At least with himself.

She had transcended the rest of her species to become someone Hasan Ildar might even respect, given time.

That thought was the most galling in its implications.

"Security Administrator Southavilay has reviewed the logs of the station and interviewed the staff at my orders," she continued, as if the other two weren't present. "We have a problem."

Hasan bit back the sarcastic response he wanted to flick at the woman like a wet towel, possibly drawing blood however metaphorically. She had come to him. Looked like she needed help from the *mere Human*.

What could he extract from the woman in recompense?

Hasan nodded, willing his heart rate to return to normal, when this looked like a political discussion, rather than a battle or an orgy.

"Zhubin Prakash went aboard the station alone," Thammavongsa said. "But his behavior did not fit a Gage officer interacting with others. The Executor has been modified by a telepath."

Oh. Shit.

"Please repeat that, Lady Thammavongsa," Hasan managed. "Prakash went alone, but you believe that the Odtsetseg Engine was able to affect the Port Executor?"

"That is correct," she nodded. "I have watched the video recordings. Prakash walks into the bridge and stands there. The Executor orders her entire staff to leave them alone, and then signs the necessary orders. At no point did Prakash actually say anything relevant to the woman."

Hasan was cold again. What had she done now? The Odtsetseg wasn't supposed to be able to do things like that. But then again, she wasn't supposed to be able to deny him, and that had been broken as well.

"Southavilay subsequently interviewed the Executor in private," the woman continued. "She admitted to doing things because she could not resist a voice in her head demanding them. The woman is also suffering from a variety of physical issues that I suspect are psychological in nature."

"The Engine broke her mind," Hasan whispered in sudden terror.

Thammavongsa nodded. The other two scowled, but remained silent.

"I will not suggest that the mental shield generators we Alvar occasionally wear against such things would be sufficient against the Odtsetseg, because all of us now know just how powerful she is."

It was Hasan's turn to nod. Those were proof against the sorts of Engines that Commander Genevong had access to.

Odtsetseg was without peer in the universe.

At least today.

There was a gleam in Lady Thammavongsa's eyes.

"If we are to resist your old Engine, I believe it will be necessary to have our own Odtsetseg aboard *Vanechon*," she said. "Or your Altantsetseg model, since you claim to have improved the design and extended her powers."

Cold. Brutal, killing, winter chill.

The woman could not appreciate what she was about to unleash on the universe, could she? With Altantsetseg, he could control all of them, as long as nobody was able to break her conditioning. Odtsetseg didn't have that much telepathic ability, because he had routed everything he could into telekinesis. Altantsetseg could barely count as two of the Engines on this ship.

But she could easily warp minds better than anything in the universe.

And he would control her.

"Is that wise, Noble-born?" he found himself asking.

The Altantsetseg could bring down The Gage even faster than the Odtsetseg, because the Alvar had nothing to stop her. Those electronic shields they wore were tissue paper at best.

"Leave us," she suddenly ordered the other two.

The witnesses.

They rose without complaint and left. Simple as that.

Hasan found himself alone with his worst possible nightmare. A competent co-conspirator.

She leaned forward a little, but it was emphasis, not seduction, enormous breast notwithstanding.

"Prakash and Kataragama must be destroyed," she said bluntly. "They have already damaged the emotional underpinnings of The Gage itself by defeating *Vanechon*, however temporarily that might be. They will be seen as peers to the Alvar. Humans. Others will want to know why they cannot also have such equality."

Hasan held his breath. This was verging right over onto active treason. It might even work to bring the Empire down, but he wanted the blues eliminated entirely, not just pulled from their pedestal.

"The Gage must change, Ildar," she said in a voice barely above a murmur now. "Humans need to stop being slaves and start being partners in ruling. Bio-gods such as men like you call yourself could lead that, by creating better Engines. If we do not need to breed Humans like prize stock, they can be free to pursue their dreams."

"What limits do you foresee, Noble-born?" Hasan asked around a tongue dry with nervousness.

"Humans and Alvar are the two species most compatible in The Gage, Ildar," she smiled. "Intellectually. Emotionally. Physically. Perhaps they need to join us in ruling the others. Your kind have more potential for greatness than any of the others we have ever encountered."

"You are suggesting nothing short of a revolution," Hasan stated in a voice that didn't quaver.

Much.

"Or treason, depending on who you might ask," she agreed. "If Kincaide escapes us today, he will bring down The Gage in time. I know what you and the others were up to, even if they did betray you at the last instant. I can offer you power when we return to civilization. As you have hinted, you plan to live forever. What could you accomplish if you didn't have to hide your machinations away from my kind, but we put you to building up a Human/Alvar empire to replace what we have now?"

She leaned back and Hasan found himself in the most exquisite trap he could possibly imagine. This woman truly understood him and had discovered the one prize she could offer that would turn his head.

Respect, coupled with power.

Humans could easily outbreed the blues and politely push them aside in a few thousand years on numbers alone, if they weren't limited to the Domes and a few Forward Arms Depots.

She was offering him a partnership measured in millennia, and all he had to do today was help her destroy Prakash and Kataragama.

"Oh, and I will have my technicians build me a more powerful mental shield generator device," she just tossed out there like it was an afterthought. "Something more like the warp-shielding that keeps the demons of the night at bay. But just one."

She knows the truth.

Could her hatred of those two men be even greater than his? Was that possible? Hasan was astonished to even consider such a thing, but perhaps she saw herself as a jilted lover atop everything else, rather than just a partner betrayed.

Just.

Here was a woman offering to destroy her entire culture, just so she could have her revenge on Kataragama. And enrolling him in her conspiracy, knowing what he had planned afterwards.

The room was still cold. Hasan could see the immediate benefit the woman sought.

Did she really think she could continue to outmaneuver him for the next several centuries? Having a personal shield that would protect her from Altantsetseg suggested as much, even as it put the rest of the vessel at risk.

He could have Altantsetseg take the Security Gigolo and use that man to strip Thammavongsa of such a device suddenly, leaving her at his mercy.

Hasan realized how deep the woman's plans must run. There must be contingencies in place against that somewhere, and she believed that they would be enough.

Dare he risk it?

He leaned back now and studied her, this dangerous creature, this woman offering to conspire with him. She had to have depths he had not ever even considered, let alone plumbed. Secrets hidden yet.

In the end, he came rather quickly to a conclusion.

"A hundred-year-truce, Lady Thammavongsa?" he asked. "We will stalk *Dashavatara* and see it destroyed, and then return and see what we can make of The Gage for a while before we inevitably turn on one another?"

Her sudden smile spoke volumes. Frightening depths of conspiracies, in a woman he knew had to be nearly five thousand years old. Did she still remember the Alvar Conquering Earth when she was a child?

Had he so badly underestimated her from the very start?

Hasan wondered now if his disdain for her kind had blinded him to her capabilities. His fear that she might seek him out as a sexual partner because she saw some faint echo of Kataragama in him.

Could they really turn The Gage inside out and satisfy the immense ego of Hasan Ildar?

Was that even possible?

"A truce," she agreed, as if reading his mind now. "I trust that far more than suggestions of sudden piety and fidelity on your part, Ildar. The Gage has grown stale and insular, and that needs to change. I would like your help doing so."

She held out a hand in the Human style and Hasan found himself taking it.

If he was going to live forever, perhaps he didn't need to destroy this woman first. She would be dead of old age in a few thousand years, and he would hopefully be in complete control by then. Or poised.

He might even find it beneficial to wait until she was gone, if nobody else came along as smart and cunning as she was.

What could they do to destroy the universe together?

EPILOGUE - LILITH

Lilith studied Kincaide as they entered her personal quarters.

It was just a chat. Odtsetseg had not done anything that would change her to make more interaction possible at the present time, so she took refuge in that.

She could still back out of this before they took the ultimate step.

Which course of action made her a greater fool?

Lilith gestured to one of the chairs as she settled in the nest that the crew had built for her, comfortable for her abdomen with space for all eight legs to relax. She blushed as she realized that this might be the very spot where she and Kincaide had their first encounter, given the physical and biological architectures involved.

First? That suggested a second. Or a fifth. Or more. Would she still have the ability to say no, after the first time she felt him inside her?

Kincaide was watching her from under hooded brows, but that was a side effect of her being so much taller. In the dark, he would see her as an Alvar.

But then, he had been with such a woman. She had heard the tales that Odtsetseg had told Kali. The memories stolen from Roselani in a moment of passion.

If he could approach that task like a blacksmith, anything might be possible.

Even enjoyable.

"What made you choose me?" she asked abruptly, finally realizing that the man would wait for hours for her to initiate the conversation.

Hunter, like her form had been built to emulate. Patiently sit at the center of a web and let fools and flies wander too close.

She suppressed a shiver, but understood that Kincaide Kataragama was unlike any person she had known in five centuries.

"A number of reasons," Kincaide shrugged eloquently. "First and perhaps foremost, you represent the Wives in the minds of most of the crew, so as their leader, I need to consider it from a political standpoint."

"I see," she said carefully, not adding any emotion to her voice.

She had suspected that it would not be an emotional thing, but Lilith had prepared herself for that.

At least she hoped so.

"Second, there are no ugly Wives," Kincaide said. "So I had my pick of beautiful, intelligent, *capable* women. At the same time, yours is the most exotic appearance. If I were to have chosen Ghost or Kali, that might suggest that I didn't see the rest of you as beautiful women."

He paused and stared at her until she looked him in the eye.

"That would be a mistake on their part," he said with quiet emphasis. "Plus, you are the most interesting mind present, as you've overcome everything that mere bipeds like me might feel about such a form. And you are still a Human woman, Lilith."

She shivered. Lilith remembered what *mere bipeds* had said about her. To her. The sidelong looks of disgust. Kincaide didn't have any of that in his eyes.

He had no pity either. No fear.

Nothing but honest appraisal.

Her shiver turned warm, because Lilith couldn't remember the last time an outsider had looked at her with naked interest. Possibly lust, and not backed by fear or worship.

Odtsetseg had shared tales with Kali. Lilith understood how much Odtsetseg was really one of them, even though she looked far more Human, save for that eight-banded ray on her face, as well as the second one nobody ever saw on her belly.

She looked more Human and was less. The Wives looked less Human but were actually closer to men like Kincaide that anyone realized.

It was all a matter of flipping certain switches in certain orders, and almost all of Earth's DNA was available. A man just had to have patience.

Brakiee Goaulda had been such a man. He had also been an arrogant sociopath intent on his own desires, ignoring everyone else other than wiring all the Wives such that their orgasms could enhance his own.

Kincaide Kataragama was a man of infinite patience.

"So you would still like to go through with it?" she asked him after a small pause to process his words. His meaning.

His intent.

"I would," he nodded. "As long as this is something you wish to do for yourself, and not just because it is expected of you."

"Expected?"

"You lead the Wives, Lilith," he stated. "That sort of responsibility brings a lot of weight with it, and I speak as the Foreman of this crew. But speaking as a man, I will say this, to you and only you. I've paid homelier professionals to fake their enthusiasm over taking a prettier one to bed, because there is nothing less sexy to me than a woman lying there and counting ceiling tiles while we're fucking. I realized then that it was a business proposition, but could fool myself for long enough in those days. But if we're going to do this, I would like to imagine that you went into it with some passion. I know that the programming might kick in and override everything Odtsetseg tries to do to break it, so you might not have any say in the matter after that. I'd like to think I'm the kind of guy that wouldn't take advantage of you at that point, because that's really no better than rape, even if your brain chemistry suddenly flip flops and you turn into a nymphomaniac. It's still rape if you can't willingly give consent, every step of the way."

Lilith had to remember to breathe when he fell silent. Every other person she had known outside the Wives themselves had never framed it in such clear language. What Goaulda had done to her—to all of them—was still rape, so many centuries later. They could not consent. They could not withdraw consent.

They were victims of chemistry and wiring that took away all agency, and none of them had dared risk the touch of another man since Goaulda had died, trapped by Enkya's legs and her orgasms.

She swallowed painfully, as everything had gone dry. She wondered if she'd been sitting here with her mouth hanging open in shock, but his smile was warming, not mocking.

He saw her as a woman.

What was it he had said before?

"In the dark, all women look alike, Lilith," Kincaide had said that day. "All women. Even you."

Even her.

He saw her as a woman. A Human woman. A full person, with wants, needs, desires, fears, and even hopes.

She studied his face. His eyes. Brown pools that held nothing she might have expected.

Lilith wondered what his hands might feel like on her neck. Her back. Her many legs. Her abdomen.

What it might feel like to know the touch of a lover again.

A partner, and not a rapist.

"Yes," she whispered, understanding now that the man would sit there forever, if she didn't give complete and unreserved assent.

Counting ceiling tiles, as he had said it. Putting up with the act for money and nothing more.

No emotion. No passion.

Just a business proposition.

She doubted that he would see it that way. She had approached him, rather than the other way around, so there wasn't even the suggestion that she owed the man something for having rescued them from Boston Dome and risked all their lives for the chance to be free.

That had been Prakash's idea.

Lilith was glad it had become necessary to save a man like Kincaide Kataragama from his own depression. She looked forward to what little time she might have to know him as a person as well.

He rose and nodded to her. Almost a bow before he moved to the door.

Part of her wanted to call him back, but she recognized the exquisite trap for what it was. There was a chance that the programming had died with Goaulda, and nobody would be sure until one of them tested it. She might end up emotionally and psychologically bound to the man for the rest of his life, even if that only ended up being half a century.

It would still mean pain.

So she nodded back. Rose enough to turn it into a curtsy as only one of her kind could manage it.

"I look forward to kissing you," he said from the door, just before he opened it and exited, leaving her to gasp, alone in her chamber.

Could the Wives finally, truly, irrevocably be free of Brakiee Goaulda? Was any price too high to achieve that?

EPILOGUE - ROSELANI

Roselani sat in the quiet dark of her own chamber and considered the implications and expectations of what she had done. She didn't really believe that Hasan Ildar would honor such a thing as a century of peace between them, but she would burn that bridge when it became necessary to kill the son of a bitch later.

Right now, the house itself was on fire and she didn't think even Ildar was fool enough to provoke something before the situation was contained.

Afterwards, he would absolutely turn on her, but that was the risk.

She had already composed a message to her cousin, the Grand Gage, Emperor Kapono Phetphommasouk, that would be carried on a separate vessel leaving tomorrow. If Ildar did use his little toy Engine to do anything to her, he would have to face hard and deadly questions when he returned, whether or not Roselani was there to protect him.

Insurance policies against a future she hoped to never see unfold, but The Gage had lasted as long as it had because the mayflies could not see things in such long terms. To Ildar, a century was a reasonable period of peace between them, as he built himself up a new power base. Roselani had plans in place that wouldn't even begin to look more than simply mature for another thousand or perhaps fifteen hundred years, with an expectation of perhaps twenty-five centuries before time caught up with her.

House Phetphommasouk had sat on that throne for as long as Humans had been a separate species on their homeworld, to say nothing of the first Alvar explorers crossing warp-space more than a million years ago.

She would be safe. Or she would be avenged.

Either way, Hasan Ildar wouldn't be allowed to win at his little games.

Then her mind went a different direction as she sat in the quiet and sipped at a late glass of wine.

Kincaide had feared her, rightly, but still did his duty. Given Ildar's conclusion that Kincaide had been the one to break the Engine, what must he have promised to that woman to do such a thing?

Ildar swore that both the old Odtsetseg and the newer Altantsetseg lacked the hormonal programming to reach sexual maturity, and all that came with it, so that could not be it. But Kincaide was also older Human. Roughly Roselani's age as a relative ratio of their expected spans.

How had he come to represent some sort of alternate god to the Engine? A father figure to replace the one she had lost in Ildar?

There were so many things she wanted answers to, and Roselani doubted that she would ever get them. If nothing else, she only had a few brief decades to confront the man himself before he managed to escape her forever.

He was almost the polar opposite of Hasan Ildar in that way. Kincaide didn't want to live forever. Didn't want any sort of immortality thrust on him, even unwillingly.

He had approached the concept of their fornication with a phlegmatic shrug, but then stepped up and knotted a sash around her neck and tugged, to the point that Roselani had almost achieved her first orgasm right there, kneeling on the floor in front of the man.

When she got too close to Ildar, he unconsciously recoiled from her. Where Kincaide had been willing to push her boundaries when she needed it, Ildar sought again and again to allay her and maintain as much distance and frigid rigidity as possible.

Perhaps in that the two men made the perfect spectrum against which to measure all males. At least Alvar and Human, in any case.

More than once, Roselani had considered torturing Ildar with sexual demands, but she still needed him as something of an ally for a time. No others held the same fear of *Dashavatara* escaping them as she and Ildar did.

They would fall out over something once the house fire was out. Of that she had no doubt.

Roselani was just sad that the situation wasn't reversed, with Kincaide here and Ildar fleeing before her. More than once, she had wistfully imagined a scene where she managed to catch up with Kincaide.

Her alone, without *Vanechon* or the others. Walk into a room and find him there, just so she could sit down and ask him *Why?* Perhaps even get answers, although she doubted it.

Roselani finished her wine and felt a pang that it would have to be enough to destroy the man and live the rest of her life in ignorance.

EPILOGUE - ODTSETSEG

Odtsetseg could almost feel Kincaide in the next chamber, brooding, but she kept her mind to herself. He had talked with Lilith, and it seemed to have gone well enough. At some point one of them would approach her and the next phase would begin.

Odtsetseg found herself looking forward to reaching into Lilith's mind to break things, but it would be for a good reason. She would be freeing their souls, just as Zhubin had freed their bodies from an eternity trapped in Boston Dome.

Would all of them seek such treatment? She didn't know, but they existed in a different place from her. Adults, in the true sense of the word. Possessed of sexual needs they had been unable to fulfill for centuries, while she could only approach such things from an intellectual standpoint.

She could only listen in as some women of the crew exploded with orgasmic bliss across the wavelengths that Odtsetseg could hear.

What would it be like to have such desires?

That fucker Ildar had supposedly cut such potential out of her genetic structure when he was building for power, but Odtsetseg had come to a much better understanding of that man, and men in general, from her talks with Kali. She suspected that he had instead sought to bind her to him by limiting her potential for maturity in all the ways that everyone else on this ship took for granted.

Every Human child would reach puberty and transform into a new creature. Except her.

Yet again, Odtsetseg wondered if she could somehow reach into her own code and change it. If her telekinetic abilities were strong enough, could she alter herself at that genetic level and turn herself into a woman, instead of remaining a precocious child for her entire life?

Did she want to?

What she might gain were romantic and sexual needs, and then she would have to face the fact that most of the crew saw her in the same terms that they did the so-called Monster Wives. Bizarre and frightening creatures designed to bring nightmares.

And she really was alien. Human base with cephalopod genes from a squid added in, among the crazier things, in Ildar's project to make a Human being crazy enough to drive a starship while still sane enough to be controlled.

Odtsetseg didn't want to be controlled, even when that fucker was light-centuries away. She wanted the same sorts of freedom that Lilith and Kali and the others were chasing.

The rational voice in her mind suggested that she Index herself right now, before attempting anything, just so that she kept all the things she had learned, if she managed to destroy herself in the process of growing up. The last Index had been before they left Al-Winoq.

A stray hand betrayed her and opened a comm line before she could stop herself.

"How can I help, Odtsetseg?" Zhubin asked immediately.

Now, her voice betrayed her.

"I think I should be Indexed tomorrow, Chairman," she found herself explaining.

"Oh?"

"There is an experiment I would like to attempt, but it brings dangers," she said.

"Such as?'"

She paused, unable to answer the man.

"Odtsetseg?"

"I would like to see if I can change my own genetic code," she finally managed. "Alter myself in much the same way that I will do for Lilith."

"Would you like to talk in person?"

Odtsetseg thought about it for a long moment.

"I will be right over," she said, cutting the line and rising.

Anything to escape the sudden chill darkness that this room seemed to cloak her in.

She opened her main hatch and saw Chairman Prakash already standing in his doorway, concern etched on his features.

He was a little younger than Kincaide, and perhaps more handsome on the surface of things, but Odtsetseg rarely just saw skin. As she approached, he became a complicated oil painting by one of the impressionists. She had seen such things at some point in a previous life and it had made enough of an impact on her that she tried to paint people the same way.

In her case, the images on the canvas were what her mind's eye saw.

Zhubin Prakash was a hard, cold man. Deadly in the physical sense of someone who trains for close combat on a daily basis, reaching back decades. Tall and powerful in ways that few others of the crew managed. Cruel underneath it. Only Reyhan Herath was a close companion that way.

Both men saw her alienness first when they looked at her, while Kincaide saw the woman underneath. The girl, perhaps, since woman was denied her.

For now.

Prakash ushered her into his den, replete with all those weapons close at hand. She picked the chair in the center of the room and settled, knowing he would be on the couch with a sword close by and several knives hidden and at hand.

That was who Zhubin Prakash was.

"I would ask what prompted this," he began, "but I presume the conversation earlier with Lilith and Kincaide?"

"Indeed, Chairman," she said, automatically falling into formality in her mind.

He started to correct her and then recognized it for what it was and relaxed back into his rest.

"I am alien," she continued. "I will never be an adult as your kind understand such things, and now find that to be intolerable as an outcome."

"Okay?" he offered, but it felt more like a placeholder than anything.

At least he was willing to just sit and listen for now.

"The Wives are also somewhat alien, but I might be able to break

539

that conditioning that holds them aloof from the rest of Humanity," she said. "I find myself wanting to be Human."

Again, he started to speak, but thought better of whatever words might have come out. She wasn't even listening to his emotions right now, so wrapped up in her own, but that was probably for the best.

"What would Human look like to you?" Prakash finally asked.

"Desires," she said, boiling it down into as stark a term as she could find in the language. "The Wives have them, but remain thwarted by Goaulda. Others in the crew have them and can exercise them. I cannot, and find that intolerable."

"Why?" he asked, leaning forward now. "What makes it intolerable?"

She nearly savaged him, but realized that he was asking intellectually. It was not personal. He hardly saw her as a person, much of the time.

"Ildar did this to me," she rasped, finding her jaw clenched painfully. "It was a way he could control me, along with all the others. Make me dependent on him for everything, because I could not experience most of the range of Human emotions. Some of those controls are broken now. I want to see if I can completely free myself."

"I see," he nodded, leaning back now. "So you feel that Indexing yourself is the safest bet?"

"I might destroy myself in the process, Zhubin," she said bluntly. "As far as I know, nobody has ever attempted something like this, because nobody ever had this level of power available. My last Index is months old, and that might be a problem for you and Kincaide. Doubly so if you had to approach that girl with Lilith's needs and none of the experiences or control I have developed."

"I know how much you hate that booth, Star Flower," he offered now. "Are you certain?"

She could smell the change come over the man. See that oil painting evolve before her very eyes as she spoke.

"No," she agreed. "But as Kincaide likes to say, some things are necessary and that overrides desire. I have a duty to this ship and the crew, as well as all of Humanity, and need to be able to fulfill that, even as I find myself wanting things for myself. Indexing this version of Odtsetseg into the Encyclopedia is the safest way to make sure every base is covered."

He fell back into thought and she focused on her breathing, appalled just a little at what she had decided. What she had concluded.

What she might do.

"I am willing to support you in this thing, Odtsetseg," he said finally. "But you will need to be prepared to perhaps self-terminate if something goes terribly wrong. You'll be Indexed, so it is possible to start over, but nobody here will be able to make you do such a thing, and the Human instinct to survive is a powerful force. And you are Human in all the ways that matter."

She felt a blush creep up her cheeks. Both Zhubin and Kincaide liked to pound that point home, even as the rest of the crew generally didn't think that way.

She was Human. She was one of them.

They both loved her, at least in their own ways.

A thought struck her and she found her head tilted as she studied the man.

"If I partially fail, I might need you to Decant a fresh Odtsetseg before I destroy myself," she said.

"Oh?"

"This model would be able to tell that version what went wrong," she noted. "It would give her a chance to perhaps correct my mistakes. And you will have me Indexed at the current state."

"It might be painful, seeing a different version of yourself," he offered.

"How many Odtsetsegs have you known, Chairman?" she snapped, feeling a rise of anger underneath it all.

However, wasn't that anger the thing that drove her in the first place?

"Over twenty," he nodded. "Including this version of you that we Decanted just before we escaped Al-Winoq."

"I rise each morning and understand that my memories of being Odtsetseg the Engine only stretch back a little over two years, Chairman." She ground out the words slowly. "Before that, she was someone else, locked into the Catalogue and awaiting Ildar's megalomania to be freed. Perhaps copies of me power Gage Warp Voyagers somewhere with a different face. And I have seen the inside of that Indexing booth more times than anyone you will ever know. I would like to break that cycle and be done."

"Done?"

"My squid and octopus genes might mean I am doomed to die in another two years," Odtsetseg said. "My Human genes should take precedence and grant me eighty more. I cannot know which will express dominance until I try to take them apart and put them back together in the manner that will make me a woman."

He started to speak, but fell back into himself. After a moment a wry grin appeared on one side of his mouth.

"You might need to see Sewwandi," he said. "Both because she represents Behavioral Medicine as well as the fact that she is a woman and I can't speak to that side of the equation. But I will support you. Like Kincaide, I want you to be happy. And like him, I have no idea what that takes."

"None of us do, Chairman," she said mournfully. "That's what makes us Human."

EPILOGUE - KINCAIDE

Kincaide triple-checked, but the main hatch was locked. Odtsetseg was the only one who could get in at this point, and then only by teleporting across a threshold he had no intention of opening tonight. He needed time to think. To relax. To plan.

They had escaped Al-Winoq and all the people chasing them. Including Roselani.

At least for now.

Endless galactic reaches stretched out in front of them now, assuming they could run ahead of the bow wave of their rebellion. Cross any system and escape through the next warp-shroud without having to run the gauntlet of hostile Port Stations along the way.

She would pick them up again soon. Of that he had no doubts. The run to Gemaharn originally had been to get into a quiet pocket. Had *Vanechon* not arrived, they could have mined a few comets and asteroids for raw materials. Refill the Decanter buckets.

Now, they probably had to bounce back up into Gage space. Cross those systems as the fastest way into the true darkness beyond the Line of Exploration. What they might find there would be a crap shoot, but they would at least be in a place where Roselani couldn't immediately call on reinforcements to help.

And what did it mean that Hasan Ildar had traveled with her? She had to know by now that the man was part of the original conspiracy. Roselani was too smart to miss things like that, and Ildar was too arrogant to keep his mouth shut around her.

Or would she kill him after Gemaharn? Whatever value they might have expected from him had certainly been proven wrong when *Vanechon* got its ass kicked in by Hanishka and Odtsetseg. Maybe they'd just give up.

A fellow can always dream.

After a time, the brooding wasn't enough. Kincaide just wasn't the sort of man given over to long bouts of depression, a few recent stints notwithstanding.

He needed action.

According to the roster in his head, Reyhan was on duty until midnight, so he keyed the bridge.

"Did you need someone to come tuck you in?" the man asked in a blithely sarcastic tone as he answered.

"You haven't got the legs for it," Kincaide countered.

"Try me sometime, big boy," Reyhan laughed seductively.

"Not while there are still sheep in the universe," Kincaide laughed back. "I need some data."

"Shoot."

"Assuming we kind of stick to our story about Emhax, how many hops to get us beyond Gage ken on a close line, before we deviate through some uninhabited systems?" he asked.

"Hang on," Reyhan answered.

Kincaide heard the man muttering to himself on the open line as he typed.

"So maybe thirty hops, if we were on legitimate business," Reyhan answered finally. "Several places where the road forks between here and there. When we are about four lines back, we can pivot and go through what is essentially dead space according to my records. Emhax kind of sticks out like a thumb right now. Rich system so Colonial Dispatch stalled for the last fifty years while they built the place out into a true forward base. Lots of empty buildings on the surface right now, waiting for us to deliver a bunch of Engines to them."

"I'll invest when the real estate market crashes," Kincaide chuckled. "Let's go ahead and assume that corridor for now, Reyhan. Find me spots where we can rest and refit without an expectation of someone accidentally showing up."

"Double back a few places once we get past stations where they'll remember us?"

"Something like that," Kincaide agreed. "The news will

eventually arrive, and someone will start checking what warp-shrouds we used, so we should expect Warp Voyagers coming after us. If we can get past the Line of Exploration, they won't push as hard."

"Except *Vanechon*," Reyhan reminded him.

"Only if Roselani Thammavongsa is aboard," Kincaide replied. "If she gets bored or someone calls her home, *Vanechon* stops being a threat."

"You honestly think that's likely, Kincaide?" Reyhan's voice took on a mocking tone.

"No, but I'll deal with her when I have to. The rest of you need to be planning for how we get away from the rest of those Gage Fleet dipwads."

"Okay," Reyhan answered. "All that's easy enough. What's really on your mind, Kincaide?"

"Two things," he said, before correcting himself. "No, three. First, we need a place to set up a base for ourselves. A colony for Humans and then eventually other species."

"Eventually?"

"Hey, pal, I don't trust anyone," Kincaide clarified. "The Eden Package is supposed to be filled with rebels and dreamers, separated off from the good, upstanding citizens of The Gage to protect those folks from our kind. I plan to Decant a bunch of Humans until we have a stable base, and only then will we expand into Mori, Boomer, or Mog."

"Recipe for an underclass, Kincaide," Reyhan pointed out.

"Tough," Kincaide fired back. "We have a monopoly on space flight right now, but eventually we'll need to build more ships. Humans are the most likely Engines, but I'm not going to limit it. But Humans need to be in control of things until we know how everyone else will jump."

"Okay, that's one," Reyhan stated.

"Two, find me Earth," Kincaide said. "Whatever you need to do in the Encyclopedia. We got a full navigational dump of Gage charts, so it has to be in there somewhere."

"They've hidden it," Reyhan said. "We've been looking."

"Yeah, but we were under their thumbs then," Kincaide replied. "Time to pursue every crazy idea, weird rumor, or strange bit of astronomical cultural details we can find related to Earth. The planet exists. It has to be someplace close to the Line of Exploration, from the way they came across us and pounced."

"How about astrology?" Reyhan mused over the open line.

"Are you supposed to be making sense?"

"Old Human religious belief system, Kincaide," he said. "Earth's orbit was divided into months based on a single moon, kinda like Al-Winoq. Clusters and patterns of stars got anthropomorphized and named. That sort of thing. None of the names will be the same in our data, but the shapes might be reproducible."

"Do me one better, Reyhan," Kincaide sat up now. "See if any of the old notes include even a single reference placing Human stellar cartography into Gage, or vice versa."

"Why would they do that?" the man asked.

"The Catalogue was supposed to be the be-all, end-all of Alvar knowledge," Kincaide said, feeling his heart suddenly accelerate. "If you Conquered an industrial species, you'd want to make sure you stole everything they knew, right? And where do the Alvar store it?"

"In the Catalogue," Reyhan breathed. "You think they might have translated everything?"

"Hell, anything puts us ahead," Kincaide said. "Turn Computer Hasan loose on it and see if the man's natural pissiness can be put to our advantage because he gets to put one over on the Alvar. I'm guessing that programming survived what you did to give him boobs."

"I'm getting an aggressive nod from him right now, Kincaide," Reyhan laughed. "Tomorrow I will sit down with my staff and see what we can do to come up with a search string that we can input to pull things over."

"Pole star," Kincaide said. "Polaris or something in some ancient, Human tongue. I remember that the populated northern hemisphere seemed to rotate the night sky around a single star, but I don't know what precession might have done to it since then."

"Worth a try," Reyhan said. "How soon do we need answers?"

"Like you said, that's number two, so years, possibly," Kincaide replied.

"So what's number three?" the Assistant Foreman asked in a careful, neutral voice.

"The Alvar marked that set of stars as No Trespassing, Reyhan," Kincaide said. "I looked at one point and it seems to me that the range is five stars across generally. What does that tell you?"

"A ring to avoid," Reyhan said. "Maybe a second ring that might be inhabited?"

"No," Kincaide said. "I'm guessing that the Alvar marked the star at the center, and then added the others around that to make sure that no ships blundered in there and woke someone up, or annoyed them enough that they emerged from that system."

"So what the hell might frighten the Alvar that badly, Kincaide?"

"That's number three, Reyhan," he said. "We get safe. We get home. Then we go find if there's someone out there more dangerous than The Gage."

"Shit."

Kincaide cut the comm and sat back rather than answer.

He had no doubts that the Alvar would eventually get around to putting some sort of Port Station around Earth, if only to keep him from just sailing in and recruiting whatever survivors they might have missed and giving them Alvar-class technology. He needed to have a colony or three someplace in the darkness first, so they could sail a whole fleet of Warp Voyagers into the ancestral land and annihilate any Gage that they found.

But yeah, one of these days he wanted to know if there was a dragon out there that he might recruit. Or at least piss off enough that the creature emerged from whatever slumber had kept him bottled up in one system for however many hundreds of thousands of years.

Because The Gage would be the first enemies such a monster might discover.

Be a shame if it proved their undoing.

READ MORE

To read more of my fiction, sign up for my newsletter. You'll also get a free book!

http://www.blazeward.com/newsletter/

ABOUT THE AUTHOR

Blaze Ward is a prolific Indie writer and publisher who works mostly in Science Fiction and Light Thriller, with occasional forays into lots of other genres like superheroic fantasy.

You can find more of his titles at www.blazeward.com/books, www.KnottedRoadPress.com and wherever else you buy your books.

He also edits Boundary Shock Quarterly, an SF magazine he founded in 2018, and Thrill Ride Magazine.

ABOUT KNOTTED ROAD PRESS

Knotted Road Press publishes dynamic fiction set in exotic locations. Our authors cover a wide range of genres including science fiction, fantasy, mystery, literary, and poetry. We also have unique non-fiction voices in genres such as autobiography, business, cookbooks, and how-tos. We offer both DRM-free ebooks and print books for a global readership.

www.KnottedRoadPress.com

www.ingramcontent.com/pod-product-compliance
Lightning Source LLC
Chambersburg PA
CBHW070924100726
47908CB00001B/98

* 9 7 8 1 6 4 4 7 0 5 0 9 4 *